Futuristic

Love in another

ENCHANTED

"You *have* cast a spell on me, Witch," Miklos said softly, his voice barely audible over the sounds of the lapping tide scant inches away.

It was a measure of the newness of it all that Jalissa froze for a moment, the protest already forming in her throat. But then he chuckled and drew her to him, both of them on their knees as they held each other again.

"I won't pretend that I understand all that you are," he said, his voice low and husky. "But I know that it's all of you I love."

CRYSTAL Enchantment

Saranne Dawson

LOVE SPELL ◆ NEW YORK CITY

LOVE SPELL®

October 1995

Published by

Dorchester Publishing Co., Inc.
276 Fifth Avenue
New York, NY 10001

Printed in the United States of America.

CRYSTAL
Enchantment

Prologue

"Hear me! You will not be free men and women much longer! The Vantrans and their accursed Federation will soon rob you of your liberty, as they have already robbed those of other worlds. Even now, they plot to take from you your riches and turn you into mindless slaves.

"They worship the evil gods of science, and would destroy the old gods of the soil and air and water that we revere. They would take from you the power to control your own destiny and to live in harmony with the world the gods gave you.

"They will bring in their great machines and tear apart your forests and dig great holes in your beautiful mountains where the Old Ones dwell.

"But they *can* be stopped! The Coven has the

7

power to stop them and save you. The Coven has returned! The evil science of the Vantrans did not destroy us, and the Old Ones have told us that the time draws near when . . ."

The speaker stopped in mid-sentence, his face suddenly raised to the darkening Darebi sky above, where the sun was spreading a ruddy glow before slipping away behind the mountains.

So entranced was his audience that they stood there silently, awaiting his next words. The Coven! They had not been destroyed after all! Could it be? Surely it must be true. They'd seen the blue fire.

For all those present, the Coven had been only a part of their collective memory—revered in their hearts, but absent from their lives and the lives of their parents and grandparents. No one now alive on Darebi had ever seen a Witch or a Warlock, and they were awed by the sight of this young Warlock. The old gods, who'd always spoken through such people, had saved the Coven after all. It was a great moment, one to be cherished.

When the Warlock continued to search the heavens, a few in the audience followed his gaze. But seeing nothing, they turned their attention back to him as he spoke again.

"You must leave quickly! Alone now, I cannot save you from the accursed Federation. But through the grace of the Old Ones and their servants, the Coven, the Federation will be stopped!"

And then he was gone! One moment, he stood tall upon the rocky ledge, and the next, he became as insubstantial as smoke—a pale, wispy smoke that drifted with the wind and vanished.

His audience had barely begun to let out their sharply indrawn breaths when they heard the telltale whine of the approaching hovercraft. They knew the sound well. Here in the Outer Ring, the presence of Federation soldiers was a constant irritant and often a cause for fear. They scattered quickly into the darkness of the surrounding forest.

The hovercraft landed in the clearing where they'd been gathered. In their rush to get away, the listeners had left behind an old man whose twisted limbs prevented him from escaping. He had come here hoping to be healed by the Warlock. Instead, he now became the captive of the blue-clad Federation soldiers.

He was a brave man and he refused to tell them anything. But they had their methods. Within moments, the drug was in his brain and he was repeating to them the Warlock's words.

Chapter One

The tram doors glided open and Jalissa Kendor stepped out into the bright morning sunlight. A breeze brought to her the lush scents from the flower garden and lifted her raven-black hair from her shoulders, whipping it about her delicate, fine-boned face. She smoothed it back and hurried through the gardens toward the building that sat at the very top of the hill, serene and majestic in its isolation.

She paused for a moment on the uppermost step and turned, her gaze narrowing as she stared across the wide valley that barely contained the sprawling city. On the far hill, another very similar building stood in its own lonely splendor.

It was officially claimed that the positioning of the two buildings, like white marble sentinels facing each other across a battlefield, was purely accidental. But few believed that—and certainly none of the buildings' occupants did.

As the city had grown over the years, it had become necessary to move certain Federation offices to new quarters, while leaving the gold-domed headquarters in the valley, at the very center of the city. The result was that the two most powerful forces within the Federation now faced each other over that golden dome. The irony was too obvious not to have been planned.

Jalissa turned and pressed her palm to the square set into the building's door. Instantaneously, it opened to admit her.

The lobby was large and airy, ascending eight stories to the clear roof. Exotic plants from many worlds thrived in the carefully controlled environment, each of them labeled with their world of origin. There were giant ferns, more than 20 feet high, with fronds so delicate that the slightest breeze set them into graceful motion. There were huge crimson flowers with pure white centers, nearly two feet in diameter and giving off an intoxicating fragrance. And there were strange fur-covered plants, twisted and gnarled, their ugliness tolerated here only because on each stalk was a multi-colored flower of unsurpassed beauty.

But breathtaking as all this was, the visitor's

eye—and Jalissa's as well—was invariably drawn to the huge crystal that soared nearly to the lobby's roof.

It wasn't real, of course. It had been sculpted from plasticene that was specially constructed to mimic the pale, rainbow-shaded crystal Jalissa wore suspended on a platinum chain.

The sculpture wasn't real because the true crystal was so rare and precious that none could be spared for mere public adornment. Even in the hands of the very best crystal sculptors, more of the precious substance was lost than was ever made into the hexagonal crystals worn by Jalissa and her colleagues. No machine had yet been devised that could shape the crystal, even though much time and money had been expended over the years to build machines that could improve upon the human carvers.

Jalissa stepped into one of the two glass elevators that flanked the sculpture and directed it to her floor. It glided silently up through the lobby and came to a halt at the next-to-top floor, a location that was a constant source of disgruntlement to some of Jalissa's colleagues.

"Who do they think they are?" was a common complaint. "Without us, they'd be *nothing*—and they know it."

"They" were the administrators of the Translation and Mediation Service of the United Worlds Federation, or "Trans/Med" as it was commonly called. And the "us" were Jalissa and her several dozen colleagues: the elite of the Trans/Med Service, people brought together from numerous worlds who could use the crystals to translate instantaneously from one language to another, and who also possessed extraordinary skills at mediating the disputes that had plagued the Federation from its very beginning.

Only a handful of her colleagues were present as Jalissa walked into the elegantly appointed lounge whose glass wall provided a view of the city—and the enemy on the other hilltop. At any given time, most of the "Whisperers," as Jalissa and her colleagues were called, were scattered about the galaxy, working to settle small disputes before they could explode into wars.

Officially, they were called "Translation/Mediation Specialists," but they'd long since come to be known by everyone as "Whisperers" because when they used the crystals, their own voices became mere whispers so as not to interfere with the work of the crystals. Long before Jalissa's time, those who wore the crystals had adopted the nickname themselves—largely to annoy the officious administrators.

Jalissa poured herself a cup of tea before joining the others. They were an intriguing mixture of races, with every shade of skin, from Jalissa's pale, creamy tones to the deepest black. The talent to work with the crystals was so rare that they were recruited from every world—except for one. To the everlasting frustration of the Vantrans, no one from their world—the home world to the Federation—had ever shown an affinity for the crystals.

And so, in a Federation set up and dominated by the powerful Vantrans, the Trans/Med Service stood apart. There were no Vantrans in its administration either. The other worlds had banded together and stood firm on this point.

"Do you have an assignment yet, Jalissa?" a tall, dark-skinned colleague asked.

"No, not yet. And if one turns up, I just might plead 'crystal fatigue' and take some vacation."

"That's just what I did this morning when they tried to send me to Garlov," a short, plump man of middle age said with a chuckle.

"Not Garlov again!" There were groans all around. That cold, dark world with its volatile tribal society was no one's favorite.

"We all appreciate that, Hanta," one of the others said dryly, "since it means that one of *us* will be sent there."

A tiny, coffee-colored woman touched a hand dramatically to her brow. "I feel an attack of crystal fatigue coming on right now."

Everyone laughed. "Crystal fatigue" didn't exist—at least not after the Whisperers were trained. But none of the administrators knew that; it was the best-kept secret in the Service, where the demand for Whisperers always exceeded the supply and vacations tended to be few and far between.

They began to tease each other about who the unlucky one would be. Then Serilla, the dark-skinned Whisperer who'd greeted Jalissa first, turned to her.

"You're the only one who doesn't have to worry about freezing on Garlov. They wouldn't waste you there."

Jalissa smiled. It was true. She was only 29, but such were her talents that the Top Floor would never waste her on a hopeless mission like that one. All of them were equally adept at using the crystals for translation, but Jalissa's special gift was for hearing the small nuances of speech that others missed, and then using them in her mediations.

She thought she knew where that particular talent came from, but it remained her deepest, darkest secret.

"Is anything important happening?" she asked, since she'd missed the morning newscast. She was very much hoping that for once, the galaxy wouldn't need her services for a time. She was nearly finished with her interminable reports, and in a few days she hoped to be off to Mafriti, the most beautiful of the small worlds set aside for recreation and pleasure.

"Would we know if anything *were* happening?" Hanta said pointedly, then waved a chubby hand toward the glass wall. "Why don't you call the

Palace of Charm and ask them?"

Everyone, including Jalissa, turned to stare out at the distant building, home to the Special Agency, their sworn enemy within the Federation. None of them had ever been inside that building, just as none of its inhabitants had ever set foot in the Whisperers' headquarters. But each of the Whisperers had stories to tell—and *did* tell them endlessly—about their encounters with the dread Special Agents.

One by one, they began to drift off toward their individual offices or to the classrooms where they each took turns instructing novices. Jalissa lingered for a while to finish her tea, then got up to follow them. Suddenly, she stopped, inexplicably drawn once again to gaze at the huge marble building on the distant hilltop. A cold darkness slithered through her before she turned resolutely and strode away.

"Two sightings confirmed, and two more possibles. He has to be found."

"I quite agree. He's preaching sedition on worlds where we can ill afford trouble. But as to this business of his being a Warlock . . ." The gray-haired speaker made a face, as though he'd just tasted something foul.

"Your beliefs on that subject are well-known, Paktos, but can you afford to be wrong?"

"He's nothing more than a Tevingian, trading on their former association with the Coven. It's a pity we didn't blow them up as well when we destroyed the Coven."

"We needed their minerals then."

"But we don't now. And when we find out that he *is* Tevingian, I say it's time to come down hard on them."

"Paktos, you can't deny that there have been many reports over the years that at least some of the Coven escaped."

"Bah! Myth and nothing more. Even when the Coven *did* exist, they never had the power they were credited with."

"They had enough magic to hold us off for nearly a century."

"Only because our science was in its infancy then. Miklos, you've been quiet. What do *you* think about this troublemaker?"

Miklos Panera stood up, stretching his long, lean frame. He was junior to both the others, but junior in title only. Their deference to him was obvious.

"I think we would be fools to dismiss completely the possibility that at least some of the Coven escaped. There was strong evidence that the Tevingians knew of the coming attack and would have had ample time to warn them.

"Nevertheless, I consider it to be unlikely—if only because I can't imagine them lying low for nearly a hundred years.

"In any event," Miklos continued, "we'll know when I capture this would-be Warlock. I'll be leaving in the morning for the Outer Ring."

"I'm afraid that you won't be leaving alone."

"What?" Miklos arched a tawny brow and fixed his startling green eyes on his superior, who looked distinctly uncomfortable. "You know I work alone, Paktos."

"Yes, but there are other considerations this time."

"Such as?" Miklos challenged.

"It seems that our friends across the way somehow got wind of this troublemaker and are demanding a piece of the action."

Miklos's wide mouth curled in a sneer. "Since when do you pay them any attention?"

"When it suits our purpose. Because of what they describe as our 'unfortunate history' with the Coven, they are insisting that a Whisperer accompany you—and the Council has agreed, over our objections. I'd like to know how they found out about this man. Obviously, their intelligence is getting better.

"They plan to send Jalissa Kendor."

An image flashed through Miklos's brain, but nothing showed on his face. "The obvious choice," he muttered. "One of their top people—and also a Tevingian."

"Have you met her?" Paktos inquired curiously.

"No, but I know her reputation."

"Do you know anything of her background?"

Miklos shrugged, affecting a disinterest he

didn't feel. "Only that she's Tevingian and completed her training faster than anyone before or since."

"Supposedly, as you said, she comes from Tevingi. At least that's where she was when Trans/Med recruited her. But as soon as it became apparent that she has extraordinary talents, we began to look into her background.

"The Tevingians are as close-mouthed as they come, and unfortunately not susceptible to our drugs, but we *did* manage to find out enough to cast doubts on her origins."

"What are you saying, Paktos, that she's a *Witch*?" Miklos spat out the final word derisively, but inside a small knot of fear had formed, spreading a chill through him.

"Of course not, but perhaps we can make it appear that she *might* be. If we can cast enough doubt on her, we can get rid of her. Trans/Med wouldn't dare keep a Whisperer with a tainted reputation. The Council would never permit it.

"Jalissa Kendor has already cost us several important operations, including that fiasco on Tiepla. We had the Hetsis set up to take over the government, and she managed to 'mediate' them into a power-sharing. They've been nothing but trouble ever since."

"So in addition to finding this troublemaking 'Warlock,' you want me to get rid of her."

"Not physically, of course. We can't risk that. But if her reputation can be destroyed, we'll be rid of her just the same. The briefing for you both is set for tomorrow morning."

"Miklos Panera?" Jalissa echoed, thinking back to that premonition she'd had this morning.

"I'm afraid so. Have you ever met him?"

"No. I know him by reputation only. Very fortunately, we haven't crossed paths."

"The fact that they're sending *him* on this mission suggests that they're taking this troublemaker very seriously."

"And that's why you've insisted that we become involved too?"

"Of course." Malvina Taran smiled. "I convinced the Council that if this man has succeeded in stirring up trouble—and they can't deny that he has—then we should send a representative as well. I pointed out to them that people who may be convinced that a Warlock has appeared among them are likely to respond better to a Whisperer who happens to be Tevingian than they would to a Vantran."

"I'm rather surprised that Panera has agreed to this."

"So am I, frankly. He's always worked alone in the past, picking up native translators as needed. And given who he is, I can't imagine that his superiors could put any real pressure on him." Malvina frowned with concern. "I pushed for this, Jalissa, but now I can't help fearing that the Special Agency could have a reason of their own for agreeing. It's possible that they might try to discredit you."

"Or get me killed—like Nydia."

"We never had proof of that, though I consider it likely that they *did* have a hand in it. You must be very careful, Jalissa."

Careful indeed, Jalissa thought. *I must be far more careful than you can possibly imagine.*

And yet sometimes Jalissa thought that Malvina *could* imagine her secret. They'd never spoken of it, of course, but Malvina was the one who'd recruited Jalissa—and she was also Tevingian.

She left Malvina's office and returned briefly to her own, where she quickly completed a report Malvina had gently reminded her was overdue. Then she left for her home in the hills outside the city.

Once inside her small but luxurious house, Jalissa stripped off the pale, shimmering robe her profession required and put on more comfortable clothing. The Whisperers all started out being very proud of the uniform of their high office. Its fabric had been designed to match as closely as possible the rainbow effect of the crystals. But pride invariably gave way to displeasure with the bulkiness of the garment and the instant identification it brought them.

When they were working, that identification was necessary, but here on Vantra, Whisperers tended to be greeted with the icy formality Vantrans reserved for those they didn't like but must of necessity tolerate. And in Jalissa's case, that was made all the more difficult because most Vantrans also recognized her as being from Tevingi: the old ally of their ancient enemy, the Coven.

Because it was home to the Federation, Vantra counted among its population people from every world in the galaxy. Van, its capital, was therefore the most cosmopolitan of cities and an extraordinarily beautiful place. But it was still dominated, as was the Federation, by a race that believed itself to be superior to all others, thanks to its science and military power.

After strolling a bit in her beloved garden and plucking a few dead blossoms here and there, Jalissa went into the room she used as a home workplace, slid into the comfortable chair and keyed up her comm unit, then settled back. She scrolled through the news first, ordering it to stop when she saw the item about the man she would soon be seeking.

It was obvious that the news service was downplaying the incidents, but that was scarcely surprising. All interplanetary news was controlled by the Vantrans, who had built the service employing the same crystals used by Jalissa and her colleagues. When cut in a certain way, the crystals acted as powerful transmitters—far better than anything science could come up with.

The Vantrans never actually lied about the

news, but by playing up or de-emphasizing various stories, they certainly had an impact on how people throughout the galaxy saw things. They were very clever people, in effect the rulers of the galaxy. But they always made it appear that they were firm believers in galactic democracy.

Jalissa frowned, thinking about this man she would be seeking. Was it possible that he was what he claimed to be: a Warlock? Malvina had laughed off the possibility, but Jalissa knew that she'd have to find out before she set off in search of him. She was inclined to doubt it, however. Surely if he were, she would have been told by now.

The galactic news ended and the comm inquired if she wished to review the planetary news. She declined, then issued the instructions that would link her to the Trans/Med comm. A voice print was demanded and she spoke the requested phrase. The menu appeared and she selected "Intelligence Reports—Special Agents," then ordered up the file for Miklos Panera.

Jalissa knew that biographical files always began with a holo of the subject, but that knowledge didn't prevent her from drawing in her breath sharply when his image appeared on the screen. She stared at it until it vanished as the comm went on to provide information. Then she ordered it back again.

He was a handsome man—not surprising, since the Vantrans were known for their uncommon physical beauty and athletic grace. It was rumored that long ago in their history, they had improved themselves through genetic tinkering and even selective breeding. If that was true, then they'd certainly succeeded to the greatest extent possible with Miklos Panera.

Panera's features were classically perfect according to the Vantran standards that had become more or less the standards of the galaxy. He had a boldly masculine face: square-jawed and cleft-chinned. Like all Vantrans, he had that skin tone that was midway between her own pale shade and the darker browns and blacks of other races.

His hair, worn slightly longer than was common in the rest of the military, was a deep, burnished gold and slightly wavy, swept away from his face in a manner that seemed only to increase his look of arrogance.

But for all that, it was his eyes that captured the attention: clear, vivid green eyes that she'd never seen anywhere else, save for a few Vantrans.

Jalissa had long since become accustomed to the tall, haughty Vantrans, but something about Miklos Panera disturbed her greatly. Exactly what the nature of that disturbance was, she couldn't say, but it had a strangely sensual element to it that made her move on quickly.

She barely skimmed the basic biographical data since, like everyone else, she knew who he was. He was 37, eight years older than she was. And he was the eldest son of the most powerful family on Vantra, descended from the ancient rulers of this place. The family's wealth and power were detailed at great length, but she ignored that because everyone who lived on Vantra knew the history of the Panera family.

He was single and childless—not at all surprising for a Special Agent, all of whom were Vantran. Marriage and family customs varied from world to world, but Vantrans were known to be very family-centered, and given that Special Agents spent even more time away from home than Whisperers, they rarely married until they retired. She wondered about Panera, though. Surely there must be pressures to produce an heir.

His education also was no surprise. He'd studied at the Federation Academy, the most prestigious institution of learning in the galaxy, where she herself had also studied. Then, after a year at the military school, he'd done a two-year stint of duty at various high-risk posts, mostly on the Outer Ring, the group of planets at the edge of the galaxy that were only nominally under the control of the Federation. He'd achieved top honors in school, and had a slew of decorations for bravery.

Then he had joined the Special Agency, the secretive, elite branch of the military that was at the very heart of the Federation's control of the galaxy.

Finally, onto the screen came his record as a Special Agent, with the cautionary note that it was incomplete and possibly erroneous in details. Trans/Med did their best to keep tabs on the Special Agents, but their resources were limited.

Some of what she saw was already familiar: times when he'd clashed on various missions with her own colleagues. His reputation was such that some Whisperers had been known to give up and leave when they found out he was involved in a particular situation.

Because the Special Agency was composed entirely of Vantrans, while her own Trans/Med Service consisted of representatives from the other Federation worlds, clashes were inevitable. But there was far more to it than that. Trans/Med sought to defuse potentially explosive situations through mediation, while the Special Agency—despite its noisy disclaimers—was known to foment rebellion if it suited their purposes. On multi-ethnic worlds, they frequently courted the most compliant group, and then set about making them the rulers.

Jalissa was fuming silently at their unconscionable meddling when a date and place caught her attention and she ordered a halt to the slowly scrolling recitation. She read the brief information on the incident, then sat there frowning.

Eight years ago, when she was a 21-year-old novice, she'd been among a small group of other novices sent with a Whisperer to what had seemed at the time to be a minor territorial dispute on a hitherto peaceful world. But the situation had escalated suddenly into horrendous violence. Later, they'd discovered that the territory in dispute held valuable rare mineral deposits unknown to the combatants, but almost certainly known to the Special Agency.

At one point, Jalissa had been cut off from her colleagues—right in the middle of a laser battle that shouldn't have happened.

Horrified by her first glimpse of such violence, she hadn't at first realized that she could take herself away from it. After all, she'd never had to use her secret talents before. Then, just as she remembered that she could 'port beyond the range of the weapons, something had struck her from behind, sending excruciating pain through her body before she'd mercifully passed out.

When she came to, she was hundreds of miles from the battle scene, in a park on the outskirts of the capital city. The pain had left her weak and confused, but even before she could get to her feet, help had come in the form of some children playing games among the trees.

The children claimed to have seen a hovercraft land briefly near the spot where she was found, and the oldest among them said it bore a Federation emblem. But later, when Jalissa had questioned her colleagues, she'd discovered that they hadn't rescued her.

She never pursued the matter because she thought that it was possible that she'd 'ported after all—just at the moment when she was struck. The park was a large one that she'd seen upon her arrival, and it was possible that she'd chosen it without consciously remembering that she'd done so.

Still, every time she thought about the incident, she was troubled by it. And now was no exception, as she read the brief account of Miklos Panera's involvement in the whole tragic affair. Hundreds had died in the battle—including a novice Whisperer—and it seemed quite likely that the weapons had been supplied by the Special Agency, though of course they'd denied it.

Casting off that troubling memory, Jalissa read the rest of Panera's record. It was the usual mix of fact and speculation, but it painted a grim picture indeed. Miklos Panera was both ruthless and relentless. If this man they sought was indeed a Warlock . . .

She switched off the comm unit and went to her meditation room, the smallest room in the house. The walls and ceiling and even the floor were painted matte black, as was the large cushion in the center, where she sat cross-legged as she went through the various exercises to put herself into a trance.

Before entering the room, she'd removed her

crystal and discarded her clothing. While the crystal facilitated normal communication, it tended to hinder the form she sought now. And removing her clothing helped to eliminate any awareness of her body, leaving her mind free.

She began to reach out with her mind, seeking. In a few moments, she felt the soft brush of another mind touching hers. She recognized it as being Leeda, one of the High Priestesses. After the ritual greeting, Jalissa immediately asked her question—and received the answer she didn't want.

The man she would be hunting was indeed a member of the Coven: a young firebrand who chafed at the Coven's secret life and had taken it upon himself to spread the word that they still existed. The other members of the Coven didn't dare go after him themselves, because they knew that the Vantrans would soon be on his heels. Besides, they were convinced that he'd never be believed—or at least not by the Vantrans, who were so certain that they'd destroyed the Coven long ago.

After she had come out of her trance, Jalissa sat there thinking about the situation. The Coven seemed to believe that the youth, whose name was Kavnor, would never reveal the location of their home, but Jalissa wasn't so certain. Since he obviously wanted to bring the Coven out of their long hiding, he might do just that.

Rather surprisingly, Leeda had urged her not

to join in the search for the young Warlock, saying that she was putting herself too much at risk. But Jalissa felt that she had no choice. She had to find him and get him away from Miklos Panera.

Alone in her dark little room, Jalissa felt the weight of her secret as never before. Long periods went by when she was able to forget completely what she was and throw herself totally into the work she loved. But now, thanks to this rebellious Warlock, she was being forced to confront the enormity of that secret.

Jalissa Kendor had not come from Tevingi, as everyone believed. Instead, she came from a barren world at the outer edge of the galaxy, where her people, the Coven, had long ago used their great magic to build an underground city. They'd fled there after their narrow escape from the Vantrans, who had subsequently blown up the Coven's entire world, using a weapon no one had known existed. It was the end of Coven power—and the beginning of the rule of the Vantrans, who'd then gone on to conquer every world in the galaxy.

The Coven's origins were shrouded in the mists of ancient history, but it was believed that they were descended directly from the old gods, who had granted to them all their magical powers.

They had originally lived on a small world whose orbit was close to that of the much larger Tevingi. And many centuries ago, when inter-planetary travel became possible, the Tevingians had gone exploring—and found the Coven. Tevingian legend had told of a race of "magic people" descended from the Old Ones, and so the Tevingians had immediately revered the Coven.

The Tevingians had spread the word about the Coven, and over the years and centuries, every world in that part of the galaxy had come to revere them—and even, in some cases, worship them as gods themselves.

Then came the Vantrans, who worshipped only their science and technology. They had advanced steadily through the galaxy, conquering everything in their path and setting up an empire. They immediately saw the Coven as being an enemy to their goals, despite the fact that the Coven had never shown any inclination toward worldly rule.

The battle raged for nearly a century, with the worlds who revered the Coven joining together to fend off the Vantrans, and the Coven itself finally joining in with magic. But in the end, the Vantrans' science had won out. Then, magnanimous in their total victory, the Vantrans had set up the Federation.

And now, thanks to a troublemaking young Warlock, the Coven might once again become the object of Vantran wrath, with the Vantrans acting this time through the Federation they controlled.

Jalissa hugged herself as a deep sense of foreboding came over her. Her secret, her beloved career and perhaps even the lives of her people now depended on her finding the Warlock and persuading him to go home. And opposing her was Miklos Panera, the most brilliant and feared Special Agent of them all.

The headquarters of the United World Federation sat in the very center of the Vantran capital city of Van, surrounded by acres of parks and gardens. It was a handsome marble structure with a large dome made of gold. Atop the dome sat the Federation's symbol: a stylized version of the space-relay transmitters that linked all the galaxy's worlds. It was also done in gold leaf. The Vantrans had plenty of gold.

On a clear, pleasant morning, Jalissa rode up from the underground transport that connected the city and its suburbs. Motorized transport within the city was limited to emergency vehicles in order to preserve the beauty of the city.

Clad in the pale, shimmering robe of her profession, Jalissa garnered much attention as she made her way through the gardens to the Federation headquarters. Part of it was due to her exotic beauty, but at least as much came from recognition of her profession.

Men and women moved purposefully through the park setting, some going to the headquarters as Jalissa was, while others headed toward the smaller buildings along the park's perimeter that housed various specialized Federation departments. There were people from every race in the galaxy, but no one could mistake the Vantrans among them. Their greater height and their proud carriage combined with their athletic grace to set them apart.

When she was feeling charitable toward the Vantrans, Jalissa had to admit that no one was more suited to ruling the galaxy. It was their science that had united the worlds, even if in the past that science had been employed to conquer their neighbors. And it was their constant striving for perfection in all things that set the standards for everyone else.

Furthermore, to their credit, the Vantrans truly *did* believe in democracy. Their own history of rule by the people went much farther back than that of any other world. From the beginning of the Federation, they had said of themselves that they were merely "first among equals": leaders, but not rulers. Others, however, often failed to see the difference.

The rest of the galaxy had a love-hate relationship with the Vantrans. Other peoples eagerly accepted Vantran largesse and admired the Vantrans' style, but the subjugated races hated them too—and for the very same things.

Jalissa herself felt this ambivalence, but on this morning, thanks to a fresh reminder of who she really was, the scales had tipped to the "hate" side. The Vantrans were, after all, the people who had tried to annihilate her own people—and she knew they would do so again if given a chance.

The horrendous weapon that had been used to destroy the home world of the Coven had never been used again. But it still existed—and it remained in the hands of the Vantrans alone.

She ascended the wide steps that led to the headquarters, and then passed through the open gold-leafed doors. In the center of the huge, plant-filled lobby was a model of the galaxy, and she paused for a moment to stare at it.

Her gaze went naturally to the vast area known as the Outer Ring. There were several hundred planets out there, some inhabited and others completely barren. And on one of those barren worlds lived her own people. She didn't know which one because that information had been deliberately kept from her.

Jalissa had left the world of the Coven at the age of 12, when it was discovered that she had a definite affinity for working with the crystals. She'd been sent to Tevingi, where she was taken in by a family who then presented her to the Trans/Med recruiter two years later as one of their own.

For 17 years, her only contact with her people had been through telepathy, and those occasions had become less and less frequent as the years went by. The Kendors of Tevingi became, to all intents and purposes, her real family.

She'd never understood why she'd been sent,

and when she'd asked, the only response was that the "gods had willed it." If so, they had yet to make known to her why she should have been ripped from her home and cast into the world of the Vantrans.

On this morning, as she stood there staring at the myriad small worlds on the galaxy's edge, Jalissa had to fight a cold, aching loneliness she hadn't felt since her first months on Tevingi. She was a Witch, and she was alone at the very center of Vantran power.

Shaking off the dark mood with difficulty, she hurried on to the small conference room where the briefing was to be held. *I'm not a Witch*, she told herself. *I'm a Whisperer.*

The first person she saw when she entered the room was Miklos Panera. He was standing at the glass wall that looked out to the gardens, his back to her as he drank from a gold-leaf mug. He was tall even for a Vantran, and his long, lean body was well-displayed in the form-fitting dark blue uniform of the Federation military. A series of braided golden ropes crisscrossed his wide shoulders, marking him as belonging to the Special Agency.

For a moment, Jalissa saw no one else in the room. She was astounded at her body's over-reaction to this man, who had yet to even turn her way. Then Malvina and several others from Trans/Med greeted her by name, and Miklos Panera turned slowly to face her.

She could not prevent herself from drawing in a sharp, quavery breath, but she quickly managed to compose herself as his startling green eyes bored into her. She thought that his wide, utterly masculine mouth curved slightly, but she couldn't be sure. And his gaze remained locked on her as he walked to an empty chair at the big round table, moving with that regal grace that belonged to the Vantrans alone and never failed to remind her of great, tawny cats.

The only remaining seat was directly across the table from him, and she slid into it as the Deputy Chair of the Federation called the meeting to order. Introductions were made, and Jalissa was grateful that the table was too large to permit handshakes. Instead, she and Panera acknowledged each other with small nods—and then she turned her attention to the Deputy Chair.

In short order, she learned in detail the activities of the renegade Warlock. Two sightings had been confirmed and several more were believed likely: all of them in the Outer Ring.

"Obviously, he has chosen the Outer Ring because it is there that he can have the greatest influence," the Deputy Chief stated. "I think we can safely assume that he'll stay there, so now we'll have a report on the current political situation on the other worlds of that region."

He turned the meeting over to a woman from the Special Agency whose area of expertise was the Outer Ring. From what she said, it appeared that many of those distant worlds teetered on the brink of anarchy.

Jalissa kept her gaze fixed on the speaker, but there was never a moment when she wasn't aware of the man across the table, who had yet to utter a word but still somehow managed to dominate the entire proceedings.

When the specialist had finished, Malvina spoke up. "The situation on those worlds could be greatly improved if we were permitted to go there."

"Perhaps that is so," the Chief of the Special Agency replied. "But the risk is too great at present. And as you know, it remains our policy to let those worlds go their own way unless they engage in inter-planetary war."

Malvina said nothing, but Jalissa knew exactly what she was thinking. Far from letting those worlds "go their own way," the Special Agency was among them, stirring up trouble and aiding whichever side they decided they could then control most easily.

"Do we know anything at all about this man?" someone else from Trans/Med asked. "Other than the fact that he claims membership in the Coven," he finished dismissively.

"Unfortunately, no. The description of him suggests that he could be Tevingian—and in all likelihood he is, since they're the ones who were most closely associated with the Coven."

37

Jalissa shot a glance at Malvina. They were the only Tevingians present, though of course Jalissa wasn't really one of them. But the only indication of Malvina's displeasure was a slight tautness along her jaw. Then Malvina spoke into the silence.

"Have you considered the possibility that he is exactly what he says he is: a Warlock?"

Jalissa shifted her gaze from Malvina to the head of the Special Agency as the man stared at Malvina with thinly veiled contempt.

"Yes, of course we've considered that, but we consider it to be highly unlikely. The Coven is gone. If any of them had escaped, we would surely have heard from them before now."

"Speak for yourself, Paktos," said a deep voice. "After giving the matter some consideration, I'm not so sure that he couldn't be a Warlock."

Everyone at the table turned their attention to Miklos Panera. If his superior at the Special Agency was annoyed at his interruption and the obvious insubordination, he hid it well. Glancing briefly back at the man, Jalissa felt a moment's sympathy for him. Being a superior to a Panera was to be not a superior at all.

"If any of the Coven *did* escape," Panera went on, "there's no reason to suppose that they would have changed their ways. The members of the Coven, if you recall your history, never left their home. People came to *them*. According to the old stories, they drew their powers from each other.

"If this man *is* a Warlock, my guess is that he's a renegade. Either that, or the Coven has sent him out to 'test the waters,' so to speak. In a few months, it will have been a century since that final battle. Perhaps they believe they've waited long enough. Or I should say that their gods may have decided that," he added with a contemptuous smile.

He looked directly at Jalissa as he spoke, and for a moment, she thought she might actually have to sit on her hands to prevent herself from striking out at him to wipe that arrogant expression from his face. Then Malvina spoke into the silence once again.

"Assuming that he *is* a Warlock and that the Coven does still exist, what threat does it pose— apart from the trouble that this one member is stirring up? As has been suggested, he could be simply a renegade, acting without the authority of the Coven.

"There were never very many of them to begin with, and their powers certainly can't represent a threat anymore."

"It isn't their powers," the Deputy Chief of the Federation Council stated. "It's their very *existence*. The members of the Coven ruled the hearts and minds of everyone who came into contact with them. They were worshipped as gods themselves—especially by the people in the Outer Ring."

"And what will be done if they do indeed still exist?" Malvina asked.

"No decision has been made about that," stated the Special Agency Chief abruptly.

"What you're saying is that you wouldn't rule out destroying them *again*," Malvina replied coldly. "We must insist that if they *do* exist, we be permitted to make contact with them."

"And just how do you propose to guarantee that your Whisperers won't be put under a spell? You forget the powers they have."

"It is a risk that I for one would be prepared to take," Jalissa said, speaking for the first time. "And as a Tevingian, I would be more likely to be acceptable to them than others might be."

All eyes were on her, but Jalissa felt only the touch of Miklos Panera's unreadable scrutiny. She met his gaze for a moment, then turned her attention to the Special Agency Chief.

"If this man is a Warlock and a renegade, the Coven cannot be held responsible for his actions. He should be returned to them."

"He is already guilty of the crime of sedition—and as such, he must be brought to justice," the man said, glaring at her. "It was not my idea that a Whisperer accompany Miklos on this mission, and I think it's important to state now that you are not authorized to act on your own this time, Jalissa Kendor."

Before Jalissa could reply to that, Malvina re-entered the fray, and the meeting quickly deteriorated into the usual bickering between the two groups. Miklos Panera remained silent, but his eyes never left Jalissa.

The Deputy Chief finally brought the meeting to an end, and Jalissa rose to leave with Malvina and the others. But the voice of Miklos Panera stopped her. She turned to face him, and found herself staring at his broad chest before she raised her head to meet his eyes.

"We will leave in three hours. I trust that will be sufficient time for you to prepare?"

"Yes, of course."

"The Outer Ring is a primitive place, Specialist Kendor—far more primitive than anything you've encountered before. I would suggest that you bring clothing more suited to such an environment than the robe of your office. No one there has ever seen a Whisperer, and most have probably never heard of your profession. In fact, it would probably be wise for you to wear a military uniform, since they *do* know what that stands for. I will try to find one for you."

"I prefer to wear my robe," she replied. "Then the people will learn what a Whisperer is."

Once again, she thought she saw that fleeting smile touch his lips. "Very well then. I will meet you at the shuttle base."

Chapter Two

Jalissa had no sooner arrived at the shuttle base than a young woman in a Federation military uniform approached her.

"Specialist Kendor, please follow me," she said crisply, then turned and walked briskly away.

Trundling her bag behind her, Jalissa hurried to keep up with the Vantran's long strides. As a regular traveler, she knew the schedule for the shuttle that carried passengers to the lunar space-launching station, and there wasn't another shuttle scheduled for two hours.

To the young officer's credit, she did turn at one point, and seeing that Jalissa was having difficulty keeping up with her, she slowed her pace. Jalissa didn't thank her. Vantran women were just as arrogant as the men, and despite the woman's accommodation, Jalissa was irritated— a not-infrequent occurrence when she was forced to deal with the Masters of the Galaxy.

How will I manage to get along with Miklos Panera? she wondered as they passed through the public area of the terminal and then were waved through to the military area. Obviously, they weren't taking one of the regularly scheduled public shuttles. She should have guessed that.

She'd spent the intervening hours thinking about this mission—and about Miklos Panera. The man was impressive; there was no doubt about that. She could forgive herself for having been rather overwhelmed by him. But now that she'd met him, she should be able to put that silliness behind her. Henceforth, Miklos Panera would be an obstacle, not a man: an obstacle around which she must navigate very cautiously.

They entered a small lounge and she saw him, standing alone at the glass wall, staring out at the tarmac. It was a reprise of the first time she'd seen him—and unfortunately, in more ways than one. The sunlight touched his golden hair and the twining gold braids on his shoulders. Jalissa managed to control her reaction better this time—but not those treacherous feelings.

The young officer left her there, and Panera turned toward Jalissa, his gaze sweeping over her robe. She expected another lecture on the inadvisability of wearing it, and was rather surprised when she got none.

And she was even more surprised when he reached for the handle of her bag. His own luggage wasn't in evidence, so it must already have been loaded. She surrendered her bag to him, though she didn't thank him. From anyone else, she would have accepted the help gratefully—but not from this arrogant Vantran.

The shuttle that awaited them was a small military vehicle that carried only a half-dozen passengers. They were the only two people aboard, save for the crew. As soon as they had seated themselves, the doors were closed and a disembodied voice ordered them to fasten their belts. As soon as they had done so, the seats whirred back into a reclining position. Panera had yet to utter a single word.

Scant seconds later, they were rumbling down the runway and then roaring off into the heavens, moving much more quickly than the larger shuttle she was accustomed to.

He finally broke the silence after the auxiliary engines were shut down and the noise level decreased considerably. "We'll be taking a U-77."

"Oh," she said, assuming that some response was required. Perhaps he was trying to impress her. She'd seen this newest spacecraft a few times at the lunar base. It was said to be very fast, which was good—but it was also quite small, and the thought of spending days and weeks in cramped quarters with this man did little for her already fragile peace of mind.

That announcement had apparently exhausted his capacity for conversation, so Jalissa lapsed into a memory of the conversation she'd had with Malvina after the briefing.

Malvina had continued to speculate about whether or not the man they sought could be a Warlock. "If the Coven still exists, you can rest assured that despite what was said at the meeting, there will be no opportunity for us to make contact. The Vantrans will destroy it!

"And the last thing they'll want is for us to know the truth!"

Hearing the echo of Malvina's words now, Jalissa slanted a glance at Panera, who reclined in the seat next to hers. She was sure that Malvina was right about the Vantrans' intentions, and since she knew that the man they sought was indeed a Warlock, her fears for this mission had increased even more.

What Malvina had been trying to tell her was that her own life was in grave danger, because the Vantrans would not want her to carry the truth back to Trans/Med.

But was this man beside her actually capable of murdering her? Certainly he was capable of manipulating disputes between peoples and fomenting wars, but surely cold-blooded murder was different.

She didn't know what to think.

Perhaps he could justify the death of one Whisperer if her knowledge threatened the future of the Federation.

One impression that had lingered from that briefing was the discomfort the Vantrans obviously felt when the subject of the Coven arose. The Vantrans were, and apparently always had been, a godless people who believed in nothing beyond their science. So it was understandable that they would be uncomfortable when faced with something science couldn't explain.

But what we don't understand, we fear, Jalissa thought. *And what we fear, we try to destroy in order to rid ourselves of that fear*.

The shuttle landed smoothly at the lunar base, then lumbered clumsily toward the series of airlocks that would take it inside the gigantic bubble on this airless orb.

When they disembarked under the protective bubble, Jalissa cast a suspicious eye on the nearly invisible dome. She'd never liked this place. The bubble seemed so fragile—too fragile to hold back the deadly vacuum of space. But all spacecraft were launched from here, where there was no gravity to contend with.

When she lowered her gaze, she found Miklos Panera watching her with amusement. "I thought only first-time space travelers did that."

"I've never trusted it," she stated, even though she knew that to question the Vantrans' science was a grave offense to most of them. His amusement made him seem more human, but it also irritated her.

But if he took offense, it didn't show. Instead, he turned to scan the cavernous terminal lobby, where hundreds of people were hurrying to and fro. At that moment, a child of about eight or nine careened into him as he ran laughing from a playmate.

Panera reached down to pick up the child and smiled at him. "Have you just come home?" he inquired as the boy stared at him, the child apparently realizing he'd committed a social mistake.

The boy nodded as Panera set him back onto his feet, commenting that it was hard to be confined to a spacecraft.

"We've come all the way from Mafriti," the boy told him. "It's a long way."

His playmate, a girl of about the same age, now approached, and as Jalissa stood there in silent amazement, Panera carried on a spirited conversation with them about the recreation world they'd just visited. Then their parents, a Vantran couple, hurried up and apologized profusely to him. It was obvious that they knew who he was. Vantra might be proud of its democratic heritage, but it was clear to Jalissa that a Panera was still an object of considerable awe.

By this time, a young man in uniform had approached them, and as soon as the others had departed, he announced that he had a hovercraft waiting for them.

Jalissa followed them across the terminal, thinking about what she'd just witnessed and heard. Panera had told the children that he'd taken his two nieces to Mafriti recently, and it was obvious that he was very familiar with the children's section of that pleasure world.

It reminded her of yet another attribute of the Vantrans. They were a very family-oriented people, known for their indulgence of children. On many worlds, children were raised more harshly by parents determined to teach them their responsibilities, rather than to give them freedom and love. Such had certainly been the case with her own upbringing—at least until she went to Tevingi, where traditions more closely resembled those of Vantra.

Apparently, Vantrans had no need to instill a sense of responsibility in their offspring. Jalissa thought sourly that they probably came into the world knowing what it meant to be Vantran.

They climbed into the hovercraft and exited the terminal through the locks, then skimmed the surface of the barren moon, headed toward the military base in yet another bubble. It was another luxury Jalissa wasn't accustomed to. If she'd been traveling alone, she would have been forced to wait for space on the scheduled hoverbus.

It was yet another way of letting Trans/Med

know that it was not the equal of the military. Regardless of the urgency of the mission, Whisperers normally had to take regular transport.

Unfortunately, the U-77 proved to be even smaller than she'd thought, at least on the inside. When she commented on it, Panera told her that the craft was much less fuel-efficient than other spacecraft, and therefore a great deal of space had to be devoted to the fuel pods.

But her worst shock was yet to come. There were only two tiny cabins, each with narrow bunk-style beds, one atop the other along one wall. Since both crew members were male, she couldn't see how she was to be accommodated. Panera walked into the one cabin, then turned to her.

"Which bunk would you prefer?"

What she would have "preferred" was to leave right now. This was impossible! She'd have no privacy whatsoever. Was he doing this deliberately, hoping that she'd leave? She knew that there were nearly as many female pilots as male. Had he arranged for this crew to be male?

"Jalissa," he said, using her given name for the first time, "I know this isn't the luxury you're accustomed to, but let me remind you that it was *your* superiors who insisted that you come along on this mission. If they failed to explain the accommodations, the fault is theirs."

She bristled. "How could they have explained it, when none of us has ever been inside a U-77?"

"Good point," he said, nodding. "But it doesn't solve the problem. Do you want to leave?"

She wasn't sure if he sounded hopeful or not. Miklos Panera, like most Vantrans, was very good at concealing his thoughts. But there was no way she could walk away from this mission.

"I'll take the lower bunk," she told him, hoping that was the one he preferred.

A short time later, they were space-bound and the lunar base was a tiny dot, silhouetted against the large, bluish sphere of Vantra. More than once in the intervening moments, Jalissa had almost demanded to leave. She was at the complete mercy of the military—and Special Agent Panera—now.

Furthermore, the Priesthood didn't want her to pursue this Warlock. It hadn't been issued as an order, but that was only because the Priesthood was accustomed to instant compliance with its decisions. The Coven was no democracy. But Jalissa had been away too long to accede so readily to veiled commands. So instead, she'd listened to her own counsel—and now here she was, forced to depend totally on a Vantran who undoubtedly wished to discredit her, and might even plan to murder her.

She explored the ship, and saw that it boasted few amenities. There was a tiny exercise room, an automated galley with one small table and a work area with a large comm unit. Panera hadn't said how long it would take them to reach the Outer Ring on this craft, but she knew it would be weeks on other spaceships.

She returned to the tiny galley and grimaced at the offerings. It seemed that no matter how many advances were made in space travel, no one had yet improved the food. And to make matters worse, the selections were entirely veg. The Vantrans didn't eat meat, though some of them did eat the delicious fish that populated their waters.

After collecting the best meal she could under the circumstances, Jalissa sat down at the table. A moment later, Panera walked in, and the already small space became even more crowded.

He selected a meal and took a seat opposite her. "You said at the briefing that you think this man should be returned to the Coven if he *is* a Warlock—but you haven't expressed an opinion as to whether or not the Coven still exists."

"I doubt it," she replied evenly, although she was very uncomfortable discussing the Coven with him. She was sure that Special Agent training, like her own, included teaching people to pick up on the smallest nuances of speech and body language.

"And despite what they sometimes say to off-worlders, most of my people don't either." She was referring, of course, to the Tevingians, which, as far as he was concerned, *were* her people.

"If the Coven does still exist, it's thanks to your people," he remarked neutrally.

"We've paid a heavy price for that," she stated coldly. "Even though it's unlikely that Tevingians were at fault." Tevingi had been forced to accept a huge permanent base for the Federation, where thousands of largely Vantran troops were quartered.

"It's a convenient base—then and now. I understand that it's about to be expanded."

"Not if my government has anything to say about it." Which they wouldn't, of course.

"Tevingi is a strange world," he went on in a musing tone. "Of all the worlds in the galaxy, it comes closest to Vantra in its traditions and history—and even its science. But its people are secretive."

"Tevingians have long memories," she replied. "And as long as that base is there, filled mostly with Vantrans, those memories will remain."

He nodded. "I've often thought that the mix of troops there should be changed."

"Then why *hasn't* it been?" she demanded.

He laughed. "If it were up to me, it would happen—but it isn't. I spent several months on Tevingi some years ago. I liked it, even thought I wasn't always welcomed. But the lack of sunlight bothered me."

"Yes. Most off-worlders feel that way." Tevingi had an almost perpetual cloud cover, and the effect was heightened still further by the narrow valleys and tall mountains that covered much of the planet.

For her, however, it had seemed a place filled with light, after years spent mostly underground on the Coven's adopted world.

"Do you ever return there?" he asked.

She was tempted to tell him that he was asking a question for which he must already have an answer. She knew perfectly well that her comings and goings were watched by the Special Agency, as were those of all Whisperers. But instead, she told him that she hadn't been back there for nearly two years. It was a long journey and she had so little time off.

"But you still have family and friends there?" he asked.

"Yes, of course."

"Good, because that's where we're going first."

"We are?" She was surprised, having assumed that they would go directly to the Outer Ring to begin their search.

"Since by most accounts this troublemaker appears to be Tevingian, the most prudent course is to try to find out if that's true. I have a holo drawing of him from a description given by a member of his audience on Darebi."

The description hadn't been given willingly, she thought angrily, certain that drugs must have been used on the unfortunate informant.

"I expect your full cooperation in this matter, Specialist Kendor."

Stung by his sudden retreat into cold formality as much as by his words, Jalissa stared at him coldly. "I resent your implication that I would do anything *but* cooperate to the fullest, Agent Pandera."

"I'm very familiar with your record—and cooperation with the Special Agency has not always been apparent."

That was certainly true. And in any event, arguing with him now served no purpose. "I've been no less cooperative than any of my colleagues," she replied with a smile.

Rather to her surprise, he laughed. "Well put. To state it plainly, you cooperate only when you have no choice—which is the situation on *this* mission."

The smile remained on his lips as he spoke, but that did little to soften his words. Jalissa wanted to lash out at him with her powers. She had just begun to acquire those powers when she left the Coven to live on Tevingi, and in all the years since then, despite numerous aggravations, she'd never once thought of striking out at someone. In fact, as that incident years ago proved, she had very nearly forgotten about them.

But Miklos Panera was trying her patience as no one ever had before. His Vantran arrogance, combined with that undeniable physical attraction, were creating in her a volatile melange of emotions she knew she must control.

"I fully understand my . . . limitations on this

mission, Agent Panera," she replied formally.

"Do you?" he asked, that smile still hovering about his finely sculpted mouth. "A glance at your record would suggest that you've never had occasion to know your limitations, Specialist Kendor.

"It *is* a remarkable record, by the way. For someone so young, you've achieved quite a lot."

"Thank you," she acknowledged in that same formal tone.

"But sooner or later, even the best come up against something they can't handle."

"Has that happened to you?" she inquired archly.

His green eyes glittered with something that might have been amusement—or might not have been. "Not yet," he replied.

"I'll expect you to use your contacts on Tevingi to see if we can find out anything about this man," he went on. "And to see if he could be part of a conspiracy."

"A conspiracy?" she echoed. "What are you talking about?"

"We have reason to believe that there could be a group on Tevingi that is hoping to form an alliance with some of the Outer Ring worlds and break away from the Federation."

"That's ridiculous! It seems to me that Vantran intelligence-gathering can't be as good as you claim if you believe that. My people are as much a part of the Federation as every other world is.

"What's *really* bothering you, Panera, is that you haven't been able to infiltrate Tevingi as you have the other worlds—despite your huge base there."

"Believe it or not, I admire your people's fierce independence. But that's on a purely personal basis. On a professional level, I worry that the Tevingians could be planning to cause trouble for the Federation."

She stared at him in silence. It seemed to her, improbable as it was, that he spoke the truth about his admiration for the Tevingians. But that wouldn't stop him from causing serious problems for them. No group defended the Federation more fiercely than the Special Agency, which had been created to do just that.

"I also happen to think that my people made a mistake by punishing yours over the Coven episode," he added. "There was never any real proof that the Tevingians interfered, and punishment without a determination of guilt is counter to all that Vantrans stand for."

Once again, she was nearly certain that he spoke the truth, but she reminded herself that among his many talents was certainly the ability to lie convincingly.

"That's ancient history, Panera," she replied dismissively. "And not worthy of discussion at this point."

"Nevertheless, 'ancient history,' as you put it, colors the present—and the future as well." Then he paused and smiled again. His sudden shifts of mood were disorienting—perhaps intentionally so.

"Since we're going to be spending a great deal of time together, do you think we could settle on given names?"

"Very well—Miklos." How she wished that his smile didn't have such a devastating effect on her. And she feared that he knew it too.

"Tell me about your family."

"They're landsmen," she replied. "They own seven thousand acres of prime farmland and several large mines in the Far West, where they mine gold and grow a variety of crops and raise livestock. My mother is also a leading breeder of Madri horses."

"Madris? They're beautiful animals. I've seen them a few times when I've been on Tevingi. It's a pity that your people won't allow them to be exported."

"They're sacred among my people. In our legends, they were the horses of the gods. To this day, they choose their riders, instead of the other way around."

Jalissa smiled at the memory of galloping across the meadows on her Madri, awaiting that moment when it would unfold its great wings and soar into the sky. She'd lived on Tevingi for only two years, but the memory of those times remained sharp and clear.

"Would a Vantran be acceptable to them?" he

asked, breaking into her reverie.

"I'm not sure. Off-worlders *have* ridden them, but not often. I think that part of the reason is that the Madris can sense the fear off-worlders usually have of horses that can fly."

He nodded. "To most people, that would mean giving up too much control."

She was surprised at his perceptiveness, but said nothing. Instead, she remarked that they'd scarcely have time to ride in any event.

"We'll make time—that is, if you're willing to take me there. I'm a firm believer in mixing pleasure with business whenever possible. Our troublemaker will probably lie low for a while after the episode on Darebi, where he came quite close to being caught. Do you have any brothers or sisters?"

"One each—but they're both off-world. My brother is on Stada, where he works in my uncle's business, and my sister is at the artists' colony on Celos."

"Then your parents should be happy to have you visit."

They would be, Jalissa knew. And even though they weren't her *real* parents, she felt as though they were. At times, she had trouble conjuring up an image of her true parents, with whom she'd spent little time in any event. Coven children were raised together, by those who had a particular affinity for working with them. Jalissa had been shocked to discover that on Tevingi, parents and children actually lived together.

The conversation continued in the same casual vein, but she knew what he was really doing: probing to see who she knew and how much information she could be expected to provide. He certainly knew that he'd get only minimal cooperation from the Tevingian government.

She wondered if it could possibly be true that there was a conspiracy to form an alliance with the Outer Ring worlds and leave the Federation. If so, her adopted family would certainly know about it. Her adopted father was a powerful man, and his older brother was one of the richest men in the galaxy.

Not that she'd ever tell Panera if such a conspiracy *did* exist. But she was troubled by the thought because she'd never before faced the question of her own loyalty to the Federation. It was simply a fact of life.

When she finally grew tired of answering his questions, she announced her intention of going to the comm room to study up on the Outer Ring worlds. There was definitely a limit to her ability to withstand the onslaught of Miklos Panera's powerful presence.

Miklos watched her leave, and then realized that her image still remained. What was that elusive quality about her that so attracted him? He'd never understood it. Like most Vantrans, his standards of beauty were based on his own race.

But Jalissa Kendor, exotic with her black hair and pale skin and dark eyes, seemed to have created a different standard in his mind.

He thought back to that incident on Temok eight years ago, when he'd first laid eyes on Jalissa Kendor. She was a novice then, innocently caught up in a battle that shouldn't have happened—and *wouldn't* have happened if he'd gotten there sooner.

The moment he'd spotted her, he'd known who she must be. Reports had already reached them of a Tevingian novice who was showing great promise. The Special Agency kept close tabs on the Whisperers, and particularly on those who came from Tevingi.

He'd arrived by hovercraft, and was standing on a hilltop overlooking the wild, rugged terrain where two ancient enemies were battling over essentially worthless territory. They shouldn't have had lasers, but somehow they did. And Jalissa Kendor was lost in the no-man's-land that was about to become a killing field.

As he'd watched from his place of safety, she'd started back toward one enemy line. From his vantage point, he could see that within moments, she'd be in range of the weapons.

Recalling it now, he still wondered what had possessed him to take action. The loss of a particularly promising Whisperer was something the Special Agency would cheer—especially when no blame could accrue to the Agency for her death. He had only to let the inevitable happen.

But instead, he found himself scrambling down the steep hillside toward her. And when he saw that he couldn't possibly get to her before she wandered into the laser fire, he took out his stunner and fired. He could have called out to her, but he wasn't sure she'd hear him, and even if she did, she might run from him. No Whisperer ever trusted a Special Agent—and with good reason.

As soon as she fell, he ran to her—and then wasted precious moments as he knelt beside her. To this day, Miklos could not explain what he'd felt then. It was as though, for just a moment, the whole galaxy had ceased to exist. The closest he could come to describing the feeling was to say that it felt as though he'd suddenly come across some exotic creature long believed to be extinct. In those seconds, he felt a sense of wonder and awe that shivered through him and touched something deep inside that had never been touched before.

Fortunately for them both, he'd come out of his trance or whatever the foolishness had been. He'd carried her back up to the hovercraft, then deposited her in a park hundreds of miles away, where he knew she'd be safe until she regained consciousness.

He'd wanted to keep her with him, but he'd regained his senses enough to know that that was impossible. Federation troops were on their way and he had to direct them, and besides, he knew that no mention of the incident could ever find its way back to headquarters.

Months had passed before Miklos could dismiss that incident from his mind. But he'd finally succeeded—until Paktos had raised the question of her murky origins. And ever since he had, Miklos had been trying to ignore the thought that was whispering through his mind. Could she be a Witch?

Like other Vantrans, Miklos was very uncomfortable with thoughts of the Coven. Defeating the Witches and Warlocks had been a necessity, and destroying them completely had been the only way to achieve victory. The Coven was small, and certainly many more of its members had died in the wars of that time than had perished when his people unleashed their powerful weapon and obliterated the world of the Coven. But he knew, as did all Vantrans, that they had destroyed a unique people: a super-human race whose magic was beyond their understanding.

But had they been destroyed? He'd seen the uneasiness on the faces of those at the briefing as they discussed the possibility that members of the Coven still existed. If their magic had been powerful enough to save them from the Vantrans' ultimate weapon . . .

No, he couldn't accept that. The Coven was gone. To suggest otherwise would force him to think the unthinkable about Jalissa Kendor and that strange moment on the battlefield.

Jalissa lay on the narrow bed, knowing that it was useless to try to sleep until he appeared. She had considered switching to one of the bunks in the crew's quarters, since the crew took turns sleeping, but to do so would be to admit to Miklos Panera that she found his presence disturbing.

She'd done her best to avoid him since their earlier conversation, but it wasn't easy, given their cramped quarters and his tendency to roam around the small craft.

Earlier, she'd settled down in the comm room and called up her favorite ballet vid for entertainment. But no sooner had she begun to relax and enjoy it than he had joined her. Most Vantrans had a keen appreciation for the arts, and it soon became apparent that he was no exception.

She lay there thinking about her resentment of this man and of all Vantrans. Her contacts with them were rather limited, even though she had lived on their world for 15 years. Trans/Med people were clannish and tended to socialize mostly among themselves. And her isolation from the Vantrans was even greater, since she spent so much of her time off-world.

She knew that some of her resentment had to do with their history, but as she thought about it now, she realized that it had more to do with the kind of people they were.

Vantrans were unfailingly generous with their technology and their great wealth, dispensing it liberally to all the poorer worlds. And off-worlders who visited or lived on their world were treated with great kindness—which was certainly not the case on many worlds—including Tevingi.

But the result of all this was a deep, if carefully hidden, resentment, and Jalissa wondered if the Vantrans knew that—and if they *did* know it, whether or not they cared. Did they know, for example, that their very name was often used by other people to signal a trait in someone that offended others? "Don't be so *Vantran!*" was an admonishment that needed no further clarification anywhere in the galaxy.

She had just begun to drift off to sleep when the cabin door opened, letting in some light from the passageway. Fortunately, she'd already turned to face the wall.

In the silence, she heard the whisper of clothing slipping from his body. But the effect upon her was as though he had shouted. Every fiber of her being went on full alert as her mind conjured up an image that sent a soft heat stealing through her. .

The situation was intolerable—and yet she'd have to endure it for weeks. She wondered what she would have done if she'd known ahead of time that she'd be forced to share sleeping quarters with him.

Then a thought struck her suddenly. If he had wanted to avoid taking her along on this mission, he could reasonably have assumed that informing her of the arrangements would have accomplished that.

She was wondering about the significance of that when she heard the door to the adjoining bath open and then close. Immediately, she felt her body begin to relax.

Could he have actually *wanted* her to join him? If so, it could only mean that Malvina was right. They wanted to discredit her—or even to kill her.

And yet she could not believe that Panera would go to such an extreme, no matter how ruthless his reputation. Or was she merely engaging in that most foolish of enterprises: self-delusion?

She drifted with her thoughts: the danger of this mission, her sudden re-awakening to her origins, her incomprehensible attraction to a Vantran who might wish her harm. Accustomed to dealing only with problems outside herself, Jalissa found all of this very confusing.

The door opened again and she held her breath, then stiffened as she felt her bed move when he climbed up the small ladder to the upper bunk.

Was he naked? she wondered. She herself generally slept that way, but she was now wearing one of her loose, comfortable tunics. She hated herself for the images that now crept into her mind, bringing with them every story she'd ever heard about Vantran men.

Sleep was a very long time coming, and when it did, Jalissa only exchanged those tales for dreams: erotic dreams with a darkness at their core—as though even in sleep, her brain was trying to remind her of the danger posed by Miklos Panera.

She awoke the next morning feeling as though she hadn't slept at all. Memories of her dreams, as fragile as cobwebs, clung to her mind, then dissolved slowly as she pulled herself from bed.

The upper bunk was empty. Apparently, *he'd* had no trouble sleeping. She was angry that she couldn't seem to escape from him even in her sleep. In fact, sleep was even worse, since at least when she was conscious, she could rein in her wayward thoughts.

Exercise, she thought as she stumbled toward the bathroom. *That will make you feel better*. She groaned as the mirror reflected back to her the image of a woman with tousled black hair and dark-ringed eyes.

After putting on the brief, second-skin suit everyone wore for exercising, Jalissa opened the door into the passageway and peered out cautiously, hoping that Panera wasn't about to put in one of his sudden appearances. Probably he was catching up on the galactic news: the secret Special Agency version, that is.

But when she walked into the exercise room, he was already there. She stopped in the doorway, fighting the urge to turn and leave. The room was adequate for two people at the same time—but not when one of them was the man who had just finished haunting her dreams.

He was wearing only a pair of second-skin briefs, and his bronzed body was glistening with sweat as he worked with the series of weights designed to exercise all muscles. Even in the much larger exercise facilities aboard the giant spacecraft, he would have drawn her attention— but here, in this cramped space, he was overwhelming.

His gaze swept briefly over her as he greeted her, but she could read nothing in it. She realized that this was the first time he'd seen her in anything but the voluminous robe of her profession. It wasn't likely, though, that she impressed him. She was so much smaller and more curvaceous than Vantran women.

She returned the greeting, then turned her back on him and went to the exercise mat, where she immediately began the series of stretching exercises she did every day. Her body was very limber, thanks to the rigorous dance training all children of the Coven went through almost from the time they could walk.

Halfway through her routine, she realized that

the sounds behind her had ceased, and she paused, then turned, hoping that he might have left. But instead, he was sitting on the weight bench watching her.

"You've studied dance," he said, making it a statement and not a question.

She nodded, concealing her uneasiness.

"I didn't know that Tevingians went in for that sort of thing."

"They don't, as a rule—but my family did." If she stretched it a bit, it was true. They had encouraged her to keep up her practice and her adopted sister had joined her. But in general, he was right. Tevingians had almost no appreciation for any of the arts, which had often made life difficult for Genna, her adopted sister. That was why she'd left Tevingi for an art colony on a distant world.

"I still go to classes at the Academy," she added, referring to the prestigious Academy of Dance on Vantra. "When I'm not off-world, that is."

"My mother sits on their Board of Governors. She was once a principal dancer."

"I know. I've seen vids of her performances. She was wonderful." Her appreciation was sincere. Davin Panera was almost as good as the best of the Coven's dancers.

Jalissa turned away and completed her routine, then got up and went over to one of the pieces of equipment. But she quickly realized that the proportions were wrong for her. It had clearly been designed for the much bigger Vantrans.

He came over to examine it, bringing with him the not unpleasant odor of masculine sweat. "I think it can be adjusted. You're the first non-Vantran to travel on a U-77."

It was an honor she could have done without. She stepped back as he began to make some adjustments, and at that moment, the ship's comm unit came to life.

"Sir, there's some news you should look at immediately."

Their eyes met, the question hanging in the small space between them. Had there been another sighting? He excused himself and hurried off to the comm room.

Jalissa was tempted to follow him, but she didn't know if the news had come over the regular channels or the ones limited to the military. She hoped that it wouldn't mean a change of course, since she'd been looking forward to a visit to Tevingi, even if it wasn't under the best of circumstances.

She also hoped fervently that the wayward Warlock hadn't been captured. If he had, she would have to think very carefully about the possible dangers of her further involvement. The Warlock would certainly recognize her as being a Witch, and while it was unthinkable that he would give her away, he was already doing the unthinkable.

Panera was back within a few minutes. "I'm afraid you'll have to cut your exercise short. We've just had a report that our man might be on Torondi, so we're changing course and going there."

She hid her relief that the Warlock hadn't yet been captured, and instead gave him a confused look. "Why should I stop my exercises?"

"You're about to discover the secret of the U-77. The only reason it hasn't been announced yet is that its usefulness is very limited. Do you know anything at all about propulsion systems or time-travel theory?"

She shook her head.

"All right then. I'll just say that this ship has a totally new propulsion system that allows it, for brief periods of time, to exceed the speed of light far beyond anything we have been previously capable of. During that period, the laws of physics operate differently, and the net result is that we can cover the distance that would normally take a week in a few hours."

She stared at him in astonishment. She might not know much about physics, but what she was hearing was obviously the biggest advance in space travel in many decades.

Panera allowed himself that small smile of satisfaction she'd seen before on Vantrans when they'd just dazzled the rest of the galaxy with their scientific prowess.

"The problem," he went on, "is that the maneuver requires enormous amounts of fuel, so its usefulness is quite limited at present. But I've decided that it's justified in this case if it means we can get to Torondi in time to capture him, or failing that, to get some fresh first-hand reports.

"It will stretch our fuel supply to its limits, but we can refuel on Torondi.

"We'll have to be strapped into our cots during the whole maneuver, and I must warn you that it's a bit disorienting, which is another problem we're working on."

Her expression obviously mirrored her fear at becoming part of an experiment because Panera smiled at her. "Don't worry, Jalissa. It's perfectly safe. You might experience some dizziness, but that's all."

Then he chuckled, a pleasant sound that vibrated through her. "Of course, since you distrust bubbles, I'm sure you *will* worry, despite what I say."

"How long will this take?" she inquired as she followed him back to their cabin.

"About five hours. You could take a sleep-drug."

It was a tempting thought, but she disliked them and decided against it.

"When we return to normal operations, we'll still be about ten hours from Torondi. That's because there's a safety factor built into the calculations. We can't afford to enter Torondi's gravitational field at X-speed."

"I think I'd rather not hear all the details," she muttered.

He laughed. "Sorry. I guess I'm being too 'Vantran.'"

She stopped in her tracks and stared at him and he chuckled. "Did you think that we don't know how others see us? Climb into your bunk and I'll show you how to strap yourself in."

She did as told, her estimate of him moving up several notches. He was certainly arrogant, but at least he had a sense of humor, a trait she would never before have associated with his race.

He showed her how to fit the straps over her body, then went over to the comm unit and announced that they were ready. "You'll feel a slight shudder in the ship. It's nothing to worry about. It's been designed to withstand far more than this."

Seconds after he had climbed into his bunk, a loud chime sounded—and a moment later, the ship did indeed begin to shudder slightly. Then she heard a high-pitched whine that was very near the limits of her hearing.

His disembodied voice floated down to her as he repeated the report he'd received. It was sketchy at best, but it *did* sound like the man they were seeking.

Torondi was one of those worlds everyone else tried to avoid. It was as primitive as many of the Outer Ring worlds: a swampy, dark place populated by small clans of leathery-skinned people who ignored any attempts to improve their lives. No Whisperer had set foot on it during her time in the Service, though she knew that a few had done so in the past.

"I'll admit that it's a likely place for an uprising," Panera said. "They have no love for the Federation. But there have never been any problems there in the past—except among themselves, of course. We've by and large left them alone. There's a small Federation force there, of course, but they've never done any real exploring because the place has never seemed worth it.

"On the other hand, they *were* once under the sway of the Coven, so they could appeal to this supposed Warlock."

"I'm not sure how effective I can be there," she admitted. "Their language is very difficult even for us. I worked with it when I was in training, but that's all."

"I've been there only once myself, and that was also years ago during *my* training. Two months of foul-smelling swamps and man-eating snakes and that accursed whistling of theirs."

Jalissa smiled at his candor. It was the first time she'd ever heard a Vantran speak ill of another world. And then he surprised her again.

"I'm sorry that we have to delay our trip to Tevingi, since I know you must be looking forward to a visit with your family. But I think we should establish quickly that this isn't our 'Warlock.' He'd have to have better transport than I think he has to have gotten there so quickly."

She said nothing. A strange feeling had come over her: a tingling sensation throughout her body and a vague nausea. When she didn't respond, he spoke her name sharply.

"I . . . I feel strange."

She heard a sudden movement in the bunk above her, and then he vaulted to the cabin floor, not bothering with the ladder.

"You'll be fine," he said. "It shouldn't get any worse. Are you certain that you don't want a sleeper?"

She nodded, wondering why the presence of a man she couldn't trust seemed so reassuring. Something tickled her mind, a fleeting memory that she couldn't quite reach.

He sat down on the edge of her bunk, still clad only in his exercise briefs. "It seems to affect some people more than others. For reasons we don't yet understand, women are often more affected than men. Do you feel ill?"

She shook her head. "I did for a moment, but I'm fine now, except for that tingling sensation. Shouldn't you be strapped in?"

"Those are just safety regulations. It isn't really necessary most of the time. Occasionally, the ship can shake a bit more than it is now."

Then, as if to prove his point, the ship suddenly began to shudder more violently. He leaned over her, bracing himself against the post at the corner of her bunk. Their eyes met—and for one breath-snatching moment, Jalissa saw what she had never expected to see in him: the naked, primitive desire of a man for a woman!

The ship settled down and he moved away, now avoiding her gaze. After murmuring a few words of reassurance, he climbed back up to his own bunk.

She wanted to believe that she'd been mistaken. The rational side of her mind told her that she must be. Vantrans did occasionally take lovers from among other races, but it was a rare occurrence.

Then she recalled with a sudden chill the disgraced Whisperer who'd taken a Vantran Special Agent as a lover. Could he intend to seduce her in order to discredit her? Was Miklos Panera capable of such a vile act? It surprised her to be able to deny that. She didn't know this man, but her instincts told her that what she'd seen, however fleetingly, had been *real*.

Chapter Three

"We're in orbit around Torondi now, sir."

Jalissa was jolted out of her dreams by the voice on the comm. But this time, the dream remained sharply etched on her mind, and she felt herself grow warm as the images tumbled about in her brain. Still groggy, she tried to sit up, only to find herself immobilized. For a few seconds, the dream and the reality merged, and it was Miklos Panera, his bronzed, naked flesh glistening and his green eyes glittering with raw, primitive desire, that held her down.

Then, just as she realized that it was the restraining straps instead, Panera appeared, once more vaulting down from his bunk. The eyes that met hers briefly were unreadable now. Seeing her struggle against the bonds, he reached to undo them and his bare arm brushed lightly across her breasts. He seemed not to have even noticed, but she was barely able to stifle a cry.

"If you want to get a look at Torondi, come to the command center," he said as he turned to leave. "It's a rather striking sight."

She said nothing, since she didn't trust her voice. His touch had been so brief and casual, and yet her nipples were hardened and straining against the thin fabric of the exercise suit she still wore.

She began to doubt her earlier certainty: not that she'd seen desire in his eyes, because she was sure of that. But now she doubted that it had been genuine. Or was he merely struggling as she was, to avoid complications?

No, she thought. There would be no complications for him. His superiors would welcome the opportunity such a liaison would produce. Discrediting her would help his career—not that it needed any help.

She pulled herself from those thoughts with difficulty and got up to follow him to the command center. Torondi was indeed a striking sight as it filled the now-opened viewport. A veritable rainbow of colors surrounded the planet, with the predominant one being a shade of green that was a perfect match for his eyes. She'd never seen anything like it, and told him that.

"The colors are the result of rare gasses in their

upper atmosphere that fortunately stay there. If they didn't, we'd be forced to wear breathers. Below it, there's a layer of clouds, so you don't see the colors from the planet itself, except at sunset, and even then, it's not as striking as it is from up here."

Several hours later, they were aboard a Federation hovercraft, skimming just above the surface of the mist-shrouded swamps, en route to the isolated town where a stranger had been reported. The reports were sketchy and the man was supposedly gone, but both of them doubted that it was the man they sought.

"Have you ever seen vids of the snakes?" Panera asked.

"No," she replied, and was about to add that it was an education she could do without, but he was already bringing the hovercraft even lower, so that it barely skimmed the surface of the dark waters where odd, twisted trees reached up with dark branches.

"There's one now!" he said, pointing.

He put the craft into a sharp turn—and then she saw it! An involuntary cry escaped from her as she stared at it in horror. He reached out to lay a hand briefly over hers—a gesture that was nearly unnoticed as she gaped at the sight just below them.

"Don't worry. They're intelligent creatures, and

they have enough sense not to attack a hover-craft."

She didn't answer because she was staring into the yellow eyes of the creature as it reared up on the front part of its body and watched them warily. Its black head measured at least five feet across, and its body was only slightly less thick. She couldn't even begin to guess its length, since most of it was hidden beneath the murky waters of the swamp.

"That's not a particularly large one," Panera remarked as he circled above the snake and it turned its wedge-shaped head to watch them. "It's probably about twenty feet long."

"I've never seen anything so . . . evil-looking in my life!" she gasped, wishing he would stop circling it.

"Some of the Torondis still worship them," he said as he finally resumed their journey to the town. "But they see them as evil too. They deny it, but we suspect that some of them might still be sacrificing children to the 'snake-gods.' Supposedly, that stopped when they fell under the sway of the Coven, but we think it may have resumed."

She was truly appalled. "I've never heard that. Why do you allow it to go on?"

"First of all, we have no proof that it does. And secondly, Torondi has just never worked its way to the top of the agenda."

"Because it has nothing you need," she stated angrily.

He shot her a brief glance. "Nothing *we* need, Jalissa. You benefit from our science too."

His tone was surprisingly gentle, but it did little to calm her anger. "Someone has to find out if they're really sacrificing children—and if they are, it must be stopped! This is unconscionable, Miklos!"

"Speaking personally, I agree with you, of course. It's time the Council pays some attention to Torondi. If I can persuade them, we'll undertake a mission to find out the truth. If not, I'll try to look into it on my own. Would you be willing to come back here with me?"

She was caught completely by surprise, and just stared at him.

"Well, if I'm going to find out the truth, I'll have to bring a Whisperer along—and a very good one, because of the difficulty of their language. I'll fund the expedition if the Council won't."

"I'll come," she said quickly. "Even if I have to use vacation time. But what will we do if we discover that the rumors are true? The Council still may not do anything about it. They're so reluctant to interfere with religious matters."

"What I'll do is try to reason with the Torondis. And if that doesn't work, I'll threaten to kill every last one of their scaly 'gods.'"

"The Council would definitely never approve of that," she said, knowing that the destruction of any species was forbidden, no matter how much of a problem it was.

"By the time the Council found out, all they could do would be to voice disapproval. And I can see to it that you aren't implicated."

"You surprise me, Miklos. That is, if you really mean what you say."

"I *do* mean it. Those stories have always bothered me, but I knew I couldn't verify them without a Whisperer. I hope that threats alone will work, though, because I agree with the Non-Extinction Policy."

"If anyone else did such a thing, he or she would be sent off to a penal colony," she mused. "But you could probably get away with it."

He nodded. "I could get away with it. There are some advantages to being a Panera."

"Are there any *disadvantages*?" she inquired archly.

He laughed. "There are some—including one that you yourself must be familiar with. It's difficult to go anywhere unnoticed."

"But at least no one treats you with hostility," she said.

"I wasn't referring to your being a Whisperer, though I'm sorry if you've encountered any hostility. It's really only envy. Many Vantrans are overly sensitive about their lack of affinity for the crystals."

Once again, his candor shocked her, but she hid it carefully. "Then what *were* you referring to?" she asked curiously. Surely he couldn't mean because she was an off-worlder. Vantra was filled with them.

He turned to her briefly again, a smile hovering on his lips and in his eyes. "Your beauty, of course: a very exotic sort of beauty to us."

Jalissa looked away quickly, embarrassed because it now sounded to her as though she'd begged for a compliment. Even the most trivial conversations with Miklos Panera had become fraught with nuances. His words had suggested nothing more than a general statement, but his eyes seemed to indicate otherwise—and that brought her back to her earlier thought that he might try to seduce her.

She was a sophisticated woman, a galactic traveler whose work frequently brought her into contact with powerful men on a variety of worlds. And as a Whisperer, she was a member of a small elite corps that had an allure all its own. Furthermore, since she was well-schooled in the art of diplomacy, she knew how to deflect attempts at seduction, and had often done so.

But never before in her career had she been faced with a situation like this one. Miklos Panera was the most dangerous man she'd ever met, and it seemed that she was drawn to him as the moth is drawn to the flame.

"There's the town," he said, interrupting her confused thoughts.

* * *

By the time the hovercraft had settled down on the rough stones of the town square, dozens of Torondis were hurrying toward them. Panera was wearing a stunner attached to his belt, but she was pleased to note that he kept his hand away from it.

The square was elevated, formed by many layers of small stones. Beyond it, stretching for some distance, lay the homes of the Torondis. All of them stood high on stone columns and were connected by elevated stone walkways. It was certainly one of the stranger sights Jalissa had ever seen, but she had to admit that it was an excellent adaptation to living in a swamp.

The dark, opaque waters lay all around them and gave off an unpleasant smell that made her want to wrinkle her nose. She wondered what these people would think of clean, fresh air. Perhaps it would smell bad to them.

Jalissa and Panera stood side by side as they waited for the people to approach them. Jalissa saw no overt hostility, to her very great relief. But after casting wary glances at Panera, they all stared unabashedly at her—not surprising, since no Whisperer had set foot on Torondi in a very long time.

She scanned the small group of men who continued to advance toward them while the others hung back. When it became apparent which of them was the leader, Jalissa addressed herself to him through the medium of the crystal.

"We come in peace, to seek information. No harm will come to you." As she spoke, Jalissa used her body to convey her peaceful intentions, though she was certainly hampered by having an armed Special Agent at her side.

The reaction of the man to whom she addressed herself was completely predictable. Anyone encountering a Whisperer for the first time was invariably either confused or frightened—or, as in this case, both. The problem was in the way the crystal worked. She spoke in Vantran, for Panera's sake, but the man heard her in his own language. It took great skill to prevent the language she was actually speaking from overwhelming the translation. Add to that a half-second delay in the translation, and it was no wonder that first-time listeners were overwhelmed.

She hurried on to explain who she was, not bothering to introduce Panera. They knew *what* he was, if not his name, and as far as she was concerned, he was irrelevant at the moment.

The man fixed his strange amber eyes on the crystal as she explained what it was. Then he began to move closer to her, and from the corner of her eye, she saw Panera stiffen. His hand began to inch toward the stunner on his belt.

"Step back," she told him. "He wants to touch the crystal, but he's afraid of you."

Panera hesitated, but finally did as told. That gesture seemed to reassure the man, and he put out his hand as she held the warm crystal to him, stretching it to the limit of its platinum chain.

She continued to speak encouragingly to the man, and her speech caused the crystal to glow with faint colors. The Torondi touched it, then drew away as though burned. Murmurs arose from the crowd and they pressed closer, now surrounding her and separating her from Panera. She glanced his way and saw him standing there rigidly, his hand now resting on his belt, next to the stunner.

Several others touched the crystal as well, as she continued to speak words of reassurance. At the same time, she tried to gauge the mood of the crowd. It seemed that they were more curious than hostile, and they were all but ignoring Panera at this point.

Then the leader spoke for the first time in his strange, whistling tongue. "Is it magic?" he asked, pointing to the crystal.

She smiled. "In a way. But it's good magic, since it allows me to talk with you. Please tell me your name. Mine is Jalissa."

He gave her his name, which she did her best to repeat. Then, apparently emboldened, he asked if she'd come because of the stranger.

"Yes," she replied. "What can you tell me about him?"

"He was very sick, we think," came the reply. "Sick in the head." He touched his own head and there were murmurs of agreement from the others.

"How did you know that?" she asked, fairly certain now that it couldn't have been the Warlock. These people would surely remember the Coven, and they wouldn't mistake magic for mental illness.

They knew he was sick because he had behaved very strangely, yelling at them in a language they couldn't understand and then becoming very agitated at their failure. He had, it seemed, a pronounced facial tic, which the Torondis imitated for her, as well as some spasmodic jerking of his limbs.

"Could you describe him?" she asked, and they told her that he had dark hair and blue eyes and that he was very thin.

Jalissa knew now that he wasn't the Warlock, and she also knew what the poor man's problem was: space-sickness. It was seen most often in space travelers who used ancient craft with malfunctioning ventilation systems. Deprived of the oxygen it required, the brain began to deteriorate. And the physical description the people gave told her which world he was likely from: a poor place where many traders took to space in vehicles that should have been scrapped decades ago.

Finally, she asked what had happened to him, and learned that he had simply walked off into the swamp, leaving behind his hovercraft.

"He sacrificed himself," the Torondi said solemnly, to the accompaniment of sober nods from his companions.

Jalissa felt ill, but nothing showed on her face. "How do you know that?" she asked, hoping they were only making an assumption.

"When the snake-god has accepted a sacrifice, he roars. We all heard it."

Jalissa's mind was filled with the image of that snake they'd seen, and for once, her aplomb nearly failed her. But whether deliberately or not, Panera distracted the Torondis by once again moving to her side. She couldn't be sure if he'd overheard the conversation—at least not until he asked her to find out where the hovercraft was.

She asked, and they pointed toward a largish building that sat at the other side of the town square, the only building not elevated on stone blocks, since it sat on the square itself. Panera took her arm and began to lead her in that direction. He bent close, his breath fanning warmly against her ear.

"You're doing fine. We'll get out of here as soon as I have a look at the hovercraft."

His words, almost certainly meant in kindness, had the opposite effect on her. She became angry with herself. If he could tell how upset she was, then she'd failed. Maintaining a cool neutrality no matter what the situation was essential to Whisperers.

The hovercraft was an old model, one she hadn't seen in years. Panera searched it for any personal belongings, but found nothing. She suspected that whatever had been there had been taken by the Torondis and hoped that Panera didn't intend to make an issue of it. The man certainly couldn't have had much.

The Torondi leader then inquired rather timidly if they could keep the hovercraft, since its owner had "gone to the snake-gods." Panera overheard the conversation as he was climbing out of the vehicle.

"They can keep it. It was rented from a place I know, near the base. I'll take care of it."

She translated for the Torondis and they all smiled, then made a high, keening sound that she took to be pleasure. Obviously, Panera had known that his gift would be greatly appreciated.

As they walked back across the square to their own hovercraft, Jalissa was having a difficult time controlling her anger with these people. She was no stranger to wars between groups who spilled each other's blood with abandon, but never before had she encountered a situation like this, where people had allowed a mentally ill man to wander off and be eaten by a snake.

"We have to look for him," she said frantically the moment they both were airborne. "He could still be alive out there."

"Our backup will be here in a few minutes," he told her, then picked up the comm speaker and ordered whoever was on the other end to commence a search in the area to the west of the town.

"We should help," she said, already scanning the dark swamp below them. "There are some dry places. He could be—"

"He's dead, Jalissa," Panera said gently.

"How can you be sure of that?" she demanded, her voice rising.

"Because the snake roared. They only do that when they've captured a human."

"I know that's what they said, but they could be wrong," she insisted.

He shook his head. "In the two months I was here, I saw more of those damned snakes than I ever wanted to, but the only time I ever heard one roar was after it caught one of our men."

She swallowed hard and stared at him. He reached over to take one of her hands in his, covering it warmly.

"I'm sorry, Jalissa. I know you haven't had much experience with primitive people like this."

For one brief moment, Jalissa allowed herself to feel the warmth of his touch and the gentleness in his voice. The horror and the anger receded as a part of her felt that pleasurable ache, that hunger for more. In the clear, deep green of his eyes, she saw that same hunger. His hand tightened around hers, sending shivers of promised ecstasy through her body.

And then she shattered the moment—willfully

but not willingly. She pulled her hand from his only to discover that it did no good. She could still feel him holding it.

Two more hovercraft came into view, circling slowly over the dark waters. She wondered if he had summoned them only for her sake. He seemed so certain the man could not be alive.

"They called it a 'sacrifice,'" she said when she could trust her voice. "The stories must be true."

"Not necessarily," he replied, the hard edge back in his voice. "They apparently believed that he went willingly to the snake and simply used that term for it."

"The man was mentally ill, Miklos, and they knew it. He was suffering from space-sickness."

"Among many primitive peoples, the mentally ill are believed to have been touched by the gods. From their point of view, that could have made him an appropriate sacrifice."

Jalissa said nothing. She was beginning to understand just how much she was out of her depth here. The worlds she had until now considered to be primitive were in fact highly advanced compared with Torondi. And it could be even worse in the Outer Ring.

"He wasn't the man we're looking for," she said, forcing her mind back to their mission as he headed toward the base.

"How can you be sure? I couldn't hear all of the conversation."

"Because they said he had blue eyes and blue

eyes don't exist among members of the Coven."

"How do you know that?"

She froze for a moment, then relaxed quickly, hoping he hadn't noticed. "Every Tevingian knows that. Witches and Warlocks are invariably described as having dark hair and dark eyes—like most Tevingians."

He was silent for a moment. She didn't turn toward him, but she could feel his gaze on her. "You're right," he said finally. "The man we seek was described as having dark eyes, and nothing was mentioned about facial tics or spasms."

"Well, what do you think?" Miklos reached over to turn off the recorder. They were back aboard the U-77 and headed toward Tevingi. He had just played a recording made of the witness's account of the supposed Warlock's speech.

She stared at the recorder distastefully. "They used drugs on him."

"You know as well as I do that those drugs don't harm anyone. And they promote total recall."

"From the description, it sounds as though he could be Tevingian. He's probably delusional and actually believes himself to be a member of the Coven. Such delusions aren't unheard of on Tevingi. A form of Coven worship persists to this day among some of the rural folk. They even celebrate Coven festivals. I can remember attending one as a child."

"But you don't personally believe that they still exist?"

"No. I already told you that. But it seems to me that the Special Agency must not be so sure. Otherwise, why would *you* be sent after one deluded man?"

Miklos decided to answer her honestly. "There are those among my people who have *always* suspected that the Coven still exists. And there have been enough unsubstantiated rumors over the years to keep that fear alive."

" 'Fear'?" she echoed derisively. "What could Vantrans possibly have to fear from the Coven now—even if it does exist?"

"Quite a lot, actually. Its magic may no longer be a match for our science, but the hold the Coven could have on the minds and hearts of people could be enormous."

She didn't respond, so Miklos lapsed into silence as well, thinking about the part of the recording he hadn't played for her. He'd edited it carefully, so all she'd heard was the physical description of the man and his speech. But the other part included the witness's testimony that the man had "called the fire" and had then vanished in a puff of smoke just before the troops arrived.

The lightning could easily have been a trick, but he knew of no way he could have pulled off that vanishing act. Creating the smoke would have been no problem, but he'd seen a vid of the spot where the man had stood, and he agreed with the man on the scene that there was no way the troublemaker could have disappeared as their witness had described.

Still, he knew that the drug wasn't perfect, even though it was close to that. Their captured witness could have seen what he *wanted* to see. The very fact that he'd been drawn there by rumors of a Warlock suggested that he expected to find one.

Miklos cast another glance at Jalissa Kendor as she turned her attention to the galactic news on the vid. His mind spun back to that time he'd first encountered her, then fast-forwarded to their meeting with the Torondis.

Miklos had spent enough time with Whisperers over the years to be very familiar with how they worked. He'd even seen the famous Petrov, supposedly their best until Jalissa came along. But there was something different about the way she worked. He'd been almost literally spellbound watching her.

He knew that Whisperers employed every trick in the book to disarm their subjects psychologically: body language, tone of voice, eye contact. He'd learned those tricks too, as part of his own training. But there was something beyond all that with Jalissa Kendor, though he couldn't say what it was.

And then there was the matter of the Torondis' reaction to her. He knew them well enough to know that what he'd seen wasn't normal for them. They were suspicious of strangers and they treated their women as little better than property. Not even a Federation uniform impressed them when it was worn by a woman.

Part of it could simply have been her talents as a Whisperer, but Miklos was unwilling to ascribe it all to that.

He continued to stare at her as she watched the news. Dark tales of Coven magic whispered through his memory, stirring up that fear he'd spoken of. But he was a man of science, and rumors notwithstanding, he didn't believe in the existence of the Coven.

What he *did* believe, though, was that Jalissa Kendor was rapidly becoming a very unwise obsession for him.

The snake was huge as it reared up on the forepart of its scaly body. Jalissa knew she couldn't outrun it. Any minute now, it would overtake her in the noxious swamp and grab her with its curved yellow fangs!

But even in her mind-numbing panic, it seemed to her that there was something she could do to save herself. What was it? What was she forgetting? It was there, tickling her memory but refusing to come forth.

She continued to run through the mucky swamp, but her legs kept getting tangled up in something, slowing her down. Surely the snake must be nearly upon her now! And then she heard a voice, calling her name! Miklos! Was he trapped too?

"Jalissa! Wake up! You're safe here."

Her eyelids seemed to be glued together. She could hear strange whimpers. Were they coming from her? Her heart was pounding so noisily in her chest that she thought it would burst.

"Jalissa! Wake up!"

Something touched her, grabbing her shoulders and shaking her gently. At first, still half-caught in the nightmare, she fought it, lashing out with her fist. But instead of encountering the snake's scaly body, she connected with hard, smooth skin and thick hair.

Her eyes flew open just as he cried out in pain, and a moment later, both her hands were imprisoned in one of his as he bent over her. The nightmare snake slithered away and reality washed over her, bringing with it a sharp awareness of him.

He was nearly naked, his bronzed body so close to her that she could feel its heat and see reflected in the low light of the cabin the curling golden hairs on his chest.

Even though he surely knew that she was awake now, he continued to hold her hands imprisoned above her head as he stared at her, his eyes dark in the dim light. The moment spun out into a seeming eternity. His gaze shifted to the wildly beating pulse point at the base of her throat, then back to her eyes once again. Very slowly, he started to lower his face to hers. Her lips parted, anticipating his kiss—and wanting it.

Then he released her and abruptly moved away from her. A small cry of protest died away in her throat as the moment moved beyond reach, leaving in its wake the aching emptiness of denial.

"You were having a nightmare," he stated unnecessarily.

She nodded, hating the tension that now filled a space occupied only seconds ago with a desire more powerful than anything she could have imagined.

"I'm sorry I woke you," she said with an attempt at polite formality in the midst of this intimate scene. Then, when she saw him rub his temple, she remembered striking out at him and apologized.

His mouth twitched with amusement. "I hope you were still fighting the snake when you did it."

She nodded, then shuddered as she recaptured the dream. "I was running through the swamp and I knew it was going to catch me. I kept thinking there was something I could do to save myself, but I couldn't re . . ."

Her voice trailed off as she realized what it was that her dream-self had forgotten. Of course! She could have 'ported her way out of danger! She frowned, realizing that the dream had a parallel in reality: that time on Temok when she'd almost been killed because she'd forgotten that she possessed the magic to save herself.

Then she realized that he was watching her, waiting for her to continue. She managed to smile at him. "I should have accepted your suggestion to use a sleep-drug."

"No harm done," he said, standing up and revealing all of his long, lean body, except for the part hidden by a pair of dark briefs. She averted her gaze quickly—but not before she saw what it had cost him to stop. And then she wondered why he *had* stopped.

"Maybe I'll take something now," she said, pushing off the tangled covers and getting out of bed. If she didn't, she was certain that the snake would be replaced by a very different kind of torment.

"Good idea," he said, his gaze passing slowly over her lightly clad body and then coming to rest on the crystal that nestled between her breasts.

He stepped aside for her to pass him in the small cabin—but for one explosive moment, it seemed that he wouldn't move and she would walk straight into his arms. She hurried into the bathroom and closed the door behind her, then leaned against the sink and waited until her body had become her own once more.

Jalissa stared down at the world she called home. It was still mostly obscured by clouds, but as often happened at this time of year, the layer had thinned out somewhat, affording a glimpse of craggy peaks covered with dense, dark forests and narrow valleys bisected by swift-running streams.

As always, she felt a powerful tug of contradictory emotions. She'd been dragged unwillingly to Tevingi and left in the care of strangers at the age of 12.

And yet, within weeks, she'd stopped crying herself to sleep at night, and within a few months she would have fought any attempt to send her back to her true home with its subterranean city.

A child lives in the here and now, with little thought of past or future—and Jalissa had been no exception. She didn't forget about her past life in the Coven; rather, she just set it aside, as a child plays with a toy and then discards it.

The woman she had become was ashamed of that child's callousness, and each time she came back here, Jalissa was reminded of that. And she was also reminded of the very great difference between her life as a child of the Coven and the very different life she discovered on Tevingi, where children were raised by doting parents and encouraged to be children, rather than being forced before their time to accept heavy responsibilities.

All of these feelings flowed through her now, as they orbited Tevingi, and so it was with some effort that she reminded herself of the dangers of this particular trip.

Panera was very eager to learn if the man they sought was in fact Tevingian. At his request, she'd sent a message to her adoptive parents, informing them of her visit and its purpose.

She assumed that they knew by now of the Warlock's escape from the Coven and of his activities. There were always Coven members on Tevingi who could receive telepathic messages and then pass them on to families like the Kendors who had been allied with the Coven for many centuries.

Tevingi spacecraft still visited the Coven's world, but only infrequently, since they risked discovery by the Federation military, who would certainly question their presence on a barren, lifeless planet.

Miklos Panera appeared suddenly at her side and informed her that they would begin their descent in a few minutes. He remarked that the cloud cover seemed thinner than he had seen it in the past, and she explained that this often happened in the spring.

As they talked, Jalissa found herself edging away from him, even as she was being drawn *to* him. She had foolishly hoped that their forced intimacy on the small craft would allow her attraction to him to dissipate. But instead, their polite formality toward each other and their attempts to avoid each other had only heightened the sensual tension between them.

How he truly felt about her remained a mystery, however. She was no longer so certain that she'd seen true desire in his eyes, though her instincts continued to tell her this was so. This ambivalence was very frustrating to one who'd learned long ago to trust those instincts implicitly.

Even as she stood here now and felt the powerful, invisible webs of sensuality that bound them together, she reminded herself that it could all be a part of a very careful seduction for the sole purpose of discrediting her.

They began to settle gently to the surface of Tevingi, drifting down through the cloud cover until the dark, rugged surface was fully revealed. Before long, she could see their destination: the huge Federation base that sprawled across one of the few flat, open areas of the planet, completely filling the space between the tall mountains.

The base was a world unto itself—completely self-sustaining since its construction a century ago over the violent objections of the Tevingians. In the early years, any Federation soldier leaving the base was risking his or her life. Now they were grudgingly tolerated by the Tevingians, but they still tended to keep to themselves. And while there were Tevingians in the Federation military, they were never posted to their home world—which was not the case at other bases.

The base abutted the vast landholdings of her adoptive family, and much of it had once belonged to the Kendors: a particular sore point since it occupied some of the most fertile land on the planet.

Thinking about this uneasy history, Jalissa wondered if it could be true that Tevingi was plotting to leave the Federation and ally itself with the Outer Ring. Certainly, Tevingians had risen to powerful positions within the Federation, but she knew them well enough to know how they still burned inwardly at the conquest by the Vantrans long ago.

A short time later, Jalissa and Miklos disembarked, and she smiled with pleasure when she saw her tall, slim, gray-haired adoptive mother among the group waiting for them. But a slight frown crossed her face as she hurried to greet her. Where was her father?

Neesa Kendor answered her unspoken question as soon as they embraced. "Your father couldn't come because there's been an explosion at the new mine. He received word just as we were leaving to come here."

Jalissa had paid scant attention to the others in the welcoming party, but she turned to them now as a Vantran general spoke, gesturing to the sky behind them.

"Here come the first of the casualties now."

They all stood and watched as three swift hovercraft settled down on the roof of a large building that Jalissa assumed must be the base hospital. One craft bore the distinctive coat of arms of the Kendors and the other two were Federation craft. She was rather surprised at this, since the base hospital was normally off-limits to Tevingians.

On other worlds, it was quite common for Federation medical facilities to treat natives, but on Tevingi, the old separation was still maintained. Apparently seeing her surprise, Neesa explained that when they'd called the base to inform them of their delay, the commander had kindly offered his facilities.

They watched as the victims were off-loaded and carried into the hospital. Then Neesa Kendor turned and introduced herself to Panera before Jalissa had the opportunity.

Jalissa saw his gaze go from her "mother" to her and back again. There was no resemblance at all between them, but fortunately she *did* bear a slight resemblance to her adoptive father, whom she now saw coming toward them. Apparently, he'd been aboard one of the hovercraft.

He embraced Jalissa warmly, then began to explain the situation to them all. "No one was killed, thank the gods, but there are some serious injuries. We don't know yet what happened—and we may never know, since the entire shaft has collapsed. If the explosion had occurred five minutes earlier or later, there would almost certainly have been many deaths. But it happened during a shift change, when there were only a small number of miners in the shaft."

The Vantran general assured him that they would do their best to save the miners, and Joeb Kendor expressed his gratitude, then introduced himself to Panera. Jalissa watched the two men take the measure of each other. Joeb was the descendant of what had for centuries been the most powerful clan on Tevingi, and was every bit as proud and arrogant as the Vantran. It was not at all difficult to see why these two peoples had never warmed to each other. The Vantrans certainly had the edge with their science, but Tevingi didn't lag far behind.

Joeb then suggested that they go home, and turned to Panera.

"Will you be joining us, Agent Panera? You're very welcome to do so."

"I would be very pleased to visit you tomorrow, if that's convenient," Panera replied. "I told Jalissa that I'd like to try to ride a madri."

"You're welcome to try, but I'm sure that Jalissa had warned you that they rarely accept offworlders."

"Perhaps I'll be lucky." He gave Jalissa a slight bow. "Good-bye, Jalissa. Enjoy your visit. I'll see you tomorrow morning."

Chapter Four

"He's very handsome—and quite charming for a Vantran," Nessa Kendor remarked as they took off in their hovercraft.

"Especially a Panera," Joeb chuckled. Even out here at the edge of the galaxy, that name was quite well-known.

"The general is his uncle," Neesa went on. "His mother's brother. He told me while we were waiting."

Jalissa said nothing. "Charming" was not a word she would have applied to Miklos Panera. She wondered what her adoptive parents would think if they knew about her dangerous attraction to him. Probably they wouldn't believe it even if she told them. Nowhere in the galaxy were Vantrans less tolerated than on Tevingi—except, of course, among her own people.

The conversation turned to the accident. By tacit agreement, no mention was made yet of her purpose in being here, or of any messages from the Coven. No one was certain just what the Federation's capabilities for spying were, so it was assumed that they could overhear any conversations taking place on—or, in this case, *over*—the base.

At the time of her last visit, Joeb had told her that he wasn't sure that the Federation might not be listening in to conversations within the house, using the comm unit as some sort of transmitter. Tevingians weren't quite so awed by the Vantrans' science as many others were, but they still had a healthy respect for it. Because of this fear, secret conversations were carried on only in the beautiful gardens and wooded glades surrounding the house.

Soon the base was behind them and they were flying low over newly planted fields and open meadows where livestock grazed and wildflowers nodded in the breeze. Jalissa cried out with pleasure as she saw a herd of madris, grazing placidly on the blue-green grass they favored.

"Bellou has been told of your visit," Neesa said. "She was out in a far pasture, but now she's staying close to home."

Jalissa's smile widened. No one was really sure just how intelligent the madris were because they were stubborn creatures who resisted any attempt to test them. But every time Bellou was told of Jalissa's impending arrival, she hung around the home paddocks, waiting.

The madris came and went pretty much as they wanted. The pastures were fenced in for other animals, but of course the madris could simply unfold their great wings and fly over them. In the heat of high summer, they favored the cool mountains, and could often be seen drifting above the peaks on the thermals. When winter came, they spent much of their time in their comfortable stables.

Jalissa was eager to see the new foals. Pregnant mares always came back to the home paddock to give birth, and then remained there until their offspring had mastered the art of flying and could clear the fences. The stallions never came inside the birthing paddock, but they often flew over it or pranced about beyond the fence, calling to their mates. Madris mated for life, and if one died, the other never took a new mate.

But as much as she wanted to see her beloved madris, Jalissa decided that she'd better concentrate first on the business that had brought her here. So as soon as they landed in front of the huge stone house, she suggested a walk in the gardens.

"Has the Coven contacted you about the renegade Warlock?" she asked as soon as they set out on the pebbled paths.

"Yes. We're all very worried about it," Neesa replied. Joeb had gone inside to call the hospital and check on the condition of the miners.

Neesa gave her a worried glance. "We were told that you had been instructed to stay away from this matter."

"That's true—but there's no way that I could. For me to have refused this mission would only cast suspicion on me. Besides, it's important that *I* be the one to find him. I may be able to persuade him to return to the Coven."

"But what about Panera? We know his reputation, Jalissa. He's a very dangerous man."

Indeed, Jalissa thought—and in more ways than one. But she didn't reply because Joeb was hastening along the path to join them. He reported that all the miners would survive, and then Neesa repeated their conversation.

Joeb nodded. "I think you have the right of it, Jalissa, but I'm not so sure that you'll be able to persuade him to go back to the Coven. In fact, we think it's possible that he might have left with their blessing."

Jalissa stared at him in shock, recalling what Panera had said about this man's having been sent out to "test the waters" for a return of the Coven.

"Would they do this without telling you?" she asked. "Have you asked them?"

Both of her adoptive parents looked at her as though she'd just said that the sky was falling.

She'd forgotten just how Tevingians regarded the Coven. They'd never question anything.

"We *do* know that in recent years, there have been more and more members of the Coven coming here and then entering the service of the Federation—mostly into Trans/Med, but also into the military and other branches."

"What?" Jalissa said, stopping in her tracks. "I thought I was the only one!"

Neesa smiled gently. "No, dear. You weren't even the first. And we shouldn't be telling you this now, because we were told to keep it from you because of your position. But we're really very worried—for the Coven and for Tevingi as well."

"You're the only one who's ever become a Whisperer," Joeb confirmed. "But there are other Coven members in Trans/Med. And we're telling you now only because of a coded message we received from one of them.

"It was very carefully worded, since we can't be totally certain that the Special Agency isn't capable of decoding. But the message was very clear. The Special Agency suspects you of being a Witch."

Jalissa felt a sudden chill and wrapped her arms around herself. "But how? Why?"

"I think it may be because you're so very good at your profession, Jalissa," Joeb said. "*Too* good. That might well have prompted them to check into your background. We took every precaution we could to make it appear that you were our daughter, but we can't be certain that they didn't uncover something—or persuade someone to talk. Vantran gold can loosen tongues—even here."

"This makes your mission even more dangerous," Neesa said. "Regardless of what it means for the safety of the young Warlock—and even the Coven itself—you must think of your own safety first, Jalissa, and do nothing to give yourself away."

"Or to give all of *you* away," Jalissa added. If she were exposed, it would be disastrous for her adopted family—and for *all* Tevingians—because the Federation would then know that they'd been aiding the Coven.

"Yes," Joeb said quietly. "There is that problem as well. We have been secretly arming ourselves as best we can."

Jalissa was recalling Panera's suggestion of a conspiracy between Tevingi and the Outer Ring worlds. "Where have you been obtaining weapons?" she asked, knowing that the Federation had very strict controls about the production and transport of weapons—especially on Tevingi.

"From the Outer Ring worlds. Danto is having them brought back on his merchant ships."

Danto was Joeb's brother. He controlled the Kendor family's vast inter-planetary shipping fleet. She'd heard that weapons were far more available on some of the Outer Ring worlds, where a clandestine market was supposedly operating along the very fringes of Federation power.

"Panera told me that they suspect some sort of secret alliance between Tevingi and the Outer Ring. They believe you may be planning to lead Tevingi out of the Federation."

"It may come to that if we must fight to protect the Coven," Joeb replied.

"Why is the Coven doing this?" Jalissa cried angrily. "This is madness!"

"They haven't told us their plans, Jalissa," Neesa said gently. "No doubt the gods have given them their instructions."

"I don't care what the gods tell them," she stated angrily. "If the Coven tries to wage war against the Federation, they will be destroyed!" She gestured toward the distant base.

"You've seen their power. You must know that Coven magic—even Coven magic combined with smuggled arms—can't possibly defeat Vantran weaponry. My superior asked the Deputy Director of the Special Agency what they would do if they learned that the Coven still existed, and he refused to rule out the possibility of destroying them. She told me later that she thinks that's exactly what they will do."

Then Jalissa paused, thinking about Malvina. It was probably she who had sent the message about the Special Agency's suspicions.

"My superior is Malvina Sangtry—the woman who recruited me. Do you remember her?"

They both nodded, and Neesa confirmed her sudden suspicion. "She is a Witch."

Jalissa was stunned. Had she strayed so far from her origins that she couldn't immediately recognize another Coven member? She'd always felt a special fondness for Malvina, but never once had she suspected the truth.

"How many worlds besides Tevingi and the Outer Ring would side with the Coven?" she asked Joeb, knowing that because of the family's business, he would be familiar with the private thoughts of those on many worlds.

"Danto believes there could be as many as five, most of those who were touched by the Coven. On many worlds, the Coven is no longer worshipped openly in order to avoid offending the Vantrans, but the feelings are still there." He paused.

"But by far the most important one is Ker."

"Ker?" she gasped, her mind reeling. Ker was the one world in the galaxy where the precious crystals could be found. It had no native population. Instead, it was home to people from various worlds who possessed the skills required to cut the crystals.

The crystals wouldn't be so important to the Vantrans if they were used only by Whisperers, but they had other uses too. They powered the Galactic Communications Network, and also powered the navigation and other systems aboard spacecraft.

"According to Danto, most of the population on Ker now comes from the Outer Ring. Few others are willing to live on such a primitive, unpleasant world."

"But the Federation military has a huge base there as well."

"Yes, but among them are a substantial number of people from worlds sympathetic to the Coven. That is so because of the Federation's policy of trying to post people either on or close to their home worlds."

A policy Jalissa knew the Vantrans had agreed to only after considerable pressure from the other members of the Federation. And now she understood why.

Jalissa stood at the fence, watching the madri foals at play, a sight that would normally have claimed all her attention. But her brain was still whirling with the information she'd received and its terrible implications.

She was still stunned at her failure to recognize that Malvina was a Witch. And how many others had she met as well, without realizing what they were?

She had moved so far from that world of dark magic. In the long intervals between telepathic contact, she simply never gave any thought to her differentness. She was Jalissa Kendor, a respected Whisperer who used her skills to make peace out of chaos and hatreds.

And somewhere along the way, she'd to all intents and purposes forgotten that she was also a Witch: a possessor of magic and a descendant of the old gods.

But she could no longer afford to forget that. There was so very much danger: for her, for her adoptive family, for the Coven—and even for the Federation.

It surprised her to include the Federation on that list. It was so much a fact of life that she'd simply never questioned it. But as she did so now, she realized that she didn't want the Federation to be destroyed. It might not be perfect, but the alternative was total chaos and incessant wars.

Her bleak thoughts were interrupted by a familiar whinny, and she turned to see Bellou, her madri mare, galloping toward her across the meadow.

"Bel!" she cried as the sleek white animal slowed to a trot and then a walk and finally nuzzled into her shoulder, making the snorting, chuffing sound madris made to show their affection.

"Oh Bel!" she cried, wrapping her arms around the mare's graceful neck. "Each time I see you, you grow more beautiful."

She rubbed the knobby joints of Bel's folded wings, and the mare shivered with pleasure. Then she went into the stable to get a bridle. The galaxy's problems could wait for a while.

*   *   *

"How will I know if one of them will accept me?"

Jalissa found herself barely able to restrain a smile. From the moment when he'd first seen the madris, Miklos Panera had been wearing the expression of a delighted child. And now he sounded like a child who fears that the toy he wants won't be his.

"Just approach whichever one you like. If it accepts you, it will let you know."

"But what if I choose the wrong one?" he persisted, his gaze scanning the grazing herd.

"It's not an individual thing," she explained. "They seem to be of one mind where humans are concerned. Either they *all* accept you—or no one does. That's because they're herd animals by nature."

He was now staring at the madri she'd known he would select: the magnificent black stallion, Wansa. Not only was he the largest madri in their herd, but he was also the most perfect example of the species she'd ever seen. And he was still young—only eight. Madris lived longer than ordinary horses, many of them to 40 or more years. Her Bel was nearing 20.

Panera cast a quick glance at her, then began to thread his way through the herd to the stallion. She followed, but at a distance. Strangely, her feelings had undergone a reversal. Instead of hoping that the madris would reject this arrogant

Vantran, she now found herself wanting him to be accepted.

Miklos had surprised her by showing up without his impressive uniform. Instead, he wore form-fitting pants and a loose shirt the exact shade of his eyes. It was the first time she could recall seeing a member of the Federation military out of uniform on Tevingi.

He'd shown up just as she was sitting down to a late breakfast with Neesa. Joeb had already left for the base hospital to check on his miners. Neesa had invited Miklos to join them, and Jalissa had watched bemusedly as he'd proceeded to charm her adopted mother, who certainly had no affection for Vantrans.

Even more surprising was the fact that Jalissa had sensed his charm was real, and not the practiced diplomacy she'd seen before with Vantrans in their social contacts with off-worlders. Still, she didn't doubt for one minute that beneath the casual exterior remained the steely, determined Special Agent.

Panera stopped before the stallion. It lifted its head and stared at him. He put out a hand slowly and touched the animal's sleek, curved neck. Most people unfamiliar with madris approached them more cautiously than they would ordinary horses. Partly, it was the wings, but it was also their size. Madris were nearly half again as big as other horses, and the stallion, Wansa, was probably twice as large. But they were also very gentle by nature, and once they'd decided to accept a rider, they never caused problems.

After studying Panera for several moments, the stallion suddenly lowered its head and nudged against his shoulder, snorting softly. Jalissa expected the Vantran to turn to her questioningly, or even to be frightened by the stallion's behavior, but he seemed to understand immediately what it meant, and began to stroke the animal and talk to it.

"They like to have the joints of their wings rubbed," she told him as she now approached them.

He did as instructed, then laughed as the animal shuddered with pleasure. Turning to her with a wide, boyish smile, he asked if they could ride now.

She nodded, and slipped the bridle she'd brought along over the stallion's head. "His name is Wansa. He's the father of that palomino foal you were admiring. That's why he's here, instead of out in the high pastures."

"Does that mean he won't want to leave?"

"No. He won't mind leaving for a time."

Panera stared at the great folded wings. "How do you get them to fly?"

She laughed at his eagerness. "You don't. You can point them in the direction you want to go, but how they get there is up to them."

"Then he might not fly at all?"

"Oh, he will. They love to fly, though they can't

116

fly great distances. They also need a rather long straight stretch to get up enough speed. The reason that this is such a perfect place for them is that there are long meadows, and then good thermals once they're airborne. We'll just ride out into the meadow, and they'll take off when they're ready. I hope you feel duly honored, by the way. It's really rare for them to accept offworlders."

He chuckled and rubbed the madri's wing joints again. "Thank you, Wansa, for being more tolerant than most Tevingians."

She decided to let that barb pass, and handed him the reins. "Just remember what I told you, Miklos. When you climb on a madri, you give up all control. He'll bring you back here if you say *docen*, which is Tevingi for 'home,' but other than that, *he's* the one in command."

Miklos nodded and turned to the stallion. "All right, Wansa. My life is in your hands—or your hooves, as it were." Then he swung gracefully onto the madri's broad back.

Jalissa laughed and turned to Bel, who obligingly knelt so that she could mount. Then she pointed the mare into the open field, and off they went, thundering through the meadow.

She watched Panera for a time to be certain he was comfortable. He'd told her that he rode often at his family's country estate, and it quickly became apparent that he was a very accomplished

117

rider for whom the lack of a saddle and stirrups posed no problem.

Both animals began to increase their speed until they moved from a canter into a flat-out gallop. Wansa quickly drew ahead, and Panera turned briefly back to her. His handsome face was wreathed in a smile of eager anticipation. Jalissa knew that somehow this moment would be locked forever into her memory. The feeling was bittersweet, however, tainted by the knowledge that it was a moment and nothing more.

Wansa's great wings began to unfold, followed a moment later by Bel's. She felt the mare's muscles begin to contract—and then they were airborne and soaring into the heavens, where patches of bright blue could be seen amidst the fluffy white clouds.

Because of the madris' 20-foot wingspan, they had to stay farther apart now, but she could still see her own joy mirrored on Panera's face. The wind created by the madris' wings and their movement through the skies lifted her hair and tore at her loose shirt. The sunlight glistened on Panera's tousled golden hair as he turned to her again, smiling broadly.

Miklos could not recall any time in his life when he'd been happier in the moment than he was right now, soaring above the meadows to the dark mountains in the distance.

He turned to stare at Jalissa Kendor. Her shining black hair streamed out behind her as she lifted her face to the wind. The loose shirt she wore was pressed against her full breasts, and her slim, muscular legs curved around the madri's flanks. It was a sight that he drank in like fine wine, even though he felt a totally illogical fear as well. Despite her ease on the madri's back, she seemed so small and helpless.

For one brief moment, his mind slipped back to that first time he'd seen her—when she *had* been helpless. And when he'd been spellbound, caught in a moment he still didn't understand. Then he was back in the present and her mare had moved farther away, its wings flapping more slowly now as they found the thermals and began to ride the winds up over the mountains.

Seeing her riding the near-mythical horse of the gods, Miklos felt a sense of awe. An inner voice whispered to him that this was no mere woman. But he quickly silenced the darker voice that tried to tell him just what she was.

The madris circled the tall peaks several times, then descended slowly, amidst much fluttering of their great wings. Finally, they drifted down to a sloping meadow, where yellow and purple flowers bloomed amidst tall bluish grasses. Several other madris were already there, and they raised their heads briefly, whickering to the new-comers.

Jalissa's mare knelt to let her dismount, and

119

Panera slid down from his stallion. His burnished gold hair was tousled and his smile was still intact: the grin of a delighted boy.

"If more off-worlders rode these animals, the pressure to export them would be enormous," he said.

"Then I'm glad they don't," she replied. "Even though I often wish I could bring Bel back to Vantra with me."

"If your mother ever decides to sell any off-world, I'd pay whatever she asks. And I think they'd like Tralisa, our country home. The land there looks much as it does here."

"She'd never sell them, and neither would any other breeder."

"Because of their association with the Coven?"

She nodded as she sank down onto the grass. "If the Coven hadn't given some to my ancestors, there wouldn't be any madris. They would have been destroyed along with the Coven itself."

He was silent for a moment, then said quietly. "It must have seemed the only possible course of action at the time. If we hadn't destroyed them, the wars would have continued and many more lives would have been lost than the number that died when we blew up their world."

"That's a self-serving statement if I've ever heard one, Miklos Panera! You could have stopped that war anytime you chose. The Coven weren't the aggressors!"

"Spoken like a true Tevingian defender of the

Coven," he said with a smile as he lowered himself down beside her. "So I assume that your family still worships them."

"I wouldn't say that they exactly worship them—but they *do* revere them. All Tevingians do. The Coven was a part of our legends even before the first space traders found them. Some of our historians believe that the Coven *was* Tevingian, and that they used their magic a long time ago to take themselves off to another world in order to avoid our bloody conflicts here. Back then, the various clans were always at war.

"They cite as evidence the fact that we appear to be of the same race and our languages are quite similar."

"But if that's true, then surely some of the magical powers of the Coven would have appeared in your own people," he pointed out.

"They have—but to a much lesser extent. There are many among my people who have a talent for precognition and clairvoyance, for example." She was sure he must already know that, even though Tevingians tended not to talk about it to off-worlders.

"But what about the other powers they supposedly had: teleportation, the blue fire, casting spells?"

"Some think they might have been learned skills, and with no one to teach them here, they were never developed."

"Doesn't the thought that we could be chasing

a Warlock frighten you?" he asked after a brief silence.

The question caught her off-guard, and she took a second to compose herself before turning to face him. "No. Why should it? I'm Tevingian, Miklos. We don't fear the Coven."

"But it means that the man isn't *human*, Jalissa."

"The Coven *is* human," she said, rather more sharply than she'd intended. His words hurt. "They are born and die like all other people. They simply have powers that others don't. Why is that so difficult to accept? *You* have knowledge that *I* don't have, Miklos—about spacecraft and weapons and other such things."

"But those things were developed through sciences that can be understood by anyone who wants to study them."

"Nevertheless, *I* don't understand them and you do, and that doesn't make you different to me."

"I think we're talking at cross-purposes here," he said with that half-smile.

"Probably we are. Vantrans and Tevingians have a tendency to do that."

He laughed, leaning back in the grass to rest on his elbows. "Maybe you're right. You're really the first Tevingian I've ever gotten to know."

And you don't know me, she thought with a sharp pang of regret that had no business being there. She turned to look at him as he continued to recline in the grass, watching her with a lazy smile that was either very real—or the practiced charm of a seducer.

"You can be very charming, Miklos. I think you even succeeded in charming my mother."

"I'm glad if she likes me, but what about *you*?"

Jalissa was startled by the unexpected question, and she saw that he knew it. She turned away quickly.

"You're a Special Agent, Miklos—and I'm a Whisperer."

He sat up suddenly, bringing himself far too close to her. "Are you saying that you think I'd try to seduce you for that reason?"

"It's happened before."

"Not with me, it hasn't."

She got up and started to walk through the meadow, intending to pick some wildflowers. He followed her, but thankfully remained silent. His denial echoed through her mind with the unmistakable ring of truth. Besides, she would certainly have heard about it if he *had* attempted to seduce one of her colleagues. His name certainly came up often enough in their conversations.

They continued to wander through the meadow, and Jalissa found herself wishing they could shed their professions, and become instead simply a man and a woman, both of them bent on seduction.

Still, she thought sadly, even if they could forget their professions for a time, she could not afford to forget what she was. And neither could he if he knew the truth. He'd said it himself: She wasn't human. She wished those words hadn't hurt so much.

"Have you asked your parents about the man we're looking for?" he asked suddenly, breaking the long silence between them.

"Yes," she replied, though of course she hadn't needed to. "They've promised to make some inquiries. I gave them a copy of the holo drawing."

"Would they admit it if they *did* learn anything?"

"Yes. They understand how dangerous he could be."

"But they could be betraying one of their own—or betraying the Coven," he persisted. "I'm certainly not getting any cooperation from the government."

"They would tell me because they trust my judgment."

"In other words, they might tell you, but you might not tell *me*."

"That would make no sense, Miklos. I care about the Federation too, you know. Besides, I'm not allowed to take any actions on my own."

Miklos decided not to press her anymore on the matter, even though he knew that if there were some sort of conspiracy afoot, her family was almost certain to be involved. He'd learned from his uncle, the commanding general at the base, that Jalissa's uncle was suspected of bringing contraband weapons to Tevingi on his ships.

At this point, the general was unwilling to confront Danto Kendor. The situation was very delicate. The Kendors were very powerful, and there would definitely be problems with the Federation Council if false accusations were made against them. There was a tendency on the part of the other worlds to sympathize with the Tevingians, who'd been treated so badly after the Coven episode. Memories were very long in the galaxy, especially when it came to complaints against his people.

Miklos watched her as she wandered among the flowers, plucking some for her bouquet. It was a picture he knew he would hold forever in his memory: the breeze that lifted her shining black hair away from her delicate face, the colorful flowers, the madris grazing in the background.

She looked as though she belonged here, walking the meadows and riding the madris, and yet he was increasingly certain that might not be the case. The time he'd been spending in the company of Tevingians had only served to make him more aware of the subtle differences.

That dark voice began to whisper to him again—and with it this time came a sudden recollection. Some years ago, he'd seen old paintings of the Coven in the Tevingi capital's art museum. At the time, he'd been reluctant to study them too closely because the Coven was always a difficult subject for Vantrans. Now he asked her about them.

"Yes, there are several of them. Why?"

"I thought that perhaps we could go to see them. Weren't they supposed to have been painted by an artist who'd actually visited the Coven?"

"Yes, they were."

Miklos saw no evidence that she was disturbed by his suggestion. He wished that she weren't so skilled at her profession. Whisperers were highly skilled at concealing their true thoughts, a necessary talent in their work, as it often was in his as well.

"I'm not sure what value that would have," she went on. "But we can certainly go there this afternoon if you wish. I wanted to go into Drasas anyway, to see my uncle. He controls the family's shipping and trading business, and I planned to take the drawing to him."

"Good idea. We can also ask him if he's heard anything about a conspiracy involving the Outer Ring worlds. His ships travel there regularly, don't they?"

She confirmed that, then suggested they return to the house. Miklos agreed, but still found himself strangely reluctant to leave this place. An opportunity had been lost here—a chance to create a small space for themselves. It was a strange feeling to him, a longing for something more than just the pleasure of her body. Stunned by the direction of his thoughts, he hurried to catch up to her as she started back toward their madris.

Moments later, they were airborne once again. Jalissa had neglected to tell him that up here in the high mountains, the madris simply ran off the edge of a cliff, then fell for a time until they caught the wind beneath their wings. Miklos wasn't truly frightened because he realized almost immediately what the animals were doing, but it was still a very unsettling experience.

She turned back to him once they had begun to soar, and gave him a look that seemed to be about equal parts amusement and apology. He could not resist teasing her about it when they landed in the meadow near the Kendor stables.

"I'd say that ranks right up there with the more unsettling experiences I've had," he told her dryly.

She laughed, a low, husky sound that sent ripples of pleasure through him. "I truly did forget to warn you, but hearing a Vantran admit that something has 'unsettled' him is an interesting experience for me too."

They smiled at each other—and in that moment, despite their unwillingness to admit it even to themselves, something began to change for them both.

* * *

Miklos stood before the huge paintings, struck by a sense that he was seeing ancient history come alive. Or was it ancient history? If the Coven still existed, he suspected nothing would have changed. They had seemed always to have lived outside time.

"They're just as I remembered, remarkably detailed," he said, turning to her.

Unfortunately, she thought, feigning interest in them herself as she wished he hadn't remembered them.

"The artist actually lived among the Coven for several months," she told him. "And during that time, he did all the sketches that he later turned into these paintings."

"I'm rather surprised they permitted that. They were supposed to have been very secretive."

"That's not true. They almost never left their own world, but they always welcomed visitors and hid nothing from them."

"Nothing?" he queried, turning briefly from his examination of the paintings to face her. "I thought they had secret rituals."

"Not that I've ever heard of. Their magic was simply a part of their lives, something they took for granted. Until the Tevingians and then others showed up, they had believed that all people must be like them."

It felt very strange to Jalissa to be discussing her people as though they were nothing more than a part of the distant past. And stranger still, they actually *did* feel that way to her. It was a measure of just how far she had strayed from the ways of the Coven.

But seeing these depictions of her people going about their daily lives also awakened in her a longing that surprised her. The paintings were nearly 200 years old, and yet they were an accurate portrayal of how her people still lived, right down to the dress. The only difference was that they now lived underground on a barren world that was very different from the place portrayed in the paintings: a small world of unsurpassed beauty, not unlike the much larger Vantra.

"The children are always pictured in groups, and not with their parents," he remarked as he turned back to the paintings. "I understand that they didn't believe in families as we know them."

"They didn't," she said. "Individuality was frowned upon by the Coven. The Coven itself was the unit, not families. Children were raised in one big nursery, as you can see."

"But they did have marriage, didn't they?"

"Oh, yes." She indicated a wedding scene. "But husbands and wives didn't generally live together, and they didn't select their mates either. The gods, speaking through the priests, ordained who could marry whom."

"A very strange society. And how were the priests selected? I assume these are priests?" He pointed to a group of black-robed people who wore elaborate headddresses.

"They are. The priests were selected by the gods, and always included both men and women."

"And did they have power in all things, or just in religious matters?"

"In all things because their religion was their life. The Coven was not a democracy, Miklos. No one would challenge the authority of the priests."

He turned to her again, and too late, she realized the implications of what she'd said.

"Then that would suggest that either our quarry isn't a Warlock—or that the Coven has approved what he's doing."

"Yes," she said carefully. "It *would* suggest that. But of course, he could be a rebel. Even among the Coven, they could exist."

"I'd find that hard to believe. It's been my experience that rebellion generally occurs among small, isolated groups like the Coven only if there's been contact with the larger world. Otherwise, fear of being cast out overcomes any desire to rebel."

She couldn't dispute that, since she too knew of numerous cases in the galaxy that proved his point.

Miklos bent to examine a detail of a large painting that depicted a group of Coven children, playing under the supervision of several adults. At first glance, there was nothing unusual in their play—until you realized that some of them were *levitating*.

Then he noticed something odd in another play group. They seemed to be playing catch with a big ball. But upon closer scrutiny, he could see that none of them had their hands raised to catch it as the ball was suspended in the center of the circle. He turned to Jalissa and pointed that out to her.

"They're not trying to catch it. The object of the game is to keep it in the air by using their magic. It was a game, but it was also training in working together. As I said, the Coven stressed cooperation, not competition."

"You seem to know quite a lot about them," he observed neutrally.

She shrugged. "No more than most Tevingians. There is a time in childhood when everyone is fascinated by them. They were fairy tales—with the added advantage of having been *real*."

"And perhaps they still are." He glanced at his watch and saw that it was time for them to leave for their meeting with her uncle. He'd invited himself along, and while she'd agreed, it was clear to him that she wasn't happy about it.

As they climbed back aboard the hovercraft for the short trip to the outskirts of the city where Danto Kendor had his offices, Miklos's thoughts remained on those remarkable paintings. The Witches and Warlocks of the Coven were just as he'd remembered them: dark-haired and fair-skinned, but with a delicate bone structure and overly large dark eyes that set them apart from Tevingians, whose looks were generally somewhat coarser.

The woman who sat beside him in the hovercraft could easily have posed for those pictures. He'd been greatly tempted to point that out to her.

Miklos was becoming more and more aware of his failure to listen to the dark voice of his suspicions, even though he was a man who had always trusted his instincts. But he thought back to those moments in the meadow and the ride through the heavens, and he decided that he wouldn't forward his suspicions to headquarters just yet.

Danto Kendor welcomed them to his spacious office with its glass walls that provided a panoramic view of the tallest mountains on Tevingi. He was a tall, well-built man with thinning dark hair that was even more liberally sprinkled with gray than it had been the last time Jalissa had seen him. Soft-spoken by nature, he was still a commanding presence.

Danto was a brilliant businessman, and a sophisticated man who wasn't overly impressed by a visit from a Special Agent—even one with the last name of Panera. Jalissa liked him very much, because beneath that gruff exterior lay great gentleness. He had come personally to take her from her childhood home to Tevingi, bringing with him his youngest daughter, who was only a few years older than Jalissa.

Danto's daughter Kelse was also on Vantra, where she worked for the Federation as a staff aide to the Council, and the two women had remained best friends.

Following the introductions, they talked for a time about their far-flung family, and particularly about Danto's first granddaughter, Kelse's four-month-old baby, whom he had yet to see except by comm.

"The world has become entirely too big a place," Danto said with a sigh. "Or perhaps too small, depending on your point of view." He turned to Panera. "I hear that there is talk again about mounting an expedition to the Raga Galaxy."

"There's talk," Panera acknowledged. "But most of the Council thinks we still have much to do to put our own galaxy in order first."

Danto nodded. "Ahh, yes, the ever-troublesome Outer Ring." Except for a few people in the Special Agency, Danto Kendor was the leading expert on the Outer Ring, since his ships traveled there regularly.

"What's your assessment of the political situation there?" Panera asked.

"Not good," Danto replied succinctly. "At least not from the point of view of the Federation. Except for the usual ongoing little wars, it seems remarkably peaceful right now. But I think that's deceptive."

"How so?" Panera asked.

"I think they may be planning to set up their own federation. You're probably aware of at least some of the secret meetings that have taken place. If you're not, you should consider replacing your spies."

Jalissa couldn't tell from his expression whether or not this was news to Panera, but she suspected it wasn't, or Danto wouldn't have mentioned it. He was careful to cooperate with the Federation, but like most Tevingians, he held back what and when he could.

"We've had some reports," Panera acknowledged. "But I'd welcome any additional information you can give me."

Jalissa listened as Danto detailed what was happening on one world after another. It meant little to her since she knew next to nothing about the Outer Ring. They'd spent little time during her training on the history and cultures of those worlds because Whisperers had never been permitted to go there.

"The belief among most of them is that the Federation would do little, if anything, to stop them," Danto finished. "And I suspect they're right. There isn't much there that we need or want."

"The Special Agency's position is that that should not be permitted to happen. We don't know what they have, since many of those worlds haven't been fully explored. And we also oppose any separate organization within the galaxy."

"I've heard rumors that there might be tactite on Debnos," Danto said, watching Panera closely.

Panera smiled. "Your reputation does not exceed reality, Danto Kendor."

Jalissa watched the two men. Nothing more was said on the subject, but it seemed to her that Panera had confirmed the rumor. Then she realized that what had just happened was a trade. Panera had confirmed a rumor of great business importance to Danto, and now he expected something in return.

Panera told Danto about the man they were seeking and showed him the holo drawing, saying that they believed him to be Tevingian. Danto stared at it and nodded, then gave Panera a smile.

"Or he might be a Warlock, as the rumors suggest."

He went on to say that he would send the holo to his various offices and ship commanders in the hope that someone could identify the man.

Panera thanked him, then went on to tell him about the other rumor: that Tevingi might join the Outer Ring if they rebelled against the Federation.

"I've heard no such story," Danto said, shrugging. "Of course, there have always been Tevingians who wanted to leave the Federation. But speaking personally, I'd be a fool to get into trouble with the Federation, since I depend on their re-fueling and maintenance bases, and nearly two thirds of my trade is with Federation worlds other than the Outer Ring."

What he *didn't* say, and what Jalissa knew, was that Danto Kendor was already one of the wealthiest men in the galaxy and could easily afford to lose business if he believed that joining with the Outer Ring was the right thing to do. Furthermore, she knew that Panera knew that as well.

And Danto would definitely do just that if the Coven decided such a rebellion should take place. His ties to them were stronger than any others on Tevingi.

"We're very much concerned about the possibility of problems in the Outer Ring," Panera stated. "And if that concern increases, it may become necessary to stop all commerce with the Outer Ring in order to avoid the possibility of contraband being smuggled in and out."

Panera's voice was even, but there was no denying the implied threat. He either knew or had guessed about the arms smuggling and was ordering Danto to cease immediately.

"That would be very unfortunate," Danto replied in the same tone. "Not only would it mean a substantial loss of income to several worlds, but it could also have a very negative effect on the Federation's request to expand the base here."

Jalissa could barely restrain a smile. Miklos Panera might just have met his match in the veiled-threat department.

"Naturally, we hope it won't come to that," Panera stated. "But as you know, when it comes to matters of galactic security, the Council can only advise."

Of course Danto knew that; *everyone* knew it. Under the terms of the Federation agreement, the military—and the Special Agency that controlled it—could invoke emergency powers and override any decision of the Council. Those powers had never been invoked, but the very fact that Panera was mentioning them now told her how seriously they viewed this situation.

Danto's reaction, though he tried to conceal it, told her that he too was thinking about that. And this was not just any Special Agent speaking either. If the Vantrans controlled the Special Agency, the powerful Panera family controlled Vantra.

Following a retreat by both sides into less threatening conversation, they took their leave of Danto, who told her that he would be seeing her later, since he planned to come out to the "homestead," which was what all the Kendor family called the house where Joeb and Neesa lived.

Jalissa was glad that she would have the opportunity to speak to Danto again, without Panera being present. If she had any hope at all of finding the rebellious Warlock and persuading him to return to the Coven, she would need the assistance of Danto's contacts on the Outer Ring worlds.

And it was also possible that Danto had private thoughts about the likelihood that the Warlock wasn't acting on his own. No off-worlder knew the Coven better or was more trusted by them.

Chapter Five

"An impressive man," Panera commented as they left Danto's headquarters.

"Yes, he is," Jalissa agreed. "Is the situation really so serious that you would cut off trade with the Outer Ring? It seems to me that would only make it worse."

"It could *become* that serious very quickly," he replied. "But our objective now is to find that would-be Warlock. I had little hope of finding out anything about him here, so I'm not disappointed. We will leave in the morning for the Outer Ring."

She hid her disappointment at their hasty departure. And in view of his comment, she wondered why he'd bothered coming here in the first place.

"Then why did we come here at all? Was it so that you could deliver that threat to my uncle?"

He seemed surprised at her candor—but only for a moment. "It seemed wise to let him know personally just how seriously we take this situation—and also to remind him that his niece is intimately involved."

She stopped in her tracks and stared at him, her anger rising. "Exactly what are you saying, Miklos Panera?"

"Only what I have already said. His actions could have repercussions for you as well."

Jalissa was appalled—and she was also deeply hurt. Could this be the same man with whom she'd just spent a pleasant morning—the same man she had thought she actually *liked*? Those feelings vanished rapidly now, buried beneath a layer of hot anger.

"How dare you threaten me, Miklos Panera? If you think the Special Agency could write off the death of another Whisperer to an 'unfortunate accident,' you can forget about it. The Council would never stand for it!"

He looked genuinely shocked, although she quickly reminded herself that he could not be trusted to be genuinely *anything*. Then his shock gave way abruptly to an icy anger that also seemed very real. He stared at her for a long moment, then leaned toward her, his voice cold even as his green eyes blazed.

"If arranging an 'unfortunate accident' had been my goal, Jalissa Kendor, I could have done that on Temok eight years ago."

She was stunned—too stunned to speak. He turned sharply and strode off toward his hovercraft, anger apparent in his every step. And as she watched him, an uneasiness came over her that seemed for one brief second to hold a tiny fragment of memory.

She thought again about her separation from her colleagues and her return to consciousness far from the scene of the battle. The memory remained beyond her grasp, but she knew from his bio that he'd been there somewhere.

She thought about the hovercraft the children in the park had seen. One of them had said that it was a Federation craft. Could it have been Miklos Panera who had saved her and then brought her there?

A city-bound shuttle appeared, and she hurried across the plaza to take it. She'd already told him that she intended to visit family and friends in the city. As soon as she had boarded, she watched his craft lift off and turn in a wide arc toward the base. Even from this distance, it was easy to identify it as a Federation craft because of its dark blue color. She recalled that when she'd questioned the children, she'd doubted their ability to distinguish a Federation craft from one of the many private craft that could have been in the area of that park.

By the time she reached the city, Jalissa had almost convinced herself that Panera had merely used his own knowledge of her missions to make her believe he had saved her. The incident on Temok had been widely publicized, not just because of the sudden, terrible battle, but also because a novice Whisperer had lost his life.

She made her rounds of her adoptive family and friends, but her mind kept veering back to his words. It seemed too much of a stretch to believe that he could have come up with such a story on the spot. And yet she knew that he was highly trained to think on his feet and to take advantage of situations—just as she herself was.

Jalissa simply could not believe that if he'd found her there unconscious in the path of the battle, he would have done anything to help her. No Special Agent would forgo an opportunity to get rid of a Whisperer. And in the hearings afterwards, Trans/Med had become convinced that one of the other Special Agents present at that time could have prevented the death of her colleague.

Furthermore, even though she was still a novice at that time, it was common knowledge within Trans/Med—and almost certainly within the Special Agency as well—that she showed great promise. If Miklos Panera had found her there, he would have left her there to die.

Jalissa was now forced for the first time to confront the incident honestly. She'd tried over the years to convince herself that she'd somehow managed to 'port herself out of there just as the stunner had struck her. But she admitted now what she'd always known deep down inside: It hadn't happened that way. She'd only just remembered that she could 'port herself when the stunner had struck her.

For most Witches and Warlocks who regularly 'ported from place to place, thinking about it and actually doing it required only a second or two. But she wasn't that skilled. It would surely have required more time for her to compose herself than she had been given before the stunner struck her down.

That evening, in the gardens of her old home, the talk was all of Panera's threat to Danto.

"You'll have to stop bringing in the arms," Joeb told his brother. "And the trips to the Coven as well. Jalissa told me about the new propulsion system on the U-77. Who knows what else they have that they're keeping quiet?"

Danto nodded soberly. "There's been talk for some time that they've perfected the new tracking system for all spacecraft, even though they claim to be having problems with it."

"But if they *have* perfected it, then they might

already know of your visits to the Coven," Jalissa said with a gasp.

"No, I doubt that very much. If they knew, they would certainly have demanded an explanation. But just as a precaution, I started sometime ago to use only the smallest freighters to go there. What I've been able to find out about the new tracking system suggests that it's still incapable of spotting smaller craft.

"Still," Danto finished with a heavy sigh, "it's all coming to an end—or a new beginning."

Joeb nodded solemnly. "I think you're right. Whether or not the Coven intends it, they're about to make a re-appearance. And now they will face a Vantra far more powerful than before."

"But perhaps somewhat more restrained, thanks to the Federation they created," Danto reminded him. "They're smart enough to know that their power is greatest when they don't use it."

"What do you think are the intentions of the Coven?" Jalissa asked Danto. He certainly had the closest ties to them—far closer than her own.

"I don't know," he replied, shaking his head. "And I can't even begin to guess. But I'm surprised that they haven't told *you*."

"I wish you hadn't disobeyed them, dear," Neesa put in.

"I disobeyed them because they didn't know what they were asking. They've lived in isolation too long to understand the danger they're in now."

"But dear, to disobey them is to disobey the gods," Neesa protested.

"They sent me away from them," Jalissa stated stubbornly. "They should have guessed that their hold over me would lessen. Now I'm a Whisperer, not a Witch."

She almost added that her loyalty now was to the Federation, not to the Coven. But that wasn't entirely true either. The part of her that "wasn't human," as Panera would have put it, was still drawn to that magical, mystical race—and it always would be.

"I think they knew you would come to feel that way," Joeb said, nodding.

"Yes," Danto agreed. "I can remember your uncle, High Priest Kamor, saying just before we left that you were destined always to walk in two worlds."

"It must be part of their plan," Neesa said to her.

Jalissa doubted that, but she didn't want to shock her devout, Coven-worshipping adopted mother any more than she already had. She hadn't yet told them about Panera's threat, and now decided not to as she listened to them discuss the possible rebellion. She didn't want them to worry about her any more than they obviously already were. Then, to her surprise, Danto brought up the subject.

145

"You must be very careful with Miklos Panera, Jalissa—especially since you're going to the Outer Ring. As charming as he may be, he is also ruthless when it comes to pursuing what he believes to be the Federation's interests.

"I'll give you the names of people I trust completely on each world—people in whom you can even confide your true identity, if that becomes necessary. I know you have an excellent memory, so memorize their names and then destroy the list."

He reached into his pocket and produced the list, together with a tiny silver-colored rod. "I have this for you as well. It's the latest weapon developed in the Special Agency's research labs: the smallest stunner they've come up with yet. And it's made of a new alloy that can't be detected by any weapons scan."

He showed her how it worked and told her about its range. She thanked him and pocketed it, together with the list. Only the gods knew how he'd managed to get hold of the stunner, but she was grateful.

"But if all else fails, use your powers," Joeb advised her. "The secret of the Coven's existence isn't likely to be a secret much longer in any event."

And my career in Trans/Med will be over, she thought bitterly. After all this time, why should the Coven surface now? She hated herself for her anger, but she could not control it. She wanted to remain Jalissa Kendor, Whisperer—not Jalissa Kendor, Witch.

Jalissa sat up in bed, instantly aware of what had awakened her. At first, she wanted to close off her mind—but the habits of a lifetime cannot be so easily broken. Furthermore, she'd fallen asleep amidst uneasy thoughts about just how far she'd strayed from the Coven.

This time, the mind that brushed against hers was that of Kamor, the most powerful of the Priesthood that governed the Coven. She conjured up an image of the man, knowing that it was 17 years old and that he would have gone from early middle years to old age in the interim. But his mind was clearly as powerful as it had ever been.

Kamor was her uncle, her mother's older brother and a Warlock so powerful that others found it difficult to be in his presence for long. Others said that Kamor might well be the most powerful Sorcerer the Coven had ever produced—even more powerful than the Priests who had combined their talents to help the Coven escape from the Vantrans a century ago.

His words whispered along the corridors of her mind. He wanted to know what progress had been made in finding Kavnor, the renegade Warlock. She told him they'd made no progress at all, but were about to leave for the Outer Ring. It surprised her that he made no mention of the fact that she'd disobeyed orders to stay out of the search.

She also told him of Panera's suspicions that a conspiracy might be forming, and about Danto's decision to halt the visits to the Coven. But she told him nothing about the Special Agency's suspicions regarding *her*. She knew that there was a chance he could glean that information from her without her knowledge, but she was counting on the Coven's long-established ban against probing each other's minds.

Then she asked the all-important question that had been tormenting her: Was the Coven planning to re-emerge after all these years?

"We do as the gods tell us, Jalissa. You knew that once, but perhaps you've forgotten."

There was a pause, but she could feel his presence. Then he went on.

"The gods do not always tell us their ultimate goal—merely the steps along the way."

"Why did you send me—and the others—away?" Jalissa asked.

"Because the gods decreed it. You are a child of the Coven, my dear niece—but even as a child, you did not belong to our life here. So it was for the others as well."

Jalissa was startled at that, but chose not to pursue it. She could tell that Kamor was tiring, so she asked him one final question.

"Did Kavnor leave on his own, or was he sent by you?"

"The gods told him to leave, and we did not stop him. Be careful, Jalissa. May the gods be with you."

And then he was gone, leaving a strange emptiness in her. She pounded the pillow in frustration. He'd told her almost nothing, and what he *had* told her was anything but encouraging.

But he was right about her not belonging there. She'd always been a dreamer and a rebel. The fact that she'd adjusted to life outside the Coven proved that he was right: She didn't belong there. And now she'd grown so far from their ways that she could not comprehend their willingness to follow a course blindly, trusting that the gods would take care of the future.

How she wished that she could find them and force them to listen to her. But she could not ask Danto to take the risk of going there now, and even if she could, she knew that her words would fall on deaf ears. The Coven was unchanged and unchanging. The gods spoke—and the Coven listened. If the gods had decided it was time for the Coven to emerge from its long isolation, it would happen—and many people would go to their deaths.

"I'd like an explanation, Miklos Panera, and I'd like it *now*."

He had been avoiding her ever since their departure from Tevingi nearly four hours ago—and that was no mean feat aboard the small spacecraft. Jalissa had had ample time to decide if she wanted to pursue his cryptic remarks, and while she recognized the dangers inherent in doing so, what it had come down to was that she *had* to know. There were too many unanswered questions in her life just now.

She sat on the edge of her bunk and stared at him. It was time for them to enter their sleep cycle. She was tired because she'd slept poorly the night before, and because the atmosphere and gravity force within the craft was being adjusted to that of Dakton, their destination in the Outer Ring.

Panera had delayed coming to their shared cabin, which suggested to her that he was determined to avoid any conversation with her. She suspected that he regretted his outburst, and she was determined to take advantage of that.

To his credit, he didn't ask what it was she wanted him to explain, but neither did he immediately offer any explanation. Instead, he just stood there, looking, she thought, as though he'd rather be anywhere in the galaxy right now but here with her. She took a secret pleasure in knowing that even Miklos Panera couldn't hide his thoughts *all* the time.

Finally, he seemed to settle for putting as much space between them as the tiny cabin would permit.

"What do you remember of what happened on Temok?" he asked.

"I went there as a novice Whisperer with several others to mediate a dispute that no one expected to turn violent," she replied, then added angrily, "Of course, we didn't know that the Special Agency would be there to undermine our efforts."

"We *weren't* there to undermine your efforts. We were there because we *did* believe that the situation could get out of control. But I wasn't referring to what happened in general. I want to know what you remember about what happened to *you*."

"I found myself cut off from the others and right in the middle of a laser battle," she said, suppressing a shudder at the memory. "Something struck me. It must have been a stunner, since if it had been a laser weapon, I wouldn't be here. And when I woke up, I was miles away, in a park at the edge of the city."

"How did you explain that to your superiors?"

Now she knew why she shouldn't have pursued this. The files of Trans/Med were supposed to be safe from the prying electronic eyes of the Special Agency, but no one knew for certain that that was in fact the case.

"I never told them," she answered truthfully, if a bit defensively. "As far as they know, I found my own way back to them." Which she had, but by a very circuitous route.

"I hired a private hovercraft to take me back to the area," she explained. "By that time, they were fleeing the battle zone, and I simply rejoined them."

She was sure that he would ask why she'd lied, but he didn't. Apparently he believed her, but it wasn't true. As soon as she'd recovered from her ordeal, she'd taken a hovercraft partway back, then dismissed the pilot and 'ported herself the remainder of the way. In the confusion, no one had questioned her lengthy absence or her great good fortune in finding her way back to safety.

"I know you were on Temok at that time," she told him.

He nodded slowly, his gaze sliding away from hers. "I was on a hillside when I spotted you down in the valley. I could see that the battle was moving quickly in your direction and that the Federation troops wouldn't get there in time to prevent your being caught in the cross fire.

"I started toward you, then realized that when you saw me, you were likely to start running in the other direction—straight into the battle. So I hit you with the stunner and then carried you to my hovercraft."

He stopped talking, and even though he wasn't looking at her, she could tell that his mind was far away, re-living the incident. She knew that she should be thanking him for having saved her life, even though he really hadn't. She would have 'ported herself out of there before the battle reached her, but he couldn't know that.

She shuddered again. If she *had* 'ported, with

him there watching her . . .

"I didn't know where your colleagues were, or even if they were still alive," he continued. "When we got back to the hovercraft, I learned that the troops were only minutes away, so there was no need for me to remain there any longer. I informed the commander of the situation, then took you back to the city. I knew you'd be safe in the park until you came to, so I left you there."

"Why?" she asked, knowing instinctively that it was the one question he didn't want to answer. When he said nothing and continued to avoid looking at her directly, she pressed on.

"I know that Special Agents have left Whisperers to fend for themselves—even if it meant almost certain death. We were taught in training that we could never depend on any of you.

"I can also guess that even then, the Special Agency knew I was exceptionally talented. So why did you save me, when by simply doing nothing, you could have gotten rid of me? Your superiors would certainly have wanted you to do just that."

"Perhaps," he admitted. "But I chose differently."

"You're talking around the issue, Miklos. I've read your file and I've heard about you from other Whisperers. You've never shown any tendency toward helping us in the past—or since then, for that matter."

Finally, he *did* turn toward her, and she drew

153

back from the intensity of his gaze. She felt as though she were teetering on the very brink of an abyss that beckoned seductively.

"I saved you because I wanted to, Jalissa," he said softly. "And I knew who you were."

As he spoke, he walked slowly toward her, then stopped so close that she could feel the warmth of his body. Her own body was pulsing wildly as her senses were filled with him. He didn't move, although she felt as though he were straining to get beyond the awkwardness of this moment. Then, finally, his hand came up to touch the shining black curls that tumbled over her shoulders.

"Now you have your answer," he said huskily. "But I doubt that you'll find much comfort in it."

His fingertips traced a line along her cheek, then dropped suddenly to his side. The moment shattered silently. What had been about to happen would not happen. He turned abruptly and disappeared into the bathroom. A few moments later, she heard the shower running.

She got into bed and turned to face the wall, not wanting to see him when he emerged. Her skin still registered his imprint and her body cried out for what hadn't happened. He was right: She couldn't take any comfort from his words.

"We'll be in orbit around Dakton in about two hours."

Jalissa turned from the vidscreen, and as she

did, her shoulder brushed lightly against his hand as it rested on the high back of the chair. She moved away quickly, and he withdrew his hand with the same speed. It was merely the latest in a series of such episodes. For three days, they had not spoken beyond what was necessary, and when they came into contact with each other, both of them reacted as though the other was on fire. The tension between them had reached the point where even the crew had noticed it. Jalissa had seen them watching their two passengers with bemused glances.

Instead of leaving the tiny comm room, Panera took the other seat in front of the big vidscreen. "Whatever you've read there about Dakton probably hasn't prepared you for the reality. And we may be visiting even more primitive worlds."

"I'm sure I can manage," she replied coolly. Anything would be preferable to being confined on this ship with him.

"These people have never even heard of a Whisperer, let alone actually seen one," he went on. "And a female Whisperer is likely to cause them even more consternation. Women on Dakton are treated little better than slaves."

"That could change—if the Federation gave the matter some attention," she stated angrily.

"Yes, it could," he agreed. "But we must deal with what we have now. As you probably know, we keep only a small force there. But what you may not know is that it is all male."

Saranne Dawson

"What?" She asked in shock.

"We need Dakton as a base, so we've avoided doing anything that might stir up the native population against us. It was decided a long time ago that the presence of women working and living alongside men wouldn't be tolerated there."

He gestured to her formal robe. "At least your uniform will be acceptable to them, although we'll have to come up with some sort of head-dress. The women on Dakton wear long, loose robes and cover their heads and faces in public at all times. Supposedly, it's because the sight of a scantily clad female would arouse men to violence."

Jalissa glanced back at the screen, realizing that the information from Trans/Med files that she'd been studying was totally inadequate. *And no wonder*, she thought angrily. *We've never been allowed to come here.*

"Frankly, I'd prefer to have you remain at the base," he continued, "but I need your skills. We know our man was here, but no one at the base has been able to obtain much information because no one speaks their language very well.

"And there's another problem as well. Our agreement with the Daks prevents us from using hovercraft, except on the base itself. They don't like machines that fly. To them, it seems that we are trying to imitate the gods—or their messengers, the Coven."

He leaned back in his chair and studied her,

156

his expression thoughtful. "You know, it occurs to me that we might be able to use their worship of the Coven to our advantage."

"How is that?" she asked, hiding her uneasiness.

"You could pass for a Witch, you know. When I saw those paintings, I realized how much you resemble them. And I'm told that the only off-worlders they'll deal with are Tevingians, because of their historic alliance with the Coven."

"Then the fact that I'm Tevingian should be enough."

"Perhaps. But they'd be even more likely to cooperate if they believed you to be a Witch."

"And just how am I to convince them of that?" she inquired, now suspecting that he had a double purpose in mind.

"Oh, that could be arranged. We can duplicate the lightning effect easily enough. Given your appearance, that should be enough to convince them."

"I dislike such deception, Miklos. That's more *your* line than mine."

"But your superiors agreed that you would cooperate—and that *I'm* the one in charge."

"I'm sure they didn't have *this* in mind."

"Why would it bother you to impersonate a Witch?" he asked, his eyes boring into her.

"I just told you that I dislike deception."

"Nevertheless, that's what you will do," he

stated, then got up and left the room before she could reply.

Jalissa glared at his broad back, thinking that she'd like nothing more than to show him right now that she could do a very good "impersonation" of a Witch without his help.

She was certain that despite his casual tone, he'd had this scheme in mind all along. If she did as ordered, he could find some way to use it against her—perhaps claiming that it wasn't an impersonation at all. Or if he really did suspect her of being a Witch, he undoubtedly hoped that she'd give herself away.

Still, there was little she could do about it. He was right. She had agreed to his being in charge of this mission, and she couldn't back off now, because she had to find the Warlock.

"I've never seen one of these, except in pictures," Jalissa said in astonishment. "I thought they hadn't been used for centuries."

"They haven't—except for a few places here in the Outer Ring," Miklos replied. "They're powered by gasoline engines, the kind that used to pollute every world. But this is the only kind of transport the Daks will let us use, so we manufactured enough for our own use, then gave them some as well.

"We tried to persuade them to let us use solar-powered land vehicles after they said no to hovercraft, but when they couldn't hear the sound of an engine, they accused us of trying to usurp the Coven's magic."

"How far do we have to go?" Jalissa asked, staring uneasily at the boxy little vehicle that was spewing forth noxious fumes.

"It'll take the better part of the day to get to the town and then back again. Their roads aren't good to begin with, and at this time of year there are often washouts: places where rocks and mud have slid down to cover the road."

A short time later, they drove through the gates of the base. Miklos was wearing his uniform, which he said Daks more or less respected—especially when it was accompanied by the silver stunner that hung from his belt. The Daks regarded it as being evil magic, but they feared it. Since their landing, she had learned that there been numerous unpleasant incidents between Federation troops and the Daks, though none had ever been reported to the public.

Jalissa was wearing a high-necked black robe similar to the formal garments worn by the Coven. Her crystal pendant sparkled on her chest. Despite the fact that women on Dakton wore headcovers, her own head was bare. Witches did not cover their heads.

True to his word, Miklos had found "lightning" for her in the form of two thin, nearly invisible bracelets. When she rotated her wrists in a certain way, blue fire arced from them. She'd practiced alone before a mirror, and then had summoned the true Witches' fire to compare the effect. The bracelets were a poor imitation, but they would do.

Before they left, Miklos had insisted that she demonstrate the effect for him. The look on his face still haunted her. He'd tried to hide his fear, but she'd seen it, and what should have given her some satisfaction had instead left her badly shaken as well.

What does he truly believe? she wondered, casting him a covert glance as he focused his attention on the bumpy road.

The Federation base was in a wide valley, surrounded on all sides by craggy peaks that were thickly covered by dark firs. The road was hard-packed dirt, muddy in places from recent heavy rains. Miklos pointed to the mountains, and said they had to cross the one ahead of them and then two more before they'd reach the town, a regional marketplace where the Warlock was rumored to have appeared.

Jalissa found herself turning several times to stare back at the base. She wasn't at all happy about venturing out into this primitive land in a noisy, ancient vehicle. She was accustomed to traveling regularly in strange lands, but in modern hovercraft and in the company of responsible local officials. Furthermore, in the past, she'd always known everything she needed to know about the people involved.

But despite all that, she knew that what troubled her most was that she was now wholly dependent on the tall Vantran beside her. Whatever happened, she dared not use her talents to save herself—not with Miklos Panera watching her every move.

"I didn't intend to frighten you with my stories about the Daks," he said, breaking the silence between them. "We're safe enough. If I thought we weren't, I would have left you back at the base."

"You couldn't leave me at the base," she reminded him. "You need me to translate."

He shot her a brief glance. "There are a few soldiers at the base who can speak their language well enough. I wouldn't put you at risk, Jalissa."

His final words, spoken as he turned his attention back to the road, were uttered softly, and, Jalissa thought, almost begrudgingly, sounded as though he were reluctantly speaking a truth. His behavior thoroughly confounded her, coming as it did from a man who seemed so sure of himself, so in control at all times—so *Vantran*.

She thought again about the incident on Temok, how he'd saved her life—certainly in contravention of Special Agency policy. It was still difficult for her to believe that he could be so attracted to her, and yet the evidence was mounting that this was indeed the case.

Jalissa knew that she was beautiful, but she also knew that unlike other races in the galaxy, who intermingled freely, Vantrans never married off-worlders, and only rarely took lovers from among other races. They obviously believed themselves to be superior to all others, and if that was true of Vantrans in general, it must surely be even more true of a Panera.

On the other hand, it was equally impossible for her to believe that *she* could be attracted to *him*—and yet she clearly was, despite the grave danger he posed. Was it merely the attraction of the forbidden—or something more? Even now, as they set out on an uncomfortable and possibly dangerous mission, desire whispered through her mind and left her weak and aching.

There was something frighteningly raw and primitive in those feelings. They were both highly sophisticated, civilized people, and yet it seemed that the longer she was in his company, the more that veneer wore away, leaving only the most basic and elemental of human needs.

As they made their way down the winding road into the next valley, he slowed the vehicle and stared out the side window. "I don't like the looks of that. Those rocks could slide down at any moment."

He drove on, and she looked out the rear window. The hillside above them was bare of trees and covered with huge boulders. Small streams of water gushed down, spilling into a ditch at the side of the road.

They were making their laborious way up the second mountain when suddenly something struck the side of the vehicle with a sharp "ping" that was then repeated several times. She turned to him questioningly.

"Just some Daks, shooting at us," he said, swiveling his head to scan the hillside. "They have old-fashioned rifles and the bullets can't pierce the armor or the glass. They know that, but they shoot anyway, just to show their displeasure."

Several more bullets struck the rear windshield before they rounded a curve. Jalissa turned in her seat, but saw no one. She shuddered, thinking that it felt as though they'd stepped through a time warp.

"They only shoot when we're safe inside this," he went on. "If I had stopped and gotten out, they'd have disappeared."

The car descended into a narrow valley, crossed a rickety bridge over a swift-running stream and then began to climb yet another mountain. It was a beautiful place that resembled parts of Tevingi, but Jalissa couldn't enjoy the scenery. Panera seemed so calm, so certain that they were safe—but she herself wasn't so sanguine about it. He might be accustomed to such things, but she was used to being an invited guest on hostile worlds, an honored representative of the Federation whose safety was always guaranteed by both sides. That incident on Temok had been the only time she'd ever encountered such danger.

By the time they had reached the top of the mountain, they were enclosed in a thick fog. Miklos slowed down as the headlights just barely pierced the heavy gray mist.

"This is the last mountain," he told her. "If it weren't for the fog, we'd be able to see the town in the valley below."

"What sort of reception will they give us?" she asked nervously.

"That depends on whether or not they believe you're a Witch," he replied, turning to her briefly. "If not, they're likely to be as unpleasant as they dare."

"And just how unpleasant is that?"

"They won't try to harm us, but they'll probably call us names and spit at us. That's what they usually do."

"How can you be so certain that they wouldn't dare to harm us?"

"Because they know the consequences," he stated.

"And what are those consequences?"

"Death. No trial, no penal colony. That's the law on all the Outer Ring worlds. And before you start to protest, try to understand that there's no other way to deal with these people. We simply follow their own laws, which are basically the 'survival of the fittest.' And *we're* the 'fittest.' "

"There has to be a better way to deal with these people, Miklos," she said, appalled at his callousness.

"No, there isn't—and that's why we've never permitted Whisperers to come here. They have no interest whatsoever in mediating their disputes. Their code of justice—if you can call it that—is very simple and brutal. For ordinary thievery, they cut off the offender's hands. Adulterous women are stoned to death, and the man may be killed as well, depending on just how offended the husband is. In the case of murder, they kill not only the one who committed the crime, but his entire family as well—even the children."

"This cannot be allowed to continue!" she cried. "Miklos, this is contrary to every law of human decency!"

"I agree, but a decision was made long ago to let these people find their own way to a more civilized society."

The Coven could put an end to this, she thought, but of course didn't say. Surely this kind of thing hadn't happened when the Coven had influence over them. Then, as though he'd picked up on her thoughts, he went on.

"Historians say that when the Outer Ring was under the influence of the Coven, they had a more just society—and perhaps they did. But when the Coven vanished, they apparently reverted to their old ways rather quickly. There's the town below us now."

She peered through the thinning mist and saw strange little rounded houses below them, topped with thatched roofs. Then, as they continued their descent into the valley, another hail of bullets struck the vehicle. Panera chuckled.

"Thank you. We're happy to be here."

Jalissa turned to him, unable to understand how he could be so casual about the situation. But before she could say anything, he turned to her with a grin.

"Are you ready to do your Witch act?"

"What I'm ready to do is *leave!*" she replied.

"Then tell that to your superiors when you see them. It's *their* fault that you're here."

By now, they had reached the floor of the valley and were approaching the outskirts of the town. People working in the fields stopped to stare at them, and even from a distance Jalissa could feel their hostility. Several shook their fists, and a few spat in their direction.

That hatred became ever more apparent as they made their way slowly along the narrow streets of the town. Although she did her level best to hide it, Jalissa was terrified. Never before had she encountered such hatred directed at her.

She started nervously as Panera's hand covered hers. "You're safe, Jalissa. Remember that. It's important that you not let them see your fear. A Witch wouldn't be afraid of them."

This Witch is, she said silently, staring out through the tinted window at the crowd that surrounded the vehicle as they drove into the town square. But if his gesture did little to soothe her fears, it still managed to send a shiver of pleasure through her.

"Stay inside and let me come around to open the door for you," he instructed. "I want us to stay together at all times."

The crowd pressed even closer to them, straining to see through the tinted glass. When he had shut off the engine, she could hear them muttering in their guttural tongue. No translation was required for her to know they were hostile.

Panera opened his door and got out without hesitation. Jalissa was astonished at his bravery, and wondered just how many times he'd faced situations like this. She'd always thought of Special Agents as troublemakers and nothing more, but she now realized she might have been wrong.

He closed the door and stood there for a moment, towering over the short, squat Daks. His back was to her at the moment, but she could see his head move as he scanned the crowd. His arms hung loosely at his sides, his hand not even near the stunner, and there was no sign at all of tension or fear.

Surely, she thought, he *must* be afraid. And yet even she, who had been trained to pick up the most subtle hints of such things, saw nothing. She was amazed—and filled with a reluctant admiration as well. This was a man whose great wealth allowed him to do as he wished with his life, and yet here he was, in a situation that most men would gladly have avoided. And certainly not for the first time either.

He began to walk casually around the front of

the vehicle to her door. The crowd moved back slightly, but there remained an ugly undercurrent in their voices, and she could see the hatred on the faces of those closest to the vehicle.

Then he opened her door and reached a hand inside to help her out, turning his back on the muttering crowd. One man took the opportunity to step forward and spit at him, but if Miklos was aware of it, he gave no indication. He even smiled at her as he took her hand. His hand was warm. Hers felt as though she'd just dipped it into ice water.

The moment she stepped out of the vehicle, the crowd's angry murmurs died away into a brief silence followed by a collective gasp. And then she heard on many lips the word "Witch." It was the same in all languages.

She stood beside Panera and let her gaze travel over the throng. Their earlier hostility had vanished. What she saw on their faces now was respect and awe. For the first time in her life, Jalissa was *proud* of being a Witch. Here, on this primitive world, she understood at last the true power of her birthright: the power to control the hearts and minds of people who had for centuries looked to the Coven as the very embodiment of the old gods.

And she knew something else as well: She could not deceive these people with Vantran tricks. To do so would be to betray her heritage.

Chapter Six

Very slowly, Jalissa raised her hands until they were stretched high above her head. Her gaze traveled over the silent, expectant crowd. Nowhere did she encounter even a hint of hostility. Eyes that had only moments before glittered with hatred now shone with reverence. Jalissa Kendor, the Whisperer, had become a Witch, revered as a member of a race that went back to the dawn of time.

She rotated her wrists very slightly to activate the bracelets, but at the same time, she called upon the ancient fire, believed by her people to be the sacred fire of the gods.

An eerie blue light immediately engulfed her hands as the powers she invoked sang through her body, filling her entire being. And for one brief moment, she was transported back to the Coven—and to her 12-year-old self. The gift of fire, or the "blessing of the gods," as it was known among her people, was conferred upon children of the Coven when they reached their 12th birthday. She'd received it only a few months before she left them.

Memories of her life there now came back to her: memories she'd ignored for years. She could hear the low, rhythmic chants of the priests, smell the pungent incense, and see the dark forms leaping and dancing as no human could possibly do.

Then the images faded and she was once more staring at the Daks as they gazed upon the fire with rapturous expressions. And in that moment, she also became aware of the silent man at her side.

She closed her fists, extinguishing the fire to a soft sigh from her audience. Fear skittered along the edges of her mind as she belatedly realized the danger in her actions. But she was too filled with the power of her true self to be genuinely alarmed.

"I am Jalissa Kendor!" she said, projecting her voice so that all could hear her. "I seek your help, Believers. I must find my brother Warlock who visited you recently. Tell me what he told you."

Those nearest to her began to speak at once in their eagerness to help her. Jalissa realized that they weren't even curious about her use of the crystal. No doubt they thought it was just another of her powers. Or perhaps they hadn't even noticed. In olden times, at least some Coven members knew the languages of all the people who worshipped them, and apparently the renegade Warlock Kavnor had studied them.

She directed her attention to one man, who quickly stepped forward, making the sign of the Coven as he did so. He told her that Kavnor had urged them to take up arms against the Federation "when the time comes," and promised that the Coven would lead them to freedom.

"Did he say when this would be?" she asked.

The man shook his head and stated that they would be ready to do as asked. With a defiant look at Miklos, he said that they desired to be ruled by the Coven, "as we were before the accursed Federation came."

Jalissa looked at the group of women at the rear of the all-male crowd. They were completely covered by dark robes and veils, but even so, she could see their submissiveness, their deference to the men who had pushed past them.

She thought about the power she had, power the Coven could use to make life better for them. Wouldn't that be more important than anything she could do as a mere Whisperer?

"Do you know where the Warlock went?" she asked, turning her attention back to the man in front of her.

Once again, the Dak shook his head. "He told us that he will travel to all worlds where there are still Believers."

The man abruptly sank to his knees, and within seconds, every other man in the crowd did likewise. "We are all ready to die in service to the Coven, Blessed One."

Jalissa merely nodded, knowing that she shouldn't thank them for this display of loyalty. They wouldn't be expecting that. Instead, after a moment, she extended her hand and made a gesture to tell them to rise again.

As they did so, there was a sudden commotion at the back of the crowd, where the group of women stood. Then the men began to move aside to make way for a woman who was carrying a child of about two years. Even before the woman reached her, Jalissa knew what would be requested of her. She should have anticipated this.

The child, a little boy who might have been older than he appeared, was obviously very sick. He was naked from the waist up and his ribs stood out starkly against his brown skin. His arms were nothing more than skin stretched over bone, and as the woman brought him to her, he began to cough weakly.

Consumption, she thought with horror: a disease that had vanished centuries ago elsewhere in the galaxy.

The woman's eyes pleaded silently, and the crowd watched Jalissa expectantly. She faced a terrible dilemma. No Witch or Warlock ever refused to heal, and these people would know that, as surely as they knew that her ancestors had cured this particular disease many times. But if she used her powers to cure the child, Panera would know that she was truly a Witch.

The woman laid the coughing child on the ground in front of her, then stepped back. Jalissa knelt beside him, staring into his fevered eyes and hearing his raspy breathing. And she knew that she had no choice.

She placed her hands lightly on the child's chest and rotated her wrists to activate the bracelets. Then she called upon the healing powers, and the blue fire surrounded her fingertips with a gentle glow. The warmth spread from her hands to the child, and within seconds, his breathing became quiet and regular.

She was not a Healer, in the highest sense of the word. She had only the basic talent they all possessed—but she knew that it was enough in this case. The fever left the child's dark eyes and in seconds, he closed them in sleep. She removed her hands and stood up, then picked up the slumbering child and gave him back to his mother.

Tears of joy streamed down the woman's face as she clutched the child. She thanked Jalissa profusely, as did several others, including a man who must be the boy's father. He knelt before her, making the sign of the Coven.

"Live in peace," she said, touching the man's

head lightly. "Your son is well."

Then, finally, she turned to face Miklos Panera, her head high and her eyes challenging. He met her gaze, but his expression revealed nothing. She had expected hatred and fear—or perhaps triumph at having now gained the evidence he sought to confirm their suspicions about her.

"Favored of the Gods," a voice said hesitantly, using one of the old terms for her people.

She turned to face an elderly man, who made the sign of the Coven and then asked if she would bless a place for them where they could pray to the old gods.

Jalissa nodded. This too would be expected. In the past, her people had rarely left their home, but when they did, it was customary for them to perform such tasks. Given the fact that her own belief in the old gods was tenuous at best, Jalissa did wonder if she should be doing such a thing. Furthermore, she hadn't the slightest idea how to go about it.

It was disconcerting, to say the least, to be among people whose knowledge of such rituals was greater than her own.

"Where is this place?" she asked, and the man pointed to a building at the far side of the square. It appeared to be the largest building in town, and was probably already a gathering place.

When she started toward it, Panera began to follow her. She turned to him and said quietly that she thought it would be better if he remained where he was. She was sure that the Daks would not want him in the building.

To her surprise and relief, he merely nodded and walked back to their vehicle. When she reached the building, she turned and saw him leaning against it, his arms folded across his chest as he watched her.

She wondered why the Daks seemed so impervious to his presence. Why didn't they question what she was doing traveling with one of the enemy? Then it occurred to her that perhaps they believed him to be her captive—a spellbound slave to do her bidding.

She had to admit that the idea was not without a certain appeal.

Miklos didn't like the idea of having her out of his sight, but he knew she was right. If he insisted upon accompanying her, it could cause just the kind of trouble they'd managed to avoid so far. So instead, he waited uneasily and tried to think rationally about what he'd just witnessed.

He felt chilled to his very bones. He was a man of science, but for a few moments, he'd felt what these primitive people must have felt: a sense of something far beyond human understanding.

Miklos had watched her practice with the bracelets and the effect had been impressive. In fact, it had been downright unsettling to see her in the role he'd assigned to her. It was like watching one of the figures in the paintings come to life.

But here, he'd felt something different—something very powerful. He reminded himself that acting was part of a Whisperer's training, just as it had been part of his. He wanted to believe it was no more than that. But when the woman had brought the child to her . . .

Miklos knew that the poor child must have fallen into a coma. It was obvious that he was near death. But once again, he'd been as ready as the parents to believe that she'd cured the boy.

It had to be nothing more than fine acting, but that knowledge sat on him very uneasily. He wondered if he could possibly be guilty of wanting the exact opposite of what his superiors wanted. They wanted to cast doubt on her by suggesting that she was a Witch, but he was increasingly certain that he wanted just as much to prove that she *wasn't*.

Lost in thought, he watched her disappear into the building, surrounded by what were apparently the town elders. He still disliked the idea of having her out of his sight, but he was sure they wouldn't harm her—not after the display she'd just put on.

Then suddenly, a thin, strong strip of leather was being drawn tight around his neck. Before he could reach for his stunner, his arms were pinned to his sides and one of his captors had slipped the stunner from his belt.

Unable to make more than a strangled sound, Miklos cursed himself for a fool as he was dragged away by his captors. He clung desperately to the hope that they wouldn't kill him without consulting Jalissa first.

Jalissa did her best to invoke a blessing on the place. Away from the watchful, suspicious eyes of Miklos Panera, she was free to use the sacred fire. She raised her hands and sent it arcing into every corner of the big, open room. She stood in its center, and the Daks huddled near the doorway, silent and awestruck. Since she lacked the proper words, she chose instead to invoke the Coven's ancient blessing of the harvest, reasoning that since most of the town was dependent upon the surrounding farms, that would suffice. Then she told them that she must leave, that there were other worlds to visit in her search for her brother Warlock.

When she emerged from the building and saw that Panera was no longer standing beside their vehicle, she at first assumed that he must be inside. But when she reached it and peered in through the darkened windows, a jolt of fear shot through her. Where was he? She was certain that he would never have wandered off on his own.

"Where is the man who accompanied me?" she asked.

The Dak leader looked at her with a proud smile. "We have captured him, Blessed One, and we have taken away his magic."

For one horrified moment, Jalissa thought he meant that they'd *killed* Miklos. Then she realized that the man was probably referring to his stunner.

"You must let him come with me," she said firmly. "It is not yet time to declare war on the Federation, and this man is very important. If anything happens to him, the Federation soldiers will come here and destroy you."

The man hesitated. He was clearly disappointed at not being able to kill a hated Federation agent. Jalissa held her breath. If necessary, she would use her powers to free Panera, for she felt responsible for this predicament. The Daks would never have taken him captive if she hadn't come here as a Witch.

Finally, the Dak told the others to bring him back, and a few moments later, Panera reappeared, his hands bound behind his back and a leather thong made into a noose around his neck, still held securely by a powerful-looking young Dak.

Only later would Jalissa realize that it was a moment she should have savored: The life of a Federation Special Agent was literally in her hands. But in that moment, all she could feel was relief at seeing that he was alive and unhurt.

It was clear that the young man holding onto the leather noose was very reluctant to let his captive go. He gave the leather thong a vicious twist that snapped Panera's neck backward, nearly knocking him off balance. But in a lightning-fast movement, Panera kicked out at the man and sent him tumbling to the ground with a cry of pain.

The men with him immediately surrounded Panera, and he began to fight them with kicks as well, since his hands were still tightly bound behind his back. They all fell to the ground in a cloud of dust.

"Stop!" Jalissa cried, raising her hands to call down the fire again.

The struggles ceased as the Daks stared at the blue fire arcing from her fingertips. Panera struggled to his knees and then to his feet. She closed her fists on the fire and hurried to him to undo his bonds. She was clumsy because her fingers were trembling.

"Get the stunner," he said in a calm, quiet voice intended for her ears alone.

She finally succeeded in freeing him, and scanned the silent group of men, searching for the stunner. It was of less consequence to her than to him, but she certainly didn't want to have to resort to magic to get them out of here.

"Give me his magic," she said. "I will keep it so that he can't harm you."

The young man who'd been trying to strangle Panera stepped forward and handed her the silver cylinder. "Now you will have his magic as well as your own, Favored One," he said triumphantly.

"Thank you," Jalissa said, taking it from him. "May the gods bestow their blessings on all of you."

She opened the door and got into the vehicle and Panera slid into the driver's seat. Not one word passed between them as they drove out of the town, past the silent crowd. Jalissa shot him a covert glance and saw the taut muscles along his firm jaw. It took little guesswork on her part to know what he was thinking. The proud Vantran was obviously struggling with what for him was surely a novel emotion: humility. Now that she knew they were safe, she could enjoy that.

And she very much hoped that after what had happened to him, he might have forgotten what he'd witnessed when she'd so foolishly loosed the fire on her own and then healed the child.

A tense silence continued as they drove up the winding road to the summit of the mountain that overlooked the town. The fog had blown away with the afternoon breeze and she stared back at it, shuddering as she thought about what might have happened. If Panera hadn't forced her to play the role of a Witch, they might both be dead. Kavnor, the Warlock, might well have stirred them up to rebellion even before her arrival here with Panera.

He pulled off the narrow road at the summit and turned to her. "Now we are even. I saved your life once—and now you have saved mine."

Jalissa nodded, not even trying to hide her smile. His words sounded rehearsed, and she suspected that was just what he'd been doing—in addition to berating himself for having been captured.

"I . . . I don't understand how they could have captured you," she said, thinking about his bravery when they'd arrived in town and how it had given her courage.

He explained what had happened. "I failed to realize that the situation changed the moment they accepted you as being a Witch. If that hadn't happened, they would never have attacked me."

"They might have in any event," she told him. "The Warlock had already stirred them up and made them believe they could attack the Federation."

He merely nodded, avoiding her eyes. "Still, the mistake was mine, for believing that we could present you as a Witch without suffering the consequences. You did an excellent job, by the way."

In the brief pause before he added those last words, Jalissa could feel his thoughts turning in the direction she feared.

"Of course, I don't know what they'll think when that child dies," he went on, still turned away from her. "He has consumption. I've seen it before out here, but they won't accept our medicines."

"They may simply believe it to be the will of

the gods," she replied. "Not even the best of the Healers in the Coven were always successful."

She suddenly became aware of the fact that she was still clutching his stunner, toying with it nervously. She handed it back to him with an attempt at a smile. "Your 'magic,' Miklos."

He took it from her, and their eyes met briefly before he reattached it to his belt. It was an odd moment she couldn't quite define: breathtakingly intimate, but still fraught with danger. The very air between them seemed to vibrate with unspoken words and a fragile sort of sensuality that sent her pulse racing.

"I think it would be wise if you had one as well," he said. "I'll see to it when we get back to the base."

She thanked him, not about to admit that she already had one, courtesy of her uncle. It was in the pocket of her robe, and she'd forgotten all about it. She thought wryly that it seemed she was always forgetting about one "weapon" or another—perhaps because she had become two people: a Whisperer and a Witch.

They set out again, and he once more lapsed into silence. Each time she cast a sidelong glance at him, she saw that his jaw was still set rigidly. Was he still berating himself for his mistake, or was he assembling in his mind the evidence against her?

The unthinkable began to creep into her mind. No proscription was more powerful among the

Coven than the one that forbade reading another person's mind. The priests called it their "curse": the one gift from the gods they had received but were not to use.

Among themselves, the temptation was not too great. They tended to know each other's thoughts simply because they knew each other well to begin with. But now she was faced with a nearly overwhelming temptation—and one she could actually justify on the basis of her own safety.

But she couldn't do it. It would be a violation of his privacy—a form of rape, really, a heinous crime that was almost nonexistent in the galaxy now, but that had been widespread among some societies once. And for all their faults, the Vantrans had fought hard to see that all citizens of the galaxy enjoyed those individual liberties.

Disaster struck as they were descending the second mountain on a particularly narrow and winding stretch of road. To the right lay the steep, rock-strewn hillside, while to the left, the mountain dropped off sharply for several hundred feet.

They rounded one of the blind curves and saw ahead of them a large pile of boulders that had slid down the mountainside in a stream of slick, dark mud. It was one of the spots he'd commented on earlier, and apparently the heavy rains that had preceded their arrival had loosened the earth.

He got out to examine the barricade, and she climbed out too. He turned to her with a wry grin, his earlier dark mood apparently gone. "I don't suppose you could include levitation in your act—to life us up over this."

She laughed—a genuine laugh, even though she knew she should be worried every time he mentioned her Witch talents. "I'm afraid that I'm a bit out of practice."

It was true actually. There were certainly those among the Coven who could have used their talents to lift the boulders out of the way, or even to lift them both, vehicle and all, over the blockade. But it took practice, beginning with much smaller objects, and she'd never advanced beyond that.

He chuckled as he turned to stare back the way they'd come. "I could call for help, but it wouldn't be a good idea to have a hovercraft out here right now. The Daks are stirred up enough as it is. I think I saw a path back there a mile or so, probably an animal track. It might lead us around this."

They got back into their vehicle and he turned it around. She hadn't noticed the path, but he found it again without difficulty and they began a steep, bumpy ascent up the face of the mountain. At the summit, the path disappeared down over the back side of the mountain, so Miklos left it and began a very slow, careful descent through bushes and saplings and over rocks.

They nearly made it. He pointed out what he thought was the road below them, just barely visible beyond a screen of shrubs and some trees. And then suddenly they were sliding out of control, as the rocks beneath the wheels slid away on the soft ground!

Jalissa cried out in alarm as they plunged headlong toward a thick grove of dark firs. Miklos merely grunted as he fought the wheel in a desperate attempt to avoid a collision.

"Get out!" he shouted suddenly, reaching across to open her door and give her a push.

In a flash, she realized what he meant. A few broken bones in a jump from the vehicle was preferable to crashing headfirst into the trees—especially as the vehicle was steadily picking up speed in its wild descent.

She flung herself out, remembering at the last possible moment that she could use her powers to soften her fall. So instead of tumbling down the rocky slope, she floated gently, and came to rest at the base of a huge old tree at the exact moment she heard the vehicle collide with the trees above her.

Miklos, she thought wildly. Had he gotten out safely, or had his effort to save her prevented his own escape? She struggled to her feet and began to call out to him. But her voice was weak and she found that she couldn't keep her balance.

She sank to the ground again, knowing that what she felt must be a combination of the adrenaline coursing through her system combined with the unaccustomed use of her powers. It would pass quickly.

"Jalissa!"

She raised her head and saw him coming toward her, scrambling awkwardly down the steep rocky incline. She sank back again, sighing with relief. Fearing for the life of Miklos Panera was rapidly becoming a regular part of her own life.

He knelt beside her, his handsome face etched deeply with lines of concern. "Are you hurt?"

She shook her head. "Just a few bruises. I . . . I was afraid that you hadn't gotten out in time."

A silence hung between them, and within it was an unspoken mutual acknowledgment of something it seemed neither of them wanted to name. He reached out slowly to smooth away the strands of dark hair that had fallen across her face.

"I'm sorry," he said softly. "I shouldn't have tried to get around the rockslide. I'm used to taking chances because I generally work alone."

Then he withdrew the hand that had caressed her cheek, and she very nearly cried out in protest. These moments of unexpected tenderness touched her deeply, filling her with something she'd never felt before.

For a long moment that held time in suspension, they stared at each other, seeking answers to questions that had yet to be asked. He began to move toward her—and then a shot rang out!

Before, when the Daks had fired at them, Jalissa had heard only the metallic ping of the bullets striking their vehicle. So this time, when she heard the sharp crack of a rifle, she didn't immediately know what it was. But it was instantly clear that Miklos knew.

He threw his body across hers, crushing her against the rocky ground. There was another crack, and a bullet struck a large boulder only a few yards away. Miklos swore and wrapped his arms around her, then sent them both rolling down the hillside to the safety of a grove of trees.

Jalissa was frightened, but not even fear could completely prevent her from registering the lean hardness of his body against hers and her own quaking response as they both came to rest in the safety of the dark, fragrant firs.

"My laser gun is up there," he said, indicating the wrecked vehicle above them. "You're safe here. I'm going up to get it."

His face was close to hers as they lay on the soft pine needles, arms still wrapped about each other. He started to move away from her, and then stopped.

It was over almost before she could register the imprint of his mouth on hers: a quick, hard, urgent kiss that bruised her lips and parted her teeth to admit his tongue. The contrast with his gentleness of a few moments ago was dizzying—and strangely erotic.

He began to move away from her again, and

she grabbed his arm. "No! If I'm safe here, then so are you. And if they come closer, you have your stunner."

"It's *me* they're after, Jalissa—not you."

"You said they wouldn't dare to actually harm you," she reminded him, still clutching his arm.

"I could be wrong. That damned Warlock has stirred them all up."

Then his expression softened and he rested his fingertips for a moment on her lips, which were still tender from his harsh kiss.

"That wasn't what I intended," he said huskily as he leaned toward her again.

The difference was electrifying. This time, his lips and tongue teased hers gently, then moved on to trace a slow line down across her cheek and throat to the pulse-point at its base. Her fingers clutched at him, weaving themselves through his thick, golden hair. Their bodies seemed to be melting into each other, chafing against the confines of their clothes. Passion was a steady throbbing drumbeat, urging their writhing bodies toward a complete union.

And then another volley of shots rang out, shattering the moment. They stared at each other, each seeing reflected in the other's eyes a desire that could not be fulfilled—perhaps even a surprise that the world beyond them existed at all.

Miklos leapt to his feet and began to make his way through the trees toward the vehicle. Jalissa huddled against a tree, her body still heavy with wanting and her mind now filled with fear for him as he dodged round after round of rifle fire.

He won't make it, she thought with horror. The grove thinned out closer to the vehicle. He couldn't get to it without exposing himself, and they would surely know where he was headed, which gave them an even greater advantage.

She had to do something! Hidden behind the thick trunk of an ancient fir, she was invisible to Miklos. If she could get up to the hilltop and stop the attackers . . .

She 'ported, landing some 50 feet behind the three Daks, who had their backs to her as they continued to fire at Miklos. She could see him below her, darting from tree to tree as he drew near the vehicle.

The blue fire arced from her fingertips: three thin, shimmering lines that struck the men simultaneously. All three fell heavily to the ground, still clutching their rifles. She hurried toward them, hoping that she hadn't killed them. Her skills weren't fine-tuned. Growing up as she had in the total safety of the Coven, she'd had no reason to learn how to defend herself.

She bent over them, checking each man. They were still alive. But now she realized that Miklos was bound to get his laser gun and come up here after them.

She 'ported back to the spot behind the tree, then began to scramble up the hill as Miklos finally reached the crashed vehicle and crawled into it to get his laser gun. When he climbed out again with it, he saw her and immediately put himself between her and the hill where the Daks now lay unconscious. Then he fired blindly in that direction.

After firing a second time, he urged her into the vehicle. She'd been so preoccupied with saving him that she'd paid scant attention to its condition, but now she saw that it was very heavily damaged. The entire front end had collapsed into the passenger compartment, cracking the dashboard and leaving barely enough space for her to fit inside. And on his side, the steering wheel was now crushed against the back of the seat.

We would surely have been killed, she thought, horrified at their second brush with death that day.

"I think they're gone," he said, crouching down beside her at the open door. "Either that, or I managed to hit them. I'm going up there to have a look."

Before she could try to stop him, he was off and running up the hill. She knew the men would still be there. They couldn't have recovered that quickly. She could only hope that he'd think the laser had struck them down. But if it had, wouldn't they be dead, instead of just unconscious? She wished desperately that she knew more about weaponry.

* * *

Miklos advanced cautiously up the ridge, laser gun at the ready. His instincts told him that their assailants had fled, though after his blunders this day, he didn't trust them as much as he had before.

He saw the three Daks as soon as he reached the top. They lay on the ground with their weapons still clutched in their hands. Setting down his laser gun, he took out his stunner and approached them cautiously. Something was wrong here. If the laser had struck them, they should be lying on their backs—but all three were face-down, as though they'd been struck from *behind*.

He picked up the laser gun again and scanned the woods, but saw no one. Then he checked the three attackers. All had the slow, steady pulses of deep sleep. They definitely did not look like men who'd been struck down by a laser. Even a glancing shot should have left them near death.

He pried their rifles from their grasps, then stood there, staring uneasily down at the vehicle, his mind re-playing other incidents of this day.

Her eyes asked the question the moment he reached the vehicle. "They're unconscious, but I think they'll be all right," he told her as he reached for the comm unit, which fortunately appeared to have survived the crash. Another mistake. He'd forgotten to bring along a personal unit.

"I'll have to call for help," he told her, picking up the mike.

"What about them?" she asked, her gaze traveling up the slope.

"We'll take them back to the base. Then it's up to the commander to decide what to do with them."

Jalissa felt cold inside. Gone was the tender man who'd sent torrents of fire through her. The cold, calculating Special Agent had returned. Was it because he was suspicious about the condition of their attackers—or was he regretting what had happened between them?

He spoke to someone at the base, then replaced the unit and told her that a hovercraft would arrive within 15 minutes. After that, he began to walk around the vehicle, feigning an interest in its condition.

She kept casting glances up at the top of the ridge, hoping that the three Daks would recover and sneak off before the soldiers arrived. But she had no idea how long it would take them to recover. She was as ignorant of the effects of her own "weapon" as she was of his.

By the time the hovercraft arrived, the silence between them had become so heavy that she could hardly bear it, and with each passing second, she became more and more convinced that he knew something other than the laser had struck down the Daks. But if so, why wasn't he accusing her? He was far too intelligent not to have put this together with the incidents in the town and come up with the truth.

He led the soldiers up to the top of the ridge. She waited nervously, wondering what the Daks would say when they woke up. They hadn't seen her, but if they knew they'd been struck from behind, any doubts Miklos might have would be gone.

She could scarcely contain her relief when they returned without the Daks. One of the soldiers said that they probably lived in the area and should be easy enough to find.

"Let them go," Miklos ordered. "Specialist Kendor has been through quite a bad experience, and I want her to get back to the safety of the base."

Jalissa was only too happy to agree, even though his sudden concern for her now seemed false.

He materialized suddenly out of the deep shadows as though her thoughts had conjured him up. But now that he stood before her, Jalissa wanted him to be gone. Whispers of danger hung in the cool night air of the gardens just as powerfully as the scent of the night-blooming flowers around them.

She had come out here seeking a peace that continued to elude her. The day's events had unnerved her. She felt herself being thrust back into a life she had thought forever in the past. She didn't want to be a Witch—and yet she'd become one.

Furthermore, she was certain that Miklos Panera knew—or at the very least, strongly suspected—her true identity. How could he not? Was it possible that his mind was so closed to the idea that the Coven still existed that he simply refused to see the evidence she'd given him?

No, she thought as he walked toward her. *This is not a man given to self-deception. He knows— but for some reason, he doesn't want me to know that he knows.*

"How are you feeling?" he inquired politely.

"I'm fine," she replied with a cool formality that matched his. But the coolness was on the surface only. All she could think of now was the feel of his body against her, his lips on hers—and how she wanted it to happen again.

A sudden burst of laughter drew her attention to a group of officers seated some distance away on several of the stone benches that decorated the gardens. And for once, she was glad of the presence of Vantrans. They frowned on public displays of affection, except where children were concerned, and Jalissa knew there could be no repetition of that earlier scene.

Miklos held out a tiny silver object and she froze, certain that he had somehow found out about the stunner that Danto had given her.

"This is a new model," he said. "Because it's

194

small, its range is very limited, but it's easily concealed and makes an excellent personal-protection device."

"Thank you," she said, taking it from him. She'd completely forgotten his promise to get her one.

His wide mouth twisted wryly. "Giving it to you is an admission of my failure to protect you, Jalissa, but I will do my best to see that you don't need it."

He hesitated, and even someone less observant than she would have seen his discomfort. She wondered if he was about to apologize for what had happened—and wondered what she would say if he did.

"It troubles me to think that you might believe I deliberately put you in danger. In fact, that troubles me as much as my own carelessness does."

She stared at him. "I hadn't thought of you as being careless, Miklos. In fact, I remember thinking how very brave you were when you got out of the vehicle to face those Daks and their hatred."

But even as she spoke, what she was really remembering was the sight of him bound and helpless. She should have enjoyed that, she thought.

"Besides," she rushed on, "I could scarcely accuse you of trying to get yourself killed just to put me in danger."

He laughed. "There *is* that."

"Still, it wouldn't do for your superiors to find out that I rescued you," she went on, thinking that surely he must be concerned for his career.

"Or that your portrayal of a Witch was so convincing," he added, his light tone belying his words.

She continued to stroll along the path. "It isn't so difficult to convince primitive people who *want* to believe."

"I am neither primitive, nor do I want to believe—and yet I too was almost convinced."

She fought down her rising panic. "I'm Tevingian, Miklos, and my people know the Coven better than any others. Besides, I've been trained to do what is necessary to calm a dangerous situation."

He said nothing for a long time as they continued to walk deeper into the gardens. The voices of the Vantran officers were fading away, and ahead of them loomed the dark forest that ringed the base. Jalissa waited fearfully for him to make his accusation. But when he finally spoke, it was to ask if she felt ready to leave tomorrow.

"It's possible, even likely, that the man we seek could be on Dradar. I checked the spaceport records, and I think he may be traveling on an old SA-30. If so, his range without re-fueling is very limited, and given the difficulty he would have in navigating the asteroid belt with that old craft, my guess is that he would head for Dradar."

Greatly relieved at the change of topic, Jalissa

asked him how the man had been managing to elude capture by the spaceport authorities. On all the worlds she'd ever visited, comings and goings were strictly controlled by the Federation's Inter-Planetary Command.

"The controls out here are very lax," he explained. "There's so much small-craft traffic, and any attempts we've made to control it have met with resistance from the natives. The most we can do is to prevent any large flects that might signal an inter-planetary war.

"Furthermore, the SA-30 is small enough to land just about anywhere, and all of the Outer Ring worlds have vast open spaces. I'm quite curious about where he could have gotten hold of one—especially one that's space-worthy."

She could have easily answered that question. The SA-30 was the only craft owned by the Coven, and since they hadn't used them in a century, they remained in excellent condition, preserved by the dry desert air of their present home.

He went on. "I've sent orders to all the Outer Ring worlds to be on the lookout for an SA-30, and to hold the pilot regardless of the sensibilities of the natives. But if he doesn't land at a spaceport, they could easily miss him."

Jalissa hoped fervently that Kavnor would find another landing place. If he was captured before she could get to him, she had no idea what he might do or say.

Once again, Miklos lapsed into silence. They had reached the end of the gardens, which were lighted at regular intervals by low, round glow-lamps. The path continued into the woods, but she stopped and said that she was growing tired and wanted to turn back. He nodded, and they turned onto the perimeter path, where they encountered a young Vantran couple, both of them officers, locked in an embrace. They sprang apart quickly, and both looked devastated when they saw Miklos. They snapped to attention quickly and said in unison: "Good evening, sir."

Miklos merely nodded and moved past them. Jalissa smiled. "I'm afraid you've ruined their evening."

"They should consider themselves fortunate that it was me, and not their commander," he replied, smiling. "As far as I'm concerned, life on these outposts is difficult enough without the military's rules."

"If you dislike such rules, why did you join the military?"

"Because I don't dislike most of them—and because I believe in the Federation. The man we seek *is* a Warlock, isn't he?"

Jalissa was caught unprepared, even though she had earlier anticipated this question. They had yet to discuss what she'd learned from the Daks.

"Not necessarily," she replied. "After all, *I* was able to convince them that I'm a Witch."

"Yes, but you've had training, as you said—and you also had the bracelets to imitate the fire."

"If he's Tevingian, he would know what I know about the Coven, and he could have acquired the bracelets as well."

"Possibly, but they're not easy to find and they're expensive." He paused and lifted his head to the night sky, where the planet's small twin moons shone brightly.

"He *is* a Warlock, Jalissa, and we both know it. The Coven still exists out there somewhere." He continued to scan the heavens as though seeking the Coven now.

"There are more than two hundred barren worlds in the Outer Ring," he said. "All of them have been scanned for possible resources, but few of them have been thoroughly explored. I spent several hours this afternoon studying the photographs of them, hoping to find something that could point to one of them being the Coven's present home."

"And?" she asked, feigning nothing more than curiosity.

"And nothing," he said disgustedly. "I think it's possible that they could be living underground on one of them. If their magic is as powerful as your people believe, they could have created a home for themselves.

"What I don't think they could create is an atmosphere—so that narrows it down. Plus I have to assume that it couldn't be too far from their old home. And that leaves me with about ten planets."

Jalissa was horrified. She'd never expected that their search could take this turn. Furthermore, she wouldn't know if her home world were among the ten, because she had no idea where it was.

"What does Agency Headquarters think?" she asked.

"I haven't told them."

"You haven't?" She was shocked.

"If I tell them that I'm convinced this man *is* a Warlock, and also tell them my theory that the Coven must be on one of those planets, they'll have troops crawling all over them in no time."

She was confused. "I don't understand, Miklos. We're supposed to be searching for this man because he could be a Warlock, and yet you don't want the military to find the Coven?"

"Not yet. I've sent a coded message to my father, asking him to inform those members of the Federation Council he feels can be trusted. I want them to start thinking about what to do if I'm right."

"You're afraid that the military might act without the Council's approval?"

He nodded. "They could. All they have to do is to declare the situation a threat to the security of the Federation, and then they can ignore the Council. If that happens, I think they may use the anti-grav bomb again."

"And you don't want that? But you're part of the military, Miklos."

"I am, but that doesn't mean I agree with all its policies. I'd like to know just what the Coven has in mind. And I'd like to be sure that this Warlock is acting on their authority."

So would I, she thought, then wondered if all this was a ruse to get her to admit that she had secret knowledge. She wanted desperately to believe what he was saying, but she couldn't afford to take that chance.

"So are you saying that we should give up our search for this man and check those worlds you mentioned for the Coven itself?"

"No, we'll continue our search because it's important to capture him before he stirs up too much trouble. When I made my report earlier, I included a suggestion that the troop strength in the Outer Ring be doubled, just in case."

"Tell me about Dradar," she asked. It was their next destination, and she knew nothing about it.

"It's a cold, watery world. Nearly two thirds of the planet's surface is covered by seas that are frequently stormy at this time of year. The population is quite small, and many of them live out their entire lives on their boats. They're every bit as primitive as the Daks, and deeply religious. They worship the old gods with even greater faithfulness than the Daks, which would make them very receptive to this Warlock.

"Still, unlike the Daks, they're not a hostile

people. They tolerate the Federation presence there. But right now, there are some very delicate negotiations going on regarding the mining of trinium. They have huge deposits beneath their seas and we need it. Knowing that, if I were this Warlock, that's exactly where I'd be headed."

Jalissa knew that trinium was essential to the construction of spacecraft, but she hadn't thought it was in short supply. "But what about the mines on Galessa?"

"They're nearly played out, and we haven't found any in large quantities elsewhere."

"I didn't realize that."

"It isn't public knowledge."

"But then this Warlock—if he *is* one—couldn't know that either."

"He could." Miklos stopped suddenly, and she stopped too.

"If the Coven still exists, Jalissa, the Tevingians know about it—and probably visit them. Danto Kendor has a network of agents and spies that nearly rivals the Special Agency. I'm sure he knows about the trinium situation."

"I know nothing about it," she said, forcing herself to return his stare.

"Trust is a very fragile thing, Jalissa," he said softly. "And for us, it may be impossible. But I wish it could be otherwise."

He raised his hand, as though to touch her, then abruptly dropped it and walked away quickly, leaving her alone in the garden with his words echoing in the night.

Chapter Seven

Jalissa shivered beneath her heavy cloak, trying not to think about her queasy stomach as the Federation boat made its way slowly out of the harbor. The water in this protected bay was calm, but far out at sea, beyond the narrow fingers of land that protected the harbor, she could see its restless anger.

She had been to sea only once, with some friends on Vantra. But the ocean there was calm and blue, disturbed only by gentle swells. The world of the Coven was barren, with no seas at all, and Tevingi had nothing more than large lakes.

Dradar was the most unpleasant world she'd ever set foot on: cold, damp and dreary. The sea was an ugly green-brown color, overhung with gray clouds. It made her wonder how some people could be so unfortunate to be born into such ugliness, and yet, since the Dradars were not a space-faring people, she supposed they didn't realize just how unlucky they were.

At the base, she'd learned that Dradar was one of the worst of the "hardship postings" that meant extra pay for military personnel willing to come here. The Vantran base commander had told her that even with that added inducement, it was difficult to persuade soldiers to sign up for the standard year's tour of duty.

Because the majority of the native population lived out their lives on their boats, contact between them and the base was minimal. The damp, forested interior was almost completely uninhabited, and only a few small towns dotted the rugged coastline, existing as trading centers and gathering places for this sea-faring people. Roads were non-existent on this strange world, and like the Daks, the Dradars did not approve of hovercraft. So Jalissa and Miklos were forced to use this boat to journey up the coast to the largest of the towns.

No reports had reached the base of any appearance by the Warlock, but the base commander told them that if he did put in an appearance, it would most likely be in the town of Dra-Kenth, where a large festival was about to commence.

Jalissa, who hadn't celebrated the Coven's holidays since childhood, had had to be reminded that the High Summer festival was nearly upon them. Here as elsewhere in the world once dominated by her people, such festivals continued to be kept, adapted to the local calendar.

She turned from the chest-high rail along the deck and hurried back to the warmth of the big, glass-walled lounge. The Federation boat was large and luxuriously appointed, and she was grateful to have a comfortable cabin to herself. The journey from Dakton had been very difficult—for them both, she thought.

The lounge was empty when she entered, but a few moments later, Miklos appeared, shedding his long blue cape as he headed for the refreshment bar.

"The weather report is fine—or as good as it gets here," he told her with a wry smile. "Have you been to sea before?"

"Only on Vantra—the South Coast." She wondered if he found these casual conversations between them as difficult as she did.

"Even the North Coast is calm by comparison with the seas of Dradar. Perhaps you should consider taking a motion-sickness drug."

She shook her head. "Only if it becomes absolutely necessary. I checked their side effects, and I don't want to be groggy."

He poured himself a steaming mug of tea, then offered to pour one for her. They took seats on sofas that faced each other across a long, low table. Jalissa thought that the silences between them were even worse than the conversation.

"I've decided that we should go into the town alone," Miklos said just as the silence had become unbearable. "The Dradars aren't hostile, but the presence of soldiers might make them uneasy. And if our Warlock is there, he's more likely to find out about our presence if we bring in too many people."

"But surely he'll see the boat?"

"We won't go into the harbor. The captain knows of a small cove only a few hours' walk from the town, and they'll put us ashore there. According to him, the town will be filled with people who've come ashore for the festival. I had some appropriate clothing made up for us. You should have no problem blending in with the local population. They're small and fair-skinned and generally dark-haired."

"What about you?"

He chuckled. "That's a problem. I can dye my hair and lighten my skin a bit, but there's not much I can do about my height. We'll just have to hope for the best."

"Miklos," she said carefully, "just what do you plan to do if we find him?"

"I'm not sure at this point," he admitted, seeming unconcerned. Then, when he saw her consternation, he went on.

"As a Special Agent, I've learned not to make

too many plans and to just go with my instincts. But before there's any approach at all, I'd like to be certain that he is what he says he is."

"So you still have doubts?"

"Rationally, no. I think he *is* a Warlock. But a part of me just isn't yet willing to accept that."

"Because you can't accept that Coven magic might have escaped even your most powerful weapon," she stated, unable to hide her anger.

"No, Jalissa, it's not that. I'm not proud of what we did—or tried to do—even though there was no other way." He paused, obviously searching for words, and Jalissa had the strong sense that it was very important to him to make her understand.

"You've lived on Vantra for long enough to have some understanding of my people," he finally said. "If, as a Tevingian, you come from a tradition of worshipping supernatural gods, we Vantrans come from a tradition of worshipping science—our own minds. We're very uncomfortable with the idea that anything exists in this universe that cannot be understood in the context of science."

"But the Coven was—or is—*real*, Miklos. You can't deny that."

"As I said, rationally I *do* know that. But they don't fit in with our understanding of this universe."

"And that's why you would destroy them," she said bitterly.

"That's why some among my people would destroy them," he amended. "I've received a message from my father. He's spoken to several Council members, to alert them to the possibility that this man *is* a Warlock. But they cannot act on that information without putting me at risk as being their source. What I would like you to do is send a message back to Trans/Med. That way, they can go to the Council as well."

"But the Special Agency will intercept the message," she protested. "We know they can break our code."

"We won't use your code. I'll send it the same way I sent the message to my father, and he'll see that it gets to Trans/Med. All you need to do is to include something that guarantees its authenticity—something that will assure the person at Trans/Med that it comes from you."

Jalissa considered that. What he said certainly made sense, and might well be the only way to prevent the military from making war on the Coven. But could she trust him? Did he have some other purpose in mind? Could this be part of a scheme to discredit her—or to get her to admit that she herself was a Witch?

"Jalissa," he said, "whatever our differences, we have the same goal here: to prevent war and the possible breakup of the Federation."

"Let me think about it. I think I can come up with something that will prove the message is coming from me."

*   *   *

Back in her cabin, Jalissa continued to think about the risk she was taking. Through her mind kept echoing Miklos's earlier statement about wishing they could trust each other. How she wished that!

There was only one thing she did trust about Miklos Panera, and that was his total devotion to the Federation. But perhaps in this case, it was enough, especially since she couldn't see how the message could be used against her.

He could change it, whispered the dark voice of her mind. He could take from it whatever you use to identify yourself and change the rest to build a case against you.

She paced around the cabin, thinking. Miklos was right: It was essential that Trans/Med and the Council know that the Coven still existed. That knowledge could be their only salvation. But if she was going to be forced to trust Miklos, then it was time that he returned that trust.

She went to find him. He was no longer in the lounge, and as she looked out the windows, she saw that the boat was nearly out of the harbor. Already, the floor beneath her was shifting constantly as they moved into heavier seas. The captain had told her that this boat was specially built to handle the rough seas of Dradar, but that did little to calm her.

She picked up the comm to see if he might be on the bridge, but she was told that he wasn't, so she went to check his cabin, which was just down the hallway from her own. He answered her knock very quickly—just as the boat was lifted suddenly.

Jalissa put out a hand to steady herself against the door frame, but Miklos slid an arm around her and drew her inside. "We're just coming out of the harbor. The boat will settle down in a few minutes."

He led her to a chair and released her. She sank into it, but would rather have had his arm around her. She hated herself for feeling so safe and protected with this man she couldn't trust. It seemed that she'd become too Vantran: unwilling to accept any weaknesses in herself.

"I've been thinking about our plan to go into the town and try to blend in," she told him, trying to ignore both the boat's movements and the remembered feel of his arm around her.

"You said that I would have no problem fitting in, so I think that I should go into the town alone. My crystal will still work even if it's concealed, and if I'm careful, they may not realize I'm using it."

"No!" he said, rather more sharply than she would have expected—and apparently more sharply than he'd intended. "I won't put you at risk."

"But you said that the Dradars aren't hostile," she pointed out.

"I didn't say the same about this Warlock."

"Miklos, I'm Tevingian. He'll see that immediately and he'll trust me."

He said nothing as his green eyes bored into her.

"The problem is that *you* don't *trust* me," she said softly. "I have to trust *you* if I send this message. You could easily change it and use it to build a case to discredit me."

His expression altered slightly, and it seemed to her that he was surprised. But was he surprised that she should have guessed his intentions—or had that never been his plan?

"If I wanted to discredit you, I already have evidence: your act with the Daks."

"An act you yourself suggested," she flung at him angrily. "Miklos, you know that what I'm suggesting makes sense. There's no way you can disguise yourself adequately, and if we find him, he will know immediately that you're Vantran."

"I will consider it," he said begrudgingly.

"Fine," she stated as she got to her feet. "I'm going to my cabin to write that message."

Nearly an hour passed before there was a knock at her door. During that time, Jalissa had composed her message. Most of it was very straightforward. She said that she was virtually certain that the man they sought was in fact a Warlock, and therefore the Coven must still exist. She said that it could not be assumed that his attempts to foment rebellion had the Coven's blessing, but that she hoped to determine that when she found him.

Then she finished with a reference to the High Summer festival she would soon be attending, adding that she wondered if the Dradars played certain games she mentioned by name.

The message would go to Malvina, and would definitely establish that it came from her. The games in question involved magic, and despite their Tevingian-sounding names, were played nowhere else but among the Coven. When she read it, Malvina would realize that Jalissa now knew that she too was a Witch.

Jalissa opened the door and found Miklos there. She stepped aside to let him enter, then gestured to the small table. "I have written my message. It is to go to Malvina Taran, a Deputy Administrator at Trans/Med. She's also Tevingian, and will recognize those games as being ones that we both played as children at High Summer festivals."

As he picked up the message and read it, a sudden thought struck Jalissa. By sending the message to Malvina, she could well be casting suspicion on her. Why hadn't she considered that?

Perhaps it didn't matter. If the Special Agency discovered that Jalissa was a Witch, every Tevingian in the Federation services would soon be suspected as well.

He folded the note and put it into his pocket.

"I'll send it immediately." Then he regarded her solemnly.

"I have decided to let you do as you've suggested, though I still don't like it. Have you considered just how dangerous this Warlock could be, Jalissa—especially if he's acting on his own? The fact that you're Tevingian may not make a difference. In fact, he might well believe that the Coven has sent you after him."

"I realize that, but it's a chance I must take. Regardless of whether he's acting under Coven orders, I don't believe he would harm me."

"Just as a precaution, I'm sending one of the ship's crew with you. He can pass easily enough for a Dradar, and he'll pretend to be a deaf-mute. According to the captain, such defects are not uncommon on this world, given their excessive inbreeding and lack of modern medical technology."

"Where is he from?" Jalissa asked, unhappy at this turn of events but unable to think of a way out of it.

"His father is Tevingian, but his mother is from Tarlogga. Fortunately for our purposes, he looks Tevingian."

"That should work, then," she said, wondering how she could manage to get rid of the man. If he were Tevingian, she wouldn't be too concerned, but a man of divided loyalties couldn't be trusted.

Miklos was pacing restlessly around her cabin,

his usual Vantran reserve nowhere in evidence. Jalissa regarded him curiously, wondering what it was that was bothering him so. Probably he disliked being forced to stand aside while *she* went to seek the Warlock. It was undoubtedly a novel situation for a Special Agent.

Suddenly, he stopped and stared at her. "Are you doing this because you feel you have to prove something?"

Startled, she shook her head. "What would I want to prove?"

His green eyes continued to bore into her, and then he shook his head and made a dismissive gesture. "Nothing."

He turned abruptly and walked out of her cabin, leaving her to stare after him in confusion. Did he believe she felt the need to prove her bravery—or her loyalty to the Federation?

The more she thought about it, the more she was inclined to think it was the latter. He might well have guessed that she knew of the Special Agency's suspicions, and was undertaking this mission to prove that her loyalties lay with the Federation—not the Coven. Even as a Tevingian, she would be suspected of divided loyalty when it came to the matter of the Coven.

And if that was what he suspected, he was right, she thought uneasily. Her loyalties were badly torn right now. She wanted to protect the Coven—but she also wanted desperately to prevent a war that could destroy the Federation.

*   *   *

Jalissa did not see Miklos again until he appeared at her side as the boat made its way through choppy seas into the more serene waters of a small cove. Off to the starboard side, the land bulged out, making it impossible to see beyond the low, thickly forested hills. Presumably, the town lay in that direction.

The cove was a pleasant place, where the waters lapped gently at a narrow strip of dun-colored sand. When Miklos appeared, she asked him if the strip of beach continued all the way to the town.

"Yes. That's the way you'll take. As soon as you get around that bend, you should be able to see it, though you'll have to walk several miles. Do you have your stunner?"

She nodded. In fact, she had two of them, one in each pocket of her long, full skirt. She was dressed in coarse, dark clothing, topped with a thickly padded and unpleasantly bulky jacket, the crystal now resting between her breasts beneath the clothing. On her feet were heavy leather boots. She felt awkward and clumsy, but didn't doubt that she would fit in with the native population. Even her lustrous black hair had been plaited into two thick braids in a style common to women of this world.

Miklos looked her up and down approvingly. "The costume is perfect. Just remember that women here are inclined to be submissive."

He added the last with a definite gleam of humor in his eyes, then added that she should take care to walk several paces behind the soldier who would be posing as her husband.

"Avoid making eye contact with anyone, especially men. No Dradar woman would do that. Your safety lies in the fact that the town will be crowded and a lot of the townsfolk will be drunk. As long as you do nothing to draw attention to yourself, you shouldn't have a problem."

"What about money to buy food and such?" she asked.

"Canar has that. As your husband, he would make any purchases. Ahh, here he comes now."

Jalissa saw a man coming toward them, dressed much as she herself was, except that he wore slim-fitting pants. He was only a few inches taller than she was and slim, and his features showed none of his Tarloggan heritage. Miklos introduced them, then indicated a small boat that was being hoisted from its cradle at the stern.

"We'll go ashore in that."

" 'We'?" she queried, fearing that he'd changed his mind about coming along.

"I'll wait on the beach. The boat will sail back up the coastline and return for us. If it hung about here, it could arouse some suspicions."

"But what about you?"

"I'll haul the boat out of the water and hide it in the woods, then stay out of sight. I want you both back here by dark. Is that clear?"

Canar issued a crisp "yes, sir," but Jalissa said nothing. Miklos turned to her, arching a blond brow questioningly. "Jalissa?"

She ignored him and started to the stern, where the little boat awaited them. The three of them climbed in and were hoisted over the rail and lowered into the water. Miklos aimed the small craft at the beach, and within moments they bumped into the soft sand. As soon as they had climbed out, he told Canar to drag the boat into the woods far enough that it couldn't be seen from the water. Then he turned to Jalissa.

"I want you to promise me that you'll stay with him—and come back here before dark."

"Stop giving me orders, Miklos! You're beginning to sound like a native."

A smile flickered across his face, then dissolved into seriousness again. "I'm only thinking of your welfare."

"I'm quite capable of thinking about that for myself."

He lifted a hand and touched one of the thick braids that curved around her neck and fell nearly to her breasts. She drew in her breath sharply and her eyes raised to meet his.

"Are you angry about what happened on Dakton?" he asked softly, his fingertips now grazing her cheek.

"No," she said huskily as the images floated in her mind's eye and her bones began to melt from

217

the heat that was spreading through her.

He began to lower his face to hers and her lips parted eagerly, already feeling his imprint. Then he suddenly glanced behind her and quickly straightened up again. She turned and saw Canar coming out of the woods toward them.

Jalissa turned just before they rounded the curve on the beach, and saw that he was still there, watching them. Then she put up a hand to touch her lips, thinking about the kiss that hadn't happened and knowing that if circumstances had been different, the kiss would have been only a prelude.

Then she turned away as Canar emitted a low whistle. In the distance, they could see the town, sprawling across a series of low hills. But it was the harbor that had drawn his attention. It was completely filled with boats, so close together that it appeared from here that the occupants could simply walk from one deck to another all the way across the huge harbor.

"I guess we don't have to worry about anyone paying much attention to us," he said as they continued to walk along the beach. "I wonder if the 'Warlock' will be there."

Jalissa noted the derisive way he spoke of their quarry. "Were you raised on Tevingi, Canar?"

"No, on Tarlogga. But my father used to talk a lot about the Coven. It seems to me that anyone from Tevingi could imitate a Warlock pretty well."

"That may be true, but Mik . . . Agent Panera and I believe this man truly *is* a Warlock. And that could make him very dangerous."

He half-sneered. "Warlock or not, I'll get him."

Jalissa came to a stop, and after taking a few more steps, he did too. "We are to bring this man back *alive*, Canar. Surely Agent Panera told you that."

"He did—but he also said that if I had to kill him to protect you, that's what I should do."

"I'm sure that won't be necessary," she stated firmly. And by the time they reached the town, she had decided that she had to find some way to get free of this over-zealous soldier. It was clear to her that not only couldn't he be trusted, but he had also taken Miklos's orders too much to heart.

The town was as crowded as they'd expected—and then some. Jalissa had more trouble than she'd anticipated in portraying herself as a shy Dradar woman. Accustomed to walking tall and erect, she constantly had to remind herself to adopt the hunched, head-down manner of walking that she noted in the women they passed.

Furthermore, the noise level was horrendous. People were talking excitedly, merchants were hawking their wares and children ran free, creating their own distinctive noise. Her crystal proved to be of only limited use as she strained to catch the translations of those speaking around her. Under ordinary circumstances, the crystal would translate the speech of only the person to whom she was addressing herself; now she was forced to try to filter out the background noise in order to hear anything.

Words and phrases came to her, but as they moved through the crowds, she heard nothing about a Warlock. Still, it seemed likely to her that he would show up here. On a world where people rarely gathered in large groups, this could be his only opportunity. He wasn't likely to try to travel the seas from boat to boat.

Market stalls were everywhere, and items were being offered from individual homes as well. Jalissa saw some lovely weaving, and was entranced by a stall filled with tiny carvings of people and animals. At first, she didn't know what they were made of, but then she realized they must be fish bones. The workmanship was wonderful and she tugged at Canra's sleeve as he scanned the crowds, clearly uninterested in the wares being offered.

"I'd like to buy a few of these," she told him, speaking softly in Tevingian.

Without bothering to turn to her, he withdrew a pouch containing gold coins from his pocket and handed it to her. She approached the slender, dark-haired youth behind the stall and indicated her selections, then asked the price.

The youth's gaze went from her to her "husband" in surprise. She hurried to explain that he was a deaf-mute, and the young man nodded, then told her the price. She added an extra coin, and told him that they'd heard a rumor that a Warlock would be here, saying she hoped that he might cure her husband of his terrible affliction.

"A Warlock?" he said in surprise, drawing Canar's attention. Jalissa shot Canar a warning glance, reminding him that he shouldn't have been able to hear the merchant's words.

But the young man apparently didn't notice as he called out to a man at the next stall, repeating her words. Jalissa winced. She knew how word traveled, and now, thanks to her mistake, she'd be hearing a rumor she had started. She hurried on, forgetting that she was supposed to be following Canar instead of leading him. He caught up with her quickly and leaned close to her.

"You shouldn't have done that. Now we won't know if what we hear is true."

"I know," she replied. "I didn't think until it was too late."

Rather to her surprise, he grinned. "I'm not very good at being deaf either. Agent Panera would have both our hides. Have you heard anything at all?"

She shook her head. "It's very difficult for the crystal to work properly in such a crowd."

"What did you tell him when you asked about a Warlock?"

She explained and he nodded. "That's good thinking. If he *does* show up, we can use that to get to him."

"Not if you continue to forget that you're supposed to be deaf." She smiled, giving back to him the bag of coins from which she'd managed to extract a few for herself.

They continued to stroll through the town, moving slowly through the ever-thickening crowds. Within an hour, Jalissa was growing tired and uncomfortable in her bulky clothes and stiff, heavy boots. They bought food and drink at a stall, and found a spot to sit down on an old stone wall that lined the market square. Canar kept an eye on the crowds while she lowered her head shyly and concentrated on listening to the talk around them.

Suddenly, Canar grabbed her arm and pointed. She looked in the direction he indicated and saw a group of people crowding eagerly around an older man, who was gesturing wildly. They both got up and hurried over. As they reached the edge of the group, Jalissa saw an old woman make the sign of the Coven. Then the people began to move together off down a narrow street. Following along in their wake, Jalissa strained to catch their talk.

Canar needed no translation. The words "Warlock" and "Coven" were being shouted by everyone as they poured through the street. Jalissa turned and saw that even more people were now following them.

Within moments, they were caught up in the eager, pushing mass of Dradars, and Jalissa saw her opportunity to get away from Canar. When they reached a corner and turned, she slipped out of the crowd and darted into the narrow space between two buildings. There was no way Canar could turn and follow her, even assuming he knew she'd left the crowd.

She peered out from her hiding place, astounded at the number of people now hurtling past, eager expressions on their faces. She could only hope that it wasn't a false alarm precipitated by her earlier question to the merchant.

Withdrawing more deeply into the shadows until she couldn't be seen at all from the street, Jalissa composed herself. She had no idea where the people were going, and so decided to 'port herself up onto the hillside above, where she hoped she could see better.

She closed her eyes, willed herself there—and she *was* there. After quickly checking to see that no one was around to see her suddenly materialize, she looked down on the central part of the town. The crowd she'd been part of wasn't difficult to spot. The lead group had reached another, wider street and was now headed up the hillside toward her.

Jalissa scanned her surroundings once again, and this time saw what appeared to be an open space, a sort of meadow, not far away.

Deciding not to risk 'porting again, she began to hurry in that direction, hoping that it might be the destination of the crowd. And she knew she was right when she reached the end of the row of small houses.

About a dozen people were gathered there, forming a rough semi-circle around a young man who stood slightly above them on the sloping hillside. She came closer, then stopped where he could easily see her.

"Kavnor!" she said, sending the message silently. "I must speak with you."

The young Warlock's head swiveled in her direction, and she saw the confused look on his face. She repeated the message, adding her name this time. In the distance, she could hear the crowd approaching. Canar would soon be here. She had to get him away.

He came toward her, and the small group around him parted to let him pass, then turned to stare at her. Fortunately, however, they remained where they were as the young Warlock came up to her, his thin face now showing both puzzlement and fear.

"Jalissa—*our* Jalissa?" he asked, staring at her.

She nodded. "Kavnor, you must get away from here now! In that crowd coming up the hill is a Federation soldier. He's been told to capture you alive!"

They both turned as the crowd noise increased, and now they could see the people making their way past the last row of houses. Kavnor turned to her defiantly.

"They won't let him capture me. They know I'm a Warlock."

"Then he'll kill you. He has weapons."

The youth hesitated. "I want to talk to them—to tell them that they can join us."

"Don't be a fool!" she said sharply. "You won't get a chance to talk to them." She pointed to a nearby hill that was somewhat higher. " 'Port yourself over there and wait for me."

"What about you?"

"I'll join you there, but I can't 'port from here. They know you're a Warlock, and if any of them had any doubts, they'll certainly know it if you suddenly vanish."

He nodded—and then was gone. Nothing remained but a faint wisp of gray smoke that soon dissipated in the breeze. The small group nearby cried out. Jalissa couldn't blame them for being awed. She was too. It had been a very long time since she'd seen anyone 'port.

The main portion of the crowd was now pouring onto the meadow. Jalissa hurried back down the hillside to the safety of the row of houses one street away from the oncoming rush of people. Then, after slipping into a small garden behind one house, she 'ported herself to the other hilltop.

Kavnor was standing there, his jaw jutting out

defiantly. "Why are you here?"

"To save your life. Did you really think that you could just wander about the galaxy trying to start a rebellion and not be chased by Federation soldiers? There's a Special Agent waiting just outside town for you."

"Did the Coven send you?"

"No. They told me to stay out of it."

"And you *defied* them?" he asked with a mixture of incredulity and awe.

"Yes, I defied them. Did they send you, or did you defy them as well?"

"I didn't defy them—exactly," he admitted. "I told them that the gods had called me to do this, and they let me go."

"And is that the truth, or did you simply hear the gods tell you what you wanted to hear?"

"They *told* me," he insisted. "They told me to be the messenger—to go to all the places where people still revere the Coven and keep to the old ways."

"And did the gods tell you to start a rebellion?"

He was silent for a moment, then shook his head. "But they told me to tell everyone that we're still here, that the accursed Vantrans didn't kill us after all."

Jalissa sighed. It was one and the same thing. On these volatile worlds, simply letting people know that the Coven still existed was enough to start trouble.

"You must go back, Kavnor. You must return

to the Coven and tell them that they cannot hope to defeat the Federation. The Vantrans will find you and destroy you."

"I don't want to go back," he said stubbornly. "I'm tired of living underground and hiding. And so are some others. We want to live like other people."

"You *can't* live like other people, Kavnor, because you *aren't* like other people." But her voice had softened. She, perhaps more than anyone else, understood what he was saying. "The Vantrans won't permit it."

"*You* live like other people," he pointed out stubbornly.

"Yes, but I also don't use my powers. Besides, I left the Coven when I was still a child."

"I don't want to leave the Coven. I want the rest of the Coven to come with me. We could live on Tevingi. They'd welcome us."

"Yes, I'm sure they would, but they can't protect you from the Vantrans. There's a huge Federation base on Tevingi."

"I'm not going back. And others will follow me as soon as I tell them to come."

Jalissa shivered at the thought of a group of renegade Warlocks roaming about the galaxy, stirring up trouble. So far, the Federation was acting with some moderation. But if they learned that there was more than one Warlock on the loose . . .

"Kavnor, the Federation cannot be destroyed.

Before it came into existence, there was constant war—and that's exactly what will happen again."

"We don't want to make war," he protested. "All we want is to be able to live as we once did."

Jalissa walked over to the edge of the hilltop. A huge crowd was now gathered in the meadow they'd just left, and no doubt Canar was searching for her.

"I know you don't want war," she told him. "But it will happen anyway."

"Because of the Vantrans," he said, spitting out the hated name.

"Yes, because of them. But they're not really bad people, Kavnor. Out here, you haven't seen what their science has done—how good people's lives are now. They don't really want war either—but they will not share power with the Coven because they fear us."

"Good!" he said stubbornly, his jaw jutting out again. "They *should* fear us. They're godless, evil people!"

"So you won't go back to the Coven?"

"No!"

"Would you at least take me there, so I can talk to them?"

"No. And I know you can't go there on your own."

"Then will you at least get off this world before you're captured? I can't protect you, Kavnor."

"I don't need your protection. You're not even one of us anymore!"

And before she could reply to that, he vanished. She turned again to stare down at the milling crowd, his final words echoing in her mind. Maybe he was right. But for now, she had to get back down there and find Canar. At least she didn't have to worry about his finding out that she'd talked to Kavnor. No doubt the crowd was full of stories about the woman he'd been with when he vanished, but since Canar couldn't speak the language, he wouldn't know.

Chapter Eight

Finding Canar proved to be impossible. The crowd in the meadow had by now swelled to fill the entire space on the hillside. Hundreds, perhaps even a thousand people milled about, asking questions and passing on rumors. Everyone seemed to know that a Warlock had been present, but that he'd disappeared after talking to a woman. As Jalissa had guessed, Kavnor's disappearance had established beyond a doubt that he was in fact a member of the Coven.

She continued to make her way through the crowd, seeking Canar, until she realized that a few people were staring at her. When one of them began to point toward her, identifying her as the woman the Warlock had spoken to, she slipped away quickly and hid herself in the rear garden of a nearby home.

She was reluctant to leave the area for two reasons. First of all, she knew that Canar had to be here somewhere and would expect her to be here as well. And secondly, she feared that Kavnor might return. She had no idea what she would do if he did in fact show up again, but she knew that she had to remain there nevertheless.

After a while, the crowd began to disperse, first in a small trickle, and then in a wave of humanity, pouring down the two streets that led to the meadow. From her hiding place, Jalissa watched the people who came down the street near her, but still saw no sign of Canar. Finally, she stepped out and joined the throng as they made their noisy way down to the center of the town.

All around her, she heard the sounds of disappointment, but it was a disappointment mingled with hope and excitement. A Warlock had been seen! The Coven still existed! Here and there, a few men muttered darkly about the Federation, but most appeared to be filled with excitement, rather than hostility.

They are so eager to be led, she thought. *It would take very little to transform that excitement into anger against the Federation.*

She thought about Kavnor's statement that others were prepared to follow him away from the protected underground world of the Coven. How could she fault any of them for that, when she herself could not imagine returning there? And yet, if they did as he said, her own position, the life she had so carefully built, would tumble down around her.

Back in the big market square, Jalissa continued to search for Canar as she heard the story of the vanished Warlock spread from stall to stall on ripples of excitement. Perhaps he would reappear tomorrow, they said. Plans were made to go to the meadow at dawn, to await his arrival.

He might just do that, Jalissa thought, knowing that she herself would have to return as well even if she couldn't do anything. Or was it possible that she *could* do something? Kavnor was young—probably no more than 16—and Coven members didn't come into their full powers until 21 or so. He could perform the simple feats of magic that any child could manage, but that was all.

She, on the other hand, had long since come into full possession of her powers, even if she rarely used them. If he *did* return, she might be able to use those powers to discredit him and convince the Dradars that he was an impostor.

That thought did not sit easily upon her. It would be cruel. Coven members never turned their magic on each other. And yet, if she did, it might well convince him to return to the Coven and give up his dangerous quest.

As she considered this, she continued her search for Canar with increasing desperation. It was important to find out what he'd learned, though given his lack of knowledge of the Dradar tongue, it wasn't likely to be much.

The merchants began to close up their stalls, and there was a steady flow of people back to their houses or boats. Dim sunlight gave way to soft dusk. Jalissa belatedly realized that most of the remaining crowd was male—and many of them were drunk. She reverted to her slouched imitation of Dradar women and kept her eyes downcast as she hurried along the streets toward the edge of town. A few remarks were sent her way, but no one tried to approach her—until she passed by a noisy, crowded tavern whose patrons had spilled out onto the street.

Even though she kept her head down, she was aware of many eyes on her and of the lewd remarks sent her way. Then the noise of the tavern was behind her and she was entering a quiet area of what appeared to be storage facilities of some sort at the far end of the big harbor. Lost in thought, she didn't hear the approaching footsteps until it was too late.

They were upon her even before she could turn: two men, their breath foul with alcohol, their eyes devouring her greedily. One of them lunged at her, catching her off balance as she turned. The two of them tumbled to the ground, accompanied by the sound of drunken cheering from the second man.

Her attacker wasn't all that big and was drunk

as well, but it still took considerable effort on her part to push him off. She scrambled to her feet and began to run, but now the other man was hurling himself at her. She hit the ground harder this time and cried out in pain. His clumsy fingers began to tug at her long skirt, and his companion was now moving toward them.

Jalissa managed to roll away from her current attacker. Angry beyond all reason, she raised her hand—and let fly the blue fire!

The man closest to her had only a moment to cry out in surprise and terror before he collapsed in a heap. With the fire still surrounding her fingertips, Jalissa turned to his companion.

"No, Witch! We meant no harm! We didn't know!"

Jalissa glared at him as she got to her feet. "Meant no harm" indeed! They meant to rape her! She could still feel the man's hard fingers on her leg.

The other man fell to his knees and continued to plead with her, calling upon the gods as his witness. Before she could succumb to the temptation to strike out at him, she closed her fist upon the fire and then turned and walked away. After she had gone some distance, she turned briefly and looked back. In the gathering night, she was just barely able to make out the two figures: one still prone on the street and the other bent over him.

By the time she reached the strip of sand, her

anger and disgust had turned to fear—and then to shock, as she realized that unlike the other times when she'd been in danger, this time she'd used her magic without thought. Furthermore, she'd done so even though she had not one, but two, stunners in her pocket.

She was so overcome with the horror of it that she sank down onto the sand. She had truly become a Witch! Aroused from their long sleep, her powers had now become second nature to her.

And once she got over that shock, she began to think about the results of her actions. Drunk or not, those men had known what she was, and they would quickly spread the word, no doubt claiming that they were innocent in the matter.

Still, neither Canar nor Miklos could speak the language, so it was unlikely that they would learn about the incident.

Miklos. Jalissa sat there in the darkness, staring out at the sea, where whitecaps glowed in the light of the rising moon. How she longed to be with him, in his arms. The drunken Dradar's lecherous attentions had awakened in her a fierce need for Miklos's kisses.

She actually smiled as she thought about his question. No, she was definitely not angry about that kiss. She was angry only that it hadn't been repeated.

She got up and started back to the cove, only then realizing that her skirt had been torn and the sleeve of the padded jacket was hanging by

only a few threads. Tired, hungry and uncomfortable, she trudged along the beach, her
thoughts not on her dilemma, but on Miklos Panera.

In the bright moonlight, Jalissa could see the
place where the strip of beach disappeared
around a sharp bend. Beyond that, Miklos would
be waiting. It was well past dark by now, and she
knew he would be worried about her. That he
would also be filled with questions she didn't
want to answer simply didn't occur to her. Right
now, there was nothing in the galaxy she wanted
as much as she wanted to feel his arms around
her.

And then she saw him! There was no doubt in
her mind that it was Miklos, even though the
dark figure that appeared from beyond the bend
was as yet indistinct. With a burst of energy she
didn't know she possessed, she began to run toward him—and a moment later, he too was running.

They didn't just meet; they collided, falling into
each other's arms, bodies pressed together. He
held her quietly for a long time, the only sounds
the rapid beating of two hearts and the soft lapping of sea against shore.

Then, keeping one arm securely around her,
Miklos fumbled the comm unit from his belt and
spoke into it, reporting to someone that she was
back. Then he replaced the comm and held her

slightly away from him, staring at her.

"What happened? Are you all right?"

She nodded, moving into the circle of his arms again and pressing her face against his chest, still not questioning what she was feeling.

He drew them both down onto the hard-packed sand, cradling her in his arms as she related the incident with the two drunken men. But when she got to the part about how she'd managed to escape them, the ugly reality of her secret confronted her.

"I used the stunner on one of them, and that was enough to keep the other one from attacking me again," she said, hating the lie that drove a wedge between them.

He pressed his lips to her brow. "I'm sorry, Jalissa. I never should have permitted you to do this. I was just about to order troops into the town to find you."

She turned slightly, bringing her mouth close to his—and then closer still. For one brief instant, it seemed that he hesitated, but in the next second, their lips were touching tentatively as they slowly fell back to the hard-packed sand. His hands slipped beneath her bulky jacket to caress her as their tongues intertwined in an erotic dance. The kiss went on and on, their breaths intermingling as their bodies once more strained against confinement.

Jalissa was lost in the moment, and wanted never to find her way out of it, knowing that in the next moment or the one after that, it would all vanish again.

When Miklos began to withdraw from her, she wrapped her hands around his face and drew him to her again. He smiled gently, a silent acknowledgement that he too wanted to stop time. His lips brushed against the sensitive palm of her hand, then trailed along her neck to the pulse-point at her throat.

She wanted more. She wanted to feel his smooth, bronzed skin against hers, wanted to yield up her softness to his hardness, wanted to feel him deep inside her. Desire was an aching presence between them, a silent clamoring for fulfillment.

Miklos lifted his head again, and his eyes, drained of color by the moonlight, gleamed darkly as he stared at her. She threaded her fingers through his tangled blond hair, which was swept with a silvery glaze.

"Mafriti," he said huskily. "That's where I want to be now—on a private beach, alone with you."

She smiled as her mind conjured up that lush world given over to pleasures of all sorts. She'd been there several times, but always alone or with a group of friends.

But his soft words, meant to conjure up a future, served instead to bring them both back to reality. The Federation ship was somewhere close by, and Canar . . .

"Where is Canar? Did he return?"

238

Miklos was slow to nod, obviously as reluctant as she was to be tumbled back into the present. "He said you were separated in the crowd when you went to find the Warlock. He searched for you, then gave up and came back here just before dark."

She waited for him to ask questions, to destroy what little was left of the magic that had held them. But instead, he brushed her hair from her face, touched his lips to hers once more, then stood up and drew her to her feet.

Holding hands, they walked along the moonlit beach. When they had rounded the bend, Jalissa saw the Federation boat, a nearly invisible dark bulk in the silvered waters of the cove. Canar awaited them in the small launch on the beach.

Miklos continued to hold her hand as they approached the waiting soldier, and only when she saw Canar's gaze go to their interlocked hands did she realize the importance of the moment. By morning, the Special Agent's strange behavior would be common knowledge on the ship—and a report might even be on its way back to headquarters.

She started to withdraw her hand from his grasp, but he merely tightened his grip as he helped her into the boat. Before Canar began to pepper her with questions, she sent Miklos a warning look, but his response told her that he knew exactly what he was doing.

Back on the ship, Jalissa stumbled off toward

her cabin, but before she had gone more than a few steps, Miklos's arm was around her waist. Knowing that she was only compounding the danger, she still leaned gratefully against him as they made their way below.

Surely he'll want a report, she thought, hoping that she could keep her wits about her long enough to be credible. But he merely hooked a finger beneath her chin and drew her face up for a soft kiss, then let her go.

She stumbled into her cabin, dazed from the day's events and still half-lost in those moments on the beach.

Miklos waited until she had closed the door to her cabin, then turned around and went back up onto the deck. The ship's lights were out, so that it wouldn't be seen by any passing Dradar vessel. The moon had slid behind clouds, and a chill wind whipped around him as he stood at the rail.

He pictured her in her cabin, stripping off her ugly disguise, baring that pale, creamy body he could only imagine. Would she lie in bed listening for his knock at the door? It wouldn't happen, but only because he'd drawn on his deepest reserves of willpower, draining them dry.

Despite their outward reserve—or perhaps because of it—Vantrans were a deeply romantic people. And Miklos Panera was no exception, although until now, he'd thought he was. The women who had passed through his life were mostly women he'd known since childhood: members of other powerful families. He'd had his share of lovers, but none of them had ever reduced him to the befuddled man he saw he was now.

He wondered if the danger was part of it—the knowledge that nothing good could come of such a liaison. It was possible, he thought, and it could be the same for her. The thrill of teetering on the very brink of a dark abyss.

Part of him wanted to believe it was just that— but another part insisted that there was more. Caught between these competing claims, Miklos turned his thoughts to the report he'd received and what she would tell him in the morning.

Whatever she said, he knew, sadly, that it wouldn't be the truth. Truth just wasn't possible between them—and never would be.

Jalissa slept late, and then breakfasted in the privacy of her cabin, expecting a knock at the door at any moment. Surely Miklos would be demanding to know what she'd learned.

Reluctantly, she began to sort through various lies and half-truths, trying to decide what to tell him. He couldn't have learned much from Canar, so there was no one to contradict her.

She knew too that there was no way she could return to the meadow today alone. Canar would be very careful this time not to "lose" her. And she was very reluctant to use her powers to prevent Kavnor from delivering his message with the Federation soldier standing there.

Perhaps Kavnor had left. He wouldn't give up his mission; that was clear enough. But her warning might have sent him from Dradar. Unfortunately, that only transferred the problem to another world—and probably to one more willing to take up arms against the Federation than this one.

When she knew she could delay her confrontation with Miklos no longer, Jalissa left her cabin and went to find him, her steps dragging as she faced the unwelcome prospect of lying. He wasn't in the lounge, and neither could she see him through the windows of the enclosed bridge. That left only his cabin—the last place she wanted to go.

The scene on the beach floated before her as she went below again, then flooded through her with a sensuous heat when she saw him outside her cabin door, his hand just raised to knock. He heard her approaching and turned toward her, powerful and remote once more in his uniform. Still, as she drew closer, she could see a lingering trace of his own memories of the night before in the eyes that locked onto hers.

She stopped a few feet from him and a silence hung between them, a silent acknowledgment of what had gone before and what must follow now. She wondered if he could possibly want to turn back the clock as much as she did.

"I didn't want to disturb you too early," he said, finally breaking the silence between them. "Did you sleep well?"

"Yes. Thank you." She heard both their words and what was unspoken as well, an eerie analogy to the way she worked with the crystal.

She opened the door to her cabin and invited him in. Immediately, the cabin seemed over-filled with him. Staring at his dark blue uniform with its gold braid trim, Jalissa was struck by how intimidating he'd once seemed, and how, even now, some of that lingered. She felt that she was coming to know Miklos Panera the man, but the Special Agent remained remote and threatening.

Perhaps, she thought, he would feel the same way if he knew the truth. He might believe he knew Jalissa Kendor, Whisperer, but Jalissa Kendor, Witch, was altogether a different matter. Whatever he might feel for her now would surely vanish beneath a wave of revulsion.

"Tell me what you learned yesterday," he instructed her in a voice that did not make it easier for her to tell her story.

"The Warlock was there, but he vanished. I saw him, but only briefly. He hadn't yet begun to speak because the crowd was just beginning to gather. It's possible, I suppose, that he might return today. At least the crowd seemed to have that hope."

"Why did he leave without speaking?" Miklos

asked, his gaze intent upon her.

She shrugged. "I have no idea."

"What did he say to you, Jalissa?"

The question was asked softly, but it might as well have been an explosion. Fear clutched her spine with icy fingers. How could he know they'd spoken? She was sure Canar hadn't seen them together. He hadn't been there yet.

She let the silence drag on until she knew it was too late to deny that she'd spoken to the Warlock. Her mind spun as she tried to re-formulate her story, finally settling on an option she'd discarded earlier.

"He's not acting with Coven approval. He claims that the gods spoke to him directly and told him to spread the word of the Coven's existence."

She paused, her eyes pleading now. "He's very young, Miklos—only sixteen. He's rebellious and also very naive. He truly doesn't understand what he is doing. I tried to explain to him that he is risking war, but he wouldn't listen."

"You weren't going to tell me this, were you," he said in that same soft voice. Had she really heard understanding there—or was she only hearing what she *wanted* to hear?

"No, I wasn't. I was afraid that you would think I was being disloyal to the Federation."

"You could have used your stunner to keep him there until Canar arrived," Miklos pointed out, but without anger.

"I . . . I didn't even think about it. I was still trying to reason with him when he vanished." The chill within her grew deeper as she realized she'd just admitted that Canar hadn't been there.

"Why did he single you out to talk to?"

She wasn't prepared for this dangerous question because she hadn't intended to admit that she'd talked to the Warlock. She affected a shrug.

"I don't know. He seemed to know that I was Tevingian, despite my disguise. How did you know that I talked to him?" She decided it was time to divert his attention and forestall any further questions.

"Canar couldn't have seen us," she went on when he remained silent. "He hadn't gotten there yet."

"Which makes me wonder how you managed to get there ahead of him," Miklos replied coolly.

"We were separated. I must have gotten ahead of him. If he didn't tell you, then who did?"

"I sent someone else, a man who has some knowledge of the Dradar language and could also pass for one of them."

Stung by his deception, Jalissa now ignored her own. "Why did you do that?" she demanded.

"Mostly for your protection," he replied smoothly. "And also in case he was needed to deal with the Warlock."

"Then why didn't you tell me?"

"For the same reason you didn't tell me about

245

talking to the Warlock—because neither of us trusts the other."

The words hung there between them, cold and accusing. But when she met his gaze, Jalissa knew that beneath those accusations lay pain for them both. It was in his eyes.

"He returned here and reported to me. Then I sent him back, to see what he could learn of the mood of the Dradars. He didn't come back until just before dawn, and he brought a very interesting story with him."

Jalissa stiffened, knowing what was coming next. She did her best to look merely curious, but she was now chilled all the way through.

"I'm not sure whether this tale can be credited, since he heard it in a tavern filled with drunken men. But the story was that there was also a Witch present."

"No," she replied quickly. "He was alone."

"This happened later. According to the story, two men approached a woman who was walking alone after dark. They apparently claimed that they were merely offering their assistance to see her safely home. But she struck at them with Witch's fire."

He paused, staring hard at her. But she knew him well enough now to see the nervousness that lay beneath his steady gaze. *He doesn't want to believe,* she thought. *He wants me to deny this.*

"I think it likely that their story was self-serving. They probably tried to attack the woman—and got far more than they'd bargained for," he said.

"It's more likely that they made up the story entirely," she replied. "Given their drunkenness and the stories about the Warlock, that isn't so surprising."

Then, into the silence that followed, she voiced the suggestion that she should return to the meadow in case the Warlock returned.

"Canar and the other man have already gone to town. You will remain here."

And before she could respond to that, he strode out the door. Jalissa closed the door behind him and sat down to think. It was very difficult, given the fact that her mind felt as frozen as her body. He knew. The evidence against her was too overwhelming now. She wondered if she were a prisoner. But if he believed her to be a Witch, he must know that he couldn't hold her captive.

Forcing her thoughts away from Miklos Panera, she began to worry about Kavnor. If he *did* return, the two soldiers would capture him. Disguised as Dradars, they would have only to make their way to the front of the crowd and then use their stunners.

She locked the cabin door, then changed quickly into the clothes she'd worn yesterday, ignoring the torn skirt and ripped sleeve on the jacket. After re-braiding her hair, she composed herself quickly and 'ported to the hillside above the meadow.

The crowd was even larger than yesterday, but there was no sign of Kavnor. She waited, pacing back and forth along the hilltop, staying out of view of the crowd in the meadow as much as possible.

The minutes dragged by as she thought about Miklos coming to check on her and finding the cabin empty. Did it really matter? He knew what she was. Still, it seemed cruel somehow to force him to acknowledge it.

With a strange sort of detachment, she wondered what he would do. Could he be planning even now to have her returned to Federation headquarters to be exposed?

The crystal felt hard and cool against her skin. It wasn't likely that she'd ever use it again. Her career was over. And yet that bothered her less than the certainty that Miklos would betray her. She thought that he would protect her to the extent he could, but his loyalty lay with the Special Agency and the Federation.

She had no idea how much time had passed before she suddenly sensed a presence and spun about to find Kavnor standing just behind her, staring down at the crowd.

"Kavnor! You can't—"

The rest of her words were cut off as he 'ported down to the meadow, where she saw him standing tall on the hillside above the crowd. Even from this distance, she had heard the noise of the crowd, but now all was silent, hushed with expectation. And she knew exactly how the young Warlock must be feeling.

"Kavnor," she said, sending her thoughts to him with as much force as she could muster. "There are soldiers in the crowd, armed with stunners! You must leave before they capture you!"

He had raised his arms high and she could see the faint blue aura. Then he stopped and his head turned in her direction. A second later, he was gone. She waited for him to reappear beside her, then sighed with relief. Apparently he had believed her and had gone away.

Miklos stood at the rail and stared unseeing at the dun-colored sea. Several times, he began to turn to go below, then checked himself.

He'd never thought he could be guilty of that common human failing of self-deception. Both his nature and his training went against it. And yet he'd spent the past hour trying to convince himself that the truth wasn't the truth.

Jalissa Kendor was a Witch. That cold, hard fact stared him in the face, and he shifted his gaze, trying to avoid it. The woman he'd held in his arms, the woman whose body he longed to possess, was not a woman at all.

But for all that fact implied, the only question he could ask himself right now was whether she had used her unnatural powers on *him*. He felt cold and sick and angry just considering that possibility. And yet how else could he account for what he felt toward her? If the most beautiful and brilliant women of his own race had failed to arouse him to such emotions, then he *must* be under the spell of an enchantress.

His eyes felt strange, and he belatedly realized that they were stinging with unshed tears. The feeling was strange to him because Miklos Panera had never cried in his entire life. He blinked them away, then turned abruptly and went below, determined now to confront her.

There was no answer to his knock at her door, so he called her name. When he still received no response, he tried the door and found it locked. She must be there. The cabin doors could be locked only from the inside. Theft was no problem aboard a military vessel, so the inside lock was there only to insure privacy.

Suddenly, cold sweat prickled his skin. Could she have gone—vanished in a puff of smoke like the Warlock they were hunting? He turned away, unable to face that possibility. But she must know that he suspected her.

He went to his own cabin, and his gaze fell on the small kit of specialized tools and weapons he always carried with him. He could ask the crew for a key, but he didn't want anyone else to find out what he feared he was about to discover. A part of him wondered at his fierce need to protect her even as he took out the tool he needed.

Back at her door, he rapped again, but the only

sound he could hear was the rapid thudding of his own heart. He pressed the tool to the lock. There was a faint popping sound, and then the knob turned easily beneath his shaking hand.

The small cabin was empty, though her belongings were still there. The door to the adjacent bath was closed and for one brief moment, he permitted himself the desperate hope that she could be in there. He hesitated, listening for a sound that would prove him wrong, then knocked at the door and finally pushed it open to find that last hope gone.

For all that he knew he should be considering at the moment, Miklos's thoughts centered on one fear: that she had vanished forever. Her pale, shimmering Whisperer's robe hung in the small closet, and his hand reached out of its own volition to touch it as images of her flooded his mind.

Finally, he decided that she had undoubtedly gone into town, to warn the Warlock if he returned. She would be back, and he thought about waiting here for her. But the thought of having her suddenly materialize before his eyes quickly drove him from the cabin. He had faced all sorts of dangers in his life, but he wasn't willing to face the proof of her witchcraft.

Jalissa sank down onto the bed, waiting for the brief spell of dizziness to go away. She supposed that if one 'ported regularly, there would be no reaction, but none of them did that. Since the

Coven had retreated into its isolated world, there'd been no need for such a talent.

Now that she was back aboard the ship, her thoughts turned to Miklos. He knew what she was, but he didn't *want* to know. The fact that he hadn't yet confronted her proved that. But what would he do with this knowledge? Was there any hope at all that she could convince him that they shared a common goal: the preservation of the Federation and the prevention of war? She doubted it, but she knew that she had to try.

Still uncertain as to exactly what she would do or say to him, she got up to go find him. When she pressed the button to unlock the cabin door, it felt strange. Then she realized that it was already unlocked!

He had come in here during her absence! There could be no other explanation. She envisioned him coming here and discovering that she was gone—forced to face what she knew he didn't want to face. Wracked with a terrible sadness, she opened the door—and found him coming toward her down the hallway.

"Get your things and come with me," he said without preamble. "We're leaving right away."

She backed into the cabin and did as told. He followed her in. They both carefully avoided each other's eyes as she asked where they were going.

"We've been looking for his spacecraft, but we didn't find it. He showed up again, then vanished.

I think he's going to leave—and we're going to follow him."

She merely nodded and finished her packing, then followed him up to the deck, where a small hovercraft had landed. Within moments, they were airborne, headed back to the base.

"I'm leaving the U-77 here for the time being," he told her as they disembarked from the hovercraft. "We'll take this."

He indicated what she knew was the smallest spacecraft in the Federation fleet. She'd never been aboard one, since they were used exclusively by the military for short voyages. She'd half-feared that he intended to take her back to headquarters, but clearly she was wrong.

They boarded the tiny craft and strapped themselves into the big, comfortable seats. While he checked the systems, she craned her neck to see the rest of the tiny craft. There was a small galley and a closed door that was probably a bathroom. A third seat was behind the co-pilot's seat that she occupied. Apparently, passengers were supposed to sleep in their seats.

The sleek craft taxiied only a short distance, then swept into the heavens at a steep angle that pressed Jalissa deep into the heavily padded seat. A moment later, the information Miklos had requested came over the comm.

"The scanners showed that a small craft broke through the atmosphere thirty-five minutes ago," reported the disembodied female voice.

Miklos muttered a curse under his breath before acknowledging receipt of the information and hanging up the mike. She noticed that he still didn't look at her as he spoke.

"That's him. Wherever he had it hidden, he got to it quicker than I expected."

"He would have 'ported," she said in a neutral tone.

"How far can . . . they 'port?"

Jalissa heard the slight hesitation and knew that what he'd almost said was "you." She shot him a quick glance, then looked away as he started to turn toward her.

"There's no limit," she replied. "At least as far as I know. It isn't like jumping or running. It doesn't require any physical energy. You just think yourself somewhere else—and you're there."

"What about in space?" he asked, his tone cold and clipped.

"I . . . I don't know," she replied. It was true. She'd never thought about it. As far as she knew, her people had never tried it.

Then she glanced at him, belatedly realizing that he probably wasn't asking because of Kavnor. He was wondering if *she* would be able to do that.

"Hasn't anyone ever tried it?" he asked, still avoiding her eyes.

"Not that I know of. The Coven never traveled

much, and when they did, they traveled mostly on Tevingian craft."

"Then it must be dangerous."

"Perhaps."

A heavy silence fell between them. She wondered if he was waiting for her to promise that she wouldn't suddenly 'port herself out of the craft. She opened her mouth to promise him that she wouldn't, then closed it again, unable to take that final step.

He busied himself with the various controls and screens, then made a sound of satisfaction. "I think I've got him!"

After watching the one screen for a moment, he turned very briefly to her, his gaze meeting hers for one brief, electrifying moment before sliding away again.

"This craft has a very sophisticated tracking device, but even so, I wasn't certain that we could follow him. It's still experimental, and hasn't always been effective with the smallest craft. But I think it's locked onto him."

"Will he know that?" she asked.

"No. With the crude system on his craft, he wouldn't know if he was being followed by a T-101." The T-101 was a giant cargo freighter, the largest of the space-going craft. A civilian version was used for the most popular inter-planetary passenger routes.

"What are you planning to do?"

"For now, I'm just going to follow him. Then,

when I'm sure where he's headed, I'll contact the base there and have them waiting for him. There are only two possible destinations: Gavon or Ker."

"Ker?" She echoed. Ker was the crystal world. She recalled the conversation with Danto about the possibility of the Warlock's going there. "Surely he wouldn't go there? Doesn't it have the largest Federation base in the Outer Ring?"

"Yes, but of all the worlds of the Outer Ring, it's the one he must want most. I ran a check earlier on the civilian and military populations there. The civilians are almost all from Outer Ring worlds, and most of the military are from worlds that are sympathetic to the Coven. At least a third of them are Tevingian."

So Danto had been right, she thought. The most important world in the Outer Ring could easily be taken over by the Coven, who would then be able to hold its precious resource hostage. She fingered her crystal nervously. He apparently saw the movement, even though he wasn't looking her way.

"There's only one way he could know how important Ker is," Miklos said in that cool, formal tone. "He's had some assistance from Tevingi— probably from Danto Kendor."

She noticed that he didn't say "from your uncle," and wondered if it was deliberate. The air in the confined space seemed to be draining away, drawing them into a dark vacuum.

"He's the one most likely to have kept in contact with the Coven, wherever they are," Miklos went on. "We know that he makes occasional trips in a craft similar to this one—one he's had specially adapted for longer voyages. We haven't followed him, because we're sure he also has the new tracking system and would be able to spot us.

"After I talked to him, I ordered the base to keep an eye on him and follow him if he left again. But he hasn't. I suppose that he's able to contact the Coven through . . . other means."

She said nothing. Her heart seemed to have leapt into her throat, and she was certain that she wouldn't be able to speak even if she could find the words.

"Now I want the truth, Jalissa."

Chapter Nine

Two powerful emotions tugged at Jalissa simultaneously: relief and fear. A part of her was relieved that the deception would be over. But an equally strong part felt a paralyzing fear. Her feelings, she knew, came from the two parts of *her*. The Witch wanted to tell him proudly of her heritage, while the Whisperer wanted desperately to deny it and continue to conceal it.

The question, of course, was what he would do with the knowledge. Would he immediately regard her as the enemy, or would he understand that she too wanted to save the Federation?

The difference between them was that in order to save the Federation, he would be willing to destroy the Coven, while she still sought a way to save them regardless of their foolishness.

There are very few times in an individual's life when a step taken instantly becomes irrevocable—but Jalissa knew that this was one of those moments. She was convinced that he didn't want to believe she was a Witch, and therefore she could probably convince him that she wasn't, despite the evidence.

Even her disappearance from the cabin could probably be explained somehow. She could tell him that she swam to shore and went into town, and if he found the cabin door locked from the inside, then it must be because the lock was defective. He might even believe that, given his desire to do so.

And she could admit to being a Tevingian sympathizer who'd known all along about the existence of the Coven. He'd believe that too, since he already knew about her uncle's activities.

Jalissa weighed all this in her mind in the tense seconds following his demand for the truth, and thought as well about his statement that trust might never be possible between them. And finally, she knew that she wanted to prove him wrong.

"You already know the truth, Miklos, although I think you would prefer that I deny it."

They were seated side by side in the cramped confines of the craft, both of them staring straight ahead into the blackness of space: ancient enemies from different worlds. He existed solely in the Vantran world of science and reason, while she teetered precariously between that world and another darker, magical world he could neither understand nor accept.

"You're a Witch," he said, his voice so devoid of emotion that she knew it concealed something.

"Yes."

He was silent for a long time, and she risked a quick sidelong glance at him. His profile revealed nothing.

"I think I knew that on a subconscious level when I first saw you on Temok. Something happened that day. I . . . felt *something*."

Her mind went back to that time. "It's possible that you felt something because I was just about to 'port myself out of there when you used the stunner on me. In the old days, Tevingians and others often said that they could 'feel' our magic.

"You see, I very nearly forgot that I could take myself away from the danger. I left the Coven when I was twelve, and from that time on, I never used my powers except to communicate with my people."

"Why did you leave?" he asked, still not looking at her even though she had now turned to face him.

"I didn't have a choice. The priests had determined that I had an affinity for the crystals, so they decided that I should become a Whisperer."

"But surely your parents must have protested.

Are the priests that powerful?"

"My parents *didn't* protest," she replied, finding it hard to keep the bitterness from her voice. "Children are raised communally in the Coven. They don't live with their parents, who often don't live with each other either. I never knew it could be any other way until I went to Tevingi. But later, when I thought about it, I realized that it must be because they wanted us to see the whole Coven as being our family, not just our parents and siblings.

"It wasn't as bad as it sounds," she said hurriedly when he turned to her and she saw the look on his face. "We were treated well, even though we weren't indulged the way Vantrans and others indulge their children."

And now *she* was the one who refused to meet *his* gaze. He couldn't understand, and hearing this must only add to his disgust with the Coven—and with her.

"Were you the only one who was sent away?" he asked after a brief silence.

She shook her head, growing sick at the thought of giving him information that could destroy so many lives. She shouldn't have told him the truth. She'd been selfish—and foolish as well. She'd wanted him to understand her and accept her, but he wouldn't—and now others would suffer as well.

"But the others aren't Whisperers, are they?" he asked.

She was surprised that he would know that, and turned to face him again. Still, she saw no hint of his feelings—not even in those green eyes that were fixed so steadily upon her.

"I think that's why you're so much better than the others at your profession," he went on. "I've seen other Whisperers working, and there's a definite difference with you. You're using your . . . talents."

She winced at his hesitation, but nodded. "You're probably right. I don't consciously use my talents, but I could be using them subconsciously."

"So the others are in administrative positions in Trans/Med and other agencies?"

"Yes, but please don't ask me to name them. And don't think that every Tevingian in Federation Service is a Witch or Warlock. There aren't many of us—and I don't even know who they are. Until recently, I thought I was the only one."

She took a deep breath, then went on. "Miklos, you must trust me and believe that I don't want war between the Coven and the Federation. I know I could have convinced you that I'm not a Witch because you didn't want to believe it anyway. But I told you the truth."

He merely nodded, and his gaze strayed to the small screens before him. After watching one of them for a few seconds and then keying up a display, he told her that it looked as though the Warlock must be headed for Gavon.

She breathed a sigh of relief that Kavnor wasn't going to Ker. Perhaps he hadn't yet realized the significance of Ker to his plans, or maybe he didn't know that the population there would be sympathetic.

Miklos picked up the mike and contacted the base on Gavon. She listened as he ordered them to capture the Warlock and warned them that he wasn't to be harmed.

"If you can't capture him unharmed, then let him go and just keep an eye on him until we get there."

Jalissa was relieved to hear his instructions about not harming Kavnor, but as soon as he finished his conversation with the base, she asked him what he intended to do.

"I don't know yet. I'm hoping that we can capture him and keep him drugged so he can't escape while I have a talk with your priests."

"You won't be able to do that if he's drugged," she pointed out.

He turned a stern expression toward her. "You're going to take me to the Coven."

"I can't, Miklos. I don't know where they are." And then, when he gave her an incredulous look, she explained.

"How long did it take you to reach Tevingi?" he asked.

"I don't remember. It seemed to take a long time, but I was so unhappy and scared. I was only twelve."

"Think, Jalissa! Twelve isn't so young that you wouldn't have had a good concept of time."

She disliked his peremptory tone of voice, and wanted to tell him that. Instead, she focused on his intention to go to the Coven.

"They could kill you, Miklos. If the priests believe that the gods have ordered your death, they *will* kill you."

"You can contact them and tell them that I come in peace."

"I'm not sure that would make any difference, because I don't think they really trust me."

He stared at her in silence, and for the first time during this conversation, she thought she detected a softening of his attitude. Was it possible that he could understand the position she was in—caught between two worlds and trusted by neither one?

"Try to remember that journey to Tevingi," he said in a much gentler tone. "It could help us find them—and we *have* to find them."

She nodded and turned away from him, then adjusted her seat into a near-reclining position. How she wanted him to trust her. Never before in her life had Jalissa wanted to cling to someone—but she wanted that now. She'd hoped Miklos could be the one sure thing in her increasingly uncertain world—and yet, by telling him the truth about herself, she'd destroyed that hope.

* * *

Miklos glanced at her as she reclined in the seat, her eyes closed. Then, fearing that she would feel his gaze on her, he turned away again. He wanted desperately to know if she'd cast some sort of spell on him, but he couldn't bring himself to ask—and in any event, if she had, she wasn't likely to admit to it.

His thoughts churned sluggishly and he seemed unable to focus them. Through his brain whispered every dark story he'd ever heard about the Coven. He stole another quick look at her, and saw in the very desirable body of Jalissa Kendor a weapon of unbelievable power—a power that terrified him because he couldn't understand it.

A long time ago, Miklos had seen the weapon that had been used to destroy the Coven's old home. It was hidden away at the most secure and secret base on Vantra, in a compound where the security was the strictest his people had ever devised. He could still recall the thrill he'd felt at seeing the most awesome creation of Vantran science, even though he deplored the purpose for which it had been invented.

But he had understood it. He was conversant with the science that had allowed it to come into existence. He knew how it worked and why, and his awe had been tempered by that knowledge.

Jalissa Kendor was altogether another matter. He had no understanding at all of the magic weapons she possessed because they had nothing at all to do with science.

And yet he wanted her still. Surely that meant that she had cast a spell on him. How else could he account for the fact that even though he now knew what she was, his hunger for her hadn't lessened?

He tried to force himself to consider what he must do, but found that he could not get beyond the moment. He knew that he should contact his superiors at the Agency at the first opportunity and tell them about Jalissa and the others who'd infiltrated the Federation. He knew it and yet he also knew that he wouldn't do it—at least not yet.

He felt an overwhelming need to protect her— a ridiculous urge, given the fact that she was quite capable of protecting herself. And yet, as he glanced at her again, all he could see was a small, beautiful and vulnerable woman who was walking a dangerously fine line between two worlds.

He was still staring at her when her eyelids fluttered open. For a long moment, they simply stared at each other, and then he looked away, fearing that she would see his confusion.

"I think it was four days—maybe five," she said into the charged silence.

His gaze swung back to her. It took him a moment to recall the question he'd asked her, and she apparently saw his confusion.

"You asked me how long it took to reach Tevingi," she prompted.

"Do you remember anything about the type of craft?" he asked, relieved to be back on firm ground again, back to something he could understand.

She nodded. "It was the same type that Danto still uses to travel there—perhaps an older model."

Miklos nodded and keyed up the computer, typing in the data as she raised her seat up again and watched. "That narrows it down," he said with satisfaction. "But it could still be any one of four worlds. What do you remember about the place itself?"

"We lived underground," she said, her voice muted as though her thoughts were far away. "It's not a large world, and its surface is totally barren and mostly flat."

He asked more questions: about gravity, about moons, about the temperature on the surface. She answered them all, but he found her responses perplexing. The computer showed no match with any of the uninhabited worlds.

"I don't understand," she said, leaning close to him to stare at the screen herself. "Maybe your information is inaccurate."

He shook his head. "None of those worlds has been fully explored, but we know the basic information about them. Could you be wrong about the length of the journey?"

"I don't think so, but I suppose I could be."

Miklos continued to study the data, frowning.

None of the worlds in that region seemed a likely home for the Coven. In fact, not one uninhabited world within a two-week range of Tevingi fit the description she'd given him.

"I'm telling you the truth, Miklos," she said quietly.

He turned to her in surprise. "I believe you."

She gave him a tentative smile, then lapsed into silence again. After a while, she said, "I wonder if . . ." Her voice trailed off uncertainly and he could see unshed tears glittering in her eyes.

"What is it, Jalissa?" he asked gently, barely able to resist taking her into his arms.

"I wonder if they stole my memories—and replaced them with false ones."

"Could they do that?" he asked, not even trying to hide his horror at such a possibility.

"Maybe. I don't know. There . . . there are secrets known only to the Priests."

Miklos could actually feel the struggle going on within her, the battle between her birthright and the world into which she had been thrust at an early age. The urge to take her into his arms now overwhelmed him, and he reached out to her.

She made no move to resist him, but her rigidity was itself a form of resistance. He held her for only a moment, then let her go. At first, it seemed that she would move back into his arms, but then she moved away instead and turned her face to the viewscreen.

"They could have done that," she said in a slow,

careful voice, as though denying it even as she spoke. "*All* my memories could be false."

"But not your recollection of the time it took to reach Tevingi," he pointed out. "You were beyond their influence then."

When she said nothing, he went on. "If we're unable to capture this Warlock and discover the Coven's whereabouts from him, we'll search the planets within a five-day journey from Tevingi."

She merely nodded, and Miklos finally turned his attention back to the screen. Their quarry would reach Gavon within hours, and they themselves wouldn't be far behind if he pushed their craft to its limits.

"He landed here, on a plain," the base commander said, indicating a spot on the huge planetary map in his office. "But by the time we got there, he was gone. We were there within minutes, but there was no sign of him."

"He 'ported himself out of the area," Miklos said.

The look on the face of the Vantran commander pained Jalissa. His horror and disgust were plainly evident.

"It's true then, that he's a Warlock," the man said, clearly hoping that Miklos would deny it.

"Yes. Specialist Kendor and I will take over from here. All that we require is a fast hovercraft."

The commander shot a look at Jalissa. "Don't

269

you want some troops? I can give you a squad of my best men."

Miklos shook his head. "It's better if we go alone. I know Gavon fairly well."

The commander nodded. "That's right. You were here during the last uprising."

Jalissa frowned, but said nothing. She'd never heard of an uprising on Gavon. It was a small world, notable mostly for its mines, which produced several valuable ores. As soon as they were airborne, she asked Miklos about the uprising.

"It resulted from a foolish mistake on the part of the mining company. The Vantran who was in charge was overly eager to please his superiors back home and refused to give the Gavonese miners time off for a festival. They celebrate the old Coven festivals. This one was the Festival of the Sun—a strange name for a festival held at that time of year."

Jalissa smiled. "Perhaps the title loses something in translation. It's a festival celebrated to persuade the sun to return, and is held when the sun is at its nadir."

"I see. In any event, we discovered that the supervisor had been working them far more hours than is permitted under galaxy law. By the time I arrived, troops had put down the rebellion, but there was a heavy loss of life. I was here for nearly three months, trying to stablize the situation."

"What do you mean by 'stabilize'?" she asked suspiciously.

"Not what you're apparently thinking," he replied. "I saw to it that the supervisor and his henchmen were removed and that the families of those who'd lost their lives were reimbursed. The Gavonese are probably the least primitive people in the Outer Ring, and some of them had been educated on Tevingi, so I had little difficulty in communicating with them.

"We set up a system to permit them to bring their grievances to the base commander, and promoted some of them into new positions of responsibility within the mining company, which happens to be owned in part by my family."

He must have seen her skeptical expression because he smiled at her. "I know you think that Special Agents do nothing but stir up trouble, but that's not true. Our mission is to maintain stability."

"Even when that means stifling democracy," she finished for him disgustedly.

"Sometimes," he admitted. "Democracy is always our goal, but the path to it isn't always as clear as you might think. In the case of Gavon, however, there is a long tradition of tribal democracy. Unfortunately, there's an equally long tradition of tribal warfare. But things have been quiet since then."

A short time later, they landed beside an ancient hovercraft that was surrounded by Federation troops. Miklos got out of their own craft and went over to examine it, then turned to the woman in charge of the troops.

"Destroy this so he can't use it to get away. He could 'port back here and be gone before you captured him."

The young officer wore the same expression Jalissa had seen on the commander's face earlier. "Are you saying that he *is* a Warlock, sir?"

"Yes. And remember that you are *not* to kill him. If you can use the stunners, do so. If not, then let him go. At least he won't be able to leave Gavon."

Jalissa said nothing, but she felt a quiver of sympathy for Kavnor. He was trapped now—and so was she. She had no choice but to work with Miklos and trust that he wouldn't harm Kavnor himself.

"We'll start with the closest towns," Miklos told her when they'd returned to their hovercraft. "Can you reach him?"

"Telepathically, you mean?" she asked, then went on after he nodded. "I'm not sure. Since he knows I'm looking for him, he could be shielding himself from me."

"Then he doesn't trust you?"

"No, I don't think he does—and he certainly won't if he sees me with *you*."

"I refuse to allow you to hunt him on your own, Jalissa."

"Because you don't trust me," she said angrily.

"Because he might try to harm you."

"He wouldn't do that," she protested.

"How can you be so sure? You said yourself that he doesn't trust you."

"The Coven abhors violence," she stated firmly.

"The Coven also does what their gods tell them to do, and if you were to get in the way of his carrying out what he believes to be orders from the gods, he wouldn't hesitate to kill you."

Jalissa turned away. She felt sick. There just could be some truth in what he said. She was about to tell him that even if he tried, Kavnor couldn't kill her, but then she checked herself. She couldn't be certain about that because as far as she knew, no Witch or Warlock had ever turned magic against one of their own.

"Try to reach him," Miklos ordered. "Explain that we simply want to talk to him."

She did as told, closing her eyes and willing herself into a semi-trance, then sending her thoughts out in a wide circle. For one brief moment, she thought that she'd touched something, but the feeling was vague and she couldn't pinpoint the direction. If it was Kavnor, he'd quickly reinforced his shields—but now he knew she was here. She explained all this to Miklos a few minutes later.

"It doesn't matter if he knows we're here. He would have guessed that in any event. What I need to know is just what he's capable of."

Jalissa stared at him, shocked not at his question but at her failure to consider it herself. "I'm not really sure," she said after a minute.

"We all have certain basic skills: using the fire, 'porting, casting some spells."

"What sort of spells?" he asked in a taut voice.

"I don't really know." She wondered why he seemed so uncomfortable. Until now, it had begun to seem to her that he might be accepting her. *A foolish hope,* she thought. *I'm just deceiving myself.*

"We never use spells," she went on. "Or at least not on each other." She did, of course, use them on herself, to bring about the trance that allowed her to communicate with the Coven.

"I know that spells have been used on our enemies. That's in our histories. Kavnor, the Warlock, could be using them to reinforce the feelings of his audience, for example."

"And you use them in your work," he said.

"Not deliberately. I already told you that. It's a fine line, Miklos, and not so easily discernible. We're both trained to use certain powers of persuasion."

"Then you could be casting a spell and not even be aware of it?" he asked.

She thought it was a strange question, but she shrugged. "That's possible—even likely where my work is concerned."

"And other times as well?"

She frowned. "I don't understand." But then

suddenly she *did* understand. "You think I've cast a spell on *you*."

His silence and his failure to look at her provided an eloquent answer. Jalissa felt a chill that penetrated to her very bones. How could she convince him when he'd expect her to lie about it?

"I haven't cast any spell on you, Miklos—either intentionally or unintentionally." But her words were spoken with far more conviction than she felt. How could she be sure? She'd been attracted to him from the beginning. What if she'd subconsciously cast a spell on him?

He said nothing, and she retreated into her thoughts. She'd left the Coven at such an early age—too young to fully understand the subtleties of her powers. Besides, until she left the sheltered world of the Coven, she'd had no need to understand certain things. In that world, there'd been no need to question whether or not one was using one's magic.

Jalissa thought now about the few times when she'd been attracted to men and how they'd invariably returned those feelings. She knew she was considered to be beautiful by most men, and knew too that her position as a Whisperer gave her a certain allure. But what if their attraction to her hadn't been a result of that? Maybe she *had* subconsciously cast a spell.

Perhaps he is right to be concerned, she thought with a shudder. *Maybe I have cast a spell on him.* Certainly, she'd never felt toward any other man what she felt for Miklos Panera.

"If I *have* cast a spell on you, it wasn't my intention," she said, surprising herself. Her outburst took the unmistakable form of a plea for understanding.

He turned to her, and his green eyes seemed to be seeking something, but whether or not he found it, she couldn't say, because he abruptly turned away and announced that a town lay just ahead.

The difference between the Gavonese and the inhabitants of the other worlds they'd visited became apparent the moment they entered the town. People stared unabashedly at them, but nowhere did Jalissa see the hostility they'd encountered on other worlds.

Very quickly, she realized that it was *she* who was attracting the greater attention. She was clad once more in her Whisperer's robe, with the crystal prominently displayed. No Whisperer had ever visited Gavon before, but from the comments translated through the crystal, she knew that they understood what she was.

Miklos had landed the hovercraft in a field adjacent to the graceful town square, and they walked across it toward a rather large building that she assumed must be the seat of local government. But before they could reach it, two men came out and started toward them, their expressions welcoming.

"Agent Panera," the older of the two men exclaimed, putting out a hand to Miklos. "It's a pleasure to see you again, but I hope that your appearance does not signal trouble."

As he spoke, his eyes moved to Jalissa. "And you have brought a Whisperer as well."

Miklos made the introductions. The older man was the town's tribal chieftain, and the other man was in charge of security. It was obvious that they both knew and liked Miklos.

Since they were all conversing in the Tevingian tongue, Jalissa had no need to use her crystal. Both men, as it turned out, had been educated on Tevingi. Jalissa knew that many Gavonese came to Tevingi regularly, and she had met some of them. It amused her to think that on Tevingi, the Gavonese were considered to be a backward people, but after what she'd seen here in the Outer Ring, they now seemed very civilized indeed.

They were ushered into the tribal council building, where they were quickly surrounded by what Jalissa assumed were the tribal elders. There were no women among them, but Jalissa was treated well and her presence wasn't questioned. In fact, they treated her with that excessive gallantry that she'd encountered in other worlds that were in transition from primitive, male-dominated societies to a more egalitarian way of life.

When Miklos explained why they had come to

277

Gavon, there were gasps and looks of utter astonishment.

"The Coven still exists?" the tribal leader asked, clearly as astounded as the others.

"Yes. There is no doubt that this man is a Warlock. We need to find him, so that he can lead us to the Coven."

"For what purpose, Agent Panera?" the leader asked, his voice now sharper than before.

"So that we can try to reason with them. We don't yet know if this Warlock is acting on their authority or on his own."

"He *must* be acting on the authority of the priests," the leader stated. "This is a very grave matter. My people revere the Coven. In fact, none of us would be here now if it weren't for them."

When he saw the puzzled looks on the faces of both his visitors, he went on. "More than a century ago, a terrible sickness swept our world. People were dying in the streets. Word reached the Coven and they came—dozens of them. They couldn't save everyone, but they did their best, working day and night until their hands screamed in pain from their healing efforts.

"We owe the Coven our lives—and we would do nothing to betray them," he stated firmly, to nods all around. "We are also grateful to you, Agent Panera, and to your family's intervention that saved lives during the unfortunate incident with the mines—but our first loyalty is to the Coven."

"I understand your position, Chief Tabbos, but I give you my word that we mean no harm to this Warlock. We merely wish to speak to him."

Miklos glanced her way as he spoke, and she froze, wondering if he intended to tell them who she was. It might have bolstered his case, but he didn't do it.

"Chief Tabbos," she said, "You must know that Whisperers and Special Agents are generally at odds with each other." She paused and received a nod, then went on.

"But in this case, we are working together. I too wish to speak with this Warlock, and because I am Tevingian, I think he might be willing to talk to me."

"That is true," the chief agreed. "Tevingians were always the strongest ally of the Coven. But how is it that they have continued to exist and yet no one knew it?"

"Some of us on Tevingi have always known," Jalissa said. "But the Coven preferred to keep it secret."

The chief eyed her thoughtfully. "Your family name is Kendor, a name I recognize."

Jalissa nodded. "Danto Kendor, of whom you may have heard, is my uncle."

He nodded. "Yes, I know the name, although we do not trade directly with him. He has an agent in Da-Hiran, a man named Shem Lattos."

Jalissa recognized the name as being one that

Danto had given her. "How far away is that?" she inquired.

"Several hours by hovercraft," the chief replied. "The chief there is an ally of mine."

He turned back to Miklos. "The Warlock you seek is not here, but even if he were, we could not help you, Agent Panera—unless he wished to speak with you himself. No one in this world would give up a Warlock to a Vantran—not even to one who has helped us in the past."

Then, obviously in order to soften his rejection, the chief invited them to stay for a meal. Jalissa thought that Miklos would refuse, but he accepted. The chief led them to his home nearby, where they were joined by his wife and a teenaged daughter whose soft brown eyes kept straying to Miklos even as she attempted to make polite conversation with Jalissa.

Both women spoke Tevingian, but without the fluency of the chief. They had been taught, the older woman explained, by Gavonese teachers who'd learned it on Tevingi. The pleasure they took in showing off that fact to her told Jalissa that speaking Tevingian was obviously a mark of great distinction on this world. Accustomed as she was to seeing Tevingians being regarded as inferior to Vantrans, Jalissa was amused at their elevation to such high status here.

Through careful and discreet questioning of the women as the men discussed mining and other matters, Jalissa decided that to the Gavonese, Vantrans were regarded with considerable respect and awe, but perhaps with an undercurrent of resentment as well.

The Gavonese had good reason to resent the Vantrans: *two* reasons, in fact. The Vantrans had destroyed—or tried to destroy—their saviors, the Coven, and the Vantrans controlled the mines that formed the bulk of wealth on this world.

The two women were as shocked as the men had been at the news that the Coven had survived. The mother made the sign of the Coven as she beamed.

"The gods saved them after all," the woman breathed happily.

The gods and the Tevingians, Jalissa thought, but didn't say. For all their powers, the Coven could not have saved themselves from the Vantrans' weapons. It was the Tevingians who had removed them from their doomed world, after receiving the information that the Vantrans intended to explode their world.

"What do we do now?" she asked Miklos as soon as they were back in the hovercraft. "Going to the other towns will do no good, Miklos. They will protect him."

She paused for a moment, then forged on, hoping he would agree to her plan. "If I go alone to seek him and show the Gavonese my true identity, they would bring me to him."

"No," he said the moment the words were out

of her mouth. "You cannot take that risk, Jalissa."

"What risk is there? The Gavonese would never harm a Witch."

"That isn't the risk I'm thinking of," he said, circling low over a meadow and then, to her surprise, setting the craft down in the midst of a field of brilliant purple flowers, interspersed with tall, lacy ferns.

"Why are we landing here?" she asked.

"So we can talk," he said over his shoulder as he got out of the craft.

She got out too, and stood there for a moment, enjoying the beauty of the spot. It was a far cry from the ugliness she'd seen too much of recently. Miklos too was silent as he stared out at the scene. Then he turned to her.

"I am the only one who knows your true identity—and it should remain that way. That is, unless you want to return to the Coven."

She stared at him. "You mean that you won't tell your superiors?"

"Not unless it becomes absolutely necessary."

"Why, Miklos?"

He glanced briefly at her, then turned away again. "Tell me, could you cast a spell to make me forget who you are?"

"I . . . I don't know."

"If the priests could take away your memories, then it must be possible," he persisted.

"Perhaps, but I don't know how to do it. And

why would I want to do it in any event, since you've promised to keep it a secret?"

"Then you trust me to do that?"

"Yes," she said as he turned back to her. "I *do* trust you. But I still don't understand *why* you would risk your career by lying to your superiors."

He shrugged. "I'm not really risking my career. As long as we're both careful, there's no way they'll find out. Did you, uh, use your powers on those Daks who were shooting at us after our accident?"

"Yes. I was afraid that they would kill you as soon as you came out of the woods."

"So you 'ported up there and used the blue fire on them?"

She nodded, not really wanting to talk about it but knowing that, for some reason, he did. "I was afraid that I might have killed them," she said. "It takes practice to wield the fire carefully."

He said nothing, and began to walk through the field, parting the waves of purple and pale green. She started to follow him, then stopped, knowing instinctively that he wanted to be alone. Instead, she climbed onto the hood of the hovercraft and watched him in his dark blue uniform. The sun reflected off the heavy gold braid.

What is love? The question formed in her mind, catching her by surprise and sending a frisson through her body that left in its wake a strange, melting warmth.

Love is trust, she thought, *and I trust him*. How she'd gotten to this point, she didn't know. He was a Vantran and a Special Agent and it shouldn't have happened. Perhaps she'd been so busy denying that she could ever trust him that she simply hadn't noticed that she *did*.

And love is taking risks. The sort of risk he was taking now, by not informing his superiors of her true identity. Despite what he'd said, she knew that his career did indeed hang in the balance. Because he was a Panera, he would probably be permitted to resign, rather than be discharged. Or perhaps he would be shunted off to some specially created but essentially meaningless position. But he would never be allowed to continue his present work if his dishonesty became known.

And yet, he was willing to risk that to protect her, a Witch.

Tears stung her eyes as she watched him stop in the field, stand there for a moment with his back to her and then turn around and make his way back.

We love each other, she thought incredulously, wondering how such a thing could have happened. Had she failed to recognize it because she'd never felt it before—and had never expected to find it? Was it the same for him?

"You asked before why I'm doing this," he said, stopping about ten feet from her. "I'm doing it because I love you, Jalissa. I don't know if it's because you've cast a spell on me, but I know that if you did, it wasn't intentional."

He paused, and his gaze drifted away from her. "There was a time long ago—thousands of years ago. . . ." His voice too drifted off into silence. Then abruptly, he focused his gaze on her again.

"I studied the classics as a child. They were filled with the ancient glories of war, which of course appealed to me since I didn't have enough sense to know what war truly meant. But they were also filled with poetry and songs written by men about women they loved but could never have. I ignored them because they seemed so far removed from the world I lived in. I was wrong."

His final words hung there in the air between them, and Jalissa found herself nodding. "I love you too, Miklos. And I understand."

He took a few steps toward her. Her heart thudded wildly and she stopped breathing. But then he stopped, and for a long time, they stared at each other across a small space that had been transformed into a yawning abyss. In their silence, they both acknowledged that it could go no further.

He was Vantran and a Special Agent. He could not marry an off-worlder, and certainly not a Whisperer. She was both a Whisperer and a Witch, balanced precariously between two worlds, never to be entirely free of either of them. Love would destroy both their careers, and if their present mission were to reveal her true identity, she would have no choice but to return to the Coven.

Together, they might save the Federation and the Coven—but at a terrible cost.

Chapter Ten

"What will we do now?" she asked as they climbed back into the hovercraft.

He turned to her with a smile that acknowledged the double meaning behind her words. But he chose to focus on their mission.

"You're right about the Gavonese hiding him, so there's no point to our staying here. Instead, we'll try to find the Coven. Can you . . . contact them?"

"Yes—or at least I think so," she replied, hiding the pain she felt when she heard that small hesitation in his voice. Even if they had no other problems, he would never be able to accept what she was.

"They could choose to ignore me, but I'll try."

As he took off, she settled back in her seat and tried to send herself into the necessary trance. But his presence was too disturbing and his declaration of love echoed through her mind. When she knew that she wouldn't succeed, she told him that she would try when they returned to the base.

"Why can't you contact them now?" he asked with a mixture of curiosity and impatience.

"Because you're here," she replied simply. "You . . . interfere."

He smiled an apology, but said nothing, and they returned to the base in a silence that was oddly comforting. Jalissa had thought that their mutual declaration of love would make it impossible for them to enjoy each other's company, but that seemed not to be true. Instead, she basked in the warmth of that love, knowing it to be impossible, but cherishing it just the same. And when their eyes met, she saw that it was the same for him.

Back at the base, he told the commander that she required a room in which to rest for a time, and she was shown to a comfortable guest room. Still, it took her some time to set Miklos from her mind.

Her senses were over-filled with him. All that she'd felt and tried to ignore now poured forth, inundating her as she sank down onto the bed. The things she'd once disliked about him had been miraculously transformed into reasons to love him: his Vantran pride, which no longer seemed arrogant, but which had instead become a deep, powerful sense of integrity; and his careful check on his emotions, which now made even more precious those rare times when he let down his guard.

Thinking about this, Jalissa laughed aloud. She'd harbored a deep resentment of Vantrans from the moment of her first encounter with them, and she'd regarded Special Agents as the worst of the lot—sly, cruel enemies of Trans/Med and therefore her enemies as well.

And now, incredibly, she'd fallen in love with one of them. And not just *any* one of them, but a member of the most powerful family on Vantra and the most feared of all Special Agents. If she'd unwittingly cast a spell on Miklos Panera, perhaps he had cast a spell of his own.

She settled down and gradually drew into herself, shutting out everything else. And then she cast her mind free, sending it out across space to a place she didn't know but could somehow reach.

She waited, patiently at first and then with a mounting impatience that threatened the mind-focus. Nothing happened. There was no soft brushing of her mind against another.

She came out of her trance into an icy chill. The Coven had closed itself off from her. She fought the panic that welled up in her as she felt herself now cast adrift from that world.

What would happen now if she and Miklos found the world of the Coven? Depite the priesthood's often austere manner, Jalissa had always regarded the Coven's leadership as being essentially benevolent. But now, for the first time, she saw the dark side of a race that lived in isolation and listened to no one but the voices of the old gods—voices that, unlike the others, she herself had never heard.

She saw now that something in her had always resisted direct communication. She heard herself as a child, incessantly questioning how they could be sure that the gods were always right. She felt again the annoyance of the elders when she dared to voice those questions.

I have never really believed in them, she thought. *If I had, I would never have questioned. Something was wrong with me from the very beginning. Perhaps that's why my parents paid so little attention to me.*

And she began to wonder if somehow the priests had conspired to give her the talent to work with the crystals—as a way of getting rid of her.

Scenes from her childhood, long forgotten until now, tumbled through her mind. The one thing the memories all had in common—which she hadn't seen until now—was her isolation, the distance she kept from the other children. Even when she had joined in their games, she hadn't been part of them.

A deep coldness settled into her, chilling her to her very bones. She was a Witch. She possessed all the unnatural talents of her kind. But what did it say about her that she herself considered them to be unnatural?

She got up and fled from the room, seeking Miklos, needing the warmth of his presence. Running headlong from her fears, she very nearly collided with him when she reached an intersecting hallway.

He reached out to her, then let his arms fall back to his sides. She stumbled to a halt, raising her own hand to him, and then instead using it to brace herself against the wall. Anyone seeing them would have thought that they risked death if they had touched each other—and wouldn't have been far from the truth.

"What's wrong?" he asked. "What did they say?"

"Nothing. I couldn't contact them."

"Has that happened before?"

She shook her head, still fighting tears. "They're angry with me, Miklos. They told me to stay out of this and I ignored them. Now they've turned their backs on me."

"Why did you ignore them?"

"Because I don't want to see the Federation destroyed, and I don't want war." She paused, choking back a sob. "And I don't want the Coven to be destroyed either."

He raised his arm again, and this time, his

thumb glided softly over her cheeks, brushing away the tears that had spilled over. A kiss could not have had a more powerful effect upon her as her mind carried them both far beyond that small gesture.

"We want the same things," he said in a low, husky voice. "I too don't want war—or the destruction of the Coven. But above all else, I want the Federation to be preserved."

She nodded, knowing what he meant. If it came to a choice between the destruction of the Coven and the preservation of the Federation, he would sacrifice the Coven. It was clear to him—but far less clear to her.

"Will they attack us if we find them?" he asked.

"I don't know. They might. If the gods tell them to kill us, they will."

"But what about *you*? What if the gods order *you* to kill?"

She knew what he was really asking. What if the gods ordered her to kill *him*?

"I would never attempt to harm you, Miklos, regardless of what the gods said." Then, in a desperate attempt to lighten the moment, she laughed. "The gods have never spoken to me, in any event—probably because I've doubted their existence. Even as a child, I doubted the existence of beings who refused to show themselves to me."

He too smiled. "You were a renegade."

"Yes. I didn't see that before, but now I think

maybe the priests gave me the talent to work with the crystals as a way of getting rid of me."

"You don't believe in the gods, but you do believe in your powers," he said musingly.

"Of course. I can see them—and feel them."

"But how did you acquire them, Jalissa—if not from the gods?"

She stared at him in astonishment. "How could you—of all people—be saying that the gods exist?"

He looked decidedly uncomfortable, but affected a casual shrug. "Perhaps I too was a renegade. My people have never believed in anything beyond the science we created ourselves, but there have been times when I've wondered." He stopped, shrugging again. "How else can one explain the powers the Coven has—that you have? If they're not gifts from the gods, then what are they?"

She had no answer to that, so she turned instead to more practical matters and asked what he intended to do now. The thought that he might actually believe in the gods was too unsettling to contemplate.

"The Warlock returned to his hovercraft, but he vanished again before they could even get out their stunners. By now, he's probably stolen another craft and is long gone. I've sent orders to all bases that if he's spotted he's not to be killed. If they can capture him using stunners, they will; otherwise, they'll let him go.

"It would be a waste of our time to try to catch him, so we'll go on with the plan to search for the Coven itself. There are two uninhabited worlds about the right distance from Tevingi. They don't fit your description, but we'll go there first."

And I will find out if the Coven stole my memories, she thought grimly.

Jalissa was falling, floating down through a darkness, her body buffeted by silent winds. She could hear faint sounds: the chanting of the priests far off in the distance. The voices were indistinct, but she recognized the chant. It was the ritual chant with which they had always greeted the oncoming night, even in the depths of their underground city where night was distinguishable from day only because the lights were dimmed.

Every child of the Coven learned this chant first: a call to the gods to ward off the demons of night. Jalissa had learned it and spoken it since she had first learned to talk. But she'd never once believed that the demons existed.

It was the belief of her people that the gods had created their race when they withdrew from this world, and that those who belonged to the Coven had been given their powers not only to help their fellow humans, but also to prevent the demons from returning to claim their share of the world.

Once in a while, someone claimed to have felt the cold touch of a demon's presence—but no one had ever actually seen one. She'd once questioned a playmate who'd claimed to have felt that unutterably cold presence, and had finally reduced him to tears with her sharp demands and her disbelief.

She continued to float through the darkness, but now she began to feel a coldness rushing up at her, reaching out to her with icy fingers. Beyond her, or below her, the darkness began to thin toward a dim twilight—and she saw the grotesque, inhuman figures waiting for her.

"No!" she cried, then flinched as something touched her arm. She was already awake and staring into Miklos's concerned green eyes when she realized that the touch was warm and human, not cold and demonic.

"You were moaning. Were you having a nightmare?" he asked gently, removing his arm. "It sounded like you were chanting something."

Jalissa blinked in the soft light of the spacecraft's console. The cabin temperature was pleasantly warm, but a chill had settled into her that not even his brief touch could banish. She stared into the vast darkness of space beyond the viewscreen.

"How long was I asleep?"

"Perhaps five hours. I slept for a time myself. We should have Xyton in sight soon."

She nodded. Xyton was the first of the two

worlds he considered to be a likely home for the Coven.

"Do you know the history of the Coven, how we believe we came into existence?"

He nodded. "The Coven was created by the old gods when they decided to leave this universe. The old gods were the forces of good arrayed against the demons, the forces of evil. The Coven was created as guardians, in case the demons tried to return once the gods were gone."

She was surprised, then told herself that she shouldn't be. He might even have looked up the story recently, after discovering that the Coven still existed. She told him how each approaching night was greeted with a chant designed to ward off the demons, who preferred darkness, and how some Witches and Warlocks claimed to have felt their touch from time to time.

"But I never did, so I didn't believe in them either."

He smiled. "There's a certain symmetry there. If you don't believe in the gods, you can't believe in demons either."

She laughed, but to her own ears at least, her laughter sounded hollow. That knot of icy cold seemed to have taken up permanent residence in her stomach, spreading its tentacles all through her. She got up quickly, to forestall any further conversation, and made her way back to the tiny galley.

The simple logic of Miklos's statement

haunted her. If she didn't believe in the gods, then of course she couldn't believe in the demons who were their opposite. And yet, she felt certain that her "nightmare" had been more than that—that it had been a premonition or a warning.

She carried food back to the cockpit for the two of them, and as they ate, they talked, mostly about life on Vantra. Safe conversation, personal but impersonal. And they talked of galaxy politics, both of them smiling as they realized that despite working for two agencies that regarded each other as being enemies, they shared the same views. Only their methods were different.

Can we come out of this as friends? Jalissa wondered. It was far less than they wanted, but it might be possible.

Then, sadly, she knew it *wasn't* possible. They might not agree on anything else, but the Special Agency and Trans/Med would certainly be in agreement that their two "stars" could not be friends. They might see each other from time to time in the course of their work, but that would be all.

When they reached Xyton, Jalissa stared down at the small, barren world and knew instantly that this was not the home of the Coven. She told Miklos that, but he was determined that they should land there in any event, reminding her that she couldn't trust her memories. She knew that her certainty came from something other than memory, but didn't argue the point. A small part of Miklos might have taken a few steps toward an acceptance of the illogical, but she knew that his actions would be based solely on rationality.

The atmosphere on Xyton held less oxygen than they were accustomed to, and its gravity was lower as well. They landed on a flat, dun-colored, featureless desert, and Miklos brought out a tiny hovercraft that was stored in the spacecraft's hold. It was low-powered and barely big enough for the two of them, making the small spacecraft seem huge by comparison.

Jalissa tried to concentrate on the land below them as they skimmed the surface of the planet, but it proved to be impossible with him so close that their shoulders nearly touched. At first, she thought that he seemed unfazed by this forced intimacy, but when he reached across her to activate some device, his hand brushed against her arm and withdrew with such rapidity that he might have been burned.

"What is that?" she asked, as a tiny screen glowed to life.

"It's a device that searches for life-forms. If there is anything alive on this world—or under it—it should register."

They spent hours criss-crossing the ugly, barren world, but the screen showed nothing. Obviously frustrated, he wondered aloud if the Coven could interfere with the device.

"I doubt it," she replied. "I don't think they're

capable of such a thing. Their powers are intended to work against people, not machines."

"People and demons," he corrected.

She said nothing. He seemed to be focusing on demons even as she tried to forget about them. And it occurred to her that she had spoken of the Coven as "they"—and it wasn't just a figure of speech. She had truly separated herself from them.

"We must refuel before we go on to Noros," he told her as they returned to the spacecraft. "I've arranged a rendezvous with a tanker so we don't have to travel all the way back to the base at Gavon."

Noros. Jalissa tested the name in her mind, turning it over and over, hoping that the name alone would tell her whether or not it was the world of the Coven. But the name meant nothing. It was just one more vaguely remembered name from her galactic geography classes.

Jalissa was jolted awake and turned immediately to Miklos, assuming he must have spoken to her. But he was staring intently at the spacecraft's many monitors. Blinking away the remnants of her dreamless sleep, she saw the tense set of his jaw, and was about to speak when she became aware of a very strange sensation.

That earlier coldness she'd felt after her dreams of the demons was back—and it was far worse this time: a deep, aching chill that made her feel as though her insides had frozen into one solid block. And coexisting with that strange sensation was one even stranger: a burning rage.

She pressed the button that brought her seat into an upright position, and the movement caught Miklos's attention. When he turned to her, she saw that she had not been wrong. He was clearly disturbed by *something*—and now fear was added to the volatile mixture of emotions churning inside her.

"What is it?" she asked, her voice still husky from sleep.

But by the time she got her question out, his expression had undergone a rapid transformation to blandness. "Nothing. Just a minor problem with the controls."

However, even as he spoke, his gaze had gone back to the glowing panels. Jalissa drew in a sharp breath. "Don't lie to me, Miklos."

He turned to her again. "The readings are off, that's all. They don't conform to the course I set after we re-fueled."

"I don't understand. Are you saying that we're not going where we're supposed to be going, to Noros?"

He nodded with obvious reluctance, then bent over the keyboard, punching rapidly at the keys, then staring at the monitors. Jalissa stared at them as well, but of course they meant nothing to her.

The chill and the accompanying anger within

her continued to build. She shifted about in the seat, aware of an irrational urge to do something, even though there was obviously nothing to do. Anger made her voice sharp as she spoke again.

"If we're not headed toward Noros, then where *are* we going?"

His head swiveled quickly to her and he reached out to take her hand. "I don't know—but don't worry. I'm sure it'll correct itself."

Jalissa knew that he believed what he was saying. He trusted his science. She recalled all the information she'd heard and read about space-craft, all of which were designed and built by Vantrans, of course. Fail-safe mechanisms. Backups to backups. No expense had been spared in the design and construction of the craft, or in the maintenance either. The few crashes that had occurred had been during the course of experimental flights—and even then, not one life had been lost. Even to someone like her, with no knowledge of such things, it was an impressive and reassuring record.

And yet something had gone wrong.

Moments passed, as Miklos continued to scan the monitors and punch out orders. The lines of tension deepened along his jawline. Jalissa remained silent, fighting her growing sense of dread and trying to ward off a certainty that was growing just as fast.

She stared out the viewscreen into the eternal darkness of space. There was no sense of motion.

They could have been standing still. But all spacecraft were like that. With some of the older craft, one had a sense of motion from the low hum of the engines, but on a newer one like this, the ship moved through space in total silence.

Then suddenly, the small craft shuddered. And before she could even turn to Miklos, she saw through the viewscreen tiny sparks of light. Miklos raised his head and saw it as well, and she heard his sharply indrawn breath.

The whole episode probably lasted less than a minute, and then the shuddering ceased and the tiny lights were gone. "What was that?" she asked.

"I don't know," came his impatient response in a taut voice. She knew that he wasn't angry with her, but rather was frustrated that, for once, he had no answer.

By now, Jalissa was finding it nearly impossible to fight the chill and the rage within her. She pressed the button to lower the seat again, and saw in her peripheral vision that he had turned briefly toward her again.

Desperately, she began to work her way through the exercises that should calm her and send her into a trance. This time, even with his presence to distract her, it worked. Impatiently, she sent her mind out, seeking contact with the Coven.

For one brief moment, she thought she felt that familiar touch of another mind—and then it was gone. She reached more deeply into herself and cast her mind out yet again—then recoiled in horror!

Dazed, she came out of her trance to find Miklos leaning over to her, gripping her shoulders firmly as he stared at her. The echo of a scream hung in the air, and she belatedly realized that it must have come from her.

"Demons!" she said, her voice a hoarse whisper. "It *must* be, but . . ." Her voice trailed off into uncertainty as she stared at him and at the monitors that represented the modern world of science.

Miklos released her, but continued to stare at her intently. "Did you fall asleep? Was it a nightmare?"

She wanted to tell him that was what had happened, but instead, she shook her head and stared out into the void. "There are demons out there." It amazed her that her voice could sound so calm. She shivered at the memory of that brief, terrible touch.

The expression on his face was one of denial, but she saw the uncertainty lingering beneath it. She asked if they were back on course, and he shook his head. Then, just as he was about to speak, an insistent beep sounded from one of the monitors and he turned to it quickly.

She held her breath and waited. In the short time she'd been on this craft, she'd heard that signal before. It meant that they were approaching a planet. Hoping against hope that they had somehow gotten to Noros, she peered intently through the viewscreen.

It grew slowly from a mere pinpoint of light to a well-defined orb, floating in the darkness and glowing with a bluish-white light. She continued to hope that it was Noros, but a nagging sense of wrongness kept away the relief she should be feeling.

There was no rational explanation for that sense of wrongness because she had no way of recognizing the world they sought. And yet, as it loomed ever larger, Jalissa knew with a cold certainty that it was not Noros.

Miklos was busy with the monitors, his gaze flitting back and forth between the screens and the eerie world that grew in size by the moment.

"It isn't Noros," he announced in confusion. "I don't know what it is. If the coordinates are right, there shouldn't be anything at all there."

"We're not in the galaxy anymore," she announced with cold certainty. "This is *their* world."

"The Coven's?"

She shook her head. "No, the world of the demons. They've captured us and brought us here."

"We couldn't have left the galaxy," he stated firmly.

"But we have. They exist in a different sphere, a world that is an overlay of our galaxy. Somehow, they've drawn us through to them."

His expression was definitely skeptical, but not entirely disbelieving. He reached out to silence the monitor, then began to work the keyboard again. A few moments later, he announced that they were in orbit around the world that now filled the viewscreen. Both of them stared at it intently.

"I'm going to land," he announced. "The monitors show an atmosphere and gravity that are within acceptable limits."

"No!" she cried. "Don't land! Try to get us out of here."

"I already have. We can't break free of the gravitational pull."

He picked up the mike and spoke rapidly into it, then waited for a response. Nothing but the hiss of static filled the cabin. After several tries, he gave up.

"I haven't been able to raise anyone since we went through that . . . whatever it was. I'm going to land and put the system through a thorough check."

They drifted down slowly through the thick clouds as the features of the unknown world began to take shape. Thick, dark forests covered gently rolling hills, stretching down to the edges of a restless sea. The closer they came, the darker the world seemed, until they were encased in twilight.

Miklos began to maneuver the small craft, seeking a place to land. Jalissa continued to stare through the viewscreen with dread. For a moment, she thought she saw something in the distance: dark tower-like structures. Then they were lost to view as Miklos put the craft into a wide arc and they glided down onto a barren plain that bordered the dark sea.

When they'd entered the orbit of the unknown world, Miklos had switched on the auxiliary engine that allowed him to maneuver the craft. Now he shut it down and within seconds, the total silence became menacing.

They were encompassed by an eerie twilight—not the soft natural twilight of a dying day but something very different, even though neither of them could name that difference. They stared out at the broad, featureless plain. To their left, a small portion of the dark sea was visible.

"Is it possible that this could simply be an undiscovered world?" Jalissa asked, even though she already knew the answer.

"No," he replied, his faith in Vantran science still seemingly intact.

"Then they have brought us here," she replied, her voice a near whisper.

"What do you know about them?" he asked, his gaze sweeping the landscape. She noticed that his one hand lay on the laser weapon that was fitted into a special groove in the space between their seats.

"Very little. None of us has ever seen them. According to our legends, they withdrew when the gods did. But we're supposed to be able to ward them off," she added doubtfully, then realized that she had used "we" again, once more identifying herself with the Coven. Under different circumstances, that change might have amused her.

"How do you fight them?"

"With the fire, I suppose." She wondered if she might have learned something if she'd stayed with the Coven. It seemed unlikely, though. Even the chants were merely ritual. No one truly believed they would return after all this time— nearly a thousand years, according to the Coven's records.

"Why would they do this—bring us here?" He turned to her, confusion and annoyance evident in his tone.

She hadn't thought about that, and her expression must have told him that because he went on.

"It seems to me that they would *want* us to find the Coven—or at least they'd want *me* to find them. The Coven is their enemy."

"Yes." She shrugged. "I don't have any answers to give you, Miklos."

She reached for the mechanism that unlocked the door beside her. He grabbed at her hand and frowned at her.

"I want to get out," she said. "If they're here anywhere, I'll know it."

"Stay inside," he ordered. "You're safer here."

"Neither of us is safe anywhere if they're here,"

she stated as she pushed his hand away.

She pushed open the door and stepped out into a chill wind that carried with it a faint, foul smell she couldn't identify. A moment later, he joined her, carrying the laser weapon. They both turned in a circle, scanning the area.

"Just before we landed," she said, "I thought I saw something that looked like tall, dark towers of some sort. They were on a hill in that direction." She pointed through the gloom.

"I don't want to go exploring," he said. "I want to do a thorough check to see what's wrong with the craft."

"Miklos," she said, reaching out to take his free hand in hers, "nothing is wrong with the craft. We were brought here—and we need to find out why. I think the answer may be in those towers."

He stared at her for a moment, then abruptly turned toward the cargo bay of the craft. "All right, I'll get out the hovercraft, but I don't like to leave the spacecraft unattended."

"I'll protect it," she said, ignoring his puzzled look as she turned toward it.

She raised her hands, then hesitated. Even now, when her secret was no longer a secret, she didn't want to use her powers—at least not in his presence. Knowing just how foolish she was, she turned her back on him and began to circle around the front of the spacecraft, tracing the ancient runes of protection in lines of blue fire.

When she came back around to the cargo bay

entrance, he had removed the hovercraft and was standing beside it, as still as a statue. She forced herself to complete the circle, then closed her fists and banished the fire. He continued to stare at her hands.

"I'm a Witch, Miklos. You must accept that."

He nodded, but it seemed nothing more than a reflexive action. She climbed into the tiny hovercraft, and a moment later he followed, then started the engine and sent it skimming above the plain, toward the barely visible hills.

"It isn't getting any darker," Miklos observed after a long silence.

"Demons like darkness, so this may be the constant state here."

"There!" he said suddenly. "Is that what you saw?"

Jalissa squinted through the viewscreen into the gloom. Some distance ahead of them, a hill rose steeply from the forest floor. Perched atop it were three tall, dark structures with rounded roofs.

As she stared at them, the chill inside her deepened—and so too did her anger. "Yes," she said, unconsciously flexing her fingers in her lap.

Then she stared down at her hands as she saw Miklos's gaze fall on them. Each finger was faintly outlined in blue fire, even though she had not summoned it. She closed her fists, but the glow remained. Her hands felt slightly warm, and they tingled with the forces that were now just barely controlled within her.

"What . . . ?" Miklos began the question, then stopped abruptly as he turned away from her, his sudden movement betraying his feelings about her talents.

Jalissa was angry. Some of the rage she felt toward the demons threatened now to spill over onto Miklos. Did he think she *wanted* these supernatural powers?

Then, before she could say anything, dark shapes were coming at them out of the eerie half-light. Huge wings flapped slowly, but it was immediately clear to them both that these were not birds. The bodies that hung suspended between the wings were human in form.

"Demons!" she whispered, straining to get a better look at them as they approached the hovercraft.

There were perhaps a dozen of them, and as they neared the craft, they veered off to both sides. Staring now out the side viewscreen, Jalissa gasped as she saw the grotesquely smiling, inhuman faces. They were the creatures of every child's nightmare —indeed, the living origins of those nightmares.

"I can't fire at them from in here," Miklos said. "I'm not sure that the stunners or the laser weapon will work on them."

"Your fire?" he asked begrudgingly. "Will it work?"

She knew what it cost him to ask that question,

thereby admitting that his science was useless here. "It will, but I can't risk it from in here." She wasn't at all sure that the magic fire could penetrate the walls of the hovercraft.

"We should be safe if—"

Miklos' words were cut off abruptly as they felt something buffet the craft. They both stared up at the roof of the vehicle as they heard scrabbling sounds. Jalissa thought about the long, wicked talons she'd seen on the creatures' feet.

Suddenly, two of the demons were pressing against the viewscreen, staring through the heavy glass at them. Both Jalissa and Miklos recoiled, and he drew her clumsily into his arms as he struggled to control the craft.

"They're forcing us down," he said tightly. "The others must be piled on top."

They had been flying above the treetops, and now they were sinking slowly. With the demons covering the viewscreen, Miklos couldn't see to steer the hovercraft.

"Try your fire!" he ordered. "We're going to crash!"

Jalissa hesitated. If the fire didn't penetrate the glass, it could rebound and strike Miklos. But if she didn't try, they would crash. She stared directly into the eyes of the demon that had pressed its hideous face to the glass in front of her—and lifted her hands.

The blue fire never left her fingertips. As soon as it saw her lift her hands, the demon and its companion slipped away into the darkness. But there was no time to savor that small victory, because they were still being forced down.

Now that he could see again, Miklos gave the craft more power and began to search the barely visible land beneath them. "There's a small clearing up ahead," he announced. "I'm going to set it down."

They had barely bumped against the forest floor when the ceiling above them began to crack. "Get out!" he ordered. "They're trying to crush us. Come out with me."

He grabbed the laser weapon and at the same time pulled her across the seat to him, then opened the door. They both tumbled out. Miklos rolled and came quickly to his feet, the laser weapon already up and firing.

Jalissa's legs were entangled in his seat belt, and as she struggled to free herself, the roof of the hovercraft caved in, trapping her still more. Terrified now, she made a grave mistake. Instead of loosing the fire on the demons, she struggled to free herself from the wreckage of the hovercraft.

The darkness was lit by the periodic flash of the laser weapon, but twisted around as she was, she couldn't see if it was having any effect. Then the flashes ceased and she heard Miklos shout!

Finally, she was free from the wreckage—and it was then she realized her mistake. She cried out in pain and anger as she saw Miklos being carried away in the talons of a demon, while the others trailed after him. Within seconds, they were lost in the darkness.

She stumbled into the clearing and her foot struck something. She bent down and picked up the laser weapon, clutching it to herself as though it was all that she had left of him. Tears streamed down her face, blinding her.

The towers! Surely they were taking him there. She could heal him—unless they'd already killed him. No! She couldn't let herself think that. She could save him.

She 'ported, landing clumsily on the rounded roof of the middle tower. The center was actually flat, a diameter of about ten feet, and then the roof curved. She stared into the dusky light and saw the dark shapes approaching, but still at some distance. Moving carefully, she edged over to the curved part of the roof and stared down at the side of the tower. Stone ledges jutted out at intervals from the upper half of the structure. If there were ledges, there must be doors. She 'ported down to one of them.

The ledge was barely wide enough to stand on, and behind it a tall door gaped open. Jalissa considered the situation. The three towers were huge—much taller than they'd seemed from a distance. And each of them had at least a dozen ledges. She had to know which one would be used by the demon carrying Miklos. She glanced back up toward the roof of the tower she was on, and knew that she wouldn't be able to see from there.

The towers were surrounded by a thick forest. Jalissa chose an especially tall evergreen and 'ported into it, then scrambled to find a hiding place within the thick branches. Now she had a good view of all the towers.

Moments later, the first of the demons appeared and landed on a ledge in the middle tower. The others followed. Jalissa held her breath. What if they'd simply dropped Miklos to his death?

And then she saw him, hanging limply from the talons of the biggest of the demons. It landed last, on the lowest of the ledges, dropping Miklos to the stone floor. He didn't move.

The demon picked him up in its hairy arms and carried him through the door. Seconds later, Jalissa 'ported to the same ledge, then peered cautiously around the edge of the doorway.

She could see very little of the interior. A faint glow seemed to rise up from somewhere far below. There was no sign of the demon or of Miklos. She stepped through the doorway—and found herself falling!

It was the scene from her nightmare! Far below, she could see shapes moving about as she fell. But in the space of a second, she realized she could save herself and 'ported to the forest outside the towers.

Dizzy from the fall and the 'porting, Jalissa

crouched in the forest and waited for her vision to clear. When it did, she saw what she'd hoped to find: another entrance into the tower.

A wide, tall door yawned open. Beyond it, she saw that same faint glow. She got to her feet and started toward it. Miklos was in there, and she gave no thought at all to her own danger.

Chapter Eleven

Jalissa walked through the door, her head high and determination plain in her every step. Her fingertips glowed with the magic fire as she moved through the darkness toward the ruddy glow. And then she stopped.

Before her was a large circular room. Torches burned on dank stone walls, but the glow she'd seen came from a huge pit in the very center of the room, where tongues of orange-red flame licked at the raised sides of the pit's border.

Miklos lay on the floor a few feet from the pit. She stared at him, seeking some sign of life, but unable to find it in the flickering light. She started toward him, then stopped as she heard the rustling sounds of wings. She peered into the shadows between the torches—and saw the demons, all of them watching her.

She raised her hands. "Begone! Leave, or I will destroy you!"

Her words echoed off the stone walls. The voice seemed not to be her own. But it produced the desired effect. The demons slipped away, leaving through archways at either side of the huge room.

Jalissa rushed to Miklos and dropped down beside his inert form. He lay twisted, partly on his side, with his torso pressed face-down against the cold stone. Very gently, she turned him over, then cried out with relief when she saw his chest rise and fall.

She began to summon her healing powers, then stopped as she felt something. A cold draft invaded the room, and with it came an even colder touch against her mind. Still kneeling beside Miklos, she lifted her head—and stared straight at an apparition far more terrifying than the demons.

It was very tall—taller perhaps than even Miklos. She could see nothing at all of its body, since it wore a black robe with a hood that shaded its face as well. She stood up as it began to move toward her, the robe swirling about it. The movement was strange—slow, gliding motions, as though it weren't walking at all, but was floating instead. And when it came to a stop about ten feet away, she saw, in the shadows of the hood, a pair of blood-red eyes that glowed like the fire in the pit beside her.

"Who are you?" she demanded, knowing instinctively that this must be the demons' master—and the one who had brought the spacecraft here. "Why did you bring us here?"

The eyes—all she could see of the creature—burned into her. Then a cold, hard voice spoke directly into her mind.

"I did not bring you here."

"Don't play games with me!" Jalissa shouted, still speaking aloud. "If you didn't, who did—and why?"

"Your gods," said the flinty voice. "Your gods brought you here, Witch."

"That's nonsense! They wouldn't do that!" But Jalissa was feeling the first, faint stirrings of doubt.

"You are free to leave—if they will permit it," came the reply.

"Then we'll leave," she said, turning her attention back to Miklos.

"No. *You* may leave. The human stays. It has been a long time since we have seen one of them."

"He comes with me!"

Jalissa could actually feel the creature's surprise. "Why?" it asked. "Why should you care about a mere human?"

For a moment, she simply couldn't answer. She stared from Miklos to the creature in absolute horror. What it was really saying was that she was more like *it*—not human. Then a movement drew her out of that cold terror, and she looked down at Miklos to see him opening his eyes and then struggling to raise himself up.

"I'm not one of you!" she shouted, her voice ringing off the stone walls. "I love him!"

Miklos had by now gotten shakily to his feet. And the moment he did, he saw the black-robed figure. His hand went to the stunner at his belt, and before she could say or do anything, he had withdrawn it and aimed it at the creature.

Laughter he couldn't hear echoed through her brain—and then the creature spoke aloud for the first time. "You cannot love a mere human. I could crush him to dust with one finger."

Miklos still held the stunner, but his gaze had gone from the creature to her questioningly. She met his gaze briefly, then turned back to it.

"You will not harm him! If you try, I will destroy you and your towers. He leaves with me!"

The creature said nothing, and she sensed that it was considering whether or not she could do such a thing. She wasn't certain either, but she stood her ground.

"Then take him. He is nothing."

Jalissa reached out for Miklos's hand; she had to pull him along after her. He seemed mesmerized by the tall figure, who now stood there silently.

Once outside the tower, Jalissa cast a quick

glance around to make sure that the demons weren't lurking about somewhere. Miklos stopped when she did, and she could tell that he was still dazed.

"Miklos!" she said sharply, tugging on his hand. "Come on! We must get back to the spacecraft."

He didn't move, except to turn slowly around and stare back at the tower. She grasped his shoulders and shook him as best she could. "Miklos! What's wrong with you?"

"What is this place?" he asked in a strange voice. "What was that . . . that thing?"

"It isn't important now. Are you hurt? Can you walk?"

Before he could answer, lightning flashed above the towers, followed by a reverberating boom of thunder that shook the ground beneath them. And seconds later, a hard, cold rain began to pelt them.

She hurried toward the protection of the forest, but Miklos was still moving sluggishly, no matter how much she tried to hurry him. Within moments, they were both soaked as the wind picked up and drove the rain through the trees.

Shivering, Jalissa considered the distance. The hovercraft was wrecked, and the spacecraft must be more than a hundred miles away. She stared at Miklos. The rain dripped off his face as he continued to stare at her, his eyes not quite focusing.

Could she do it? she wondered desperately.

Could she 'port with him? It seemed to her that the worst that could happen was that she wouldn't be able to do it, and they would be forced to walk all the way back to the spacecraft. That would surely take several days, and what if the spell she'd cast to protect it began to weaken? She wasn't exactly an expert on such matters.

She *had* to try it. She was convinced that if she got Miklos away from the towers, he would recover from his stupor. He had to be reacting to some force she couldn't feel herself.

"Miklos," she said, speaking slowly and carefully, as one does to a child, "we're going to 'port back to the spacecraft. Or at least I'm going to try to take us there. Do you understand?"

He merely frowned at her. "I . . . can't 'port."

"No, but I can—and I'm taking you with me. Just wrap your arms around me, and don't let go."

She hugged him to her, one cold, wet body pressed against the other, and after a second, his own arms wrapped themselves around her.

"Jalissa! Wake up!"

She struggled up from a deep well of darkness, aroused by the sound of a familiar voice. When her eyes fluttered open, she found herself staring into a pair of very worried green eyes.

Memories assaulted her: the demons, the towers, that terrible creature. Then she remembered trying to 'port—and stared hard at Miklos.

"Are you all right?" she asked in a raspy voice. He seemed to be. And she belatedly realized that they were back in the spacecraft.

"As all right as I'm likely to be," he said with a grim smile.

"Where are we?" she asked, trying to gather up enough strength to raise herself from the reclining seat. Every bone and muscle in her body protested, and she fell back again.

"On our way back to Gavon. From there, we're going on to Mafriti."

"Mafriti?" she echoed, nearly smiling as she thought about that beautiful world. "Why would we go there? What about Noros? We have to find the Coven."

"Neither of us is in any shape to go looking for the Coven now. I've arranged to have the U-77 meet us on Gavon. We'll be on Mafriti within twenty-four hours."

Mafriti. This time, she did smile. In her mind, she saw the two of them, walking along its white sand beaches, swimming in the lucid turquoise waters. . . .

Miklos contacted the command center on Gavon, then replaced the mike and stared at the sleeping woman beside him. He still wasn't sure he remembered what had happened to them. Disjointed pieces came to him, but with no context to put them in, he hadn't been able to reconstruct what had actually taken place after the demons had forced down the hovercraft and carried him off.

The only thing he was certain of was that she had saved him—and at great cost to herself. How great that toll had been, he wouldn't know until the medical specialists on Gavon could examine her.

As he guided the spacecraft into orbit around Gavon, fragments of conversation echoed through his brain. "He leaves with me!" "Then take him. He is nothing."

"He is nothing." Those words kept haunting him, even though his memory did not produce an image of the speaker. That he, Miklos Panera, scion of the most powerful family in the galaxy and the most respected of Special Agents, could be called "nothing" sent a chill through him.

The truth was that he wasn't sure he *wanted* to know what had happened. The rational world of science he understood so well was already threatening to shatter around him.

From her comfortable spot on the deck of the small beach house, Jalissa watched as Miklos came out of the water, framed by the sparkling white sands and the turquoise sea tipped with small whitecaps.

He was naked, and the sun reflected off his wet, bronzed body. She felt a very familiar stirring inside, a melting sensation that told her she must indeed be recovering and that this brief vacation from their problems was now in danger of becoming a problem in and of itself.

She had only the vaguest recollection of the trip to Gavon and the medical specialists and then the trip here to Mafriti. Most of those memories consisted of Miklos's soothing voice, telling her that she would be fine, that all she needed was some rest.

She still didn't know what he had told the medical specialists, but she knew what was wrong. She had pushed her powers beyond their limits when she'd 'ported the two of them back to the spacecraft. She, who had for years disdained her supernatural talents, had then foolishly assumed that they were limitless.

Down on the beach, Miklos picked up a towel and wrapped it around his lean waist. He stood for a moment, staring up at her, and she raised a hand to let him know she was awake. He immediately started across the beach and up the hill toward her.

They had been on Mafriti for three days now, but she'd spent most of that time dozing in her comfortable chaise on the deck. Such conversation as had passed between them had been limited to how she felt and making choices from the menus for the meals that were then brought to them.

Jalissa had been on Mafriti several times, but this was the first time she'd ever stayed in one of the private beach houses, each of which had its own strip of beach and enough land to be totally secluded. Her salary as a Whisperer was quite substantial, but not enough to afford such luxury as this.

Mafriti was an almost uncannily beautiful world that the Vantrans had laid claim to centuries ago. It had no native population, but what it *did* have were miles of lovely beaches, fascinating rain forests and some of the highest mountains of any world in the galaxy.

When peace came to the galaxy after the founding of the Federation, the Vantrans had set about developing Mafriti—but in a very careful manner, so as not to despoil its natural beauty. It became—and remained—the vacation spot of choice for those who could afford it.

Miklos climbed up the stairs to the deck, then picked up his discarded robe. Jalissa found it amusing that he would swim naked in full view of the deck, yet show such modesty now. He poured some fruit juice for both of them, and then settled down into the other chaise.

"I think I may go swimming myself," she told him. "I really am beginning to feel more like myself again."

He nodded, and she could see that he was debating with himself about something. She had no idea how much he recalled of what had happened to them. It might be better if he knew nothing, but she was sure that he would demand an explanation sooner or later.

"What do you remember, Miklos?" she asked when he continued to sit there in a brooding silence.

He gave her a look that told her he was both grateful and fearful that she'd raised the subject. "Nothing at all—at least after those creatures attacked us—or attacked *me*."

"They were demons," she said gently. "It will do you no good to pretend otherwise. I know that you would prefer to believe they don't exist—and so would I—but they *do* exist."

And then she told him the whole story, leaving out nothing. As she talked, he sat there staring out at the sea. When she had finished, he turned to her. She saw that he was striving to control his emotions. It was difficult enough for *her*, and she at least had grown up with the knowledge that such things existed, even if she had tried to deny that knowledge. How much harder it must be for him to be forced to face something for which science had no answer.

"What was it—that other one, with the red eyes?"

"A demon-master. The demons that attacked us are essentially mindless creatures who simply do their master's bidding."

"Do you believe that the demon-master had nothing to do with our being brought there?" he asked.

Jalissa was silent for a moment. He had asked the question she herself had been asking ever since she'd awakened here on Mafriti.

"I don't know. I don't see what it had to gain by lying."

"But why would the . . . gods have done it?"

She noted that even now, he had trouble admitting their existence.

"Because they wanted to prove something— perhaps to *both* of us."

"That they exist, you mean?"

She nodded.

"Then why didn't they just show themselves to us, instead of showing us their opposites?"

"I think they wanted to be certain that we knew *both* exist."

"And that they'll interfere—if they choose to do so," he said bitterly.

"Yes."

"We *must* find the Coven," he said determinedly. "I think they must be on Noros. That's why they captured the spacecraft, to keep us away from them."

"If that's true, then how can we find them?" She knew he was right, but she didn't relish the prospect of another encounter with the demons and their master.

"We can always hope that they've made their point and will let us proceed." He paused for a moment before continuing. "I wish that I could pursue this on my own, instead of putting you at risk again. But I *need* you with me."

Then he gave a short, mirthless laugh. "And

anyway, I haven't done a very good job of protecting you up to this point."

"I've never really seen you as my protector, Miklos. We're a team, and we protect each other."

Unable to risk allowing the conversation to proceed any further along this dangerous path, Jalissa got up and announced that she was going swimming. When she reached the beach, she turned back and saw that he was still on the deck, no doubt continuing to blame himself for his failures.

A little humility won't hurt him, she thought as she slipped out of her robe and walked into the warm water, conscious with every step of his gaze on her naked body.

The water was pleasantly warm and the waves mere ripples in this sheltered cove. Jalissa alternated swimming and floating as she tried to think about their next move. But images of Miklos, walking naked from the sea, kept interposing themselves between her and those thoughts.

For three days now, they had treated each other with exaggerated courtesy while taking great care to avoid physical contact. Only in certain glances or sentences left dangling in the charged atmosphere could she see beyond the formalities to the carefully leashed passion.

The truth was that she'd been feeling quite well for a day now, but she'd continued to pretend otherwise because it seemed safer that way.

Two voices were at war inside her. One said that they should continue this way to avoid the inevitable pain, while the other stated with equal force that they should seize this moment, these few precious days, to create memories that would have to last a lifetime.

Was he facing the same dilemma, she wondered, or Vantran that he was, had he already decided upon the rational solution: Since they had no future, they had no present either?

She floated with the current, caressed by the warm water, drifting with erotic fantasies. There was a dichotomy in Jalissa. In her professional life, she was often called upon to seize the moment, but in her personal life, she was highly disciplined and disinclined toward risk-taking.

She knew that she wanted Miklos Panera as she had never wanted any man—and knew too that this feeling was unique to this man and would never come again. And even though she'd avoided thinking about what lay ahead for them when they left this place, those dangers also urged her to find what happiness she could now.

Turning around in the water, she began to swim for shore—and saw him standing there, just at the water's edge, her discarded robe at his feet as he watched her.

It seemed to take forever for her to reach the shallow water, where she stumbled to her feet and began to wade to the beach—and to him. A warm breeze caressed her wet skin, sending shivers through her that had as much to do with the man who stood there watching her silently as it did with the temperature. Walking naked from the water, Jalissa felt at one and the same moment a surge of power and a soft vulnerability.

He didn't move as she reached him. His gaze swept over her with a hunger as naked as her body. She understood then that he too was locked in the paralyzing embrace of the conflict they shared: wanting and being afraid to want.

She picked up a towel and began to dry herself, casting desperately about for the right words to say—as perhaps he was doing too, since he remained silent.

When she had finished drying herself, he picked up her robe and held it out to her. She turned around and let him slip it over her shoulders, then struggled with unaccustomed clumsiness to fit her arms into the sleeves. The soft fabric pricked her heated skin. She turned again to face him. He cleared his throat, which did little to get rid of the huskiness in his voice.

"If you're feeling well enough, I thought we might go to the rain forest for dinner tonight."

Jalissa felt the moment dissolve as she nodded. Deep in the rain forest was a small, elegant restaurant built high on stilts in a small clearing. Ancient fern trees surrounded it, and the strange creatures of the jungle played beneath it and in the trees. She'd seen holos of it, but had never been there because it was necessary to make reservations many months in advance—unless you were a Panera, of course. The family probably owned it. They owned most of the resort areas on Mafriti.

Two hours later, a hovercraft dropped them off on the platform constructed for that purpose next to the restaurant. Private craft were forbidden here to avoid congestion. They stepped out of the craft into the heat and humidity of the rain forest, replete with the sounds of animals and birds going about their lives in the thick jungle. A short walkway connected the landing platform with the restaurant itself, a long, narrow glass bubble that afforded all diners window seats. Inside the giant bubble, the air became pleasantly cool and dry again, but the sounds followed them, mingling now with the low voices of diners. The special glass-like substance of the bubble allowed sound to pass through, while filtering out the heavy, moist air.

Heads turned as they entered the dining room. Jalissa felt momentarily flustered by the attention and the press of other people around them. Both of them wore the casual, comfortable clothes all vacationers wore in this enchanted place, but she knew that Miklos, at least, was probably known to most of the people on sight, if not personally. Among the 40 or 50 guests present, at least half were Vantran.

They were quickly seated by one of the young

people who staffed the resorts here. Even the most menial positions on this world were eagerly sought after by the graduates of the galaxy's best universities, who came for a year to enjoy this paradise before moving on to their careers.

Dinner was delicious, though neither of them really noticed it. After a few stilted attempts, they gave up any pretense of conversation, feigning instead an interest in their surroundings. A be-whiskered and bearded monkey-type creature cavorted in a tree, swinging from branch to branch with the ease of a seasoned performer. Below them, two great spotted cats padded silently through the dense undergrowth. The sun sank lower, casting a ruddy glow over the myriad greens of the jungle, touching the huge white blossoms of a vining plant that embraced the fern trees.

Then a Vantran couple approached them, greeting Miklos familiarly while casting curious glances at Jalissa. When Miklos introduced her, their interest turned to unabashed shock.

"Jalissa Kendor—the *Whisperer?*" the woman said, staring at her.

Jalissa nodded, waiting for Miklos to explain that they were on a mission together and had come here for a few days' rest. But he said nothing, and after the couple had departed, she questioned him about his failure to offer an explanation for their presence here together.

"Won't this get back to your superiors?" she asked.

"They know we're here, and so does Trans/Med."

Jalissa was startled to realize that she hadn't even thought about contacting Malvina, though she should have done so long before this. Vantra and the Federation seemed so far away—in both time and distance.

"Have you told them what happened?" she asked, even though she was reluctant to let work intrude on the moment.

"No. I told them that you picked up an unidentifiable virus from one of the worlds we visited and we were coming here for you to recuperate." He paused for a moment, then suddenly reached across the small table to take her hand in his.

"I don't want to talk about that, Jalissa. We'll have to leave in another day or two. Let it wait."

She stared at their joined hands, barely able to resist the temptation to glance around and see if anyone was watching. Such gestures of affection were unusual enough among Vantrans, who eschewed public displays, but between a Special Agent and a Whisperer? Why was he taking such a risk?

"We have this time, Jalissa, and it may be all we'll have. I refuse to deny my feelings for you."

She stared into those clear green eyes that seemed to hold all that was contained in the word "love"—and she nodded, then whispered,

"Yes." In the sudden spark that lit his eyes, she saw that he understood all that was meant by that single word.

Silver moonlight stippled the dark, restless water and bathed the white sand in glowing light. A cool, salt-scented breeze caressed their naked bodies as they lay entwined on the blanket Miklos had carried down from the house. Their gradually discarded clothing lay in small heaps around them.

It was not as she'd imagined it—and was better for that. After denying themselves for what seemed so long a time, she had thought that their passion would be loosed like some wild beast, consuming them both in a frenzy of lovemaking.

Instead, they simply held each other, fitting body to body, hard angles to soft curves, as they discovered each other while at the same time feeling as though they'd always known these intimate secrets. His lips and fingers unerringly found the places on her where the merest touch produced shivers of delight, and it seemed that she too knew his pleasure points.

He raised himself up, then slid slowly along her body, raining warm kisses from her brow all the way to her toes, tormenting her by bypassing that most intimate of kisses. She throbbed with wanting, ached with the need to have him touch her there.

Instead, he sat back on his haunches and

stared at her, his wide mouth curved into a gentle smile. "You *have* cast a spell on me, Witch," he said softly, his voice barely audible over the sounds of the lapping tide scant inches away.

It was a measure of the newness of it all that she froze for a moment, the protest already forming in her throat. But then he chuckled and drew her to him, both of them on their knees as they held each other again.

"I won't pretend that I understand all that you are," he said, his voice low and husky. "But I know that it's *all* of you I love."

She buried her face in the taut chords of his neck, breathing in his scent and loving him still more for what he'd said. She'd feared that he loved her in spite of her being a Witch, and had been worried that his love might fade if she were forced to use her powers during the days ahead.

They tumbled back to the blanket, this time with her on top. She mimicked him, moving slowly down his long, hard body, kissing each angle and plane until at last she reached his hard shaft. She felt him draw in his breath sharply, and felt him arch beneath her in silent invitation.

His breath was released in a deep groan as she took him into her mouth, teasing him with her tongue until he grasped her head and pulled her away, letting her know that he was caught on the very edge.

"Leave me with some self-control," he gasped, drawing her down beside him.

"Why?" she asked with a smile.

"Because I don't want it to be over yet."

She understood. They had both become addicted to the thrum of barely controlled passion that bound them, holding them both in one moment that spilled slowly into the next with new sensations all along the way.

His hand slipped between her thighs, questing fingers seeking and quickly finding the moist, throbbing heat as his mouth covered hers to swallow her cries of pleasure. And just as she knew that she could take no more, just as her body began to arch rigidly, he withdrew. She protested, and she could feel his smile against her heated skin as he traced kisses down across her throat and seized first one and then the other of her hardened nipples between his teeth, catching pleasure and pain in a perfect balance.

She moved restlessly beneath him, grasping his head and urging him lower as he took his time wandering along her curves, dipping a tongue slowly into her navel before moving lower and burying his face in her hot, pulsating core.

Jalissa was beyond all thought, her whole body a searing, formless liquid, flowing inexorably toward the final, shattering ecstasy. When he raised his head, she cried out in a protest that had barely passed her lips before he slid into her, gently at first and then with an unleashed passion that sent them both over the edge into powerful spasms of release.

The incoming tide began to lap gently around them as they clung to each other, their bodies exquisitely sensitive as they caressed each other. Neither of them spoke at first because mere words could not have conveyed what they felt. Jalissa saw mirrored in his eyes her own sense of wonder. She was a woman who knew magic—had known it all her life—and yet she had never known that magic such as they'd created could exist. It was a thing separate from them, but made of them both.

The water had now soaked the blanket and was rising around them, sending shivers of pleasure through them that mingled with the small aftershocks of their lovemaking. Miklos drew her to her feet and they walked into the sea, wading slowly until they were caught up by a wave and tumbled beneath it, sputtering and grasping for each other and laughing with pure joy.

The man and woman who'd made love now became children playing in the surf, a transition that seemed quite natural to them both. When they tired of swimming and riding the waves, they moved closer to shore and began to walk along the moonlit beach, wading through sand and water.

When they reached the curved end of the beach, where a small sign warned that they were encroaching upon another private beach, Miklos drew her into his arms. His wet hands glided softly over her slick flesh.

"I wish that our science or Coven magic could stop time in its tracks," he said in a low, husky voice. "Between us, we hold the powers of both worlds, but still, we cannot manage that."

She nodded her agreement, then pressed a finger to his lips. "But we *can* manage it for a few days," she said.

He nodded, and they started back toward the house, both of them determined to hold back the dark shadow of the future as long as they could.

Jalissa nibbled on some fruit as she watched Miklos trim the sails, setting a course that kept them far enough offshore so that they didn't intrude upon the privacy of others on the long coastline of small beach houses.

The shoreline had been sculpted to create a long series of coves, each with its own little house. Distant figures could be seen, lounging on the beach or swimming in the surf. Jalissa was certain that none of them could be as happy as she and Miklos were. But with each passing hour, she became more and more aware of the price they would pay. Living only in the moment was becoming increasingly difficult for them both.

Miklos dropped down beside her and selected

some fruit for himself. The bright sunlight made his golden hair gleam and cast his body in a deep bronze. He had not been her first lover—but as she watched him peel the fruit, she knew he would be her last.

She smiled sadly, thinking about those stories she'd heard about Vantran lovers. It was all true. This man, who could so often seem so arrogant and controlled, had for two days now been showing her the opposite side of his complicated nature: a warm and generous and very inventive lover.

He fed her a slice of the fruit, then licked the juice that dribbled down her chin before lowering his head to trace slow circles down across her throat to the swell of her breasts. When he reached for the clasp on her bra top, she protested. He chuckled, ignoring her and removing it anyway.

"No one will see you. People respect each other's privacy here."

He was already naked, but she had insisted upon wearing at least a minimal covering, even though as yet no other boat had come close to them.

She'd already discovered that her inhibitions tended to fade away with him, and it was no different now as he stripped away the tiny scraps of fabric.

They made love slowly this time, their bodies perfectly attuned to each other. Jalissa couldn't understand how each time could be better than the last—and yet it was. She loved the way he shuddered beneath her touch, giving himself over completely to her erotic ministrations. At such times, he seemed to her like a great, tawny cat, arching his body and making satisfied sounds deep in his throat.

To Miklos, Jalissa was the very embodiment of passion. Her womanly curves seemed made for his hands and lips, an erotic playground to bring to life a man's wildest fantasies. He felt incomplete when she was beyond his reach, which hadn't happened often in the past few days.

To be sure, there were still brief moments when the word "Witch" would creep into his mind, with all that it implied for any Vantran, but even then he could feel the old definition of the word slipping through his mental grasp. If he was indeed bewitched, he wanted it never to end.

On the gently rolling deck of the boat, beneath a golden sun, Miklos kissed her satiny skin, breathing in the scent of her, losing himself in the secrets of her voluptuous body. They both loved to inflict torments on each other—approaching that point of no return as closely as possible, only to draw back and start once again. The game had played itself out many times.

He drew first one and then the other of her

dusky nipples between his teeth as his hand slipped between her thighs, urging her to the brink before withdrawing. Quickly, he smothered her protest with a deep, lingering kiss, only to begin the torment all over again.

This time, he miscalculated—or perhaps he'd done so deliberately, because he loved watching her give herself over to ecstasy, holding her there as long as possible before sliding into her moist, welcoming warmth and joining her quaking body to his own.

Afterwards, her eyelids grew heavy and he watched her fall asleep in his arms, curved against him with a trust he had thought they could never find.

Slowly, his gaze turned from her to the sea, and then to the heavens. Their time here was over. They had held back the rush of hours for as long as they could. He would never tell her how close he'd come to resigning, ending his career. Life on Vantra would be impossible for them, but there were other worlds.

And yet he'd known, even as he let the thought come to him, that it wouldn't work for either of them. No matter how much they loved each other, no matter that his wealth would permit them to live as they chose, the time would come when what they had given up would seem to be more than they'd gained.

A single tear trickled down his cheek, then dropped onto her and slid between her breasts.

Out there, in the darkness of the Outer Ring, and much farther away, on the golden world he called home, the forces were gathering that would tear them apart—and perhaps the galaxy as well.

Chapter Twelve

"We've been summoned home."

Miklos's words, spoken in a flat, unemotional tone, dropped like stones into a pool of water, spreading ripples through the placid calm of the morning.

But the calm had been deceptive in any event. Jalissa had not asked how much longer they could remain here, because she didn't want to know. But it had been a small self-deception that hadn't really worked; she knew their time in paradise was coming to an end.

They lay curved into each other's bodies amidst the tangled covers, their bodies sated after long, leisurely lovemaking. Jalissa realized that he must have known since the evening before, and she loved him all the more for having given her that last precious night.

"Why?" she asked. "What do they know?" And as she spoke, she unconsciously edged away from him, fearing for him more than for herself.

"I've told them everything—except about you."

"Then they know about the *demons*?" She felt it all closing in on them now. It gave her little solace to know that he hadn't given away her secret. It would all come out—especially since they knew about the encounter with the demons.

He nodded, reaching out to take her hand, but not trying to draw her back to him. "I made it sound as though I was the one who rescued us from them."

She detected something in his voice, either a reluctance to admit that he *hadn't* saved them or guilt over having lied to his superiors.

"That isn't all," he went on, his eyes never leaving hers. "The Warlock is dead. He was killed by Federation troops on Ker—but not until after he'd managed to preach his message of revolt. And now, thanks to some trigger-happy soldiers, there's a full-scale rebellion going on there."

Jalissa was horrified. Of all the Outer Ring worlds, Ker, the sole source of crystal in the galaxy, was the one world the Federation could not afford to lose.

"But why did they kill him? I thought you had issued orders."

"I issued orders on Gavon, remember?" he

said. "Apparently, he managed to steal a spacecraft on Gavon. Don't ask me how. We're still trying to figure that out. Maybe he had help from someone loyal to the Coven. He took the craft to Ker, where he ran into federation troops. Apparently, he tried to use the fire against them, and instead of using stunners, they turned the laser weapons on him." Miklos sat up now too, and ran a hand distractedly through his golden hair.

"The commander there is a damned fool. It apparently never occurred to her that by killing the Warlock, she made a bad situation even worse. The rebels have taken over the base, aided by Federation troops that are now proclaiming their loyalty to the Coven. They shot down a ship bringing a regiment of special Vantran forces."

Jalissa swallowed hard. She'd known that there would be a price to pay for their few days together here—but she'd never expected *this*.

"It's not our fault," Miklos said, still holding her hand. "The commander on Ker should have known better."

"But we've been blamed," she said dully, her mind awash in horror.

Miklos shook his head. "No blame has been attached to either of us. A copy of my warning not to kill the Warlock was sent to headquarters. They hold the commander on Ker fully responsible."

"Then why have we been summoned back to Vantra?" she asked, confused.

"The Council itself has summoned us. They want a firsthand report—especially about the demons. A U-77 will be here to pick us up by this afternoon." He paused briefly, then went on in a very different tone of voice.

"I'm not going back now," he stated firmly.

"You're not?" Jalissa was stunned that he would disobey an order from the Council. He might be able to get away with ignoring an order from the Special Agency, but to disobey the Council? The Council was composed of members from all worlds of the galaxy, and given the fact that most of them already resented the Vantrans. . . .

"Miklos, you can't do that! Many of the Council's members already resent the Vantrans. They'd demand your resignation! They might even send you to a penal colony."

"I'll take my chances. The Council will dither and delay as they always do. And in the meantime, the situation could get worse. Finding the Coven is the only hope we have of preventing full-scale war, and it may already be too late."

"Then I'm going with you."

"I want you to come with me," he confessed. "But that's selfish. You have your own career to think of. Besides, there's the danger."

"There's more danger for you than for me," she pointed out. "The Coven might not be very happy with me at the moment, but they won't kill me."

"How can you be so sure of that? If the gods order them to . . ."

"They won't," she stated succinctly. "If the gods wanted me—or *us*—dead, we'd already be dead. They were only trying to prove to me, or to both of us, that they exist. That's why they sent us to the world of the demons."

"Maybe they thought the demons would kill us, and spare them the trouble."

She shook her head. "Neither the demons nor their master could kill me. If they'd been able to do so, they would have. That . . . creature *feared* me, Miklos. That's why it let me take you away."

"Did you know that at the time?" he asked curiously.

"No. I've never known much about the Dark World. Only the Priests have studied it."

Miklos shook his head ruefully. "You might have spent a lifetime denying your heritage, Jalissa, but it's there."

"What do you mean?"

"Your fearlessness. In the past couple of days, I've recovered most of my memories of what happened there—or at least enough to know that you showed more courage than most people would have under the circumstances."

"You forget that I grew up in a world that accepts the supernatural. The demons and their master frightened me, but not as much as they would have frightened most people. I'm going with you, Miklos."

He got out of bed and drew her into his arms. "I'd feel a lot better about it if I knew that I could keep you safe."

"We'll keep each other safe," she said, stretching up to kiss him.

"Promise me one thing," he said. "Promise me that you'll let *me* take the blame for this. If we get hauled before the Council, I'll tell them that I kidnapped you and forced you to accompany me so you couldn't tell them where I was going."

"All right, I promise." But it was a promise she hoped not to be forced to keep.

They went off to bathe in the big tub that was set amidst a garden of fragrant shrubs and flowers and open to the soft sea air. For the next hour, they held the world at bay, luxuriating in the scented water and in each other. And even now, when they both knew what lay ahead for them, they were gentle with each other.

Miklos explained that he'd made arrangements for a private spacecraft to pick them up before the U-77 could arrive. They would take it to Gavon, where he would acquire one of the small craft they'd used before.

"But what if they have orders to capture us?" she asked.

"That won't happen. The Special Agency would never order the regular military to capture one of its Agents. It's a matter of pride. If they come after us, it'll be with other Special Agents, and by the time they can get there, we'll be long gone."

"But they might follow us."

"That's why I'm going to take a craft they can't track, and I'll file a false flight plan just in case."

An hour later, Mafriti was a rapidly diminishing blue and white orb in the vast darkness of space. Jalissa sat in the small passenger compartment, while Miklos remained in the cockpit with the two-person crew.

Was this a fool's errand? Miklos seemed certain that the one remaining world they hadn't explored must be the home of the Coven, but if he was wrong . . .

And even if he was right, would the members of the Coven allow themselves to be found? Jalissa knew that the entrances to their underground sanctuary were protected by powerful spells. Even if he found the right world, Miklos could never find *them* unless they permitted it.

The spells wouldn't work on her, but they could still refuse to permit her entrance—or at least she thought they could. It had never happened before, to the best of her knowledge, but then no one had ever posed such a threat to them. She was more than ever aware of her precarious position, straddling two worlds.

Miklos appeared and told her that he'd overheard a communication from the U-77, which had apparently entered Mafriti's orbit only minutes after their departure. Long before they reached Gavon, the Special Agency would know that they'd fled.

He continued to insist that no one would try to stop them on Gavon, but by the time they landed at the base there, Jalissa was prepared to find a whole army awaiting them. What they found instead were two young Special Agents.

Jalissa and Miklos both spotted the gold braid that distinguished the two men from the other officers the moment they disembarked. Miklos muttered a curse, then told her to remember that she was supposed to be with him unwillingly.

The Agents greeted them politely, then asked if they could have a word in private. Apparently Miklos was right when he said that the Special Agency would want to keep the arrest of one of their own under wraps.

As they walked through the terminal, Miklos questioned the two men about their presence. It turned out that it was mere coincidence. They were returning from a mission to another Outer Ring world and awaiting transport back to Vantra. But it was soon apparent that the Special Agency had turned this fortuitous happenstance to their advantage.

Both Agents were clearly uncomfortable as they explained that they were to "remind" Miklos that he had been summoned by the Council.

"I'm aware of that," Miklos said coldly. "They will have their report in due time."

"But . . . but, sir—I mean, Agent Panera—you

can't just ignore a summons from the *Council*," one young Agent sputtered.

"I can—and I will. And I'm taking Specialist Kendor with me."

"We have orders to keep you both here until the U-77 arrives," the other Agent said, though in a very uneasy tone.

"And do you also have orders to use force against us?" Miklos asked in that same cold voice.

Jalissa saw Miklos's hand move toward the stunner at his belt, and saw one of the two Agents make a similar move. Quickly, she stepped between them.

"Please!" she implored. "I want to go back to Vantra. Don't let him take me with him!"

Confused, the two Agents stepped back. Miklos drew his stunner and leveled it at all three of them.

"You're coming with me, Whisperer! I can't let you go back now."

Still holding the stunner, he reached out and grabbed her roughly, then fired at the two Agents before either could reach for his own weapon. Both men instantly fell to the floor, unconscious.

"Good thinking," Miklos said, smiling at her. "That'll take care of them for a while."

"But how can we get past all those soldiers?" she asked.

"We'll just have to take the chance that they don't know what's going on," Miklos replied as he opened the door to the small office and drew her out into the terminal.

But before they'd gotten far, they both saw another Special Agent headed toward them. The man had already spotted them, and his hand began to move toward his stunner.

Jalissa and Miklos turned and ran down an intersecting hallway, with Miklos gripping her arm to keep up the pretense that she was his captive.

"What will we do now?" she gasped, having a difficult time keeping up with him as they ran through the corridors. "Surely he'll call in the troops now."

"He probably will," Miklos said grimly, turning onto yet another hallway in the labyrinthine terminal.

"Find a place where we can hide," she told him, suddenly seeing a solution to their problem.

They began to try the various doors, and finally found one that was unlocked. Behind them, they could hear the rapid steps of their pursuer, although he wasn't yet in sight.

The long, narrow room was lined with shelving containing supplies of some sort. There was no way to lock the door and no place to hide, but Jalissa wasn't planning to hide.

"We can't risk it," Miklos said, having already guessed what she was planning. "Remember what happened last time."

"That was over a hundred miles," she reminded him. "This is a much shorter distance.

Besides, it's our only chance. Just tell me which direction and how far."

Miklos pointed, though he clearly didn't like the idea. "That way, about two miles or so. But—"

He never had the chance to finish his protest. Jalissa wrapped her arms around him and 'ported.

They landed in an untidy heap on the ground between two large cargo transports. Miklos got quickly to his feet and surveyed the immediate area, then returned to her as she struggled to get up.

"I'm just a little bit dizzy," she told him, then laughed. "Maybe it would help if I were bigger or you were smaller."

He chuckled as he circled her waist with his arms. "Maybe you should cast a spell to change that."

Even in the midst of their problem, Jalissa did not fail to note that he could laugh about her powers—a very good sign, given what lay ahead.

"Now we need to find the craft I requisitioned," he said, keeping an arm around her as they made their way cautiously around the huge cargo ships.

They spent the next five minutes weaving their way through the huge parking area. Fortunately, they were able to avoid the soldiers who were loading and unloading and performing maintenance tasks. Then, just when Jalissa thought she couldn't manage another step, Miklos brought them to a halt.

"There it is!" he said, pointing. "Just walk to it as though we have every right to be here. They aren't likely to have raised the alarm yet, because they wouldn't expect us to have gotten all the way out here this quickly."

They walked calmly toward the small craft, passing several soldiers who stared at them and then returned to their tasks. Then, just as they were about to board the craft, a voice called out.

"Sir, you have to sign the requisition."

Miklos turned as the young woman approached, and took the electronic tablet from her to punch in his code. "Sorry." He smiled. "We're in a hurry. Is it ready?"

"Yes, sir. Thank you." She took back the tablet and disappeared.

Jalissa sank gratefully into the comfortable seat as Miklos ran through the checklist, then picked up a mike and requested permission to take off. They both held their breaths as they awaited an answer.

But it seemed that once again, he was right. The Special Agency didn't want to involve the rest of the military in their problem. They were spacebound within minutes, since the craft Miklos had chosen was capable of very short takeoffs and landings. He filed a flight plan for Ker, even though that wasn't their destination.

"They'll probably believe it, given what's happening there," he told her.

Seconds later, they received a warning that landing on Ker was impossible right now. No explanation was given, however. Obviously the Federation was trying to keep the rebellion under wraps.

"The warning is noted," Miklos said into the mike. "But our destination remains Ker."

Then, scant moments later, one of the screens lit up and a warning bell chimed. Miklos glanced at it and told her that the message must be from the third Special Agent, who'd apparently discovered their abrupt departure. Jalissa watched as he punched in a code that turned the unintelligible words on the screen into Vantran.

"Agent Panera. You are ordered to return immediately to Gavon. Special Agent Kundera. Authorized by General Maleda."

Miklos switched it off without replying. "They'll come after us, but they're going to have trouble tracking us in this. Besides, I think they'll assume that we *are* going to Ker."

And as he spoke, he began to re-program the computer, to change their destination. Jalissa sank deeper into the seat, exhausted from the ordeal of 'porting them both. She was already drifting off to sleep as Miklos kissed her.

"We make a good team, Specialist Kendor."

She smiled sleepily. "I doubt that the Special Agency and Trans/Med share your belief."

* * *

The meeting was historic. Never before in the history of the Federation had representatives the Special Agency and Trans/Med met alone in secret together. Despite the urgency of the situation, considerable time was wasted in determining just where they should meet. They finally chose the neutral territory of a retreat in the forest that was used by various Federation agencies for training purposes. Now they sat across a long table, glaring suspiciously at each other.

"You've lost them?" the Director of Trans/Med asked.

"Yes," replied Shar Holota, the Director of the Special Agency, in a tone that indicated someone would pay dearly for this error. "They took a small craft that can't easily be tracked. They filed a flight plan for Ker, ignoring the warning, but they obviously didn't go there."

"I must protest this strongly," Mara Tendit, the Trans/Med Director stated. "One of your agents has kidnapped our best Whisperer."

"That remains in doubt."

"What do you mean?"

"We have reason to believe that despite her statement to the two agents on Gavon, she has accompanied him willingly."

"That's ridiculous!" Tendit sputtered. "Jalissa Kendor—"

"They spent five days together on Mafriti," Holota said, cutting her off. "They were seen together several times, and they did not appear to be unhappy in each other's company."

"Are you saying—"

"I am saying that they chose to stay in a secluded beach house, rather than in one of the hotels, and when they were seen together, they gave every impression of being lovers."

"That's absurd!" Malvina stated, speaking for the first time. "Jalissa Kendor is both a Whisperer and a Tevingian. She would never become involved with a Vantran—let alone a Special Agent."

But even as she defended Jalissa, Malvina knew that it must be true because she alone knew that, if Jalissa had wanted to get away from Miklos Panera, she possessed the powers to do just that.

Malvina quickly guessed what they must be planning. They were trying to find the Coven. If so, then that meant either that Jalissa really trusted Miklos Panera, or that she herself had turned against the Coven. She could only hope that it was the former.

"If they didn't go to Ker, then where could they have gone?" Tendit, the Trans/Med Director, asked.

"We think they're trying to find the Coven," the Director of the Special Agency said.

"You're assuming that they exist?"

"Yes," Holota admitted, but very reluctantly. "Before he was killed, the Warlock clearly demonstrated his supernatural powers." At their shocked looks, he went on to describe what had happened. "And there is more."

He signaled an aide, who withdrew from his case some papers and handed them, with obvious reluctance, to the delegation from Trans/Med.

"This report was filed by Agent Panera before the two of them went to Mafriti. The Council has already received copies."

Trans/Med had already heard rumors of some strange encounters by the pair, but all of them—even Malvina—were shocked by the detailed report of their encounter with the demons and their master. According to the report, it was Miklos who had slain them and then managed to save the two of them—but Malvina knew differently. She suppressed a shudder as she thought about Jalissa doing battle with their ancient foes.

"I don't believe this!" said the Trans/Med Director. "Panera has obviously lost his senses."

The Director of the Special Agency leaned forward, staring hard at his counterpart. "Miklos Panera is the most brilliant and talented agent we've ever had. Either his report is the truth, or he's under a spell!"

"Under a spell? What are you talking about?"

"Jalissa Kendor is a Witch! It is *she* who has captured *him*—not the other way around!"

"And exactly what do you offer as proof of this absurd suspicion?"

"No proof that you would accept, but it's good enough for us. We think she is taking him to the Coven, so they can hold him hostage."

Malvina said nothing, and hid her small smile of satisfaction. She was sure they were wrong about Jalissa's intentions, but she was also secretly pleased to see that these men, who had so rudely dismissed the Coven in the past, now at least accepted its existence.

But she was left with a dilemma. Should she contact the Coven and warn them that Jalissa and Miklos Panera were coming—or should she let this play itself out?

The flight to Noros was fraught with tension for both of them. Jalissa was unable to sleep for long, and Miklos was constantly scanning the console for signs that they'd been spotted or that the demons might interfere once again. For long hours, they simply stared out at the darkness and held hands, determined but wary.

"Would you leave Trans/Med?" he asked suddenly, breaking a long silence between them.

"Wh . . . what do you mean?" she asked, the question catching her by surprise.

"When this is over, we could both leave Federation service and go live somewhere else—maybe Telera or even Mafriti."

Jalissa said nothing as she let herself imagine them spending the remainder of their days on either of those lovely worlds. But a cold certainty settled over her that it could never be.

"I love you, Jalissa, and I want to marry you."

She smiled, stretching across the space between their seats to kiss him softly. "It's a wonderful dream, Miklos. And I love you too. But it will never happen."

He frowned. "Can you see the future?"

"No, not really—or not generally. But I know it won't happen that way."

"Then what *will* happen?" he asked.

"I . . . don't know." But in that very moment, she had what she knew was a sudden vision of the future.

She saw herself in a strange place. It looked like Tevingi, and yet she didn't recognize it. What she *did* recognize were the small stone cottages scattered about in the forest and the black-clad people moving about.

It was the Coven's old home—a place she'd seen only in the paintings at the museum on Tevingi. And she was there among them, clad in the black garments of the Coven—a Witch once more.

I will go back to the Coven, she told herself, barely able to hold back the protest that welled up inside her. And if I go back to the Coven, he will not be there.

Fortunately, Miklos didn't ask her any more questions, though he kept casting worried glances her way as they moved silently through space, headed toward the last hope they had of finding the Coven.

He tuned into the coded broadcasts that allowed them to be updated on the situation on Ker. That world was now totally under the control of the rebels who swore their allegiance to the Coven. Apparently, no further attempt had been made to land loyal Federation troops there.

"What will they do?" she asked.

"My guess is that they're waiting to see what the Coven will do," Miklos replied. "By now, word must have reached Tevingi of the rebellion, through the Tevingian troops there. So the Coven probably knows what has happened."

He smiled grimly. "Thanks to those rebels, the Coven has more power now than they've ever had before. No one knows where they are, and the Federation can't possibly destroy Ker because of the crystal. It's a classic standoff."

But what will they do with that power? Jalissa wondered silently.

Noros was not the world of the Coven. Jalissa knew that as soon as it came into view. Miklos suggested that she could still be under the spell cast by the priests to deceive her, but she shook her head.

"This isn't the right world. Don't ask me how I know it—but I do."

Still, he insisted upon landing on the barren world, then taking the tiny hovercraft and scanning with the device that detected life-forms. Finally, he too agreed that this couldn't be the right place, and they returned to their spacecraft.

"Maybe we should try to contact Danto," she suggested. "He knows where they are, and I could try to persuade him to help us."

But Miklos shook his head. "We can't risk any transmissions. That would allow the Inter-Planetary Command to track us."

"Then what can we do?"

He was silent for a moment as he studied the screen that held a map of this part of the galaxy. Then he called up a more detailed view of one sector.

"There's one other possibility," he said after a few moments. "I considered it before, but it didn't seem likely. Still, the Tevingians have always known their way through it better than anyone else."

"What are you talking about?"

"The asteroid belt. Do you know anything about it?"

"Not much," she said, frowning. "I know that centuries ago, the Tevingians mined several of the asteroids, but the mines were abandoned long ago, after they took what they could. All I can remember from my studies is that it's supposed to be very dangerous for spacecraft."

"That's right," he confirmed. "There are more than four hundred asteroids, ranging in size from a few miles in diameter to some that are almost the size of small planets. Their orbits are erratic, which means charts aren't much help, and many of them contain metals that interfere with signal transmissions.

"Some years ago, a Federation expedition went there to see if they could find anything worth mining. They lost all but one of their craft, and no one has been back since.

"The interesting thing, though, is that some scientists doubted the presence of metals that can interfere with transmissions. There was a lot of arguing about it at the time."

"What are you saying—that the interference could have come from the Coven, rather than from these metals?"

"Maybe. You said once that the Coven couldn't affect the workings of machinery, but are you certain of that?"

"No," she admitted. "I just assumed that they couldn't because they've never encountered modern science."

"The only problem with the theory is that you remember being on the surface of the planet, and that would rule out anything in the asteroid belt. None of them has any gravity or atmosphere. They aren't planets."

"Then the Coven couldn't be there. Even if they gave me false memories of being on the surface, how could they have created an atmosphere for themselves underground?"

"The Coven couldn't, but the gods could have. After our unplanned trip to the world of the demons, I can believe that. How do your people account for their escape from their old world?"

"The Tevingians found out about the plan to destroy it and carried us away before the Van-trans got there. At least, that's what I was always told."

"It could be another false memory, Jalissa, designed to keep you from thinking too much about how they escaped and where they went.

"While you were resting on Mafriti, I did some research into that whole episode. That mission was planned and executed in the strictest secrecy. Furthermore, we were keeping a close eye on the Tevingians. The space-tracking system back then wasn't as good as it is now, but even so, it was impossible for the Tevingians to get enough craft to the Coven's world to carry them away, even if they had somehow managed to learn about the mission.

"What I think is that the Tevingians had nothing to do with the Coven's escape. I think the gods saved the Coven, and put your people in a place where only the Tevingians would be able to find them. They were the only ones who could navigate safely through the asteroid belt."

"But if you're right, then we can't find them."

He nodded grimly. "Trying to find our own way through would be too dangerous. I wouldn't be able to trust the readings."

"I might be able to get us through," she said after a moment.

"How? You don't remember the journey."

"No, but if you're right about the problem—
that it's a spell and not the presence of metals—
then I should be able to find our way through."

"It's too dangerous."

"So is doing nothing," she reminded him.

Miklos leaned back in his seat with a sigh. Jalissa knew exactly what he was thinking because
they were her thoughts as well. The temptation
to do nothing was very powerful. They could
both resign, as he had suggested, and spend the
remainder of their days on some quiet world un-
touched by the battles to come between the
Coven and the Federation.

But they couldn't do that. Not even their love
could survive the knowledge that they had turned
their backs on the Federation, and she, at least,
could not turn away from the Coven or its allies,
the Tevingians.

She tried to conjure up an image of the two of
them, living out their lives in some quiet spot, but
the image was blurred by its unreality, by the certainty that a cloud would hang over them
wherever they went.

Miklos roused himself from his own contem-
plation and began to punch in coordinates. The
spacecraft ascended slowly through the atmosphere into darkest space.

"We'll try to get through the asteroid belt," he
told her, though with obvious reluctance.

Jalissa nodded, then settled back to try to get

some sleep. If they were right about the spell, she would need all her energy to steer them through. She drifted off to sleep with her hand curved in his, praying to the gods that she wouldn't be sending them both to their deaths.

She awoke to a sense of something touching her mind. Her eyes snapped open and she immediately turned her head to look at Miklos, thinking he had spoken. But he was asleep, his breathing slow and regular.

Then she wondered if the priests might have reached out to her. She willed herself into a trance and waited for the sensation to grow stronger. But there were no voices—only that sense that something was there. She came out of the trance and stared out into the void, wondering if she should awaken Miklos.

She was still undecided, even though the feeling was growing ever stronger, when suddenly a chime sounded, shattering the quiet. A half-second later, the computer-generated voice announced that they had reached their destination.

Miklos awoke and brought his seat into an upright position, turning toward her at the same time.

"I feel something," she told him. "I'm not sure what it is, but it woke me up before the chime sounded."

"Could it be the spell?"

She nodded slowly. "It could be."

He merely nodded as he bent over the various screens. She could see the tension in his body. How terrible it must be for him to know that the screens could not be trusted now. His belief that everything could be understood in terms of his science had suffered some devastating blows.

"We're entering the belt now," he said. "I've switched off the auto-pilot, but the collision-avoidance system is still on—for what it's worth."

Which is nothing, she thought. Now it was all up to her.

They flew on. Miklos had slowed the craft considerably, but they had only the instruments to confirm that. She leaned forward in her seat, staring into the darkness, fearing that at any moment, one of the asteroids would suddenly appear.

That strange feeling grew ever stronger, humming through her whole body now. She started to ask Miklos if he felt anything, but the words died on her lips as she had a sudden certainty of danger. And before she could tell him that, she also knew just where the danger lay.

"Turn right," she ordered.

Miklos glanced at her, then steered the craft to the right. A few seconds later, the dim shape of an object nearly twice the size of the spacecraft appeared off to their left. No warning issued from the collision-avoidance system.

For nearly four hours, they continued that

way, watching as asteroids of varying size came into view, then faded into the blackness of space. Jalissa had lapsed into a semi-trance, her eyes closed as she slowly began to trust her instincts.

Then suddenly, the feeling was gone, leaving her as quickly as it had come. "Stop!" she ordered, sitting up quickly to stare out through the viewscreen.

"What's wrong?" he asked in a tense voice.

"The feeling is gone," she told him. "Either we've broken through the spell, or . . ." She left the rest unsaid. If they hadn't broken through to their destination, then they were trapped.

Miklos had switched off the useless avoidance system, and now turned it back on again. As soon as he did, the warning came and something showed on the screen, directly ahead of them. He began to move forward slowly as they both strained to see what lay ahead.

"There it is!" he said, his gaze traveling from the tiny world now coming into view to the screen where information was now pouring forth.

"That's the one I told you about—the biggest of them." He glanced again at the screen. "It's about half the size of the Vantran moon."

Even though it was tiny by comparison with the other worlds they'd visited, it now nearly filled their screen. Jalissa stared at the gray-brown surface, seemingly a dead rock like the other asteroids. Was this the place where she'd spent the first 12 years of her life? Shouldn't she know if it were?

They settled onto the surface and stared around them at a twilight world devoid of any life. Miklos turned to her questioningly.

"I don't know. I don't feel anything at all."

"There's no atmosphere, so we'll have to use the airlocks and get into the hovercraft inside the bay."

They scrambled from their seats into the cargo bay, then climbed into the tiny hovercraft. Miklos, she noted, seemed far more eager than she was. But then his memories hadn't been stolen from him. If this was the world where she'd been born, the Coven had committed a grievous sin against her, one she wasn't certain she could ever forgive.

They left the spacecraft and flew slowly over the cratered surface. Both of them kept shifting their gazes from the barren world around them to the blank screen that would come to life only if it detected life in some form.

The screen was still empty when Jalissa felt something: a gentler version of the feeling she'd had before. When it began to recede, she told him to turn around. He turned the hovercraft and re-traced their route, and after a few minutes, she had pinpointed the location of the disturbance she'd felt.

"Over there," she said, pointing. "That deep crater."

Miklos skimmed along its edges, then dropped down below the vertical rock walls into the bottom of the crater. It was deeper than she'd thought. As they settled gently to the bottom, she was looking up at sheer cliffs several hundred feet high.

And then her gaze fell on one particular spot, as though drawn there for no reason she could understand. As she stared at it, it began to grow indistinct, the gray-brown rock fading into a sort of mist that slowly turned bluish-white and grew, until it became an opening large enough for a craft the size of their spaceship to pass through.

"There!" she said excitedly. "A doorway! Do you see it?"

Miklos stared and shook his head.

"It's there, Miklos: an opening! We can fly through. This must be the home of the Coven."

"It can't be," he replied. "Nothing shows up on the screen."

"They could have cast a spell on it too," she insisted. "We have to go in there."

"I'm not going to fly into a wall of rock."

"You have to trust me, Miklos. I brought us through the asteroid belt safely."

He stared at her silently, then stared at the wall, obviously torn between what his eyes told him and the need to prove that he trusted her. She waited silently, knowing the conflict that was tearing at him. She no longer had any doubts that this was the world of the Coven, but she understood what she was asking of him.

Finally, he took her hand. "It still comes down to trust, doesn't it?"

She nodded, and he began to move them toward the wall.

Chapter Thirteen

Jalissa had no doubt at all that they were approaching the spellbound entrance to the home of the Coven. But she was keenly aware of the fact that what Miklos saw before them was an impenetrable stone wall. She wondered if she would be able to place as much trust in him if the situation were reversed, and was glad that she would not have to be put to the test.

Absolute trust is not something either of us bestows easily, she thought. *We're alike in that.*

The hovercraft slowed, but did not stop. At this point, Jalissa saw only the bluish-white haze of the enchanted doorway, but she knew that Miklos must see death staring them in the face. If they were to hit the stone wall even at this low speed . . .

Then she heard a startled exclamation from him as they were totally surrounded by the eerie light. And a moment later, it was gone.

The hovercraft was traveling slowly through a stone-walled corridor that angled downward. Water dripped from the cut stone on either side of them, only a foot or so away from the stubby wings of the craft. She turned to Miklos and smiled, putting her hand briefly over his as he guided the craft.

"Thank you for trusting me," she said.

His uncertain smile told her that he hadn't—quite. But she was satisfied with that, understanding how difficult this was for him.

He gestured to the bio-scan device. "It's still not showing any indication of life-forms."

Jalissa frowned. It didn't seem likely that the Coven could be affecting it in any way. Why would they? They were certainly safe enough with the spell that kept everyone but the Tevingians out of the asteroid belt, and the additional protection of the spellbound entrance to their underground home.

They continued down the gentle slope of the tunnel for another few minutes, and then it abruptly ended in a large cavern. Miklos brought the hovercraft to a halt, and they both stared at the high-ceilinged stone room. When they'd entered the tunnel, Miklos had turned on the powerful headlights of the hovercraft, but they barely penetrated the darkness of the cavern.

"Do you recognize this place?" he asked.

She shook her head, even as she continued to peer into the gloom beyond the reach of the headlights. She had no recollection of ever being in the spot where the Tevingi craft entered their subterranean home.

"I thought they landed on the surface," she told him, struggling once again with her anger at the priests for having taken away her memories.

Then she thought she saw something high on the wall just beyond the light cast by the head-lights. She asked Miklos to turn the hovercraft and aim the lights in that direction. He did so—and any doubts she'd begun to have about this being the home of her people vanished.

"What is it?" Miklos asked, his eyes also on the delicate-looking sphere that clung to the wall.

"It's one of the lights we use down here. But why isn't it glowing?"

The sphere was cloudy and giving off no light at all. Jalissa felt a slowly gathering fear. These were not ordinary lights—and they never went out. They were bits of the magic fire, captured inside glass balls. They could be made to glow brighter or become dimmer merely by focusing on them for a moment. She did that now, and the sphere suddenly began to glow brightly.

"Did *you* do that?" Miklos asked nervously, scanning the area.

"Yes. But I don't understand why it was off."

"It could be the Coven's way of not welcoming us," he suggested.

"That would be foolish, since they know that I can turn it on again. Something is wrong, Miklos."

She started to open the door to the hovercraft, but he put out a hand to stop her. "Will any weapon I have work against them—if it becomes necessary?"

"No. Either the stunner or the laser weapon might work, but you'd never get a chance to use it. They could wield the fire instantaneously just by thinking about it, while you would have to raise the weapon and aim it and fire."

She touched his cheek gently. "You must trust me again, Miklos. I won't let them hurt you."

They both got out of the hovercraft and she noticed that, despite her warning, he still carried the laser weapon with him, as well as the stunner attached to his belt. She knew that he had a need to cling to the weapons he understood, so she said nothing.

Turning in a circle, Jalissa reached out with her mind to the other light-spheres until all of them were glowing brightly again. Then she sent her mind out beyond this cavern, seeking her people. There was no response.

"They're all shielding themselves from me," she said in a whisper that still echoed through the room. "Why would they do that, when they know we're here?"

There was a slight pause before Miklos spoke the words she didn't want to hear. "Maybe they're not here."

His words, spoken in a normal tone, bounced off the stone walls, echoing through the room and through her mind as well. Surely he was wrong! Where could they have gone? Nearly seven thousand people could not have been removed that easily, especially now that she knew they could not have been picked up on the surface.

The gods could have taken them away, she thought. But why would they do that—unless they wanted to hide them from me—or from Miklos?

Carrying two bright flashlights, they walked through the stone archway into another corridor, where Jalissa saw more darkened spheres. She didn't bother to bring them back to life because the flashlights were adequate.

The corridor ended at a sight that was both familiar and terrifying. They were on the upper level of a huge room that served both as a market and a meeting place for the entire Coven. Wide walkways cut into the stone traversed the high walls, with doorways leading to living quarters. The utter silence of the place was frightening, so frightening that a few seconds passed before she saw the place for what it was: a home that had been abandoned long ago.

She uttered a small, strangled cry that brought Miklos's arm around her waist quickly. She huddled against him, seeking his solid warmth as a chill settled into her very bones.

"They're gone!" She cried. "Look at the dust—and the cobwebs! It's impossible!"

Dust lay heavily on the beautifully carved stone benches and on the many tiers of the ornate fountain at the center of the room. Cobwebs were strung from tier to tier, where water had once gurgled pleasantly.

Jalissa began walking down the series of walkways to the floor, scarcely aware of what she was doing. Every time she passed a light-sphere, she turned it on, although she wasn't really aware of that either.

When she reached the lowest level that held the benches and the fountain, she stopped and turned around to see the footprints they'd made in the thick dust. There were no prints other than their own.

Then she spotted something lying on the stone floor, and cried out as she ran to pick it up. Her fingers began automatically to push and pull the interconnected wooden pieces into place.

"It's a toy—a puzzle. We all had them."

"Is there someplace they could be hiding?" Miklos asked gently.

She shook her head. "They know I could find them. They're gone." Her final words came out accompanied by a choked sob.

Miklos drew her into his arms. "They aren't just gone, Jalissa. They must have left a long time ago. It would take years for this much dust to cover things down here."

She'd known that at some level, but hearing him say it now only made the chill deepen inside her. She nodded miserably.

Miklos continued to hold her in his arms. His hands stroked her back soothingly. "We already knew that they changed some of your memories. Maybe they changed more than we thought."

She stared at him in horror. "You mean that I never actually *lived* here?"

He nodded. "What you remember could be someone else's memories—some older person who *did* live here. The Coven must have lived here at some point."

She felt empty, drained of her very essence. It had been a long time since she'd given much thought to her childhood here, but that didn't lessen the impact of knowing that those buried memories must be false. The Coven had truly abandoned her, cut her off from her heritage.

They spent several hours walking through the silent underground city. All of it was as she remembered it, but all of it had clearly been abandoned many years ago. Miklos guessed that it had been empty for at least a few decades, although he admitted he couldn't be sure. In what she thought was an attempt to make her feel better, he said that it was possible that she could have lived here. After all, nearly 20 years had passed since she'd left this place.

But that proved to be of no consolation to her. Even if her memories *were* accurate, the Coven had still abandoned her childhood home and kept their new home secret from her. And in any event, she could not understand *why* they would have left.

She told all this to Miklos, who nodded, frowning. "I could understand it if they had left recently. They might have been afraid they would be found, given the fact that the Warlock made their presence known to us."

"Even so, they must have known you couldn't find them—unless I helped you." She added that last phrase in a choked voice.

Miklos grasped her arms. "Listen to me, Jalissa. *They're* the ones who sent you to the Federation. They must have known they were dividing your loyalties—that they could lose you. Even that encounter we had with the demons proves that. They apparently felt it necessary to prove to you the existence of the old gods."

"Or to prove it to *you*," she added.

"Yes, well, if that was their intention, they succeeded," he said with a grim smile.

Finally, they reached the children's quarters. They passed by classrooms filled with small desks and old-fashioned chalkboards that drew smiles from Miklos, who'd seen such things only in pictures. He asked what sort of education she'd gotten here, his tone indicating that it couldn't have been much.

Jalissa explained that they had been taught only the rudiments: reading, writing and simple math. "It's all we needed, really. And of course, we spent much time on history and learning to develop our talents."

"Then you must have been very much behind children your age when you went to Tevingi."

"I was," she admitted. "The Kendors found a private tutor for me, though, and I caught up."

She looked around the classroom they had entered, and shuddered. "I was happy enough here, but seeing it now is like looking at ancient history to me too."

Miklos drew her into his arms. "You don't belong with them, love. Don't even think of going back to them."

"I may have no choice," she said, fighting back tears. "But I can't very well go back if I can't find them."

She moved out of his arms and led him back down the corridor to the dormitory-style living quarters for the children. "This was my room," she told him as they paused in the doorway of one of the huge rooms where narrow beds lined both walls.

"Or at least my memory tells me this was my room," she added.

They stared at the beds and chests lining the stone walls. She saw it as Miklos must be seeing it: an impossibly grim and impersonal place, like something from an old horror story.

"It wasn't as bad as it must seem to you," she said as he looked around.

He turned to her, his green eyes lit with love. "What amazes me is that you have become the person you are after this."

She considered his words. "I think the Kendors are responsible for that. They gave me love and a sense of family. I owe them a lot.

"The Coven is not cruel, but I realize that to outsiders it must seem that way. It's just that they live in their minds more than others. Even the choice of a mate is more a matter of compatible minds than anything else.

"To understand them, you have to understand their sense of themselves—not as individuals, but as small pieces of a whole. Even the funeral rituals speak not of the death of an individual, but rather the loss of part of the whole."

"There were ancient civilizations that once believed that," Miklos said, "and they were all tyrannies of one sort or another because someone always took advantage of that belief to drive out individualism and force others to a single will."

"But that hasn't happened with the Coven— unless you consider the gods to be tyrants," she added, thinking that they were, in a way.

As they talked, they'd been walking along the

rows of beds. Jalissa reached the bed that had once been hers—or at least occupied the same spot. Like the others, it was covered with a dusty blanket. Without giving it any thought, she used her talent to send the blanket flying off the mattress in a cloud of dust, then sank onto it. She felt suddenly very tired. She glanced up at Miklos to see him staring at the blanket that now lay in a heap on the floor, and only then realized what she'd done.

Rather to her surprise, he chuckled. "Life with you is going to be very interesting, Jalissa Kendor."

She smiled, but it was a smile tinged with sadness. He saw it, and sank down onto the bed with her. "It will happen," he said softly, drawing her into his arms.

Then he raised his head and gazed off into the space around them. "Hear this, gods," he announced in a voice that echoed through the silent room. "You will not take her from me."

"I wouldn't try to anger them," she warned. "Especially not *here*."

"I intend to make them *very* angry," he replied, just before his lips claimed hers.

Jalissa felt that familiar surge of heat that seemed to melt her very bones. But she was still uneasy. The ghosts of the Coven hovered about this silent place, even if the gods themselves might be keeping their distance.

And yet she *wanted* to make love with him in

382

this place, for reasons she didn't fully understand. Perhaps it was because she wanted to assert her right to live in two worlds, rather than to be drawn once again into the dark life of the Coven.

There was an urgency to their lovemaking that had been absent before, a fierce hunger that dissolved all reason and had them both tearing off their clothing with reckless abandon.

Pale, silken skin met hair-roughened bronzed flesh in a frenzy of need that grew explosively as he entered her and she welcomed him and they succumbed greedily to the ancient rhythms of love. Proud of their passion, they defied the ghosts and even the gods, and gave themselves up to the cataclysm, a love-storm that swept them both away from their bleak surroundings.

Then, surrounded by the soft afterglow, they held each other, whispering their love, stroking exquisitely sensitive flesh until the chill in the room forced them, reluctantly, to seek out their hastily discarded clothing.

The magic of their lovemaking followed them as they made their way back through the silent corridors toward the hovercraft. But bit by bit, reality crept in. They had stolen a few moments and certainly neither of them regretted that, but their problems still awaited them.

When they were once more back aboard the spaceship, with the hovercraft stored again in the cargo hold, Miklos began to switch back and forth among the frequencies, listening to the disembodied voices and then punching in the code that gained him access to the Special Agency's secret communications.

Surprisingly, they heard nothing about themselves. Instead, the screen was filled with the situation on Ker. A large contingent of Federation troops was on its way to that vital world now, due to arrive within a day.

"But they'll be shot down," Jalissa protested.

"My guess is that they're planning a massive invasion," Miklos stated grimly. "Ker's defenses won't be able to withstand it."

"But they'll still manage to shoot down some of them, won't they?"

He nodded. "There's going to be a heavy loss of life."

"I can't believe that the Council would approve such a thing, without at least trying to negotiate with them."

"The Council has nothing to do with it. You forget that the Special Agency has emergency powers in such a situation." He paused, his expression bleak.

Then he went sadly on. "This will tear the Federation apart, regardless of the outcome. When it's over, the Council will demand that the emergency-powers clause be nullified, and my people will refuse." He leaned back in the seat with a sigh.

"I can see both sides, unfortunately," he said. "As a Vantran, I too can't accept this challenge to our supremacy, but as one who believes in the Federation, I can understand the position of the other worlds as well."

"Is there nothing we can do?" she asked.

He was silent for a moment, then began to work the computer again. Jalissa watched as mostly meaningless words filled the screen. She understood it just well enough to realize that he had called up the information on Ker's defenses.

"There might be," he said after a long silence. Then he shook his head. "No, it's too dangerous."

"What are you talking about?" She demanded.

"Because this ship is small, I could get us close to Ker without our being spotted." He hesitated, and Jalissa understood his thoughts even before he spoke them.

"We could 'port the rest of the way," she said.

"It's still more than a thousand miles. You were drained after a couple of hundred miles before."

Jalissa nodded. "Wait here for me. I won't be gone long." And before he could protest, she 'ported herself from the spacecraft and back into the home of the Coven.

She landed at the end of a corridor, where a heavy carved wooden door faced her. For just a moment, Jalissa hesitated, her Coven upbringing overriding her intentions.

Beyond the door lay the stairs to the secret place where only the priests could go, the room deep within the Coven's underground home where they sought the advice of the gods. Coven children were warned from the time they could walk that they must never open that door, though given its weight, it was doubtful that they could have done so in any event. By the time they grew to a size that would have allowed them to invade this sacred place, the strictures were too strong.

Jalissa felt the weight of those strictures even now, but she put out her hand and grasped the gold handle, telling herself that in all likelihood there was nothing beyond the door now, since the Coven had fled.

The massive door was heavy even for her, but she pulled it open and stared into an impenetrable blackness. She hadn't brought along a flashlight, so she sent out her mind, seeking the light-spheres. Immediately a soft and eerie bluish light glowed along the walls of the stairwell, revealing only a short part of its length before curving away out of sight.

She started cautiously down the steps, picking up her pace only when she thought about Miklos, now locked out of the Coven's home and undoubtedly worrying about her. She had little hope that this would work, but she knew that she had to try.

When she reached the bottom of the long staircase at last, she found herself beneath an archway that opened into a small, perfectly circular room. The only thing in the room, save for some more of the light-spheres that she set aglow, was a huge bowl with low, curved sides that took up more than half the floor space.

She began to circle it, frowning. What could it mean? Clearly it had had some purpose, though it was totally empty now. She leaned over the low side, peering at dust in the bottom, seeking some indication of why it was there.

Then, after a few minutes, she backed away from it and closed her eyes, sending out her mind to try to touch something, even though she was nearly certain there was nothing there to be touched. And within seconds, she felt something: not the gentle touch of another mind against her own, but something far deeper and more powerful.

She opened her eyes as the vibrations pulsed through her—and then gasped as she saw the bowl. It was now alive with arcing lines of blue fire, the design so mesmerizing that she couldn't have taken her eyes from it if she'd tried. And as she stood there, transfixed, the voice-that-wasn't-a-voice spoke in her mind.

Jalissa knew instantly what it was. She'd heard those who'd claimed to have spoken directly with the gods describe it.

"You have our blessing, Child. Your request is granted."

Jalissa drew in her breath sharply as the presence withdrew from her, while at the same time, the blue fire in the bowl died away, leaving only a faint glow that itself vanished within seconds.

She backed slowly out of the room, then ran up the steps. She hadn't even told them what she wanted. At the top, she stopped for a moment, gasping for breath. Then a strange giddiness came over her and she laughed aloud. In her eagerness to tell Miklos what had transpired, she suddenly remembered that she could return to him as quickly as she'd left him.

Miklos flinched as she suddenly appeared beside him. His hand had even begun to reach for his stunner before he realized that it was her. Furthermore, she was *laughing*.

"Damn it, Jalissa, don't do things like that!" he rasped, caught between his anger at her tricks and his relief at her return. "This is no time to—"

"I'm sorry," she said, but without much contrition. "Take us to Ker. When you get there, I'll 'port us down."

"It's too dangerous," he told her. "While you were playing your games, I've been thinking. I'm going to contact the Special Agency and Trans/Med and persuade them to let us try to contact the rebels before the troops arrive. We'll have to re-fuel before we can go there, so we're going to need their cooperation in any event."

She shook her head. "We don't need to re-fuel, because we don't need the spacecraft to get there. *I'll* take us there."

He stared at her, dumbfounded, wondering if

she'd taken leave of her senses. There was something in her expression that seemed almost insane—or at the very least, inappropriate to their situation. Her huge dark eyes glittered and her smile was almost supernaturally radiant. And when she lifted a hand to touch his cheek, he could see the faint bluish glow that surrounded it.

"The gods will help us," she told him. "We can 'port to Ker with their help."

He seized the fingers that were unnaturally warm against his cheek. "Jalissa, what happened? Where did you go?" He ·was really worried about her now, certain that the damnable Coven had exacted revenge against her for bringing him here—not to mention making love with him here in their place.

She told him what had happened, how she'd returned to the center of their old home to ask the gods for their help in getting to Ker.

"They *want* us to go there. They approve of what we're doing."

"Jalissa, are you sure that they spoke to you— or did you just hear what you *wanted* to hear? You once suggested that others had done that: that Warlock, for example."

"They spoke to me, Miklos. We're going to Ker."

And before he could utter another word, she wrapped her arms around him and a brilliant blue light was blinding him to everything but the feel of her body against his.

* * *

Miklos felt strange—as though he'd just awakened, even though he also felt certain that he hadn't slept. Jalissa lay beneath him on the hard ground, and was already wriggling to free herself from his weight. He pushed himself up onto his hands and knees, now straddling her. She was smiling.

"Welcome to Ker," she said, waving a hand around them. "This *is* Ker, isn't it?"

Still dazed, yet beginning to feel the first faint stirrings of desire, he got to his feet. It seemed that he had only to be in her presence to want her, regardless of the circumstances.

Making love to her in the Coven's home—or former home—had been one of those "circumstances." He'd been terrified that he might have condemned them both to death for that, but now, as he looked around them, he saw that she was probably right: They were on Ker.

Or at least it *could* be Ker. Miklos no longer trusted his senses. For all he knew, this could all be an illusion and they might still be back on the asteroid in their spacecraft. His hand went automatically to the stunner at his belt, and he wished that he'd brought the laser gun.

She had gotten to her feet and was casually brushing the red dust from her robe. He stared at her, feeling as always that powerful mixture of love and something close to awe. Maybe, he thought, that sense of awe was responsible—at least in part—for his constant hunger to possess her. A part of her was forever beyond his reach, making that which he could possess even more necessary.

"Well," she said, planting her hands on her slim hips, "are we on Ker?"

"You brought us here," he replied with a smile. Then he nodded. "I think so. This is what most of the planet looks like."

"Where are the crystal mines?"

"They're all in one area, and the base is there as well. The rest of Ker looks much like this."

They were standing on a high plateau, where the surrounding view showed no life of any kind. Beneath a milky sky, the land was all ruddy in color, like the dust under their feet. A hot, dry wind buffeted them.

"Do you happen to have a plan?" she asked, turning toward him.

"I had hoped we could make one during the journey here."

"The rebels will listen to me—once they find out that I'm a Witch."

"That's assuming they let us live long enough to find that out," he replied, only half in jest. He was liking this situation less and less by the minute. He knew he'd be recognized by at least some of the rebels—and they wouldn't be happy about seeing him.

"I'll protect us," she said dismissively.

"Maybe we should split up," he suggested, even

though he didn't like the idea much. "They won't harm you even if they don't know right away that you're a Witch."

Her dark eyes flashed. "Maybe not, but they'll kill *you*, and you have only your stunner."

Miklos frowned, trying to put himself into the mind-set of the rebels. "I'm not so sure of that. My guess is that they may already be regretting the fact that they shot down those troopships. They have to know that they can't hold out forever against the Federation."

"They may very well believe they *can*—if they have the backing of the Coven."

"But the Warlock is dead," he pointed out.

She frowned. "What worries me is that some of his friends might be here. Remember, I told you that he claimed to have like-minded friends."

Miklos hadn't considered that possibility, and didn't want to now either.

"Can you control them?"

"They wouldn't harm me, but I'm not sure how much credibility I'd have with them either. Kavnor claimed I wasn't really one of them anymore, and he's right, of course.

"I could try to contact them if they're here, but there's danger in that, because it would let them know that we're here too. What are the chances of our sneaking quietly onto the base?"

Miklos considered that. "The defenses are aimed at preventing unauthorized landings from space. Everyone lives on the base: the troops and the miners and some of their families. I doubt that they'd be paying much attention to the possibility of anyone approaching by land."

"Well, then, we have to find the base."

"How do you propose we do that?" he asked.

She pointed to a tall, reddish-colored peak in the distance. "We can begin by going there and hope that we'll see something you recognize. I can't risk 'porting us directly onto the base, because we could land right in the middle of them."

"I don't understand how 'porting works," he confessed. "Do you have to be able to visualize a place before you can go there?"

"It's certainly better that way. The truth is that I don't really know. I haven't done enough of it."

She stared at him, tilting her head sideways. "You could give me a picture of the base. That would help."

"Describe it, you mean?"

"No. You could do that, but it would be better if you let me take it from your mind."

Miklos felt a chill. "You can do that?"

She nodded. "We have the power to read minds, but we never use it. It's the strongest taboo we have."

They stared at each other in silence, and then he nodded slowly. "Then do it. It isn't wrong if I give my permission."

She took his hands in hers, her eyes searching his face. "If there were a way I could give up all my powers when this is over, I would do that."

"It's part of you," he told her. "And I love *all* of you." But he knew that if she'd been reading his mind at that moment, she would know he lied. It was certainly true that he loved her, but he also knew that there would always be times when he wished she could be an ordinary woman.

She gave him a sad smile, and he realized that even without reading his mind, she knew that.

"Picture the base in your mind," she instructed him. "Try to see it as you might see it approaching on a hovercraft. Is there any place nearby where we could appear and still be concealed?"

"Yes. Just west of the base is a series of low hills," he replied, beginning to picture it in his mind.

She continued to hold his hands, but now she closed her eyes, and after a moment's hesitation, he did likewise.

He didn't know what to expect as he tried to concentrate on his memory of the base. Despite the fact that he should be used to her magic by now, he felt a strong aversion to this. The fact that even the Coven considered mind-reading to be wrong reinforced his fear.

Then he felt something—and immediately recoiled, both mentally and physically. She merely gripped his hands more tightly as a soft warmth flooded through him, flowing outward from his mind until it touched all of him. The sensation was definitely erotic, but it was far more than that. And then, as suddenly as it had come, it was gone. He actually cried out in protest as his eyes flew open.

She was watching him warily, the question in her dark eyes.

"I . . . felt something." The words were inadequate, but he was too confused to be more precise.

She looked away. "I didn't think that would happen. I mean, I knew it happens among us, but . . ." Her voice trailed off uncertainly.

He sensed that whatever had happened, she didn't want to talk about it now. But he *did* want to talk about it. He'd never felt anything like it before, and he wanted to feel it again. Instead, however, he asked if she'd gotten the image of the base.

"Yes. I can find it now. I'll 'port us to those hills and we can walk in from there."

She slid her hands up his arms, gripping him tightly. Her touch brought back an echo of that sensual mind-touch and he felt his body respond. But he also noticed that she wouldn't meet his gaze.

Chapter Fourteen

They landed on their feet this time, with her arms still gripping his. She was already looking past him and when he turned around, he saw that the base lay several miles beyond them on the broad plain.

"It looks so . . . peaceful," she said, moving away from him as she continued to stare down at the scene below them.

"It probably is—at the moment," he replied. "The rebels control it now."

The base was huge, larger even than the sprawling base on Tevingi, because it was also home to the hundreds of miners who cut the precious crystals from their deep caverns. Only a few figures were visible as they moved across the open spaces between large buildings.

Miklos drew her into the shelter of some rocks. They were far enough away that it wasn't likely they'd be spotted from the base, but he didn't want to risk that. Then he began to describe the layout of the place in detail.

"Those long buildings closest to us are for the troops. If they haven't already killed the loyal troops, they're probably holding them there. The prison stockade wouldn't hold all of them. The miners live in the compound out near the airbase, and there are small guest quarters there too."

"How many people are there altogether?" she asked.

"Assuming that the loyal troops are still alive, about six thousand."

"How many of them would have remained loyal to the Federation?"

"Probably at least two hundred. The officers are all Vantrans, and there are some others who would probably side with them because they have no history with the Coven. But most of the troops—and all of the miners—come from worlds loyal to the Coven."

She sank to the ground with a sigh and he sat down beside her. "We should wait until the middle of the night," he told her. "That will give us the best chance of succeeding. If they've got the loyal troops locked up in one of the barracks, they aren't likely to bother with much of a guard.

"I'll take the guards and then we'll have the assistance of the loyal troops."

She shook her head. "What you're talking about is a battle, Miklos, and I don't want that. We should split up. You go find the troops and I'll try to reason with the others. When they find out that I'm a Witch, they'll do as they're told."

"But if there are other members of the Coven here . . ."

"I have to try," she said firmly.

"I don't like the idea of our being separated."

"Neither do I, but I like the idea of a battle even less."

Miklos crawled over and peered around the edge of the rock. The sun was sinking rapidly, making the landscape even more ruddy in color. He knew that her plan made sense. It was what he would have suggested if his companion had been anyone else. But he had a terrible, irrational fear of letting her out of his sight: irrational because with her magic, she was far better armed than he was.

They sat side by side watching as the light drained away. Although he'd finally agreed to her plan, Jalissa almsot wished that he hadn't. She too felt an irrational fear at being separated from him. She told herself over and over that their plan would work, that nothing could happen to either of them—and yet a part of her refused to believe it.

Overhead, the stars had come out. Ker had no

moon to dim their lights, so the dark canopy of the heavens was aglow with millions of tiny lights. The hot wind of the day was replaced by a cool breeze.

"Jalissa?" he said, breaking a lengthy silence between them, "What happened when you . . . reached into my mind?"

She lowered her head, not wanting to look at him. "What do you mean?"

"I told you that I felt something, and you said that you didn't think that would happen."

When she didn't reply, he reached out to cup her chin and draw her around to face him. "Tell me."

"It . . . happens among us, or so I was told. I was too young when I left the Coven to have had any lovers. When it happens between a Witch and a Warlock, they know they have found their mates."

"A union of the mind as well as of the body?" he asked gently.

"Yes. I felt it too."

"I want to feel it again," he said huskily as his lips covered hers. "I want to make love to you both ways."

She hesitated, caught in an uncertainty she didn't fully understand. He drew back, his eyes searching her face intently.

"You're afraid because you think you would be drawing me too deeply into your magic," he said.

Jalissa nodded. It seemed ridiculous to be worrying about that now, given what he'd already seen. He already knew about her magic, and even seemed to accept it. But this was different. This was *shared* magic, not just a display of her powers. And his next words proved that he understood that too.

"Your magic doesn't frighten me anymore, love. It's a part of you. Let me share it with you."

They made love beneath the glittering stars, cushioned by their discarded clothing. The union was like nothing either of them had ever experienced before as they opened both their bodies and their minds to each other until neither one could have said where one left off and the other began.

Each of them felt the awesome power the other had to give pleasure—and to receive it. Lips and flesh touched in passion, while minds touched with the deepest understanding of love. They were wholly absorbed in each other, bodies writhing in ecstasy while their linked minds fed that passion.

And even when their bodies had been sated, their minds remained united, making words irrelevant as they fell asleep in each other's arms, sharing dreams that echoed their love.

Jalissa awoke with a start, caught on the very edge of a dream that was already sliding away. Miklos was stirring too, and she both heard and felt his protest. Her skin was prickled with an icy fear, and she felt the mind-link, already tenuous now, shatter.

She shivered—not from the cool night air, but rather from a near-certainty that the dream she could not recall was a portent. She wanted to ask him what he had dreamed, but the words would not come out.

Miklos kissed her, a soft, lingering kiss. Then he got to his feet and drew her up with him. "It's time to go," he said as he helped her into her robe, then put on his own clothing. She heard the calm in his voice that she now knew hid deep emotions, but still she could not ask what he'd dreamed.

She almost refused to go on. Below them, on the plain, the base was lit by small points of light that seemed barely to pierce the all-encompassing darkness—a darkness that now seemed to reach into her every fiber.

But they were set on a course, and there was no turning back. So she moved into his outstretched arms and 'ported them both down to the very edge of the base, to a spot deep in darkness behind the barracks.

"I will need time," she told him in a whisper as they stood there, still holding each other tightly. "I have to find out if any of the Coven are here before I can do anything."

"If the loyal troops are still alive, I'll keep them in their barracks, and go to the air-defense installation. I can't be sure exactly when the other troops will arrive, so I have to capture air defense to prevent them from shooting down the ships."

She nodded. His was by far the more dangerous mission. Whether or not any other Coven members had come here, she was in no danger. Hers was a mission of persuasion, while his was fraught with the danger of battle. But to change the plan now was to risk many more lives.

"When this is over," he whispered, "they will either accept us or we will find a new life. But we'll be together. I promise."

She raised her face to his, barely able to see him in the darkness. "I love you, Miklos. And I know we'll be together."

Then, before he could question the tremor in her voice, she left him, 'porting out of his arms to the far side of the base to begin her search. And in that instant, it felt to her as though she had left part of her behind.

Jalissa huddled in the shadows next to the building that housed the guest quarters. From what Miklos had told her, if there were any Witches and Warlocks here on Ker, it was likely they'd be in this building.

Quietly, she began to circle the building, listening for voices. There were a few lights on inside, but it was possible that the residents were all asleep.

After creeping around the entire building and

hearing nothing, Jalissa tried the main door and found it unlocked. She stepped inside to find herself in a sort of lounge area. Only a single lamp was lit, leaving the large room in near-darkness. But then something moved in the shadows, rising from a chair in the far corner of the room. She froze, calling on the fire but keeping it contained, so that her hands glowed slightly. The figure approached her hesitantly.

"Jalissa? It's you, isn't it?"

The young Witch stopped a short distance away, her own hands glowing with blue fire.

Jalissa nodded, searching the speaker's face. There was something familiar. . . .

"It's Nedeeyah. I was only a baby when you left, but I remember you."

"Nedeeyah?" Jalissa was astonished. Her cousin had been not quite two when Jalissa left the Coven. The memory flooded through her. Nedeeyah had followed her around, a nuisance most of the time. And yet, after she had gone to Tevingi, it was Nedeeyah she had missed most.

"Before he was killed, Kavnor told us that you might come here," Nedeeyah said, her voice cautious. "He said you would try to stop us."

Jalissa wanted to reach out to this lovely young woman, but she kept her emotions in check. "What you are doing is wrong, Nedeeyah. Hundreds, perhaps thousands of people will die because of this."

"We don't want anyone to die," the girl protested. "All we want is to be able to live as others do."

"How many of you are here?" Jalissa asked, trying to ignore the girl's plea even as she imagined herself in her situation.

"Twelve of us. Kavnor was our leader—until they killed him. The Vantrans killed him, Jalissa. They still hate us. How can you side with them?"

"His death was an accident. The soldiers should have captured him alive. The Vantrans wanted him alive."

"Nevertheless, he is dead—and we're going to carry out his plan."

"And what is that plan?"

"We know that the Vantrans need the crystals here, and now that the worlds that once worshipped us know we still exist, they will help us keep control of the crystals. The Vantrans can't use their weapons here, or they will destroy their precious crystals. All we ask in return for letting them have the crystals is that they allow us to live in peace."

"Live where? Where is the Coven? I know the members have abandoned their old home because I was there. Are they all here on Ker?"

Nedeeyah shook her dark head. "But I can't tell you where they are—at least not yet. We will announce it when the time is right."

"Listen to me, Nedeeyah. The Vantrans will not permit this. They are sending a huge force to Ker. It'll be here within hours. And some of them will get through. They know the defenses here because they built them. They will sacrifice however many troops it takes to re-capture this place."

Nedeeyah lifted her chin defiantly. "Then let them try. We defeated them before, and we'll do it again!"

"The Coven defeated them only by going into hiding," Jalissa reminded her. "And you've already said that none of you wants that."

She made a dismissive gesture. "Besides, that was nearly a hundred years ago. Now the Vantrans possess weapons that are more than the equal of ours—and they too have changed. They may control the Federation to some extent, but they can no longer act without taking into account the feelings of other races.

"The Federation isn't perfect, Nedeeyah, but it works most of the time. The wars now are limited to tribal conflicts on some of the more primitive worlds, and although I don't always approve of their methods, the Vantrans are committed to peace and to the Federation.

"There are still some Vantrans who would use a battle here as an excuse to seize even more power, and that cannot be allowed to happen. We have a powerful ally among the Vantrans. His name is Miklos Panera, and his family is the most powerful on Vantra—in the entire galaxy, actually."

And as she spoke, Jalissa once again felt that

chill. Miklos wasn't far away, but it already seemed to her that he was a part of her past. She resisted the urge to 'port herself back to the barracks and focused instead on her cousin.

"Take me to the others. I must speak to them."

One moment, Miklos was holding her in his arms, and the next instant, his hands were clutching empty space. As her final words echoed in his brain, he thought that they were belied by fear. Or was that his own fear he sensed?

He tried again to reach for that dream that had awakened him—had probably awakened them both. But once more, it eluded him.

She'll be safe, he told himself. *If her people are here, they won't harm her.* And neither would any of the others who were loyal to the Coven. All he had to do was to find the troops still loyal to the Federation and restrain them. That was all-important, because among them could well be another trigger-happy fool like the one who'd killed the Warlock.

He made his way carefully along the side of the building, stunner in hand. When he reached the main entrance, he backed quickly into the shadows. In front of the next building, two guards were sitting on the ground. Miklos grimaced. So much for military discipline. He couldn't quite suppress a thought that the military had suffered by being opened to all worlds. With the Vantran officers locked up inside, these men were ignoring their training.

Still, it was what he'd expected, and it made his job easier. It also meant that the loyal troops obviously hadn't been killed and could now be enlisted to help him.

He moved quickly, felling the first one and then the second man before they could do more than half-turn in Miklos's direction. Then he searched their unconscious bodies until he found the key to the barracks door.

Once inside, he searched for the light switches, and flooded the barracks with light to wake the sleeping troops. Men and women sat up in their cots, blinking sleepily at him. He scanned the lot of them, searching for the commander, and found her just as she recognized him.

"Miklos Panera!" she said, vaulting from the cot. "What . . . ?"

"Have someone bring those guards in here and take their places, in case someone comes to check on them," he ordered as he turned off the lights again.

Then, as two soldiers hurried to do his bidding, he explained the situation to the commander.

"Jalissa Kendor is with me. She's gone to try to put an end to the rebellion."

"They won't listen to her, Miklos," the commander said. "This situation has gone far beyond the abilities of a Whisperer."

"But not beyond the abilities of a Whisperer who is also a Witch."

The commander blinked rapidly. Her officers had gathered around her and they all stared at him in disbelief.

"She's pretending to be a Witch?" the commander said. "Normally, that might work, but they're really here—a dozen of them, Witches and Warlocks."

"She isn't pretending."

It took some time for that to sink in, and Miklos could tell that at least some of them didn't believe him. That, he decided, was *their* problem. They'd find out soon enough. He went on to explain about the imminent arrival of the troopships.

"I want your best men and women," he told the commander. "We have to take the air-defense center. I'm not certain when the ships will arrive."

Jalissa was growing impatient. She'd been talking for some time now to the hastily assembled Witches and Warlocks. Only her sympathy for their predicament gave her the will to continue to speak calmly.

None of them claimed to have heard the voices of the gods, though Kavnor had said he had. They were here because they didn't want to spend their lives in the isolation and primitive surroundings of the Coven.

For years now, they'd listened to stories told to them by Danto Kendor and his crew when they visited the Coven. They knew how much the world outside had changed, even if they were a bit fuzzy on the details. And they'd succumbed to that universal longing of youth to seek out that which they didn't have.

There were more of them than were present here, they told her. In fact, it sounded to Jalissa as though the entire generation they represented was ready and eager to claim a piece of the world beyond the Coven.

"But what of your elders—and the priests?" She asked.

"They didn't try to stop us," Nedeeyah told her. "And they would have if the gods had told them to."

Jalissa knew now that there was no way she could persuade them to give this up and return to the safety and isolation of the Coven—wherever it was. The most she could hope for was to prevent bloodshed, so she concentrated on that.

"We must negotiate with the Federation Council," she told them. "And in the meantime, we have to prevent your followers here from shooting down the troopships."

"Then they'll just land and kill everyone," a young Warlock stated.

"No. I have an ally here. He's a Special Agent of the Federation military. They'll listen to him."

"Is he a Vantran?" someone asked, making the word into a curse.

"Yes, and he knows I'm a Witch." Jalissa hesitated, then decided to tell them the whole truth. Perhaps that would convince them that not all Vantrans were evil.

"He's also my lover—and when this is over, we plan to marry."

The room was utterly still as they stared at her, too shocked to do more than draw in sharp breaths. She understood their dismay. Not only had she chosen a mate outside the Coven—something that had never before happened in all their long history—but she'd also chosen a Vantran, one of their ancient enemies.

"He is a good man, and he will help us," she went on. "I want you to remain here, and keep the miners that are allied with you under control. I must find him and speak to him."

She waited, watching as they all exchanged glances, clearly uncertain now about what to do. She pressed her point.

"If you allow these troops to do battle, we will never be able to persuade the Federation Council of our peaceful intentions."

"But what about the other troops?" Nedeeyah asked. "Has he set them free?"

"He will keep them under control. Now do as I say. It's our only hope."

One by one, they nodded, and when she was satisfied that she had gained their cooperation,

Jalissa 'ported herself to the air-defense compound.

Miklos and his small contingent made their way quietly across the base under cover of a darkness that was just beginning to lighten with the coming dawn. With him was the man in charge of the air defenses, whose intimate knowledge of the compound would be valuable.

The landing area and the air defenses were on the far side of the huge base, miles from the barracks. Miklos considered and then rejected the idea of taking several of the vehicles parked nearby. It was still early for anyone to be up and about, but if anyone was, they would surely be curious about vehicles moving toward the air-defense compound.

He also wanted to avoid the area where the miners and the Coven members were housed. Jalissa had said that she would need time to convince them to remain peaceful.

As they moved quickly along the perimeter of the base, Miklos's glance kept going to the gradually lightening sky. The man in charge of the air defenses followed his gaze.

"I overheard one of my men—one who joined the other side—saying that they expected the troopships this morning. They're already tracking them."

Miklos grunted. This was not good news. He'd hoped to have as much time as possible to get things under control before he had to deal with the arriving troops.

He knew full well that if he were anyone other than who he was, he wouldn't have a chance of persuading them to stop the attack. After all, he was a fugitive now, someone who had dared to disobey a direct order from the Council. But because he was also a Panera, he at least had a chance to persuade them. If necessary, he would threaten to bring down the wrath of his family on the commander of the task force, to ensure that the commander would spend the remainder of his or her career in some forsaken backwater.

In the distance, he could see some lights coming on in the miners' quarters. The officer with him explained that they were working round-the-clock shifts right now, because many crystals were needed for the changes being made to the galactic tracking system.

"When is the shift change?" Miklos asked.

"In about an hour."

He hoped that within that hour, the situation could be resolved. The highly skilled miners could not be put at risk. It took years to seek out those who could be trained, and then still more years to accomplish that training.

"There's a lot of hatred here right now, feelings of betrayal," the Vantran officer went on as they moved along the edges of the base.

"And all it will take is one trigger-happy soldier

to bring a disaster upon us," Miklos finished for him.

"Unfortunately, there are always that kind around. The Coven must have ordered them not to kill us, but I suspect they may have better control over their forces than we have over ours."

Miklos nodded, once again regretting that some of the less dependable worlds had been allowed to provide troops. He knew there were some among them who were just barely beyond the kind of mentality that had bathed their home worlds in blood for centuries. The Vantran military command had tried to keep them out, but the Council, always sensitive to the demands of emerging worlds, had insisted that they be let in.

Miklos and the others passed by a group of warehouses, and then Miklos saw the air-defense compound in the distance. In the middle of it stood the tall tower that housed the space-tracking and landing-guidance systems. The glass top of the tower was brightly lit, and he squinted, trying to see the occupants.

"How many . . . ?"

The question hung in the cool air unfinished as they both raised their heads to stare at the heavens. For one brief second, something with the brilliance of a sun appeared up there, leaving a lingering afterimage on their eyes.

"They're here!" the officer said unnecessarily as the others gathered around them. "They've shot down one of the troopships."

413

Miklos shook his head. "The flash wasn't large enough to have been a troopship. My guess is that it was a T-43 or some other smaller ship, hoping to sneak through without being detected. But the troopships can't be far behind."

Even though they were all winded from jogging across the base, they now poured on speed and headed for the tower, taking advantage of the surrounding buildings that housed the powerful laser missiles that had just fired. Guidance was by remote control from the tower, so there would be no one in these missile silos.

Entrance to the tower itself was gained only by handprint identification, and Miklos held his breath as the officer pressed his palm against the panel. Those who now controlled the tower could have changed the coding, which meant that instead of gaining access, they'd be setting off an alarm that would not only alert those inside, but also the troops back at the barracks.

The door slid open, however, and they all hurried inside. Miklos deferred to the air-defense commander, who quickly issued orders to the group. Then they split up and began to make their various ways to the control room at the top of the tower.

Jalissa landed next to one of the buildings in the air-defense compound. A wave of dizziness came over her, and she sank to her knees, then sat down against the wall of the building. She realized that she'd been overusing her powers—and on an empty stomach as well. She'd had nothing to eat for nearly 24 hours.

She was about to get to her feet when suddenly the sky was lit by a bright flash of light. Instinctively, she sank down again. The troopships must have arrived, and Miklos apparently hadn't succeeded in gaining control of the tower.

She staggered to her feet again and moved out of the shadow of the building. Some distance away, she could see the tower and the tiny figures inside its glass-walled top. Where was Miklos? Had something gone wrong back at the barracks? She had to find out.

Drawing on her dwindling reserves of strength, Jalissa 'ported herself back to the barracks, landing just behind one of them. This time the dizziness was even worse, and she had to wait for several minutes before she dared to get to her feet. She was between two barracks, and she could hear shouting coming from them both. Someone had seen the exploding ship and awakened the others, or perhaps it was time for them to get up anyway. Dawn was fast approaching.

She listened for a time, trying to sort out the different voices, hoping to hear that one familiar voice among many. Where was he? Finally, she got to her feet, even though the dizziness hadn't yet gone away.

She made her way toward the front of the barracks, summoning the fire as she went. But her vision was blurred and her head was throbbing painfully. Still, she knew she could wield the fire if she had to. And she was determined to find Miklos.

Jalissa never saw the two men who were making their rounds as guards of one of the barracks. They were with the loyal forces, and one of them was from just the kind of world that so troubled Miklos. When he and his companion came around the corner and saw before them what was clearly a Witch, with the magic fire surrounding her hands, the soldier fired his laser gun without hesitation. His companion, a young Vantran soldier, tried to deflect the gun, but she was too late.

"I don't care what your orders are, General. Either you remain where you are or I personally guarantee that you'll spend the rest of your career on Garlov—that is, if you're fortunate enough to escape being sent to a penal colony!"

"You're a fugitive, Panera. I don't have to listen to you."

"I may be a fugitive, but I'm also a Panera. And if I were you, I'd think about the latter fact, not the former. Regardless of what happens to me, my family will see to it that you have no future in the military—or anywhere else."

Miklos stared at the large viewscreen, knowing that the general was staring back at him. Behind Miklos, the last of the defenders of the tower were being put into restraints before they could regain consciousness.

He could not allow the Federation troops to land now. Word had come from the barracks region that fighting had broken out. He didn't know what had set it off, but to permit reinforcements to land now would only exacerbate the situation. So far, from what he could tell, the Coven members and the miners were keeping to their quarters, and that must mean that Jalissa was there with them, safely away from the fighting.

The general glared at him from the screen, and Miklos glared back. He knew that the man was fully aware of his ability to carry out his threats, but he was obviously weighing that against the glory he could see accruing to him if he won this battle.

"I'll give you an hour," the man said finally. "And then we're coming in."

"Fine. As far as I'm concerned, you can come in and look like the conquering heroes. The credit for putting down this uprising will be yours."

"You're still a fugitive, Panera."

"I'm not going anywhere."

Miklos shut off the comm and turned to the air-defense commander. "What's going on at the barracks?"

"Someone apparently got trigger-happy, just like we feared, and attacked one of the Coven."

"The Coven were down there?" Miklos glanced

at the comm. Obviously, Jalissa hadn't been able to control them—or at least not *all* of them.

He rejected the notion of trying to contact her via comm. The visitors' quarters where they must be was only a few minutes away. He decided to go there. In all likelihood, Jalissa had had some success, because the miners hadn't gotten involved yet. But she could probably use his support right now, to convince them and any of the Coven who were there that he could be trusted and there would be no attack.

He left the tower and covered the short distance in one of the small solar-powered vehicles he found parked nearby. Even though his problems were far from being over, all that was on his mind as he braked in front of the visitors' quarters was seeing her again.

He pushed open the door to the visitors' quarters to face a cluster of black-robed Witches and Warlocks. They all turned to stare at him, and the magic fire glowed around the hands of several of them.

"Where's Jalissa?" he asked, guessing that she was probably in the miners' quarters, trying to keep them calm.

"Are you Miklos Panera—the Vantran?" one of them asked, a young woman who bore a faint resemblance to Jalissa.

He nodded impatiently. "Is she with the miners?"

"No. She went to find *you*."

Miklos felt the first faint stirrings of alarm, but kept them in check. Probably she'd appeared in the tower right after he left.

"When did she leave?"

The young Witch frowned. "I'm not sure. It wasn't long before that explosion in the sky. Can you . . . ?"

Miklos cut her off. "*Before* the explosion? Are you sure?" He hadn't gotten to the tower until afterwards, and she wasn't there. Fear began to crawl through him like an icy snake.

"Are you all here? Did any of you go to the barracks?" he demanded, scanning the group.

"We're all here," the young Witch assured him. "Except for Jalissa. She told us to wait here and keep the miners from leaving."

But Miklos barely heard the last part as he turned and ran back to the vehicle. If none of them had been at the barracks and a member of the Coven had been attacked there . . .

No, he wouldn't let himself think about it. He knew how facts got distorted in situations like this. Besides, Jalissa was quite capable of protecting herself.

Still, as he pushed the little vehicle to its limits, he wished that he could 'port.

He could see the sporadic flashes of laser fire as he drove toward the barracks, and soon could hear the shouts. His stomach knotted with fear, he leapt from the vehicle, clutching his own laser gun.

419

The battle was all but over by the time he joined it, and it was clear that the forces loyal to the Federation had won. Still, he had to dodge from building to building to avoid the fire of the traitorous troops who were now trying to flee, perhaps hoping to persuade the miners and the Coven to help them.

Bodies of soldiers littered the space around the barracks, and even though his conscious mind refused to consider it, he was subconsciously checking to be sure none of them could be Jalissa.

The nagging thought came to him that if she were here, she would have ordered the troops loyal to the Coven to stop—and they would surely have obeyed her.

He came to a corner of the one barracks, and peered cautiously around into the space between it and the next one. And for one frozen moment, he could not accept what he saw. And then, in the next, he was running to her.

Falling to his knees, Miklos called her name. Then he carefully lifted her into his arms. But what he saw sent a wave of horror over him that paralyzed him.

Her skin bore the telltale gray hue that resulted from death by laser. He'd seen it too many times before to deny it—and yet he *did* deny it, bending over her to feel her breath at the same time he pressed a trembling thumb against the base of her throat, seeking the throbbing pulse of life.

Cradling her in his arms, Miklos Panera felt his own life draining away, gone with hers. And he thought about that dream they'd shared and the look on her face just before she left him. She'd said that they would be together—but she'd known that that would never happen.

Suddenly, he became aware of the presence of others, and when he looked up, expecting to see soldiers, he saw instead three black-robed members of the Coven: a woman and two men. Dazed, he stared at them. They weren't any of the ones he'd just seen back at the visitors' quarters because all three were much older.

A surge of hope welled up in him. The Coven had healing powers! "Heal her!" he commanded in a voice cracked by emotion. "You can heal her!"

The eldest of the three, a kindly-looking old man, stepped forward. "She is beyond our help, Miklos Panera. We have come to take her home to the gods."

"No!" Miklos clutched her lifeless body more tightly. "You can't have her! She belongs to me!"

The man gave him a sad smile. "She belongs to the gods now."

And then, once again, Miklos was holding nothing.

The 26 members of the Federation Council, representing every inhabited world in the galaxy, were all in their ornate chairs around the curved table. In the center was the current president, a woman from Tevingi. The presidency rotated among the various worlds, but everyone agreed that it was most significant that Tevingi occupied that seat now.

Two ex-officio members of the Council were present as well, seated at opposite ends of the long table. They were the Directors, respectively, of the Special Agency and the Translation/Mediation Service. Their positioning at the table—as far as possible from each other—was *not* coincidental.

Every seat in the hall was filled, with an overflow crowd spilling into the hallway beyond. There were journalists and other writers, high-level employees of various Federation agencies, and such important personages as could obtain seats on their own. Cameras recorded the event to send it out over the airwaves to the far corners of the galaxy.

And yet, it was all for show. There was scarcely a person in the galaxy, save for some primitive worlds, who didn't already know the story. The fact that all were gathered here today, nearly two weeks after the incident, demonstrated that they all understood the historical significance of the moment.

The president read from the statement drafted by the Council. A more detailed accounting would be available in the Council's archives. She spoke, as was the custom, in Vantran, but with a readily discernible Tevingian accent.

"The Council wishes to issue a report on what has come to be called 'The Ker Incident,' but which, in a much larger sense, can be called the 'Return of the Coven.'

"First of all, the Council condemns the attempted destruction of the Coven by Vantran forces nearly a century ago. Nevertheless, that is not our purpose here today.

"The incident that occurred on Ker two weeks ago traces its origins to the emergence of a young Warlock who left the Coven to announce to the galaxy that his people had survived. Special Agent Miklos Panera and Translation/Mediation Specialist Jalissa Kendor were dispatched on a joint mission to find this young man and determine whether or not he was, in fact, a Warlock. They were told to capture him alive, if at all possible.

"Unfortunately, through no fault of their own, Panera and Kendor were unable to capture the Warlock before he was killed by a Federation soldier on Ker. That soldier has been sent to a penal colony and his immediate superior has been dismissed from the military.

"Digressing here for a moment, we must explain that during their joint mission, Agent Panera discovered that Specialist Kendor was in fact a Witch. Knowing, therefore, that the Coven did indeed still exist, Panera, accompanied by Kendor, set out to find the Coven in order to prevent a recurrence of the wars that had once plagued the galaxy.

"By so doing, they disobeyed a direct order from the Council to return to Vantra, but the Council has forgiven them this transgression, and now believes that they acted in the best interests of the galaxy.

"Unable to find the Coven, who had by then removed themselves from their underground home on an asteroid, Panera and Kendor went to Ker.

"The situation on Ker at that moment was desperate. Following the appearance and then the unfortunate death of the Warlock, a rebellion had occurred, and troops and miners loyal to the Coven had seized control of Ker. A contingent of elite Vantran troops was already on its way to Ker with the intent of re-taking that world at all costs. This action, it should be noted, was not approved by the Council. Under the Articles of the Galactic Federation, the military, controlled by the Vantrans, has the authority to act as it deems suitable in cases involving galactic security.

"Panera and Kendor arrived on Ker only hours before the Federation forces. Together, they managed to end the rebellion with only a minimal loss of life. Their bravery in the face of overwhelming odds has resulted in their being awarded the highest honor the Federation can bestow: the Order of the Galaxy.

"Unfortunately, in the case of Specialist Kendor, this award was made posthumously. Jalissa Kendor was killed by a Federation soldier, who has since been convicted and sentenced to a life term on a penal colony.

"The Council wishes to state that it regards Jalissa Kendor as a remarkable woman—both a Witch and a Federation loyalist. The ultimate peaceful resolution of this crisis has depended to a large extent on the fact that she walked in both worlds and believed in both.

"One week ago, the Council met with the Priesthood of the Coven on Tevingi, its new home. The Coven has disavowed any intent to disrupt the Federation, and has sent its members to all worlds where it has been revered to encourage their cooperation with the Federation.

"The Coven will remain on Tevingi, and its interests will be represented in the Federation by the Tevingians. The Council has voted unanimously to give the Coven the designation of 'Special Entity,' a unique status within the galaxy for a unique people. Their desire to live separately on Tevingi will be protected by Tevingian forces and by the Federation as well—for as long as the Coven chooses to remain apart.

"In closing, we would like to say that we are grateful that, at long last, a terrible blot on our galactic history has been removed. One century after that terrible incident, a Vantran and a Witch joined forces to save the Federation and bring into it a people who had suffered a terrible injustice."

Journalists pressed forward with their questions, buttonholing various Council members for their individual thoughts. Others in the audience gathered in small groups, talking in low tones about the matter.

Danto Kendor, who had come to Vantra to receive the Order of the Galaxy on behalf of his adopted niece, made his way across the room to a tall, gray-haired man who was engaged in conversation with the Director of the Special Agency.

"Ralus Panera?" he inquired politely as the man turned to him.

"Danto Kendor," the man acknowledged with a nod. "I had hoped we could meet."

"I had the pleasure of meeting your son on Tevingi and wanted to inquire after him. Will he be present for the ceremony tomorrow?"

A shadow crossed the taller man's handsome face. "I think not, although I've encouraged him to come. He has been in seclusion at our country home ever since his return from Ker."

Ralus Panera paused briefly, then went on. "I regret that I did not have the opportunity to meet her—and I deeply regret that we will be unable to welcome her into our family." Then, when he saw Danto Kendor's startled look, he smiled.

"You didn't know that they planned to marry?"

"No, I didn't, although perhaps it shouldn't surprise me. It was apparent when I saw them together that they felt strongly toward each other."

"To be quite candid with you, Kendor, I am worried about my son. When Jalissa Kendor died, it was as though a part of him died with her." He indicated the Director of the Special Agency. "But as I was saying to the Director, I believe that in time Miklos will choose to return to his work, and will undoubtedly make it his life."

They parted a few minutes later, and when Danto Kendor left Vantra two days later, he carried his secret home to Tevingi with him.

Epilogue

Jalissa Kendor stepped from her small cottage to greet the first warm day of spring. There was work to be done—but then, there was *always* work to be done. Among the children of the Coven, she had discovered a surprising number who had an affinity for the crystals.

She lifted her face to the soft breeze and smiled, thinking of Bel. The work could wait. She had no classes scheduled this morning. So she 'ported herself to the Kendor home, where she found her adopted parents breakfasting on the terrace with Danto.

All three of them looked up and smiled when she suddenly materialized at the edge of the broad terrace.

"I was just saying that I expected you to put in an appearance this morning," Neesa Kendor told her with a laugh. "Bel is in the home paddock. Will you join us for a few minutes?"

Jalissa slid into a seat and accepted a cup of tea. "How have you been, Danto? I haven't seen you for quite a while."

"Too long, my dear," Danto Kendor said, leaning over to kiss her cheek. "In fact, I was planning to visit the Coven this morning. How are your classes coming along?"

Jalissa's face lit with pleasure. "Wonderfully. I have six children at present, and they're all showing remarkable talent. Malvina will be here next week to evaluate them, and I think she'll be very pleased."

"At this rate, the Coven will be taking over Trans/Med," Joeb remarked. "That must be giving the Special Agency some headaches. How many Whisperers has the Coven contributed?"

"Eight in the past two years," Jalissa replied. "And according to Malvina, they're all doing very well. The only problem is that they are finding life on Vantra a bit difficult."

"It's only because they're the first," Danto said. "The novelty will wear off in time. I understand that it's been months now since anyone has tried to sneak into the Coven's compound."

"Yes, you're right about that. None of the intruders wished to cause us any harm, of course, but the Coven—particularly the older members—finds it unsettling." Jalissa finished her tea and stood up.

"I'm off to find Bel. I'll probably see you later, Danto."

The trio watched as she walked across the terrace—and then vanished. Neesa saw the brooding look on Danto's face, and touched his hand gently.

"She is happy, Danto."

"Yes, but it's the happiness of ignorance. I had thought that if she came across his name on the news reports . . ." He shrugged. "Does she have no interest in leaving the Coven, even just to visit her old home on Vantra?"

Neesa shook her head. "Malvina says that she always asks about her old friends, but has shown no inclination to visit them. It's the will of the gods, Danto. They gave her back her life."

"But at a price," Danto said. "I picked up some interesting news on Vantra, by the way. I had dinner with Ralus Panera. We're considering a joint venture in the Outer Ring. He told me that Miklos will soon be named Director of the Special Agency."

"Oh?" Neesa replied. "I'm very glad to hear that. From the news reports, it seemed to me that he was doing everything possible to get himself killed."

Danto nodded. "Exactly what his father said. For the past two years, he's been involved in every dangerous mission there is. But perhaps now he's made peace with himself at last.

"Having him as Director will be very helpful to the Coven. The current Director has never quite reconciled himself to the new order, even though Ralus Panera has done his best to see that Vantrans treat the Coven well."

"I wonder if Miklos has found someone," Neesa mused.

"No. Ralus said that he has given up any hope of ever having grandchildren from Miklos. According to him, Miklos has no interest at all in women." He clenched his fists.

"I tell you, I've never been so tempted to intervene in someone's personal life as I am with those two."

"But you mustn't, Danto," Neesa said gently. "Think about how hard it would be for Miklos— to know that she's alive but has no memory of him."

Danto sighed. "You're right, of course."

But privately, Danto thought that the gods had treated Jalissa very badly. They'd ordered that she be sent away from the Coven simply because she was bright enough to ask difficult questions, and now they'd given her back her life, but taken away the memory of the only man she'd ever loved.

Jalissa soared into the heavens on Bel's broad back. Nothing gave her greater pleasure than

431

these rare times when she could escape from her duties and ride with the wind.

As they caught the thermal and began to ride it up over the mountaintop, she turned to look off to her side, then quickly turned back again with a slight shiver. It seemed to happen every time she rode, and she didn't understand it. It seemed to her that she expected someone else to be there, though she had no idea who it might be.

It happened other times as well: strange interludes when she would look up expectantly, almost able to see ... someone. She'd never spoken of this to anyone, because she didn't understand it, just as she didn't understand her strange need to remain with the Coven at all times.

When she let herself think about it, she thought maybe it had something to do with her return from the dead. She still had trouble dealing with that, though she didn't doubt that it had happened. She could recall quite clearly the terrible pain of the laser ripping through her body, although her memory of what had preceded it was rather murky.

She knew that she had been credited with preventing war and possibly saving the Federation, even though, for some reason, she'd never wanted to read the accounts of that incident. By the time she'd regained her senses, nearly two months had passed, and what she did know about it had come from Danto's account when he brought her the medal she'd been awarded.

She rode the thermals until she felt Bel beginning to tire, then returned to the stables. After giving the Madri a rubdown and an extra ration of oats, she 'ported home. It wasn't far. The land given to the Coven was formerly part of the Kendor land, high in the mountains.

She spent a busy day with her students, then wrote the reports that Malvina would want. After that, she returned to her cottage to spend the evening alone, as she did most days.

Jalissa was uncomfortable with the attentions of her fellow Witches and Warlocks, who remained in awe of her return from the dead. They seemed to believe that she regularly received special communications from the gods, though she told them again and again quite honestly that she didn't.

So she lived a strange sort of life—part of the Coven and yet not part of them. And sometimes she had the sense that she was waiting for something, though she had no idea what that "something" might be. Perhaps it was nothing more than a response to the others' belief that the gods would communicate directly with her.

Her cottage, like the others in the Coven's new home, was patterned after the cottages in their long-destroyed world: rough stone with thatched roofs. This new home on Tevingi had been created for them quite literally overnight, through the magic of the gods, who had previously moved them from one asteroid to another to protect them.

The other Coven members continued to live in a primitive fashion in their new home, but Jalissa had all the modern conveniences, provided by Danto. And as time passed, the rest of the Coven—especially its younger members—were also showing an interest in such conveniences, to the dismay of the priests. It seemed that Jalissa was still a problem to the Coven.

Danto had also provided her with a comm unit, but for many months Jalissa had ignored it because she had no desire to inform herself about the rest of the galaxy. More recently, however, she had begun to pay sporadic attention to galactic news, and when she came home this day, she switched it on.

The Tevingian newscast was just beginning, and Jalissa settled down with a cup of tea to watch it. The lead story was about the changes at the Federation base on Tevingi. For the first time, the base was to have a Tevingian commander, and native troops would be permitted as well. It was hailed as a breakthrough in Tevingi's often stormy relationship with the Vantran-controlled military.

Jalissa had already known of this change, but the second item in the news surprised her—especially in view of the fact that she'd just seen Danto that very day. It seemed that he was entering into a joint venture with Ralus Panera in the Outer Ring, where they were hoping to develop some native industries.

"Panera," she murmured to herself. The first name was different, but she'd seen that last name before.

A strange feeling came over Jalissa—and it wasn't the first time. Ever since she had begun to watch the galactic news, she had from time to time seen the name "Miklos Panera," and for a reason she couldn't understand, she would find herself repeating that name, as though the very sound of it were somehow pleasurable to her.

His name had appeared fairly often in the galactic news, always in connection with some crisis on distant worlds. It seemed that wherever there was trouble, Miklos Panera was present.

As the rest of the Tevingian news scrolled past, Jalissa thought about that name. She didn't remember the man, and yet, since he was a Special Agent, it was possible that she'd met him at some point.

The Tevingian newscast ended and the galactic news began while she was still wondering why that name seemed to strike a chord in her. And there it was again!

"Special Agent Miklos Panera has been named the new Director of the Special Agency. Panera stated that he intends to focus more on cooperation between the Special Agency and the Translation/Mediation Service. This announcement was hailed by the President of the Federation Council, who—"

Jalissa ignored the rest of it. "Miklos Panera." She murmured the name over and over as a very strange feeling came over her. She *must* have known him. It felt like the memory was there— but just beyond her reach for some reason.

She leaned forward and began to press keys, trying to recall how to summon biographical information on well-known figures. And then she was suddenly staring at the face of Miklos Panera!

"Miklos," she whispered again. For one brief instant, he seemed so familiar, though as she continued to stare at his image, that sense began to fade.

She sat back and peered at the screen more objectively. He was a strikingly handsome man. Surely if she'd met him at some point, she would have remembered him.

The information slid past slowly. She scanned it, but with little interest. It was detailing his long career with the Special Agency.

Then she gasped and reached out with a trembling finger to halt the words. Miklos Panera had been involved in the incident on Ker! He had even received the same award she herself had been given. Her name was mentioned with his in the recounting of the incident.

She switched off the comm. Obviously, they had worked together. How could she not remember him—or remember him so little?

She got up and fixed herself some dinner, but ate very little. Then she went for a walk in the soft twilight. Confronting that time was still very difficult for her. Every time she thought about it, she felt as though she were reaching out into some unimaginably dark place: her own death.

But tonight, she felt a need to pierce that darkness, to stare it in the face and demand that it yield up its secrets. If she was challenging the gods themselves, then so be it. She could no longer live with that black abyss.

She returned to the comm, torn between calling up information on the incident itself and summoning her own bio. Finally, she decided on the latter. It seemed somehow less threatening, though she couldn't have said why.

Her own face appeared on the screen, but she never got beyond the initial information: her date of birth—and death!

Jalissa was stunned! For several minutes, she stared at the screen, willing it to correct itself. But there it was. According to the galactic archives, she had died on Ker. She had, of course, but why was there no mention of her return?

With trembling but determined fingers, Jalissa called up the public report on the incident on Ker. It was all as she remembered it—but with one very important exception. She had believed herself to have traveled to Ker alone. She'd 'ported there after being unable to discover the whereabouts of the Coven.

Now she saw that she had not been alone—either on Ker or in her earlier attempts to track down the Warlock, Kavnor. Miklos Panera had been with her all the time!

Jalissa switched off the comm once again and sat there for a long time. That awful darkness remained, but now she thought she saw a way to end it.

"Danto, could you arrange a cottage on Mafriti for me—right away?"

Danto Kendor couldn't hide his shock. "Of course, Jalissa. I'll be happy to arrange transport for you as well. But—"

"Thank you. I'll expect to hear from you soon."

Her image faded from the screen, but it lingered in his mind. What was going on here? There was something in her voice—and in her face as well. The Jalissa he'd seen for these past two years had been content; he couldn't deny that. But the woman whose face had just appeared on the vidscreen was radiant—and excited.

Mafriti, he thought. *Interesting.* He wondered if the gods had finally admitted their mistake and were about to rectify it. He'd argued with Joeb and Neesa many times over the past two years—but mostly with Neesa, whose belief in the infallibility of the gods was absolute.

She'd argued that if the gods wanted Jalissa to

forget about Miklos, they must have a reason, and he'd been forced to admit that could be the case. Certainly Jalissa's presence among the Coven had eased her people's transition back into the world, and her work with the children was essential. Not only did she determine which of them showed an affinity for working with the crystals, but she also prepared them for their emergence into a world that was surpassingly strange to them.

Maybe, he thought as he set about fulfilling her request, the gods have decided that she's repaid them for the life they gave back to her. There was a certain symmetry to that.

After making the arrangements for her and sending her a message to confirm it, Danto couldn't quite resist making another call.

"Ralus, how are you?" he asked when his soon-to-be partner appeared on the screen.

"Just fine, thank you, Danto. I was about to call you to discuss the contracts. Have you received them?"

"My legal people are looking them over now, but I don't see any problems. I called to congratulate you on Miklos' appointment, now that it's official. You must be very proud."

"I am indeed—and in more ways than one. His acceptance of the offer tells me that he's finally decided to stop trying to get himself killed." A faint cloud passed over Ralus's face. "But to tell you the truth, I *do* still have some concern."

"Oh?" Danto prompted.

"We were planning a family celebration for this weekend, but he's suddenly decided to take off for Mafriti. It seems a bit strange."

"Didn't he offer any explanation?" Danto asked, trying to restrain a smile.

"No. He called me this morning and apologized about the celebration, saying that he *had* to go to Mafriti, and that he might be gone for a week or so."

Danto saw his new friend's concern, and took a deep breath. "Ralus, I hope you're not going to be angry with me for withholding this information all this time, but . . ."

Jalissa walked out onto the deck that overlooked the ocean. Now that she was actually here, she felt rather uncertain. That hadn't been the case when she'd awakened yesterday morning. *Then,* she'd known that she had to go to Mafriti, even though the reason still eluded her.

She didn't really know why she was here. After reading the report on the incident on Ker, and realizing that her memories had somehow been changed, she'd decided that this man, Miklos Panera, was the key to recovering that lost part of her life. There *had* to be a reason why he'd been deleted from her memory—or nearly so.

She'd gone to bed after deciding that she would go to Vantra and find him—and had then awakened with this compulsion to come to Mafriti instead.

It had been years since she'd been here—or had it? Whispers of memories taunted her. She was sure that she'd never stayed in one of the cottages—and yet it seemed somehow familiar.

She walked slowly down the steps that led to the deserted beach. The sun was sinking slowly into the sea, dappling it with a red-gold glow. Jalissa knew herself to be in the grip of something. She felt a strange sort of peace—but also an eagerness. For all that the gods had bestowed upon her, she still didn't quite trust them. What did they have in store for her now?

As she walked slowly along the edge of the water, she became absolutely certain that something was about to happen. And she was so lost in her thoughts that she failed to notice the small sign that warned she was encroaching upon someone else's private beach.

Miklos swam through waters that glowed like liquid fire. The exercise kept him from getting too lost in his confused thoughts—or so he'd hoped. But it wasn't working at the moment.

Why had he suddenly decided to come here, even when he knew that his family had planned to celebrate his appointment? He didn't know the answer to that any more than he'd understood his acceptance of the Directorship. All he knew was that something had changed in him.

But why Mafriti? He'd intended never to set foot on this world again, so that his memory of this perfect place would be forever connected to a perfect love.

As he moved through the water with long, powerful strokes, he thought about her—and realized that for the first time in two years, he could do so without pain. Perplexed by yet another indication of change, he struck out for shore.

He was wading through the surf when he first saw her. The sun was almost down and shadows flowed across the white sand. She was walking along slowly, her pale, gauzy dress billowing in the sea breeze. As he squinted to see her better, she stopped and then bent to pick up something, probably a seashell. Her long, dark hair fell forward, and she reached up with one hand to hold it back.

Miklos stood there transfixed, even though he was aware at some level that he should cover his nakedness. For one brief, heart-rending moment, he let himself hope—then pushed that hope roughly away before it could bring back the pain.

For months after her death, he'd kept expecting her to materialize in front of his eyes. It was the curse of her magic, which had allowed that to happen before. But he'd finally accepted that both she and her magic were gone forever.

He still couldn't see the woman clearly in the gathering dusk, but it was obvious that she'd now spotted him because she stopped suddenly. He thought again about covering himself, but he didn't move. He was still caught on the sharp, painful edge of hope.

Jalissa pocketed the delicate seashell and continued her walk. But she'd taken only a few steps when she saw him. He was walking naked from the sea in the last faint, red rays of the setting sun. In that strange light, his wet hair glowed and his body shone a burnished bronze.

And then she knew! The memories that had been stolen from her flowed through her, flooding all her senses as she stood there staring at him. She felt both weak with the weight of them, and yet as insubstantial as a feather.

"Miklos," she whispered—and now it was more than just a name. Now it meant her life—her future.

They started toward each other, neither of them moving hurriedly. Jalissa wanted to savor the moment, and Miklos still could not quite believe.

But as the last of the sun's rays faded from the darkening waters, he finally *did* believe, and Jalissa was looking into the green eyes of her future and seeing the light of love that forever banished the darkness.

Futuristic Romance

Love in another time, another place.

Don't miss these tempestuous futuristic romances set on faraway worlds where passion is the lifeblood of every man and woman.

Awakenings by Saranne Dawson. Fearless and bold, Justan rules his domain with an iron hand, but nothing short of magic will bring his warring people peace. He claims he needs Rozlynd for her sorcery alone, yet inside him stirs an unexpected yearning to sample her sweet innocence. And as her silken spell ensnares him, Justan battles to vanquish a power whose like he has never encountered—the power of Rozlynd's love.

_51921-6 $4.99 US/$5.99 CAN

Ascent to the Stars by Christine Michels. For Trace, the assignment is simple. All he has to do is take a helpless female to safety and he'll receive information about his cunning enemies. But no daring mission or reckless rescue has prepared him for the likes of Coventry Pearce. Even as he races across the galaxy to save his doomed world, Trace battles to deny a burning desire that will take him to the heavens and beyond.

_51933-X $4.99 US/$5.99 CAN

Dorchester Publishing Co., Inc.
65 Commerce Road
Stamford, CT 06902

Please add $1.75 for shipping and handling for the first book and $.50 for each book thereafter. NY, NYC, PA and CT residents, please add appropriate sales tax. No cash, stamps, or C.O.D.s. All orders shipped within 6 weeks via postal service book rate. Canadian orders require $2.00 extra postage and must be paid in U.S. dollars through a U.S. banking facility.

Name _____

Address _____

City _____ State _____ Zip _____

I have enclosed $_____ in payment for the checked book(s). Payment <u>must</u> accompany all orders. ☐ Please send a free catalog.